Random House

New York

a novel by

Lael Tucker

Lament for Four Virgins

1952

I

The Four Virgins of Andalusia

3

Contents

Done and Left Undone

2

Nor for Good nor Evil

2

To Wert

I

The Four Virgins

of Andalusia

1927

1. The Town and the Church

Andalusia is a medium-small, middle-aged town south of Ogle-thorpe, which is a medium-big old town, and north of Marianna, which is a medium-big new town. Andalusia lies between a slow-moving, thick, chocolate-colored river and a main-line railroad. It has a number of pre-Civil War families of both colors, several pretty residential streets, an adequate shopping district, and several industries. During seven months of the year, the weather is variable. During the other five, it is hot.

The one large, ugly hotel, the Andalusia House, was built in 1890 and is avoided by visitors who can possibly stay at The Oaks, which is an expensive resort hotel for hunting-fishing-and-golfing in Oakland, five miles outside of town. Andalusia's families live in old-fashioned, unimpressive houses in town and spend their money, when they have it, on the cars they drive and on modern hunting lodges in Oakland.

In many ways, Andalusia is modern. Its women drink, smoke, and go naked at the midriff. Its maidens go out unchaperoned, equipped with only a set of hand-me-down convictions on the subject of behavior proper to young ladies. In other ways, it is old-fashioned. Infidelity or divorce among its married couples is rare.

The leading families are still a law unto themselves, or rather they control the law to suit themselves. The whole town knew it when Lucy Lee Cranborne poisoned her poisonous old mother, but nothing happened to Miss Lucy. The daughters of the leading families, however, are rarely considered justified in going to work, and when they marry it is with, not without, their parents' consent.

The leading families of Andalusia include both those who have acquired wealth and those who have maintained their family identity as gentlefolk in spite of downright poverty. This is a compromise between the rigid social standards of the larger towns to the south and north of Andalusia. In Marianna, the only leading families are those with money and the willingness to spend it. In Oglethorpe, no social claims postdating the War Between the States are considered valid. The leading families of Andalusia may be identified by their membership in the Andalusia Cotillion Club and the frequency with which they are mentioned on the society page of the Andalusia *Banner*.

The 1920 census recorded for Andalusia a total population of 15,426, of whom 7,723 were white. Two of these were voting age, registered Republicans. One was a Socialist. This does not indicate a lack of political liveliness, as there are always infinite political differences among Andalusia's Democrats, particularly with regard to the status and living conditions of the non-voting half of the population.

There is no question of Andalusia's militant patriotism. Wars have produced little or no division of opinion.

Theoretically, the men of Andalusia are the masters of their fates, their morals, and their families. (The town clings to this southern tradition, as it does to many others.) The extent to which the last two are no longer true is partly the fault of the men.

The moral as well as the social leadership of Andalusia centers in St. James's Episcopal Church. The titular chief is the rector of St. James's. He is backed by his vestry, which includes a banker, a lawyer, and other respected male citizens. Nevertheless, the women have taken over the church to a large extent and, in so doing, the moral structure of the town. During the course of a few years in Andalusia, one rector fled, one was forced to leave. The last is still there.

2. The Coming of Summer

Angela Madison watched the summer coming. The streaking, cold rain stopped, the raw, erratic wind died, the sunshine began pouring over the earth in bucketsful. Angela straightened her legs downward, threw back the blankets, and padded, barefoot, across the bare, wide-boarded floor of her bedroom. By the time she reached the window, summer had come. It had taken only five minutes, and there had been no spring.

The sun burned on her out-thrust, winter face. The sky was blue in depth, from horizon to horizon. In the back yard, the water oak trembled as if assaulted by the midsummer attack of the sun. The liveoak was immobile under its heavy burden of rain-soaked moss. Angela pressed her hands on the windowsill. She wanted summer, like love, to be slow in coming, to last a long time. The seasons should be guided by the calendars that men, in their finite wisdom, had handed down through the generations to give form and graciousness to the year. This yard had had no time to prepare itself for summer. Last year's oak leaves steamed on the brown ground. The sun blazed on a barren, untriumphant earth.

Angela dressed hurriedly, as if she were racing to catch up

with the arrival of summer. She wrenched open the door of her room, and then hesitated on the threshold of the long upstairs hall. Touching the door, as if to still the vibrations of her rude opening of it, she left the doorway and tiptoed along the hall toward the back steps, past her parents' bedroom. Her father would have left the house, but her mother might still be somnolent beside her breakfast tray. She did not want to see her mother yet. By noon, she would have made her private terms with the unseemly abruptness of the universe. Now she wanted only to be suspended in the new sunshine, in the limited, intimate space of her car, to acquire still-ness and acceptance by movement, to be in the company of Ellen Terra Rook, who was her best friend and who considered every-thing that happened as inevitable.

Before she reached the dining room, she heard the slam of the kitchen screen door and the crack and slap of water as Pinckney threw it in a long arc from the dishpan.

"Mama told you not to throw that water so near the house any more," she called without animosity as the screen door slammed again. The door between the dining room and the kitchen stood open and she could smell fresh-made coffee. Mama should have the sink drain fixed, Angela thought without censure.

"Yesm," called Pinckney amiably. He came in with a pot of coffee and a plate of hot biscuits wrapped in a white napkin that glittered against his brown hand. "You look nice, Miss Anglah," he said, approving the white skirt and yellow blouse she had put on in immediate capitulation to the season. "You always *was* a summahtime gal."

She smiled without speaking, without looking at him.

"Doan you want some aigs? Fat you up quick for summah."

"No. Summer can't come like this." She glanced up at Fate Pinckney's brown, lopsided head, bent, as he poured her coffee.

"Cain't," he said, "but did. Doan ketch cold, now, Miss Anglah. Better take you a coat along." His maternal-paternal atti-tude toward her was soothing and undemanding. "Want me to put yo top down fore you maw gits up and gits ideas?"

"Sure! I'll help."

"Take yo time and doan hurry yo breakfast none." He left the dining room, removing as he went the white cook's apron, the cream-of-wheat chef's hat he had constructed for himself. To put down her top, he would wear the mechanic's cap her brother had given him. He had a dramatic sense of fitness, and he felt both respect and affection for cars, especially for Angela's sleek, gray cabriolet. Angela stirred, anticipating her foot on the deep clutch, her hands on the responsive wheel, the sun on her head. Her affection for cars was sensuous and personal—akin to the affection some women in the country felt for horses, some men for hunting dogs.

She was impatient to be out and gulped at the hot coffee. Ellen Terra would be already waiting for her. Ellen Terra was prompt. It was because she was humble, for all her prettiness, for all her untidy charm. Ellen Terra meant no one harm, kept no one waiting, hated nobody, was never cross with God. Angela did not want to be alone on this disturbing morning. She was glad Ellen Terra was waiting for her.

She frowned, visualizing with physical accuracy what she would do. She would not go out by the driveway and into Norwich Street, on which she lived. She would leave the yard by the back gates and go down the alley behind the house, under the many-layered archway of oak limbs, thick with age and dripping with moss. People said it was a shame that this ancient avenue of trees shaded such a muddy little alley lined with Negro shacks, but Angela liked it. The unpainted cabins were the color of the moss and the innumerable voices of their inhabitants blended with the sound of the innumerable birds. She would turn from the alley into Somerset, which was a dull cross street of lesser houses. From Somerset, she would turn into Egmont, bringing the car up in front of the large, assured yellow and white frame house where Ellen Terra would be waiting. By taking the route she had chosen, Angela would reach Ellen Terra without unnecessary and geographical reminder of the fact that she was secretly and humiliatingly in love. Otherwise she would simply go out into Norwich, down Norwich, and up Gloucester to Egmont. But on the corner of Norwich and Gloucester stood the blue, ugly, familiar house where lived the man she loved.

Angela pushed back her chair and stood up, still holding her coffee cup. She was ashamed of this unwilling, unrequited falling in love. Like a schoolgirl. There had been, after all, no finality in becoming twenty, no milestone that left behind the tomboy, the schoolgirl, the gawky, too susceptible, unreliable behavior of her heart. She was offended at her own foolishness.

If she had been unable to help loving this man, she must at least discipline her love, mortifying it, feeding it only the meagerest crumbs of recognition and of hope. A man such as he was would demand the privileges of manhood, the right to make his choice and to woo his lady, unwooed. He could not be offered love. He must offer it, the knee voluntarily bent from the height of his pride.

So far, from this height, he had bent only his head. He had offered her no more than the courtly word, the mischievous glance, the easy compliment. Confederate currency, she reminded herself wryly, and never to be confused with legal tender.

At least summer had come. In summer she was someone. In summer she was sweet and solid, not wispy and hidden. In summer it might be that he would look at her and see not only what she was, but what she could be. In the fall she was full of regret, mournful and fearful. In the winter she huddled, miserable and hostile, beside her inadequate inner fires. In the spring she was made vulnerable by hope and expanded slowly, to lose her meanness in the summer, cleansed by rivers of sweat, golden brown of skin and glad enough to be alive. Even Pinckney knew that she was a summer girl.

Reminding herself sternly that summer was less than half an hour old and that wild speculation was the betrayer of foolish virgins, she went out into the day to look for Ellen Terra, who so calmly accepted everything as it was.

Ellen Terra Rook sat on her front porch watching the rain. She was sure it would rain until the end of time, which would be soon. She had read somewhere that the earth was moving away from the sun, into outer darkness. She saw it dripping and moving and darkening as it went. The sun came out as she watched and she moved her spine comfortably up two bones against the raffia back of the chair. The oak leaves lying all over the scrubby grass began to steam.

Mattie opened one side of the front door and stuck her head

outside. "I mos forget, Miss Ellen Terra, Miz Rook she say tell yuh should take this lettuh tuh yo revund."

Ellen Terra sat upright quickly to still the rising and falling, the prickling that occurred in her loins. She held out her hand. Mattie, still in her carpet slippers, with her sweeping-kerchief tied tight around her head, looked to see that no one was coming along the street and shuffled out to give her the note. It was on her mother's heaviest monogrammed stationery.

"Yo Maw bout dressed now, yuh wants tuh see huh, she wants tuh see yuh membe," said Mattie softly.

"Well, I don't," said Ellen Terra. "Miss Angela'll be here for me in a sec'."

"She say nothin foah shuah bout seein yuh," said Mattie agreeably.

Ellen Terra unbuttoned her topcoat with one hand, but did not move. Putting the letter in her lap, she kept the other hand on it, the fingers resting lightly on the face of the envelope. If she saw Mama now, Mama would fuss because she was going out with Angela Madison again. Mama had fussed because she saw too much of Carrie Gregory last year. Before that, she had complained about Hope Stone. She was always deviling Ellen Terra for seeing too much of one girl, always asking why she did not see more of this or that boy.

Mama did not see how it was between girls. Ellen Terra saw friendships with girls as plants: slow-growing, shaded, deep-rooted things. They needed so much time, and so much talk, to grow. There were the things you said and the things you didn't, to make them grow, in the long, long hours of the day. In the evenings, they were there—so pretty, when you had, or even when you did not have, the company of men.

The company of men was different. Friendship with boys was different. Ellen Terra sighed as she thought how quickly such friendships grew. But if they stopped growing, if they faded, there was nothing you could do about it. You could not even tell why.

Ellen Terra hunched one shoulder and rubbed the soft wool of her coat against her round cheek. There were no words for such things, to explain such things to her mother. Words were a musical accompaniment to understanding. Talk was rain on a roof already

9

snug. Otherwise it was distressing. She could not use words to create understanding, as Angela did. She rarely thought in words, but only in pictures. When she paused to focus sharply on a series of pictures, it seemed to her she was thinking. She saw her mother, now, angry, and herself helpless, unable to defend herself. She did not want her mother picking at her and Angela! She was glad when Mattie diverted her attention.

"He look sortuh like Mistuh Gilbut," said Mattie, rolling her eyes, "yo revund."

"He doesn't really," Ellen Terra disagreed, savoring the tingling that rose to make her full-blown breasts flatten themselves against her tight, boyish-form brassiere. She looked down in her lap, at the name, "Rev. Mr. E. Mark Barbee," written in her mother's sprawling hand. "Car coming, Mattie," said Ellen Terra, untruthfully, feeling the warmth rising toward her cheeks, wanting Mattie to leave.

Mattie ducked inside. She had her vanity, and before she would permit herself to be seen outside, she would change her carpet slippers for the broken black shoes that had once been a man's and her sweeping-kerchief for a faded blue bandanna.

Ellen Terra traced the name on the envelope with one forefinger. With the other hand, she absently ruffled the back of her dark, cropped head.

Hearing no sound in the quiet street, in the quiet house, she moved uneasily and got up, drifting across to the porch bannister, where she took off her coat, laying it on the bannister beside her. The sun was hot, streaming slantwise into the porch. She was glad that she was a virgin, however precariously this virtue had been retained. Fortunately you were, or you weren't. She must manage to convey her virginity to Mark Barbee.

She saw herself now at the rectory, separated from her by one block lined with oleander bushes on Egmont Street, by one naked block of Gloucester. On the corner of Gloucester, facing palmetto-lined Norwich, across from St. James's Episcopal Church, was the old, blue rectory. She saw herself invited into the rector's study, where Mark wrote his wonderful sermons at the same wide, varnished desk on which his predecessor, the Reverend Mr. Witherspoon, had composed his prosy preachings. She had seen Mark through the big windows that faced both Norwich and Gloucester, pacing beside the battered sofa where old Witherspoon had always napped in full view of the passers-by. She had watched him sit down at the desk and punch a clattering portable as if he were inspired. . . . She would trust to the moment for what she would say when she saw him now, how she would say it. She bungled things when she planned them. Words were so elusive.

She could, quite naturally, go on to the rectory, leaving word with Mattie for Angela to find her there. It would be proper to deliver a letter from her mother, even though Mark Barbee's aunt had gone back to Mobile, leaving only her gimlet-eyed ghost as chaperone. It might give her a moment with him alone, to go now. She had never seen him alone. It was only the fact of walking that deterred her. She had once walked the town streets. She remembered the children walking, she and Angela and Carrie and Hope, to the public school at the corner of Gloucester and Sussex, a matter of several blocks. They had walked to each other's houses then, and downtown together, too. To get to Oakland, they had taken the interurban streetcar at the corner of Gloucester. By the time they were sixteen, they had all been able to drive and had taken turns wheedling cars from their families. They had not had cars in Oglethorpe, where they had gone to Miss Luttrell's to be "finished," but their families had given them their own cars as graduation presents. This had been when she was eighteen, and by then the streetcar tracks had been taken up. She was nearly twenty now and she had scarcely walked at all for two years in Andalusia. She could see herself driving to the rectory, but she could not quite visualize getting her own car out now, when Angela was coming in hers. It would be natural to call on the bachelor minister with a note from her mother, but it would be queer to walk there. Her dilemma held her until she heard Angela's horn.

It was the horn Angela had found in Italy when the Madisons had gone abroad with her the year before. It sounded a jaunty *sol mi do mi* and Ellen Terra loved it. She ran down the steps and out to the curb.

Angela swung around the corner and swooped to the curb, her tires within an inch of, but not touching, the curb. Barely a second later, the car was under way again, and Angela was shifting into third. It was as neat as if Ellen Terra had been hung like a sack of mail for a train to pick up without stopping.

"Sorry I'm late, toots," said Angela. "Had to put the top down."

"Isn't it heaven?"

"The summer . . ." said Angela, her long face intent above the wheel.

"The spring . . ." said Ellen Terra, reprovingly. Her small hands curled greedily, stickily, like new leaves. Everything was wonderful in the spring. In the summer she saw herself sensible, and so sweaty, being plump. In the winter she was cold and lazy, inclined to stay in bed with cold cream on her tissue-paper skin. In the spring, she felt lovely and things happened to her. This spring, Mark would happen to her because she would burst if he did not.

Angela turned from Egmont into Gloucester, barely pausing for the stop sign that marked the through highway, and headed for Main Street. At the Andalusia House she swung into the driveway, backed out, and turned, so that she could park her car between the white lines on the sunny side of the drug store across the street. Theirs was the only car there, and before the *mi* had sounded on the horn, a white-clad youngster was smiling up at them from beside the car.

"Sure glad to see you-all looking so fine. Cokes, Angela? For both you-all?"

"Are you playing hooky this morning, Jackie?" Ellen Terra asked. She exaggerated her normal, soft, southern pronunciation of the word, saying *maaaawnin* in tribute to its warmth.

"Dad's laid up," he said, "and I'm studying between times." He loved being alone with the drug store, being youthful host to the whole town.

"Double for me," said Angela, "with a dash of ammonia."

Jackie made a sympathetic *moue.* "You, too, Ellen Terra?"

"Dope and lime, Jackie."

"AND a dope and LIME," called Jackie, as if to the counterman who did not come to work until two o'clock, walking into the empty drug store.

"Hangover?" inquired Ellen Terra sympathetically.

"Not really. I didn't drink anything. That corn of Dugdale's is lousy. He gets it in Oglethorpe, the stupid. Everybody knows you get the best corn at Oakland. They wouldn't dare give those Yankees at The Oaks real white lightning. It would kill them off. How do you feel?"

"I just never do have a hangover. I've got Mama's digestion instead of Papa's, thank goodness."

Ellen Terra faked on her drinking, and Angela knew it. She could put a bottle to her lips and swallow most convincingly without actually downing a drop. She was adept at disposing of undetected portions of a drink in handy and unlikely receptacles, looking innocent as a kitten. Angela was too inattentive for success at such tactics. Anyway, she had learned to rather like drinking. Prohibition as a law had certainly enforced drinking, she thought. She wondered what Mark Barbee would think if he knew how much she could hold. He drank himself, of course, but in an old-fashioned, gentlemanly sort of way.

Angela wheeled the window down level with the door and Jackie fixed the metal tray in place. The crushed ice had already frosted the two glasses. Jackie deftly wound a paper napkin around the bottom of each one.

"You look like Claudette Colbert, Ellen Terra," he said. "I declare you do."

"Thanks," said Ellen Terra. As he went back into the drug store, she added, "Thanks from the neck down."

"Don't you think she's pretty?" asked Angela. "I do."

"M-m-m-m," said Ellen Terra, sipping. "I almost gave up Coke for Lent."

"What did you give up?" asked Angela, sliding down in the seat under the wheel so that the sun was on her face.

"Sweets. I always do. And biscuits and corn bread. Everything fattening. I've lost nearly a pound. I'm too fat."

"You're not really," said Angela politely. Neither of them paid any attention to this ritual courtesy.

"And—you can laugh—I gave up reading fiction. It was Papa's idea. He says there's nothing wrong with my brains except I've used them for a trash basket. So instead of reading, I think. With my brains . . ." She paused.

"You're fishing," said Angela amiably. She was willing to

concede Ellen Terra's figure as an asset, especially in a bathing suit, despite its anachronistic curves, but if Mr. Rook thought his daughter was an intellectual, his opinion would have to remain unseconded. The secret of courtesy lay in exaggerating the truth, not in outright lying.

"What did you give up?" asked Ellen Terra.

"Swearing," said Angela. "I actually gave up smoking last year, just to see if I could, but Mama said if I did that again, she'd make me leave home. I was unbearable. The year before," she added inconsequentially, "I gave up Lent."

"Hope says you can't get a decent Coke anywhere in the North," said Ellen Terra. "You reckon Hope goes to the Cape every summer because she *likes* it?" Ellen Terra thought of Cape Cod as a land of angry waters and eternal snow. No descriptions from Hope of bathing and boating could dispel her mental picture. There were Yankees who swam off the Georgia coast in December, too, while you watched them horrified as you shivered in your sweater and your coat. Hope bought white, but *woolen* suits for summer wear at the Cape. There could be no summer where you could bear the touch, even the sight, of wool. For all she sounded like them and had lived just down Egmont Street since Ellen Terra could remember, Hope was a Yankee. Blood was important.

"Yes," said Angela shortly. She knew all about why Hope still went to the Cape for her summers. She knew too much about Hope Stone. Hope always insisted on telling her every last thing. It made her uncomfortably responsible for Hope.

Hope had returned from the Cape that one summer determined not to go again. "I don't belong there any more," she had said triumphantly to Angela. She and Angela had been exclusive best friends then. They were almost exactly the same age, and the six months difference between them and Ellen Terra, the ten months that separated them from Carrie, had taken on new significance when the other two had dropped behind in school. Ellen Terra had disgracefully flunked a grade and Carrie had been kept out for a new series of operations on her crippled leg. Angela and Hope were involved alone together in preparations to leave Andalusia for Miss Luttrell's in Oglethorpe.

"I can't wait," Hope had said. "I adore Miss Luttrell's. Oglethorpe is the dreamiest place in the world." Angela had said, "I hate it. Deadest place in the world, you mean. A nasty old cemetery full of flowers." Being intuitive, which Hope was not, she was preparing herself for the ghastly possibility of failure in Oglethorpe. She knew that she was secure in having a father whose name was Cecil Lord Madison, whose sister, Angela's Aunt Angela, had gone to Miss Luttrell's. She knew that she was insecure because her mother had been Hannah Miller. Miss Luttrell's was no place for the insecure. It was no place for the northern-born Hope Stone. It was Angela herself, protecting herself, who had perpetrated the gibe, for the gibe's sake, that had echoed to laughter at Hope through the school. "You can't become a Confederate," she had said, "by conversion."

Hope had become known as the "Confederate convert" and actually gained a little in popularity thereby. But it had been cruel, and Hope had been hurt. It was hard not to be cruel to Hope. She was so honest, so literal, and so dreadfully frank. She had gone back to the Cape the next summer, and the next. "They just love southern girls up there," Hope had told her wistfully. "The boys fall all over themselves. Up there, they make me feel like I really belong down here." "Well, you do," Angela had said, "in lots of ways."

The "you do" had made Hope happy; the qualification had made her wince. She was logical, Hope was, and therefore easily confused. Odd how deceptive logic was, thought Angela, especially when combined with Hope's indestructible optimism. Hope was like one of those leaded, round-bottomed toys. Bat her down, up she came again. She wondered if Carrie batted Hope down very often. Hope was vulnerable, for all her bounce, and Carrie was mean. Before she had been crippled, Carrie had been a vile-tempered and difficult child. After she had been crippled, and then had learned to manage being crippled, everyone thought she was marvelous, which she was, and that she was extraordinarily sweet, which she was not. If you knew Carrie as well as Angela knew her, you forgot she was crippled and you remembered that she was mean. Angela hoped that Carrie was not too mean to Hope.

To get away from thinking about it, Angela decided to call Hope when she got home. The four of them might go out to The Oaks tomorrow and shoot skeet, or, if it rained again, play bridge.

Whatever had happened in Andalusia, there they were, the four of them. Nothing could really happen to the kaleidoscope of their friendship that had moved forward through the years on scooters, on foot, roller skates, tricycles, and in cars, as it had begun in baby carriages. She and Ellen Terra were now shaken into place on one side of the prism, as best best friends, and Carrie and Hope shared what she and Hope, what she and Carrie, what Ellen Terra and Carrie, Ellen Terra and Hope, had shared in turn. The pattern had shifted, but it had not lost or acquired a part.

Angela called up a series of diminishing pictures of Ellen Terra, differing only in size. She was the same at nineteen as she had been at two—irresistibly pretty to coo over or to whistle at, small and round and squashy, small-boned and white-skinned, black of hair and almost black of small bright eyes, which were either sparkling like black diamonds or blank as raisins in the round face of a gingerbread girl. Her voice was a muted purr and as inviting as her snug body. She was gentle-tempered and generous and untidy as she had been when she would give you all her toys and spilled a tithe of everything she ate on her bib. She had not changed at all. It made Angela feel much the older of the two, knowing how much she herself had changed.

"Where will we go?" asked Ellen Terra. She was putting off again, shyly, the moment when she must tell Angela of the errand her mother had given her. She felt, without thinking about it, that it would be better if no one knew that she loved Mark Barbee. It would spoil something to babble about loving Mark Barbee.

"Down the Marianna road." There were only three ways to leave Andalusia: down the long, straight, shadowless road to Marianna; up the long, curving, tree-shaded road to Oglethorpe; or by the road to Oakland, which was only five miles from town. "For the sun," said Angela decisively. The sun forgave all sins.

"I—I have to go by the rectory first," said Ellen Terra. The extraordinary effort to speak casually, the glaring delay in making this so casual remark, the color that flooded from her heart into her thin-skinned, telltale face, was complete betrayal of her secret. Looking straight at Angela, wide-eyed and unwilling to have so betrayed herself, she saw in the faint color under Angela's never entirely faded tan and in the wary cloudiness of Angela's usually clear brown eyes that they shared the same secret and that Angela would never have told her of it.

By common and wordless consent, they put off Ellen Terra's errand until they should have settled their behavior, now, together.

Angela drove down the asphalt road, her eyes following it without seeing it as it stretched unbeautifully to an unbeautiful horizon. There was only scrub-pine country south of Andalusia, between Andalusia and Marianna. The landscape repeated itself mile after mile, the low, undistinguished pines scattered haphazardly on the hummocky ground, covered between trees with coarse grass, plain, ugly weeds and uglier flowering weeds, and coarser bushes. The land was no good for crops or for cattle or for pecans or for oranges or for hunting. It was no good for anything. Only barrel-bottom white trash lived on it, a family at a time, in pine-board cabins widely separated from each other in spacious desolation, as if such misery could not even bear company. Or Negroes who could find no other place on earth to exist. The pines were not even worth tapping for resin and grew not in groves or in clumps, but stunted and each one alone.

The long duologues-in-motion, the togetherness in the front seat of a car, was the essence of best friendship, thought Angela. It was difficult to withhold your secret thoughts in this special intimacy that both fled from itself and into itself with the movement of the car. There was no privacy as great as this one, at which the world was welcome to look as it fled past. There was no escape from a subject, as there was no escape from the small space they occupied, which, between walls, would have driven them restless. There was no need to change a subject, when motion provided such a causeway, with natural bridges traversing all silences; and, being no need, there was also no excuse. It was possible under such circumstances to protect a secret that was a secret. It was scarcely possible to protect one they both so surely knew.

Angela waited fearfully for Ellen Terra to speak. If she touched it with words, she could only defile this precious and delicate love, which was unlike any other and could only suffer from rude exposure to confidences between women.

"I think," said Ellen Terra without thinking, her sweet, purring voice filling the enclosed space as did the hum of the motor, "that we should, Angela, help Mark. I do care terribly about St. James's, about the church, somehow. It's shivering beautiful sometimes, isn't it? Old Witherspoon made being an Episcopalian seem like being a Christian Young Lady from Miss Luttrell's. Like old, stale orange juice."

"Boring," said Angela happily. "He was an old bore." Trust Ellen Terra. Darling Ellen Terra. A flower of a girl, closing her dark petals at night, opening them dewy and sweet to the morning sun, as natural as the blossoms that grew on the morning-glory vine. She had the pure, sure instincts of a flower or a kitten. As religion, love was undefilable. As their minister, they could talk about Mark without evasion and almost with frankness. Thus they could talk softly around their love and share a secret without cheapening or changing it. Bless Ellen Terra.

Ellen Terra paused at the word "boring." She had never been bored in her life and the word affected her as a mysterious symbol of the things she did not understand about other people. She admired it and could repeat it, but she could not quite encompass it. She nodded and said, "Boring," and went on. "We could go to all the rest of the Lent services, couldn't we?"

"Even to six-thirty communion on Thursdays?" asked Angela, laughing with delight and relief. "That would certainly jar Miss Sis! Wouldn't she be surprised if anybody else turned up? Wonder why Mark doesn't bribe her to stay away so he can sleep." She paused and picked up Ellen Terra's perfect gambit. "I agree, honey child. The church is really a kind of part of us. It's exciting . . ."

Ellen Terra regarded her slightly bemused. "Exciting" was a funny word for the Episcopal church. It sounded almost revivalistic.

". . . the ritual and all. I hate it when people talk in a language I don't know, like Catholics, or make up things in church, like Protestants. It's messy." She felt enormously happy under the bright, high sun.

High sacerdotal peace of early noon, and ebbing tide, thought Angela. That was the first line of a poem she had written during the time when she wrote poems, before she knew too surely that she would never write poems as good as those that had already been written. This one had been written during one summer she had spent with Carrie at the seashore. They had gone every Sunday to service at a sweet, ugly little chapel, very high church. They would come out of the church into the sun, still smelling the incense, and go swimming before late lunch. They would go in on weekdays, too, after swimming, out of the sun to pray. They had argued quite viciously about praying for Carrie's leg to get well. . . . "I think personal prayers, like letters to Santa Claus, must irritate God, the One Who made pine trees and poets," said Angela, following her thoughts and her remembered mode of thought, heedless of the continuity of what she was saying. She was thinking of the infinitely tall pines beside the ugly little chapel, and not seeing the scrubs they were passing.

"He made sweet little wobble-headed nigger babies, too," said Ellen Terra comfortably, settling back in the seat. She still said her prayers at night when she remembered, or rather when she forgot not to, and passionately prayed for what she wanted, ending with God-blesses like an old lullaby prefacing her still childlike slumber.

"Made you, too," said Angela, lightly. No need to be solemn. She must find a new way to handle religion, now that she was returning to it. And not all for love of Mark Barbee. Her period of skepticism had brought her only a hollow feeling of insecurity. "Since He made you, He must have a pretty eye for the flesh."

"How you do talk, Angela," said Ellen Terra, relishing the compliment. "I wish He had given me some of your brains," she added, returning it in kind.

It was the moment for familiar comfort and they dispensed it to each other now with lavish, careless generosity, taking comfort avidly from each other, winnowing the true germs of comfort from the friendly, careless exaggerations, each concentrated on what she was getting and reckless in what she gave, protesting what she was given in order to receive the more.

Ah, if Angela was not *exactly* pretty, she was fine, fine-boned, sensitive, original. If thin and tall, she was *chic*, she had an air, a quality. Her light brown hair was so fine, it had such *lights*, and her dark brown eyes were so *expressive*. Angela looked, said Ellen Terra finally, seeking to make a vocal and adequate return for Angela's larger vocabulary and the happy swelling of her own ego under Angela's extravagantly worded compliments, Angela looked, she repeated, putting the picture she had into words, like a stained-glass window.

Simultaneously they realized that this, having a particular truth, gave Angela an advantage in the unadmitted context wherein they were exchanging comfort. Angela rejoiced covertly and Ellen Terra pouted. For a fleeting second, they were bitter rivals. They did not want this. If Mark Barbee had regarded them both with approval, it was no greater approval than that with which a southern gentleman should look at attractive young women. He had not singled them out. He was equally pleasant to Carrie and to Hope.

Restlessly, Ellen Terra plucked a compact from her bag and regarded her own face. Her small black eyes blinked at her image and blinked away dissatisfied. She thought of Hope's eyes, blue and enormous as twin mountain lakes and fringed like pretty lakes with ferns.

"Hope's the prettiest girl in the *world*," she wailed, stuffing away her compact.

"Carrie," said Angela flatly, "is smarter than I am and so distinguished."

"Well," said Ellen Terra, sighing and then brightening, "we must start organizing things and getting up stuff, for the church."

"It'll be fun," said Angela, nodding.

They were on their way back to Andalusia now, Angela's foot consciously steady on the accelerator. The needle held at fifty, scarcely wavering. They were both silent at last, cozily silent, at momentary peace with the situation they found themselves in together.

They turned their heads toward the rectory as they came down Gloucester, but the position of the sun made it impossible to see inside the bright, blank study windows. As they came around the corner, they swung their gaze from the blank, blue rectory across to the gray stone church. In front of the choir-room door stood the red roadster with the powerful, custom-built engine in the custom-made body that Mr. Gregory had given Carrie two years before and that she vowed she would never change for another model. Leaning up against the red door, the sun gilding his thick brown hair, his high-nosed profile highlighted and laughing, his arms in shirtsleeves casually folded along the door of the car, was Mark Barbee, looking down on the faces upturned to his. Hope's blue eyes were opened wide enough to drown a man and the expression on Carrie's aquiline face was soft as down. The back of Carrie's roadster was loaded with flowers from the Gregory greenhouse. As Angela and Ellen Terra drove up, the two girls in the roadster moved in preparation for helping Mark to carry the flowers into the church.

It was when the four of them met on the sidewalk, casually friendly, with a cooing chatter of greetings that was as charming as the greetings of birds and as frivolous, ignoring for the moment, as was fitting, the man in their midst, that Evelyn Mark Barbee had his first impulse to flee.

"You cain't hardly blame em *at* all," said Mattie to Fate Pinckney when she got home that night, later than Fate because the Rooks ate later than the Madisons did. "Po lil things. Along he comes in duh desert, lookin like Angeal Gabriel an Mistuh Gilbut, apreachin *fiah* an brimstone . . ."

"How you find out he preach fire and brimstone?" asked Fate. "Bet he preach like Miss Nellie at Sunday school."

"He preach fiah," said Mattie. "He uh man, ain't it?"

"How you find out he's a man?" asked Fate provocatively.

"Any gal know *that*," said Mattie. "Even when he got uh lobsided haid like you is, ah knowd *that*, frum all duh way down duh rivah an *across* duh creek."

Fate said cheerfully, "Now he's got em all layin on they backs, what good'll it do anybody? What's the use being a man if you gotta marry em?"

It was a touchy point. Fate refused to marry Mattie, despite ten years of reasonable fidelity on both sides and two children with lopsided heads, indisputably his.

"Doan yuh talk lak dat sos ah kin heah yuh," said Georgianna Church, Mattie's mother. From the close-by gloom of the porch next door, the rocking chair creaked as she gave it an extra shove with her bare feet. "Doan yuh talk lak dat sos ah kin half heah yuh, nuthah."

Fate and Mattie turned toward her with their bodies and

nodded in unison, as if she could see them on their unlit porch in the unlit alley that the oak trees shielded from the moon.

"Yessum," added Mattie.

"I got me two bits on Anglah," said Fate.

"Talk up ef yuh ain gonna shut up," said Georgianna.

On the steps next door, below Georgianna, the second of her three daughters, Mercy, stirred and sighed.

"Hush, now, you Mercy," said Georgianna.

"Miss Anglah be too skinny," said Mattie, after meditation, raising her voice. She reverted to her original theme. "It's uh desert. Ah sho would hate tuh be me uh white gal in Andalusia. All dem gals, putty gals, too, an havin tuh divide em up one *man*. Po lil things."

"Ain't that Sonny Boy a man?" asked Fate. "Ain't that Logan Knight?"

"Yuh oughta say Mistuh, you Fate Pinckney," said Georgianna into the darkness. "Yuh duh devil's own, Fate Pinckney, an one day duh devil gonna fin it out."

"Ain't that Dugdale Winthrop?" demanded Fate.

"Naw," said Mattie. "Po lil things."

3. Preacher and Women

The Reverend Mr. Evelyn Mark Barbee was lost.

He awoke with a start as if from a dream to find himself in the sanctuary of a church, standing before the altar of God, his mouth open, and lost. His tongue was tense, a word vibrant on its tip. It must be a word of prayer. One did not preach, read, or announce from the sanctuary. He had no idea what word from what prayer tingled on his tongue, or whether it was the one just spoken or the one he should speak. The word was lost for all eternity, the eternity of the damned.

The prayer book, open on its brass stand on the altar, blurred before his eyes. He glanced, panicking, down at himself, but his ample white surplice was reassuring. He was not naked in front of his congregation, as he had been once in a nightmare.

His surface mind scurried frantically now, classifying bits of evidence, trying to help him find his way back into a state of grace. The two tall communion candles were lit. It was, then, the service of the Holy Communion, which, his surface mind commented, was the longest and the most difficult to reconstruct. The sun shone through the vast red stained-glass window over the altar in long, reddish, dusty rays, so angled that they must reach to the farthest pew behind him, if he dared to turn around. It was, therefore, the early service. He would preach no sermon. There would be no choir. Out of the corner of one eye, he confirmed that the organ was dark. It must be summer. It was stifling hot, even under the high-pitched dawn rays of the sun, in the shadowy vault of the church. But, glancing, he saw that his stole was black. It came to him easily, then, that it was Lent and that it was Thursday. He tried to focus on the prayer book, its clear, outsize print at eye level, but he was still sufficiently lost even if the page came clear. He had betrayed his profession and he was affronting the Lord.

Into the timeless void, piercing the panic of drumming in his ears that still echoed from the thump his heart had given when he awoke to find himself damned, sounded a voice like that of an angel. It was a teacherish, angelic voice, enunciating carefully: "Thy king-dom COME . . ."

The sweat started under the arms of his heavy black cassock as he picked up his cue. Oh blessed, lifelong familiarity of the Lord's Prayer. Oh pitfall of familiarity that had let his unblessed other thoughts carry him far away from the sacred place of their departure.

"Thy will be done. On earth as it is in Heaven!" he chanted gratefully, thanking Miss Sis, who had found him, and the Lord.

Miss Sis's voice subsided into a murmur, joined by a murmuring quartet from the other side of the center aisle that separated the rows of pews.

The quartet of soft, young voices brought back his other thoughts, as Miss Sis's penetrating tenor, which could be heard across a county when she chose to raise it, had brought him back to the ritual words of his responsibility. Sternly he suppressed them, but they continued in subdued counterpoint to the service he was reading. The four young women who knelt with bowed heads in the fourth and fifth pews on the right-hand side, the pews belonging by long tradition to the Madison and the Gregory families, had come to this service, brightly and flimsily arrayed in the too hot, too early morning, not to worship God, but to worship him.

". . . that our sinful bodies may be made clean by His body . . ."

He applied himself deeply to this final prayer before the partaking of the communion and closed his ears to the murmuring chorus which joined his "Amen."

Humbly and devoutly, he gave himself the bread and then the wine he had consecrated for the purpose. Then he turned and lifted the plate to invite such as were ready and had confessed and repented their sins to partake likewise. He did not look down as the five women rustled softly up to the rail and knelt before it. He went first to serve Miss Sis who took her accustomed place on the left, near the closed gate in the railing that separated the sanctuary from the chancel.

"The Body of our Lord Jesus Christ . . ."

Alone, together, these many Thursdays since he had come to St. James's, he and Miss Sis had celebrated the mystical eating of the body and drinking of the blood of Christ, humbly, well, and without mishap. She did not ask of him or of God that they give her more than was due from them. He loved Miss Sis. She was a spinster who lived out in a bamboo thicket where she protected her individual and private life and who came into Andalusia only for groceries and for God. She was an admirable woman, daughter of Eve, not of Lilith, and fit wife for the man she had never found. They called her eccentric because she had saved her maidenhood from waste by retaining her individuality. She was far from one of the old maids, widows, or unhappily married middle-aged who tried to get from the church and its clergy false substitutes for what they missed in life. These were the slow death of the church. Miss Sis was part of its life. She came to the Thursday services, instituted some fifty years before to try the early-morning midweek consciences of St. James's already lackadaisical congregation, in the rain or the heat, when not even the little acolytes would any longer serve the early-morning altar. He thanked Miss Sis silently for her aid this morning, and cherished her in his heart as he put the wafer in her rough, cupped hands.

The young were also part of the church's life or it would die.

As he moved to the other side of the gate, the four faces at the rail lifted to him and the four pairs of cupped hands were held out to him, formal and decorous, but still beseeching. He knew that while he was almost sincerely, almost humbly, offering them

25

the body of Christ, these four young, ripe virgins of Andalusia were accepting from him his own body and offering in return their own. The sweat dripped from his taut, young man's body, the blood rose and beat in his ears, he felt himself shy like a colt from the quadrupled impact.

Two of the faces lifted to him at the altar rail expressed the shadow of his own passionate effort to separate the occasion and the man, the man and the priest. The other two worshipped frankly at the altar of Eros. "Take and eat this. . . ." As he moved along to each one, they dropped their eyes. The dusty sunrays slanting over their heads gave to each of their shadowed faces a wild, worshipping beauty and he wanted to kiss each one of their soft, yearning mouths and he hated them all.

In the vestry room, finally alone, since no acolyte and no choir accompanied him, he lifted the trinity of his fingers high and pronounced the final benediction in ringing tones. As he turned quickly and wrested the surplice off, over his head, preparing to go out to the front to speed his departing communicants, he felt a welling impulse to laugh. He smelled, under the arms of the heavy cassock, as if he had just tackled a fullback, or completed a four-and-a-half-minute mile, which was the best time he had ever clocked, or wrestled with the devil himself.

He had heard clergymen fumble for lost places, betrayed by the very rigidity of the Anglican service which made it so unvaryingly and forever beautiful. He had heard them stutter and repeat themselves, spoiling the poetry and form of the service. In the contemptuous confidence of youth, he had been sure that he would never commit the misdemeanor of inattention, much less the sin of complete defection. But even his grandfather, in the legendary vagaries of his old age, had never committed such a lulu, such a darb. He must be laughing in heaven, the old man who had so loved human failings. The beamish son of his beamish boy. Right in the middle of the Lord's Prayer!

Mark Barbee threw back his head and laughed softly upward, thinking of his grandfather. Then, remembering what had led him into error, he lowered his head, away from his grandfather, and straightened his athlete's shoulders. Because he was, like his father, his grandfather, and his great-grandfather, an Episcopal minister, did not mean that he merely followed in the footsteps of his ancestors, or that he needed them now. He made his own decisions, in the full pride of youth and free will, prior to praying. Part of his deep excitement in entering the ministry had been because it channeled his youthful vigor and challenged his modern indiscipline. Still, it must have been easier in old Evelyn's day.

Hitching his tasseled sash tight around his thin waist, Mark paused, thinking again of his grandfather. The big-bellied, friarlike Bishop of Colorado ("No eastern diocese would have me, son, a dirty old Johnny Reb like me!") had a habit of booming his advice. "Beware the daughters of Lilith, son!" And "Marry young, son. Marry young."

Of course, he could take one of them to wife. His loins responded instantly to the thought and he tightened his sash angrily. He was damned if he would marry in order not to burn. If he was tempted by all his passionate young women parishioners, he had better be digging ditches for a living. It would be easier to be celibate if he were digging ditches, he thought, deriding himself and the pinch of his sash and the pose of his muscular shoulders. Summer had no right to come before the end of Lent, betraying him to these southern women before he could get onto the tennis court and into the swimming pool. It was easier in the North, where he had served his first parish. Common courtesy stopped so much shorter of sex and both his Easters had been cold. Now, the warm, prolonged southern summer he loved so much had come, with no spring for warning, and four virgins were offered him at the altar rail.

He snorted softly, throwing back his head, his nostrils flaring. Southern daughters of Lilith! For himself, he would choose a daughter of Eve to wife. And *he* would seek and choose her, not be sought and chosen. *And* he would seek in the hammock, in the car moving privily through the night, on the wide front porches of his beloved South, not select one kneeling before him at the altar as if she were living sacrifice to a pagan priest. *And* he would go out now— and give these four lovelies his calm, friendly benediction, promising them nothing. He wanted to see Miss Sis. Old Evelyn would have loved Miss Sis. He would send for his aunt.

Giving his sash a final hitch, he went thus girded out into the staggering sunshine to find his five parishioners.

To his disappointment, Miss Sis had not waited for him. He saw her retreating back, the black bombazine skirt that reached to the top of her high-buttoned shoes, the starched white blouse with the celluloid collar and the bow tie, the sailor straw of her youth visibly marking her eccentricity. As he looked after her, she put two fingers in her mouth and whistled so that it could be heard half a mile away. So she commanded, still entirely feminine, the attention of her friends. The friend this time was Old Bailey, on his way to work in the Madison garden.

"Hi, you, Bailey," called Miss Sis, "you come on out and cut my bamboo for me, hear?"

Old Bailey's reply was inaudible, and Mark turned to the girls. He was easy and familiar with them now and no longer frightened of them. He shook them warmly, each one, by the gentle hand, considering them as he did so. He would make himself no false promises that one might not still be the woman he sought.

Angela was the nearest to his height, tall and taut, her body responsive as an aspen tree to breeze and sun. Her mobile face, tilted toward the sun, now pretty, now plain, was full of unrealized promise. Her restless eyes, brown as autumn leaves, were sometimes clear with intelligence, sometimes cloudy with liking to be alive. As she looked up at him, her large, childishly formless and sensitive mouth parted slightly, he felt a swelling of confidence in the fullness of his twenty-six years, in the full dignity of his profession, in the rightful arrogance of his southern maleness. He considered her kindly. She was not really very pretty, nor yet grown, and she was preening awkwardly in her attempt to attract him, but the faintly distinguishable pain lines at the corner of her mouth argued her a daughter of Eve, making tearful night choices between good and evil. His mother would have known her for a lady.

He turned then to Hope, aware that he was teasing them all with his arrogant, slow regard, revenging himself a little. His appreciative, attentive and sexually lively manner, which both elevated and reduced all womankind, was bred into his bones. He knew it contained no false promises, either from him or to the southern women.

Hope stood foursquare, unlounging, compact, sturdy and prim. From the wide windowpanes of her clear, blue eyes, she promised him honestly her honest devotion. Benign and judicious, he regarded her extraordinary, perishable prettiness and wished her early marriage. She would make an excellent wife, her transplanted virtues resisting the southern sun. With Olympian kindness, fatherly, he offered her in his mind the choice among the eligible young men. Lanky Dugdale Winthrop—prop him up to his inordinate, underfed height and mend his conspicuously broken heart. Dreamy, good-looking Logan Knight, once the vainglory of his intercollegiate diving championship had diminished a little . . . Sonny Boy Lovejoy was a gay little man who would enliven the Stone household and whose infidelities would be fictional. . . . Paternally he smiled at Hope, unaware that she took his prolonged consideration as affirmative reply to the promise in her eyes.

Glancing at Carrie and glancing away, he saw her almost beautiful. Suffering had aged her and sharpened her wisdom and her wit, as it had burned the softness from her sharply boned, gallant face. For all the distortion of her body, her torso was fine and she was wide of shoulder and her head was held high. It would take an older man to appreciate Carrie.

But no man could fail to appreciate Ellen Terra, as no boy could resist a small, black, squashy ripe berry still on the vine. Who would take her, merry and somnolent, sweet, ripe and careless? Logan Knight or Dugdale? Wild Bill Bloodgood, galloping down from Oglethorpe? Abruptly he was jealous and he wanted them all for himself. He wanted to gather all four of them in this sunlit moment into his long and so long empty arms.

They stirred together, and their inter-reaction to each other spoiled even the sweet pain of his momentary possessiveness. Their linked friendship lessened their separate virtues and made plain their terrible voraciousness. Nervously he rejected them all and spoke to them, his voice deliberately humdrum.

"Thanks for coming out so early," he said.

"Some of those cold Thursdays, didn't you wish old Miss Sis would stay home so you could go snuggle back in bed?" teased Ellen Terra.

"Sure I did," he admitted, grinning and relaxing. "I hate cold weather."

"So do I!" exclaimed Angela, fervently kin to him in this.

"Do you rush out and sin after Easter, Mark?" asked Carrie in her husky, edged voice. "Go on a worldly tear?"

"And *how*," he admitted again. "Reminds me, Dugdale and Logan suggested we have a church dance after Easter. What do you think?"

"Oh, wonderful," said Hope, her voice like a silver bell. "A cotillion! Dugdale told me you were interested in livening up the parish. He's quite excited."

"Fancy, long-leggedy lazy Dugdale," purred Ellen Terra.

Carrie said gruffly, "St. James's was dead while Mr. Witherspoon was here. He was a disapprover."

"Young people," said Mark, and then stopped because he sounded unctuous.

"You sound a million," laughed Angela.

It was hard to be natural as a clergyman, thought Mark uncomfortably.

"Let's have a treasure hunt too," said Hope.

"We'll have a rejuvenation meeting after Easter," said Mark. "All of us." He was tired now, and miserably hot in his cassock. He wanted to get away from the restless, lively female faces that surrounded him. He had a great deal to do, preparing for Palm Sunday, which was only two days away, and which was followed by the most strenuous week on his calendar, Holy Week, climaxed by Easter.

"Lent must wear you out," said Angela tenderly, forgetting her companions for an instant.

"Must have," he said. "Do you know that's the first time I ever went up in my lines?" He used the theatrical parlance naturally, having been an avid amateur performer, being unafraid of sacrilege through words.

"During the Lord's Prayer, too," said Hope. "Ain't you ashamed?"

"As the very devil." He smiled at Ellen Terra's startled face. She was a plump little dope of a darling. He felt entirely at ease again. Maybe God would give him wisdom as he had granted it to Solomon with his thousand wives.

They stirred and made ready to go then, realizing that the ritual social interval on the church steps was well over, that Mark was waiting for them to go. They wanted, too, instinctively, to get away from each other, knowing that their separate charms were hopelessly reduced because they were together. Angela looked down at Ellen Terra and at Hope and felt that she never wanted to see either of them again, the one thrusting her round, uptilted breasts, the other opening her indecently large eyes at the tall minister. Die, she commanded them absurdly, feeling that she towered above them, feeling an irrational gust of hate as she had as a child. Die! Then she laughed at herself and summoned from within her pity for them both and some for herself.

The minister went into the church and the girls separated and went toward their four cars, parked behind each other near the sidewalk: Carrie's custom-built red roadster; Angela's gray cabriolet with the top down, the musical horn perched on the side, its rubber bulb surmounting a cluster of silver pipes; Ellen Terra's touring car, and Hope's coupe.

"See you later," they muttered to each other, knowing and resenting in this moment that this was true.

4. Poor Women!

In the moment that she went alone toward her car, Angela felt that it was impossible to be alone just now. If she did not want to be with Ellen Terra or with Hope, neither did she want to be in her own company, with this unreasonably long morning ahead of her, with her confused and embarrassing thoughts.

She paused until Carrie had made her slower and ungainly way to her car, until the others had driven off. "Come have breakfast with me," she called to Carrie. Carrie's reserve had the discipline of her determination to hide her physical pain from the world. Carrie would not talk about religion as if it were sex, or the other way round.

Carrie lit a cigarette with a sigh of relief.

"Don't know what possessed me to get up and come to church at this unholy hour," she remarked, dragging deeply at the cigarette. "To make up for not going next Friday maybe. I can't sit still and not smoke for three hours Good Friday. Let's go out to The Oaks and have a fancy breakfast. Birds, or something."

"Fun," said Angela, liking Carrie's deep, nonchalant voice, her prickliness. "I'll leave my car at the house and go with you."

Carrie always liked to drive. She drove extremely well, if much too fast. Unlike the rest of them, she rarely talked while she was driving.

Along the narrow, pretty road to Oakland, a few Negroes were walking, swinging their arms like pendulums and moving through the unreal early sunshine as if they were objects propelled along by some exterior force. The lodges, deep in the pines along the river, were closed at this time of the year. Only a few of them would be open for Easter. The town families came out there in the summer and the fall, and the northerners came down in the fall. Angela and Carrie glimpsed two men plodding around the still dew-wet golf course on the left, but inside the entrance to The Oaks they saw no one lurking about the elaborate, half-tended grounds. The hotel looked shambling, instead of rambling, as advertised, and almost imperceptibly run-down.

They were the first guests in the dining room. There were few visitors in the hotel at this time of year. Those who came for the limited spring hunting were out long since and would not return until later. Those who did not hunt at The Oaks lay late in bed.

The white head waiter greeted them with a head waiter's wan professional rapture. He knew them as the daughters of lodge owners, as patrons from Andalusia, but he fumbled their names.

"Mighty early in the morning," he repeated as he ushered them to a choice table by the faintly dirty window. "Now what can I offer you that would tempt you delicate ladies?"

They ordered discursively, wide-awake and hollow with what felt like hunger, and were served by Luke, a middle-aged Negro man who knew their names and their ages.

"Let's make it a champagne breakfast while we're about it," said Carrie argumentatively. "I feel like celebrating. God knows what. I feel like drinking anyway."

Angela said, "Do they have it?" She felt disturbed and distraught. She was losing all her lazy, drifting comfort in life, being so unfortunately preoccupied with her love. It made her feel ungainly and uncomfortable.

"Well, they call it champagne and they charge for champagne. Dad gave me a formidable check for Easter, so it's on me. If we don't like it, we can lump it. I think it's better than gin and ginger ale. Whoever thought up gin and ginger ale?"

33

It was brought to them by Luke, the bottle and the bucket of ice both wrapped in towels, not so much to disguise their contents as to make an obeisance in the direction of the law, or perhaps to flaunt the breaking of it. When it was cold, Luke poured it solicitously into water glasses, remarking as he did so that they were being mighty gay this morning. Both of them looked at him with light scorn. They were not being gay.

It was very bad champagne, thought Angela, from the limited sophistication of two weeks in France the year before, if it was champagne at all. Still it was cold and it sparkled and to its indifferent charm was attached the charm of the idea, of the name. If they were not gay, it was still a gay thing to do and the notion of drinking it with breakfast protested any monotony in life, or in a morning that already seemed to have lasted forever.

Under the influence of the drink and the idea, she began to enjoy her breakfast, so lavishly ordered on the theory that what she felt might be hunger. The young squab were beautiful to see and pungent to taste. Angela's mother said frequently and fervently that nobody on earth could fix squab as they did at The Oaks.

"It's such fun to eat, really," said Angela greedily. "When I get to Mama's age, I am going to do nothing but eat. It's the only graceful pleasure for your middle age."

"Do you really care what you eat?" asked Carrie. "I don't." She was thinner than Angela, thin to emaciation, and was smoking as she picked at the bird. "I like to think about it. I like to plan dinners. I even like to cook, but not to eat. I'd rather shoot birds than eat them."

Angela did not reply to this. Raised in hunting country, she was a poor shot and still suffered twinges when she did manage to hit anything small and helpless or small and on the wing. It was an attitude and an inability that aroused no sympathy in Andalusia or in Oakland.

Time began to pick up speed as the sun rolled higher and then was very high and hot. They were still alone in the dining room, although it seemed as though hours had passed since dawn. They talked, leaning toward each other as if there were others to overhear, and as if it mattered if they did. The talk was random and familiar and chopped into separate paragraphs, without continuity.

"Oh, for God's sake, let's get drunk," said Carrie after their coffee. Peremptorily she ordered another bottle of champagne. "I insist on celebrating—something, any old thing will do."

Angela said agreeably, "We can even sober up in time for lunch. The virtue of getting up so early. We can pretend it's last night."

"I hate getting drunk at night, especially on Saturday night," said Carrie contentiously. "Have you ever been drunk? I've never seen you drunk."

"Twice, really; I didn't like it. I like to drink, though. I'm liking this."

"It's rather fun. It's so silly. Have some more." Without waiting for Luke, she poured out the first glass of the second bottle. It was still warm. Neither of them minded, but watched it froth to the very edge of the glasses without spilling.

A few other people came into the dining room, hearty in hunting clothes or barely washed from bed. Several of them nodded to Carrie and Angela, or spoke, and they replied affably, agreeing that it was hot—hot, turning back together at the polite but fractional instant so that no one would join them or continue the conversation in companionably raised voices. They spoke earnestly together, as if their talk had purpose instead of merely echoing things they had said to each other a hundred times before.

"I wish I were younger or older," said Angela when the dining room had emptied again. Even the head waiter had gone, and they were entirely alone. She was not thinking of what she said, but was feeling restless, wanting to have drunk less, wanting to be moving, wishing this third bottle were empty. "Or prettier or uglier. Or something. Or something." She took another swallow, the bubbles tickling her nose. It made her laugh.

"Did you ever wish you were somebody else?" asked Carrie, eyeing her distantly over the fresh cigarette she was lighting after grinding a butt into a pile of them in front of her.

"No!" said Angela, and then hushed, startled as her voice echoed around her ears.

"I wish I were a man," exclaimed Carrie. "I hate being a woman. I hate it because it's so lousy. It's stinking. It's degrading."

"It's not," said Angela loudly. Then very quietly, "It's not. It's not. It's good to be a woman. It's fine to be a woman. It's better than anything. I like being a woman. I want to be one until I die."

"Calm down," said Carrie, surprising Angela, who had felt herself extraordinarily calm, calm and firm. "You will be. But it stinks."

"It doesn't," said Angela, more calm, more firm. "It's what's done to being a woman that stinks. We haven't learned how. It's fine to be one if you can just find out how."

"There's no way how," said Carrie morosely.

Luke peeked in through the swinging door to the pantry and then came in and poured out for them again. They waited for him to go away, for the bubbles to subside in the glasses.

"You're just trying to make the best of a lousy bargain," said Carrie, leaning toward Angela. "And you can't."

Angela said combatively, "I'm going to find out how. I'm going to be a damn good one. Oh. Sorry. I gave up swearing for Lent."

"How silly," said Carrie, the s thickened almost to a lisp.

Angela felt around for her sobriety. She wanted to argue this question well. It was so very, very, very important.

"It's not silly. It's a nice, arbitrary . . ." Arbitrary was a sober, exact word; Angela felt exhilarated and pleased. ". . . arbitrary thing to do, giving up things for forty days. It makes the year come out right. Like being cold in the winter and hot in the summer, so you can sit by fires and go swimming in the sun."

"You're a lady," said Carrie. "That you are." Carrie paused and Angela bridled, remembering that her mother had been Hannah Miller, and that it could not be taken for granted that she, Angela, Hannah Miller's daughter, was a lady.

"But I don't like you," went on Carrie emphatically. "I'm drunk, of course. I am drunk like a lady, too. I don't like me, either."

"I like you," said Angela defiantly, straightening her back and placing her hands nicely in her lap. "I like me, too."

"Do you really?" said Carrie. "Not that I give a good God damn, you understand. Not that I believe you, even. The question is academic. Let's grow up."

"We are," said Angela, "I guess." This was a facer. "You have to be at twenty. It's the rule."

"You mean, you're supposed to."

Angela nodded. That was exactly what she did mean. They both drank.

"It takes forever to grow up," said Carrie. "And then women never grow up. It's *hell* to be a woman."

"How can a man love you if you aren't a woman?" asked Angela, triumphant. This, of course, was the answer. "A *man*, I mean."

"How can he if you are?" asked Carrie. Angela felt her courage ooze. "How can anybody? That's the awful bloody bottom stinking nasty hell of it." She paused and Angela paused, too, suspended in non-thinking, unable to answer, aware that she must answer for her own sake, must answer to refute. "Well, love 'em," said Carrie reflecting. "Maybe. I suppose that's one thing. Maybe men can manage to love women somehow. But *like* them? Never. Until hell freezes over. Do you like Hope and Ellen Terra? Do you? Do you?"

"Yes," said Angela softly, her courage gone, her body shaking lightly. "Often. I do. Yes, damn, damn, damn, I do, Carrie. Honestly, I do."

"There you are," said Carrie. "You don't." Her long, fine hands went up in a despairing gesture that wavered as her eyes began to close and she slumped a little toward the table. She crooned to herself in infinite sadness. "Men don't like women and women don't like women. Poor women. Poor women."

5. Black and White

There was a midsummer thunder storm that night, violent and destructive. A section of the road through the swamp was blown away. The bridge that crossed the creek beyond the Miller and Rook Company collapsed and the telephone wires were down all over the county.

Angela woke up in the morning to find that her turbulence of spirit, which had responded to the storm in wakeful intervals during the night, had subsided with the storm. There was a fresh flush of sunburn on her face, unbecomingly uneven, and concentrated on her nose, which was immovably stuffed.

It was, at last, a fine, spring day. Leaning out of the window of her room, Angela saw her mother conferring with Pinckney and Old Bailey over the peaceful havoc in the yard. Old Bailey was stirring the strewn moss under the giant oak with his stick. Still wet, the moss was greener than the faded, unrevived grass. On the tree, it was already regaining its beardlike gray under the gentle toweling of the spring sun. If Old Bailey had come, it meant that it was truly spring. Old Bailey could not read the calendar on the wall and knew no arbitrary marking off of months and seasons. Angela's body had rejected both winter and summer because she had read on a wall that it was spring. She had been drunk, overexposed and underdressed yesterday and she had a hangover, sunburn and a cold. Bailey came simply when he and the earth were ready to produce flowers, in their own sweet time.

He was saying "Ymmmmm, ymmmm," to her mother. That meant yes ma'am in words and nothing at all in spirit. He would do as he pleased and the garden and the yard would look as he wanted them to look. So it had been every year since she was born, and neither her mother nor Pinckney, who during his eight years with the Madisons had also argued with Old Bailey as perennially as her mother did, would have anything to say about it.

"It would be nice to change the zinnias this year, Bailey. Zinnias are so *brazen*," her mother was saying. "Put the phlox . . ."

"Yummm," said Old Bailey, stirring the moss with his stick. "Yuh **UMMM**."

Such a nice, polite, old-fashioned Negro, they said, who knew his place. He did indeed, thought Angela, and giggled. You might as well argue with an obsequious mist.

She met her mother in the downstairs hall.

"I don't think Bailey has any intention of moving those zinnias," said her mother comfortably. "We get more zinnias every year. Anybody can grow zinnias."

"Yes, darling," said Angela. "I love zinnias."

"That's nice. Angela, would you go out to The Place," went on her mother. She called the Miller and Rook Pecan Company "The Place" and her absent-minded persistence in appropriating and capitalizing this generic term had prevailed until the whole town called it so. "Ask your father if he wants anything and if he's coming home for lunch and whether he wants me to send any out to him, or what? The telephone line to The Place is down and the bridge over the creek was sure to go down in that idiotic storm."

"All right," said Angela. "I'd love to."

"You've got a *cold*."

"Yes'm."

"Bundle up then, sort of. I never saw summer come before spring like that."

Angela telephoned Ellen Terra to drive out to The Place with her.

"Sweetie, I can't," wailed Ellen Terra, in mocking regret. "Mama wants me and Carrie to help her and Mrs. Gregory do the church—for Palm Sunday. Mama and Mrs. Gregory are Altar Guild this week. I promised I would." There was an almost unnoticeable pause. "You want to help?"

"No," said Angela, and presently hung up. Ellen Terra, she decided, was not an innocent flower, but a triple bitch.

She telephoned Hope, feeling glad of Hope's clear honesty, her inability to be deceptive.

"You've got a cold," said Hope on the telephone.

"So I have," said Angela impatiently, irrationally irritated.

"Do you want to go in my car then?" asked Hope, solicitous, affectionate.

"Heavens, *no*," said Angela. She hated closed cars. "On a day like this? I'll come for you in five minutes. You be ready. I'll tootle." She hated to pause on the way, or to leave the car until she had reached a major destination. "Watch for me." There was no porch on the Stone house, and there was central heating inside. It accentuated the differences between the Stones, who had moved there, who had built a new house, and the town's own.

Once they were on the way, it was impossible to be anything but cheerful. Chattering agreeably, and even urgently—as if they had been separated for a long time—they passed by the side road that led from the Oglethorpe highway to The Place and had to turn around and go back to find it. They laughed uproariously at this misadventure, using it as an excuse for laughter, filling with laughter the pine grove that crowded against the narrow road to The Place.

The grove ended abruptly, as if it were fenced, and they began to pass the raggedly cultivated farms where were grown the vegetables canned at The Place. They waved carelessly at such figures as they passed at work in the fields, making no effort to identify the figures, bestowing the gesture like young princesses, neither waiting for nor noting the response.

The Place was busy almost all year now, under Angela's papa's excellent management and because of Clementine Rook's insistence. It was possible to raise three crops yearly in this kindly country and there was always something to can, when the pecan season was not yet, or was over. For a gentleman, Mama said, Papa really had a remarkable business brain and The Place was yearly more profitable.

It was certainly not impressive to look at. It was a haphazard collection of board buildings, more or less gray as they were more or less weather-beaten, in accordance with the number of years they had stood against the weather. The two oldest buildings were no longer used and were rotting comfortably up against their newer neighbors. The third oldest was being mended at by two Negro men to whom a little boy handed hammer or nails on demand, humming as he did so. Soon it would be no longer worth repairing, either. On the other side of the group of buildings, a new wing was being added by the unindustrious labor of three more Negroes. There was plenty of labor. Paint was harder come by, and so was cement, which had been used to construct one small, snug office for the manager.

"Where's Mister Madison, Uncle Peter?" asked Angela of the very old Negro man who had the courtesy title of gatekeeper and who was bobbing his head at them in welcome.

"Duh bridge done gone un duh stohm, Miss Anglah. He down dah fixin she. He be raht back."

"Why don't they fix that bridge for good and all?" asked Hope curiously. "Seems to me it falls down every time it thunders."

"It's practically no trouble to fix the bridge every time," said Angela absently.

"Oh," said Hope, sitting bolt upright and opening her enormous eyes. "They're *singing.*"

From the biggest shed, farthest away from them in the direction of the pecan groves, came the sound of women's voices like a many-toned hum from a hive of bees.

"Not really," said Angela listening. "Not yet." There were only tentative snatches of song to be heard, silence, then several at a time, ragged and unmatched, but somehow never unharmonious. "How many have you got working today, Uncle Peter?" The old man was relaxed into immobility beside the car, husbanding his life in an unembarrassed semblance of death until it should be asked of him for some purpose to be alive again. She repeated her question.

41

The old man's smooth, wrinkleless face took on the imitative aspect of thought. "Ah reggn thutty, fohty, fohty *an* some—round thuh uhbouts. We cannin peas, Miss Anglah. Ah mos shuah we cannin us peas. If tain't tomatoes, it's mos sholy peas."

"Do make them sing, Angela," begged Hope. "Like you did the other time. I do love it."

"I can't *make* them sing," said Angela. She liked to hear the women sing. Lord, how they could sing! But Hope's self-conscious enthusiasm embarrassed her. There was no way to share an enthusiasm as deliberately unrestrained as hers. You could only echo it or reject it, irritated, your own enthusiasm paling beside it. You couldn't share it. Stop picking at Hope, Angela Madison, she scolded herself. Hope was one of the nicest human beings with whom God had seen fit to mollify the earth. Honest Hope, decent Hope, literal-minded, logical and vulnerable Hope, so pretty Hope. There was no reason to withhold something from her just because she wanted it so much. "Come on," said Angela, overcoming her essential reluctance to move while comfortable, while the sun shone on her comfort.

They went toward the far shack, passing the three Negro men who were building the new wing. Studiously unaware that the girls were passing, the men put on a playlet, a little dance, in a burst of co-ordinated and rhythmic activity, as they walked by.

"Right heah," said the biggest one, driving a nail with a blow as accurate as a bullet and almost as powerful. "An right *theah*." The second nail flashed inward to the hilt. Hammer in one hand, the other hand empty, he flung his arms high in triumph.

"You JOHN," said the second, swinging a board from a pile of lumber in an arc as beautiful as the span of a bridge.

"An take it uh WAY," sang the third, hoisting the board over his head toward the sun and pivoting toward the first man who flipped the hammer to the second as he caught the board with his arms still high.

It was impossible to tell whether the act actually forwarded the building or whether it had been composed solely for the enjoyment of the audience, or the actors, or for its own sake.

In the shack, from around the long board table where the women sat, the thutty, fohty, fohty *an* some faces turned upward toward the faces of the white girls as they entered. With their shoulders and their faces, the dark women acknowledged the alien fair women. Their hands acknowledged nothing but the work they were doing, their big hands delicately stripping the green pods, flicking the pods into a pile, the peas into three baskets each, grading them for size without ever glancing at them. The dull rattle of the peas into the baskets was like rain on the roof. The sound of "Miss Anglah—Anglah—Anglah . . ." was like the chime of distant church bells in the rain as the women greeted the boss's daughter, their brown eyes, separated from their faces by white eyeballs, rolling lightly away from her face.

Only Georgianna Church, who was forewoman, taskmaster, duenna, and protectress of the roomful of women, stopped working. Only her daughter, Mercy, continued to look straight at Angela, her face reposeful and composed. Only her other daughter, Amanda, refused to look at all, her eyes on her hands, her mouth closed.

"Good morning, Georgianna," said Angela, greeting them all, as was proper, through their forewoman, taskmaster, duenna, and protectress. "How are you this morning?"

The thin, little, almost black woman rose from between her two full-bodied, brown daughters. "Mighty nice tuh see yuh, Miss Anglah. An yo frien." She smiled at them slowly, the smile lighting up the witch wisdom of her profoundly moving face.

"May we stay a minute in here, Georgianna?" asked Angela.

There was a stir of appreciation around the table at the unnecessary courtesy of the request.

"It's uh pleasuh, Miss Anglah. Mercy . . . Mandy . . ."

The two daughters stood up, deep-bosomed, broad-shouldered, and went in muscular unison, with fluid grace, to fetch chairs for the visitors.

"Ask them to sing," said Hope in a low voice to Angela after they had sat down in the offered chairs.

"They'll sing," said Angela shortly. "They can't talk, really, while we're here. Just wait."

Some of the younger girls were giggling and whispering among themselves, but for the most part there was an uneasy silence around the table. Looking around the table, at the faces whose eyes flickered away when she looked at them, Angela thought, as she

had thought when she traveled across the high, treeless plateaus of
Spain, that there were more colors of brown than there were colors
in all the rest of the rainbow. She knew now why Spain, so unlike
home, had so curiously made her homesick.

It was Georgianna who began the singing, in her cracked,
unlovely falsetto which had musical authority, but no longer any
beauty.

*"Ahm gonna lay down mah sowahd an shield . . . down
bah thuh rivuhside . . ."*

It was a company song, a good-manners song, sung for the
entertainment of the white girls because it was a song the white
people knew and sang themselves. One after the other, the voices
took it up, singing at first conventionally in four parts, singing it
almost as the song had been adapted for white people or for trained
Negro choruses to sing. After they were all singing, the harmony
grew gradually more complicated until it departed from the limitations of whole-, of half- and quarter-note harmonies. Lacking their
men, the women supplied tenor and bass voices among themselves,
finding no limitations in their sex as they found none in the harmonies that grew so close as to be almost indivisible, so accurate
that the ear could find no faintest flaw, no accident of cacophony.

As one song fell into exhausted or triumphant disuse, someone would start a new one, in the bass, in the soprano, the tenor,
starting it anywhere and letting it grow.

Angela felt even the toes inside her shoes tender and vibrating with little nerves that responded like harp strings to the music.
Hope touched her hand and shone the great lamps of her eyes on
her to show her delight, but this did not disturb her. She felt Hope's
pleasure mingle harmoniously with her own.

The singing, the songs, grew sad as emotion flowed from
one song into another and freed itself of any belief that there was
heaven in the future, hope on earth.

The older women were leading the singing now, choosing the
songs, edging fearfully toward recognition of their approaching
death.

Pick up yo dus, boy
Put um in duh rock sack
Dyin day comin

The last line was a moan, full of fear, heavy with inevitability.

Oh say me no want yuh
Dyin day comin.

Hope felt suddenly that she might die that minute, sitting in this chair, these women chanting her requiem. She did not want to die. She knew that she would not die. She knew, also, that she was afraid to die. She felt the mocking eyes of the big colored woman who sat on Georgianna Church's left and who was not singing. The woman knew it and was glad that Hope was afraid to die. Hope could hide nothing. She had never been able to hide anything or to escape anything. She only wanted to be happy. Instead she was afraid. That woman would rejoice at her death. She was afraid of all these women, those who would moan and those who would rejoice if she died, as some day she must. She felt dizzy, leaning over the edge of the great gulf that separated white from black, who would all die. Suppose the gulf should clap to, as had the waters of the Red Sea. The black would cross the no longer existing gulf. That woman would kill her, rejoicing, while the others moaned. She did not want to die.

Amanda, sitting on her mother's left, stared in sullen silence at Hope. She was waiting for the old women to pause, for the young women who sang with the old women about death to stop their sniveling. She was afraid of nothing. Into the desolate instant at the end of the repeated and inescapable phrase *Dyin day comin,* Amanda lifted her powerful defiant contralto.

When ah come aroun, put yo man outside . . .

She looked straight at Hope, scorning her fear, looked at both Angela and Hope, challenging their womanhood, despising their pale faces, their wan virginity, their pallid dreams, throwing the coin of their marriageable virginity into their wan faces.

Angela felt Amanda's enmity and was stirred by her challenge, but rose to it within herself, and not in response to the brown woman. The gulf was too fixed, too immovable, too certain, to be bridged. Neither the death nor the violent life of these women had anything directly to do with her.

Hope cowered, wanted to run, to hide, to escape.

Most of the older women stirred and protested as Amanda flung down her song. The younger women shuffled their feet and giggled or frowned, or rolled their eyes this way and that.

"You Amanda!" commanded her mother sternly.

Amanda turned contemptuously away from Angela and Hope as if she considered them worth no more bother, wanted none of any man they might have, poor, pale virgins. She turned to challenge her own kind.

If ah fin yo man, jus yo say good-bye

"Hush yuh duhty mout, you Mandy . . ." A gaunt, furious woman with naked gums leaned across the table.

With a piercing, sweet shriek, a high lyric soprano in the body of a stumpy little brown girl farther down the table joined Amanda's trumpet contralto:

If ah fin yo man . . .

Swaying, a middle-aged woman with a light brown face, her body great with child, shut her eyes and began to sing simply, quietly, as if praying to herself:

Baby Jesus wah safe in duh arms uh He maw

Around the table, several of the older women joined her, shutting their eyes, swaying, singing their prayer. Around the table, several of the young ones joined big Amanda and the stumpy soprano, defying in song the old, the virtuous, and even their God. The songs swelled together, striving against each other. Sin outsang, for the moment, virtue. Georgianna Church sat immobile, suffering and resigned. On the other side of her, her daughter Mercy was as still as a pond, as relaxed.

For the first time, the pattering rain of peas slowed and nearly stopped. Beneath the tension and the struggle there was also discordance. Not in the dissimilar songs, which strove together: the prayer to the Babe in the arms of His Mother, and the song of the vampire woman, predatory and raging, who had turned away even from fecundity, strove together in beauty. Virtue was in perfect harmony and counterpoint with sin. The discordance came from the brown women who were still aware of their white visitors, watching them covertly to see how they were reacting. It came from the women who sided with neither good nor evil, but waited to see what would come of the struggle, from the women who disapproved of sin, but primly, and the women who approved, but slyly, and from Angela and Hope, dizzy on the edge of the gulf.

Until this moment, Angela had been lazily enjoying herself. She responded lazily to the sounds these women made, as she always had, enjoying the little harps in her toes, the pleasant sadness of contemplating unreal death. She had been amused, but not annoyed at Amanda, the bad girl among her father's employees, the fresh one. She had been pleased, not otherwise, that she would at last hear one of the naughty songs with which Mandy, the impudent, was reputed to annoy the elder women and tantalize the men, but which had never been sung in Angela's presence. Now the released emotions in the room, reaching through the thick protection of her laziness and from across the gulf that separated black and white, stirred and disturbed her with their intensity. She felt these emotions flowing into her, rousing her own, and her own emotions straining against the swaddling clothes of her white skin, the decorous restraints of her religious and social behavior. The gathered blood drew taut the membrane of her undeniable, seemingly visible virginity. Her heart beat against her small, high, decorous breasts.

Hope, unprotected and utterly vulnerable, wished for a horrified moment that she were black, fled in terror from such a wish and wished that she were dead, flew from this more dreadful wish and wished that she could faint or scream.

The singing came to a ragged, trailing, incompleted end, the rain fell again, roofing the new quiet. Angela looked up to see her father, cheerful and contained, chewing one end of his fine-haired mustache and smiling down at her.

"Mistuh Madison—Madison—Madison . . ." chimed the church bells.

"Hello, young ladies," said Mr. Madison to Hope and Angela, in a normal, infinitely polite voice.

"Oh! You scared me, Mr. Madison," said Hope. Her face was white and her big eyes blinked rapidly.

"Hello, Papa," said Angela, immediately lazy, calmed and normal.

"Come on outside." He turned toward the table of women. He was a small, thin, stooped man, with a pleasant, compact face. He was still smiling, but his voice was stern. "Georgianna, you-all keep right at it. Storm beat down vines. Tomatoes this afternoon, and more peas."

"Yas, suh," said Georgianna, bowing her head. "Heah dat, yawl?"

"Yas, suh," murmured the women, quiet and downcast, their hands quickening their tempo, the rain drumming faster and faster, although more softly as the baskets filled.

"Yas, suh," said Amanda, her voice impertinent and clear above the rest.

"Who started the trouble? Mandy?" asked Mr. Madison when they were outside.

"There wasn't any trouble," said Hope.

"It was Mandy," said Angela.

"Born she-devil! Needs . . ." He paused. He thought that Amanda Church needed a man to beat her every night and get her pregnant every June, but that was not the sort of thing you said to your daughter and her friends. ". . . a good scolding."

"Don't you like them to sing?" asked Hope.

"Oh, certainly, yes. Work better when they sing. But not when they get naughty. That's a right naughty song. Glad you didn't hear the rest of it. Need a good black revivalist and a good dose of calomel all around in the spring. . . . To what do I owe the honor of this visit?"

"Your father is sweet," said Hope, as she and Angela drove away from The Place, having found out that lunch would be fixed for him in the canning kitchen, since the stoves were fired, and that he would return home in good time that evening.

Angela nodded. She was not thinking of her father. She was thinking of Mark and wishing that he had been there this morning. She would like to know how he would have reacted. His lanky, loose-limbed body must surely have responded to the singing. His earnest approach to God must have been affected by the sweet simplicity of praying to a Baby cuddled at His Mother's bosom. She did not know what the emotions rampant in that roomful of women would have meant to him. He was good, was Mark, good and a man. What did a good man do when a vampire woman came around? He needed a good woman, thought Angela. So he could turn to his good, thin, dark-brown-eyed, light-brown-haired woman whose loins were his as her heart was his. If he would only love her, she would stubbornly give him everything he needed. She was stubborn enough to love him until he died.

She became aware that Hope was weeping in the seat beside her. She glanced over and saw the tears sliding painfully from between her screwed-up, reddening lids. If Hope cried, she should cry prettily, as Ellen Terra cried, with nice, symmetrical raindrops of tears that washed the eyes clear of sorrow. Or she should cry privately, as Angela cried, as Carrie cried, if Carrie cried at all any more. Angela had an impulse to stop the car and dump damp Hope into the ditch beside the road that was still running with rain water. Instead, she turned into the nearest track that wandered into the pine woods and, out of sight of the road from The Place that led to the highway between towns, she stopped.

"It's all right," she said meaninglessly, her sympathy in her voice, her vexation in her mind. Her thoughts were as harmonious and as antagonistic as the music had been when virtue sang against sin. Her friendship with Hope had always been thus; vexation that could rise to fury mingled and harmonizing with liking that could rise to love. Hope's virtues of honesty, of justice, of enthusiasm and academic intelligence, of logic and clarity aggravated Angela's unwilling irritation. Hope worked so hard to bring order into the irrational universe. Hope's faults of honest meanness, of unwitting tale-bearing, of stupidity in human relations aroused Angela's maternal protectiveness, her indulgent affection. Hope's insistent optimism made Angela gloomy and contradictory. Hope's brief and terrible blues made her want to run away. Nevertheless, perversely, she liked Hope tenderly and was tied to her irrevocably by the shared past and the fact that Hope had never deceived her. Still, it was easier with Ellen Terra, who was so much stupider than Hope, whose relations with the truth were nonexistent, so that even God could not tell when she was lying, since Ellen Terra never knew herself. Ellen Terra was reprehensible and fine. Hope was a fine girl, and to hell with her. Hope was a pitiful girl and she must comfort her.

"Angela, Angela, I love him so. I love him so. What shall I do? I can't sleep or eat or think or anything. It's hell. I love him so."

Angela's hands, still on the wheel, tightened in a spasm of irritation and sympathy. She did not want to be told this. She did not want to betray herself. You could not accept a gift, even of honesty, without returning it in kind. If you were unable to refuse a gift, then you must give in return. She tried to refuse.

"You have so many beaus, Hope, you're lucky."

"Sonny Boy!" said Hope in frantic derision. "But it's Mark Barbee I love!" As if Angela did not know it. The name quieted Hope and she gulped, stopped crying, and blew her nose. "He's so good, Angela, and so strong. I want to wash his socks and have ten of his children and type his sermons and scrub his floors and die in his arms when I'm ninety-six!"

You could not cozen Hope with fair words of courtesy. She took words at their dictionary value. If you told her she was beautiful, she preened. If you said she was intelligent, she would utter profundities. If you told her that she would win Mark Barbee, she would seize upon it with her natural optimism and believe you. You could only offer Hope what she offered you.

"So do I," said Angela, somber, helpless, betrayed.

And Hope, having sought a friend and found a rival, dried her tears and withdrew immediately within herself, regrouping her forces to protect herself against an enemy as she had laid herself naked to a friend.

They talked of last week's bridge game on the way in, planned a tennis match if the weather continued, made a date at The Oaks for next Tuesday. They agreed, behind veiled eyes, to meet in church for the Palm Sunday service. They said what fun it had been to hear the women sing at The Place and wished that they had heard the rest of the naughty song, which was reputed to be very naughty indeed. They agreed that it was marvelous because it was spring and not summer or winter.

Angela felt stilted and stupid and had an uncomfortable desire to giggle. How absurd Hope was. As if acting like this made any sense.

Only as she left the car, in front of her porchless house, did Hope refer again to the confession in the pine woods. She stood beside the car, her stocky body squarely planted on her spread feet, her hands folded primly, her face closed and stolid, looking empty as, thought Angela, only blondes can look empty when they are not warmed by any feeling. You could still see a long way into Hope's big, clear eyes, and you could watch the thought process by which she was rationalizing the strange morning.

"I didn't intend to," she began. She paused, rearranging her thoughts. "Those women singing," she began again, "are really very extraordinary. They got me all wrought up. I'm sorry I cried and carried on like that. I didn't intend to tell anybody, you or anybody, about—about how I feel about Mark. It is not a thing one should tell."

When Hope started using the impersonal "one," it irked Angela beyond endurance. "No, one shouldn't," she said. Hope looked hurt, and Angela went on quite gently, "One just does sometimes."

"He hasn't—well, you know . . . *Mark* doesn't know," said Hope, dropping her eyes.

"No," agreed Angela. Of course Mark knew. He was not a fool, nor blind because he was a male. That was the error they had all made. They had let him know. Even Carrie. It had been so hot. You couldn't pretend when it was hot.

"So you won't tell anybody, Ellen Terra or anybody?"

"Of course not," said Angela. "Nor you. The nonsense we talked."

Hope nodded, comforted. "No. 'Bye now." She hesitated and turned back. "Good luck," she said. She meant, I wish you luck next to me. She was not ungenerous. She was fair. We can be friends again, she meant.

Angela responded, feeling oddly affectionate, "Good luck, Hope, darling."

6. Progenitors

On Palm Sunday, everyone agreed that the weather, the church, and the service had never been more beautiful. Men and women, pouring slowly from the crowded church, waited under the blue spring sky, chatting with each other as the light, white clouds clustered and parted overhead. When Mark Barbee came hurrying out in his cassock, they shook his hand and made kindly remarks about his sermon, his service and the weather.

The next day, the first day of Holy Week, it rained. Even so, the late-afternoon service surprisingly brought forth a congregation of at least twenty. After the service Mark sat at his desk in the battered and homelike study of the big rectory, and composed in writing notice of the offer he had just received. It was an excellent offer. He almost hated to refuse it, as he was almost sure he would.

He had been asked to become assistant rector of St. Matthew's in Mobile at $3,000 a year, or $500 more than his salary in Andalusia. He would have the expectation of replacing the rector there, who was seventy. St. Matthew's was one of the South's oldest and best known parishes. It was rich in tradition and distinguished southern names and well known in the trade for its harmonious stability. No rector had ever left there as a result of unpleasantness with the congregation. This was distinctly different from St. James's, which had tempestuously lost three rectors in a row prior to the Rev. Mr. Witherspoon, who was impervious to insult and too stupid to arouse violent partisanship. The Bishop of Georgia had warned young Barbee when he accepted the call that Andalusia was a troublesome spot. The Bishop of Alabama, writing to him now of St. Matthew's, apologized for trying to take him away so soon from a Georgia parish where he was apparently doing extremely well, but said that a crisis had arisen due to the ill health of St. Matthew's beloved, but aging rector, and that this was a fine opportunity for so young a man. It was somewhat unethical to ask a man to leave a new parish in so short a time. The circumstances must excuse the unorthodoxy.

Mark, writing rapidly, conveyed to his vestrymen the bishop's apology as well as the offer presented by St. Matthew's vestry. He did not mention the contents of a letter he had received from his aunt.

I confess, she had written to him from Mobile, that I had this eventuality in mind when I arranged to have you preach at St. Matthew's the Sunday you visited me. You made me very proud that day and you made a wonderful impression on our congregation. I did not realize then how very much I would hope for you to come.

I do not, my dear Mark, like Andalusia! It's a horrid, muddly place, not even amusingly vulgar. It is—how can I convey to you what it made me feel?—a self-conscious town. Your mother might not have felt so, but your mother was easily entertained, which I am not, and she was so great a lady that knaves, fools, hypocrites and even middle-class people acted in her presence with her own grace. Her gift was extraordinary and it misled her. She raised people to her own level and then thought they were her equals.

I am an old woman and a snob, my dear boy, and I do not suppose you will listen to me. You have a great deal of your mother's gift, but if I may be frank, this frightens me. You can only be happy married to the right woman. (We used to worry most terribly about your mother before she met your father because she liked the most PECULIAR men. Did you know she cried for a week after she accepted him??? But you know how well this came out.)

53

Mark had paused when he reached this point in the letter, both to rest himself from the arduous task of translating his aunt's rapid and elusive handwriting and to wonder briefly just how happy his mother and father had been. He discovered, to his surprise, that he had no idea. His father had "adored" and pampered his mother and had been pampered by every woman in his congregation. His mother had fussed over, fussed at, and sometimes ignored his father. Her life had been very full of other people, who gathered around her like flies haunting a honey pot and who became in her aura something more, and nearly always more charming, than themselves.

Picking up the sheets of blue paper, he had continued to read with the irritated interest his aunt always provoked.

What I am really getting at is that I think you would do well to come to Mobile. A big city has more scope and I expect you to do fine things. There is a slum mission attached to St. Matthew's which is doing wonderful work among the sailors and the poor, and the best people at St. Matthew's are really the BEST.

To tell you the truth, Mark, I am just an incurable old matchmaker, too, if you will indulge an old maid. I have met a girl here who is everything I dream of for you. She is VERY pretty and VERY popular and she is also gentle and well-bred.

Never mind about that! I know what you will say!! (Still, I sometimes think these things were better arranged by families, just the same.) The important thing is that it seems to me your town of Andalusia is a very unhealthy place. I must admit I admire some of the modern young women I have met who are making a new place for themselves. But I DO NOT LIKE those who have discarded one code of manners and have NOT found a new CODE. This is SLOPPY.

Your old-fashioned and devoted
Aunt Mag

Mark frowned over the letter, laughed, and then tossed it aside. It was absurd that the question of his work should have gotten tangled up in his own as well as his aunt's mind with the question of his future marriage. It was a tempting idea to go to St. Matthew's, to inherit such a parish from its almost sainted rector, but it was clear to him that he should stay in Andalusia. He would like to make a success of this, his second job, and his first really responsible one. Three years would be a minimum of time in which to prove to himself that he could handle it as well as he should. He had a feeling that he would be succumbing to the twin weaknesses of ambition and cowardice were he to leave in this unorthodox haste. It would make him, somehow, less of a man and less of a priest.

Besides, St. Matthew's was almost too stable, too secure. A rector was not expected to leave St. Matthew's unless he were made bishop, retired, or died. Mark had other plans for himself. He wanted to experience many parishes before he finally settled down. There was plenty of variety in his profession, if you managed it right and did not let yourself grow stagnant and stay too long in one place.

He finished his tactfully worded letter to his vestry and sat back to smoke a cigarette. He was dining alone, as he had indicated to the hospitable that he would prefer to do during the strenuous and exacting Holy Week. The ancient Negro woman his aunt had hired in deference to the conventions of a bachelor establishment would tell him when dinner was ready. He had plenty of time in the cool of the spring evening. He would have liked to sit on the porch, but the passing would stop to talk. He preferred to think uninterrupted. Besides, all churches were full of bores.

His vestry, on receipt of his letter, might give him a raise. That would mean he could buy a car. And a new tennis racquet. And new tailored white linen suits for summer. He would enjoy all that. This was a good town for the things he liked best, and he could indulge in sport without becoming one of those exasperating hail-fellow clergymen who made a virtue of being like other "boys." After Easter, he must arrange some tennis with Dugdale, who played about as he did, a smashing, erratic game in which strenuousness was more important than winning. He straightened his shoulders, which had been bowed over the desk. Strange guy, that Dugdale. He thought they were making friends as men could be friends and as it was difficult for a clergyman to be friends without self-consciousness.

Tennis and some riding should help him soothe his celibacy, too. He was entirely capable of celibacy, as he was capable of fasting. He rarely fasted because it did not seem to make him clearheaded, only light-headed. It seemed neither male nor intelligent to him. He was celibate because he must be. When he married, he must find a woman who would make him more of a man, not less of one, a better priest and not a more comfortable one. He wanted a son, of course. Even God had wanted a son.

When he found his woman, he would woo her. He was not seeking a girl in the image of his mother, who was a great lady but a daughter of Lilith, with no moral code whatever. He had a lively curiosity to see the girl his aunt had chosen. Her anachronistic and ethical tastes were often akin to his own. He wanted a girl superior to the one he had already loved the most, who had married another man before Mark was graduated from the seminary. He wanted a daughter of Eve, responsible with the knowledge of good and evil, gay in virtue and strong in the return of the love she inspired.

Meantime, the devil with women. He had work to do. He must talk to the organist about being on time for choir rehearsals. Perhaps he could persuade Hope to join the choir. Her trained voice would be an asset. He should fire "Uncle Jimmy," the sexton, who was an unmitigated, drunken black scoundrel and temperamental as a goat. (He lacked the courage for this!) He wondered if Carrie's crippledness had made her kind and whether she would help him in his nursery school. The school was doing good work among the pathetic kids whose mothers worked. The Episcopal Scouts were a problem. He approved of Boy Scouts theoretically, but he had hated being one. He could scarcely confess to that, but he could arrange to merge his troop with an interdenominational one. He could offer to coach the lot at touch football. (No, that smacked of the YMCA type. He'd just get out from under.) He must get down to see the colored Episcopal clergyman; he was quite a character. He had a long list of sick calls. The poor said, in Andalusia, that the change of the moon always brought sickness. The rich seemed to get sick when they were rained on. And there had been that unseasonal heat. . . . After Easter, he could permit himself to have a pretty good time, too.

The vestry, duly informed, informed their wives of the call their new clergyman had received. There was some indignation, but more concern. Three days later, on Maundy Thursday, the vestry met to consider their response to him. Since the rector was not asked to be present at this meeting, it took place, not at the rectory, but at the home of the senior warden, who was Andrew Gregory, Carrie's father.

Before the meeting, Carrie sat with Andrew Gregory in the living room that had been cluttered with extra chairs to receive the twelve serious men.

"Your mother thinks we ought to raise the young man's salary," said Andrew to his daughter. He was a big, beefy, simple man, known as a man's man. He was contented with his big, affectionate, red-faced wife, who looked and thought very much as he did. He was at ease over his buxom oldest daughter, Susan, who lived with her husband in Atlanta. His second daughter, Caroline, had always seemed to him a scrawny witch baby. When she had been so terribly maimed, he had wished that she would die. For this, he felt an obscure guilt toward her, which he expressed by giving her anything in the world she demanded.

"I expect you should," said Carrie. "Aren't the clergy always underpaid, anyway?"

"Well, they get a house free and all that," said her father.

"Nobody'd have the rectory for anything *but* a gift," said Carrie. "You might at least paint the old barn, you tightwads."

"Who's a tightwad?" asked her father.

"Oh, you're all right," said Carrie kindly. "You're just a thrifty Scot. Mr. Stone is a tightwad and so is Alton Rook."

"Now, honey," said Andrew Gregory. His daughter had no respect for her elders. His daughter was looking at him with that sharp, condescending look, as if she were the elder. "Now, honey!"

"It's a shame if you can't pay a guy what he's worth," said Carrie.

"It's not a rich parish," said Andrew uncomfortably. "None of us are what you'd call really rich, and Alton Rook loses money on the *Banner*."

"His wife doesn't lose money on The Place," said Carrie. "And it makes me mad when any of you-all talk po' mouth."

"Well, I expect we'll offer Barbee a substantial raise, honey," said her father. "I daresay he deserves it."

"He deserves it just for not being a damn bore," said Carrie sharply. "Like the others."

Good Lord, thought Andrew Gregory, startled at the thought

that came unexpectedly into his usually predictable mind. Maybe his strange, unhappy daughter was interested in the man, Mark Barbee. Well, why not? Clergymen were supposed to be above things like legs, and Carrie was a handsome enough girl. Clergymen were supposed to be above such things, too, but she would be well-dowered. Very well-dowered indeed. He owed her that. Maybe his wife, whom he considered intuitive, had thought of this very thing. In that case, they would certainly have to see that Mark Barbee stayed in Andalusia.

"He's a very attractive young man," exclaimed Andrew incautiously, with the vocal equivalent of a blush.

Carrie looked at him with cold contempt, and he winced. He often had the feeling that she could read his thoughts. Of course, he had no right to hope so heartily that his daughter would marry and leave him by his comfortable fireside with his comfortably aging wife. He cherished his daughter and admired her intelligence, he told himself. It was absurd to be, well, unsettled by your own child. If she had been a boy, with her brains . . . The thought of a crippled son was unbearable to him and he turned away from it.

"I'm thinking of selling out my AT&T stock," he said in haste, "so I'll be temporarily flush with cash, anyway."

"I think I'll hang on to mine," said Carrie judiciously, making peace with him.

Her father had put some stock holdings in Carrie's name the year before and permitted her to handle them herself. He had been agreeably surprised at her shrewdness. It had amused her, too, and given them common ground for conversation. Carrie would never, as his wife did, pretend an interest in his business, which, being female, she could never enter. When she was interested she was, as his wife was not, undeniably shrewd.

"Maybe I'm premature, selling it now," said Andrew, almost as if he were speaking to an equal. "What do you think?"

Carrie's mind was working on two levels at once. She enjoyed playing the stock market. It made her feel able. She had forced her father to respect her financial judgment, which gave her a feeling of satisfaction. She was searching in her mind for an answer to his question which would inspire that gleam of startled respect in his eyes. Actually, she had decided to hold on to her AT&T stock merely because she thought it would go higher. But that was insufficient reason. It was quite likely that some of the other, less staid common stocks would go higher still.

On the other level, she was conscious that she must be visibly in love with Mark Barbee if her obtuse father had come close to guessing at her state of heart. The thought was sharply painful. She knew, somberly, that the other three were most certainly visibly in love with him. Mark had seen it. The heat had made them transparent, given them all away. The only thing that protected Carrie was that she alone was hopeless. This was a barricade against unbearable pain, and she could bear a lot of ordinary pain. She preferred pain to boredom. Hence she wanted Mark to remain where she could suffer what was necessary for the pleasure of seeing him. He need not run from Carrie, avoid her, fend her off. She was hopeless. But was she quite hopeless enough, since he had looked at her that way, that Thursday morning after their invasion of Miss Sis's service? Carrie swore to herself that she was hopeless. That was her only protection.

"If there's a squeeze," she said, making an effort to reach the level of her father's financial sophistication, "it seems to me people will hang on to their telephones longer than other extras."

"In the very nature of economic inflation . . ." began her father, in a voice that did its best to avoid any tone of fatherly condescension.

Carrie half listened to him. He intended it to be flattering when he talked to her like this, but he was a bore. She was glad when the doorbell interrupted him. Having no interest in greeting the vestrymen, she went out hastily, leaving him to the men.

All the vestrymen came to their senior warden's house that night. Among them were John Stone, Cecil Lord Madison, and Alton Rook, fathers to Carrie's friends, Hope, Angela, and Ellen Terra.

John Stone came first. He was a small, tightly tubby man, and always prompt. He was the treasurer of the parish, a position he considered sufficient reward for the fact that he made the largest single contribution to the church. As president of the biggest local bank and the richest man among them, he was expected to do so. If he had been born in Andalusia and raised from birth as an

Episcopalian, he would, in the nature of things, have been a warden. It irked his daughter, Hope, that he was not.

Cecil Madison, as manager of The Place and husband to its half-owner, would have been junior warden except for his firm refusal. He was often called to The Place for Sunday emergencies, during the various seasonal crises that occurred. Since The Place no longer confined itself to pecans but tinned everything that grew regionally, the crises were frequent. Mr. Madison could not guarantee his regular presence in church to pass the left-hand plate. He was forgiven for this. It was a town joke that he had not only married The Place, he was wedded to it. It was a congratulatory joke. According to the formula for such things, Hannah Miller, who had inherited her half-share of the Miller and Rook Pecan Company from her Pappy Miller, had done herself well to marry into the gentry. Cecil Madison, a sober and impecunious young gentleman of the county, had done well to marry money. It was not in the cards that the gentleman should also prove to be a first-rate and absorbed businessman who steadily improved the value of his wife's property. The town considered that their parents had done well by their older sons and by their daughter, Angela.

The excellence of The Place's management had also benefited Alton Rook. As a groom, he had sold his share in the Miller and Rook Company to his lively, blackhaired, independently wealthy bride from New Orleans. With the proceeds he had bought the Andalusia *Banner*, thus fulfilling his adolescent dream of becoming a country editor. So long as The Place brought her an increasing return, Clementine Rook refrained from bothering her head over her husband's failure to make any money on the paper. She even enjoyed his limited reputation as a wit, acquired because his one-line political quips were reprinted in the *Literary Digest* more often than those of any other small-town pundit. Alton Rook enjoyed his newspaper so much that after a while he ceased to threaten to leave his volcanic-tempered, arbitrary wife. He acquired a sense of detachment in place of an irascible valor, and yielded to her in most things. He thus sired two more children, in addition to Ellen Terra, who had been the fruit of their honeymoon, and became a vestryman at St. James's. Clementine Rook, no longer needing to expend her vitality to subjugate her husband, turned her attention to the town and became its dominant matron. It was as her husband that Alton Rook was elected junior warden. He arrived last, in accordance with his notion that newspapermen were always breathlessly late on formal occasions, and the meeting began.

Alton Rook had his instructions on the subject of the meeting from Clementine. He enjoyed following them because of a private bet with himself that three other husbands had received similar instructions.

He judged himself right in short order. Andrew Gregory, as senior warden, made the opening suggestion that Mark Barbee's salary be substantially raised. He made a rambling speech pointing out that Barbee was an up-and-comer who had managed to interest the young people, as well as many new people, in the church. The speech was heartily and promptly applauded by Treasurer John Stone and by Cecil Madison and by himself. The rest of the vestry were somewhat taken aback. They had not come prepared to be quite so generous. There were many drains on the purse of public-minded, expensively wived men these days.

Alton Rook, reveling in the humor he had learned to keep mostly to himself, impudently tested his theory. He suggested that he, Gregory, Stone, and Madison make up most of the increase. Agreement was eagerly arrived at, and still he was sure that no one except himself was aware of the reason. They four were the only members of the vestry with currently ripe, marriageable daughters, and with wives who were thus content to keep the lottery open on an eligible man even at some expense. They would spend a like amount on provocative wardrobes for these same daughters for this same purpose.

The whole matter of an offer to Mark Barbee having been thus quickly arranged, the vestry settled down to comfortable drinking of the illegally distilled whiskey, the imported brandy and the gin which Andrew Gregory himself had made with alcohol, water and drops. Alton Rook and Cecil Madison, who shared, in contradistinction to the others, a certain nervous slenderness and a dislike for male small talk, left early.

As he started home, Alton Rook reflected that he had no further bets to make with himself. He did not know which of the girls had the best chance with Mark, now that the money had been paid into the lottery. Ellen Terra's best friend, Angela, Cecil's daughter, might have a chance. She was comparatively subtle. Actually, he would have liked to know Angela better. He might find some way to help her. He reflected that he had no idea what he meant by "to help." There was nothing much sharable left in his private heart and mind. He had lost the key to human hearts. The gap between generations struck him as more formidable than that between the sexes or the colors. He could rarely even cross the smaller gap that existed between him and his male contemporaries. He believed that Angela hungered intellectually, which touched him. Probably she was just a mass of awkward emotional yearnings that meant nothing and only appealed to him because she had a long-boned, wistful face he liked.

He tried to think detachedly about his own child, Ellen Terra, whose sticky, plump, baby fingers had so mauled his already wary heart. He was fully aware of the enormity of his daughter's sex appeal. She had inherited it from her mother without inheriting her mother's destructive, massive vitality. Ellen Terra was sweet. He reflected, deliberately cool, that Mark Barbee could do worse than succumb to something so simple and satisfactory as Ellen Terra's open invitation to bed.

But Mark was a tough young man. Alton Rook found it difficult to credit any young man either stupid or religious enough to go into the modern ministry with toughness, but he thought Mark was tough. It was for this that he liked him better than he did any woman. Mark would, thought Alton Rook pleasurably, give both the gals and their mamas a run for their money.

His humor revived by the thought, he began to chuckle. Instead of going home and to bed, or downtown to his office, where the presses would be vibrating as they turned out the next morning's edition of his paper, he decided to go by the rectory. He was curious. He admitted that he was curious about the young man. He remembered his own youth with nostalgia. He had been the town iconoclast, the indigestible town wit. He had been impertinent and skeptical, even questioning the obvious. He had had predicted for him a bad end. The same sort of judgment would predict for young Mark a good end.

Mark came to the door of the rectory and welcomed him in.

Alton Rook, knowing that his curiosity was more keen than kind, was embarrassed by the warmth of the welcome.

"I won't keep you a minute," said Alton Rook, embarrassed, "I . . ."

"I'm a night owl myself," said Mark, "and I never want to go to bed. Do me the honor, sir, of joining me in a drink."

"Well, I will," said Alton Rook, rather pleased with Mark's old-fashioned manners. "In fact, I'd be delighted."

"Gin or corn?" asked Mark. "The gin is local, but the whiskey is a present from the senior warden and superior stuff."

"If you can spare it."

Mark went out to fix the drinks, both pleased and nervous over his visitor. He thought he liked Mr. Rook. He seemed to Mark odd and shrewd, and not nearly as bloodless as he looked.

When they had settled down with a polite tipping of their glasses and a "How" preceding the first sip, Alton Rook said tentatively, "I didn't come to report on the vestry meeting. You'll be informed and you'll be pleased, I think, no matter what you decide. I dropped by to ask you to let me know, if you can, what you decide before you announce it. We newspapermen—" he never, in all the years, had recovered from a youthful feeling of self-consciousness in referring to himself as a newspaperman "—always like to know things first. I'd like time to compose a bit of prose in your honor. A nice bit, if you decide to stay, or a few drum beats if you leave. It won't be embarrassing. I'll write it myself."

"Why, thanks," said Mark. "I'll be glad to let you know. But I—honestly, I don't know. It's hard." He hesitated. He did not know whether he trusted this man or not. Mr. Rook was an enclosed sort of man, but he would not, at least, mouth platitudes. "Do you mind if I talk to you a little bit, sir? You remind me of a guy—a man I liked a lot at Sewanee. He was professor of religious history and the—if you don't mind—the University bad hat. He didn't talk like the others. . . ."

Alton Rook nodded. He was flattered. He said, "I'd be flattered," and almost added, for his own amusement, "I'm old enough to be your father."

"Professor Danton," said Mark, naming his man. "We called him Pop. I got a letter from him today. It puts a third proposition to me. It makes it even harder to decide what to do. He's got a bug, Pop has, about missionary work."

"I don't agree with him," said Alton Rook immediately, touched on one of his many prejudices. "I think maybe the church had better consolidate its so-called gains before it tries to expand. There's plenty of undigested human material it claims as its own." He almost added, "like me." He was a fine one to talk like this, he thought. He had long since lost all faith except the shred of a skeptic's refusal to entirely disbelieve in anything—even in the Anglican God.

Mark laughed. "Pop would agree with you," he said. "But he thinks young men, especially me, for some reason, should do a couple of years of straight mission work and then come back with what he calls the missionary approach at home. He says the southern United States is the biggest heathen territory in Christendom."

"A man after my own heart there," said Alton Rook, "unless he's talking revivalistically."

"Lord, no," said Mark, thinking of the irascible Pop and comparing him to the man before him, whose irascibility was tucked beneath his dim and slightly shrunken exterior. "He just thinks that we—the clergy—aren't tough enough."

Alton Rook warmed warily toward the young man. "You seem pretty tough," he said.

"Pop's a misogynist," said Mark reminiscently, enjoying his listener's understanding. "He thinks women are all born immoral and that they are ruining the church."

Alton Rook grinned widely. His whole face changed. "Bring the man along," he said, "and I'll buy him a drink."

"He wants me," said Mark seriously, "to take a missionary territory in Montana that he's interested in. He wrote me . . ." Mark went over to his desk and fished the letter out from under the pages of an answer he had tried to write. Running his eye down the badly typed page, he found the paragraph and read aloud, "*I need a tough young man for this mission, Mark. They don't take kindly to the cloth. Since old Tiger Tucker left, we've had bad luck. There are few women, little money, plenty of saddle sores, and your parish-ioners carry guns. How about it?"*

"Well," said Alton Rook, "how about it?"

"I can ride," said Mark, "and I'm a better shot since I've come here. But I can't convince myself that missions are as—well—important as other things. He thinks I need it. I would have to think so, too." He laughed with embarrassment at having said so much and ran his hand through his thick brown hair.

Alton Rook shook his head. "I can't advise you, Mark," he said. "Even if what you want is advice. If I were you, I'd want to take it and probably wouldn't." He was surprised at himself. He was so absorbed in the young man's problem that he had, fleetingly, been able to imagine himself as a minister. "Seems to me that you took a hard job here, and it ain't finished. Mobile is a step up the church ladder, of course, so that's a natural temptation. And then there's the temptation to go rootin' tootin' off testing your muscles out West, wrestling with uncivilized souls. That about the size of it?"

Mark nodded. "In a nutshell," he said ruefully. "I want to say no to Pop, but I just haven't managed to, yet. Sir," he added.

"Take your time," said Alton Rook, feeling his age. He wished he could talk as well as he wrote. "Take your time," he repeated nervously. Then his liking for the young man coupled with a vision of his daughter's tempting face prompted him to add, "You in any trouble here, Mark?"

Mark wondered if he were blushing. "Well, not that I know of," he said, and did not add, "Not yet."

"If the girls are after you," said Alton Rook, completely scandalized to hear himself saying exactly what he thought, "run, Son, run!"

With this he clapped his hat on the very back of his head, in deference to his notion that this was how working newspapermen wore their hats, and said a hurried good-bye.

When Alton Rook had gone, Mark sat down alone. He was disturbed and not at all amused. Did the whole town know that the four girls looked at him with favor, or only this shrewd character who was father to the luscious Ellen Terra? It seemed to him that Alton Rook was a man, however shrunken, and he wanted his respect. He would respect Mark most if he stayed in Andalusia. If he went to Mobile, Alton Rook would have no further use for him. If he went to Montana, what Alton Rook would feel was envy. . . . He could make no decision. Well, the man had told him to take his time.

7. Treasure Hunt

Spring in Andalusia came in white and gold and lavender against a varied background of greens. Dogwood trees flowered white among pines, oaks and beeches. Camellias and Cape jasmine were as fragile and white as their leaves were strong and green. Lilies grew pale on pale green stems, with long, light-colored leaves. Yellow jasmine tumbled across the countryside, the less vivid but equally profuse honeysuckle providing scent enough for both. Wisteria hung downwards in lavish lavender curtains, draping the porches of cabins and mansions. It was a cherished and usually long drawn out season. Hope loved the spring, feeling it brisk and blonde and sweet-smelling as herself. She wore fresh clothes the color of wisteria to match it with her white skin and yellow hair.

In the year 1927, Andalusia's spring lasted one week. The two-day summer that had so strangely preceded it after the very long and unusually rigorous winter was warning. On Maundy Thursday, April 14th, three days before Easter, summer came again to stay. The dogwood blossoms turned brown at the edges, the jasmine died, and the wisteria thinned. The many bright, harsh colors of summer were burnished by the bright sun.

By Easter, most of the town had sighed and settled down to summer. If it was longer this year, it was always long. Hope was reconciled only by a moment's conversation with Mark, when she drew up beside him in her car as he was on the way to the twilight service on Holy Saturday. In the special kinship of two who were not born in Andalusia, they agreed almost surreptitiously between themselves that the weather was an outrage. Mark, raised in the gentler climate of the eastern seaboard of South Carolina and in tidewater Virginia, loved summer far best of the year, but admitted that he had not bargained on loving it so early and so long. Hope admitted, not for quotation, that she could not help thinking of Cape Cod with affection. It was a moment of breathless, promissory intimacy between them.

The lilies lasted long enough to provide Easter with its traditional decoration. The men came to celebrate the High Feast at St. James's in linen and seersucker suits, the women flocked in pastel organdies, voiles and linens. Both wore straw hats and freshly whitened shoes, and the women carried fans and the men an extra supply of handkerchiefs. Hope, cherishing her moment on the sidewalk, contained herself through the gala Sunday as part of a worshipping throng blessed equally and impartially by Mark. The three days preceding the "rejuvenation meeting," scheduled for the evening of the Wednesday after Easter, when she would see Mark himself personally again, were hot and endless.

She had planned to be the first, but she was the fifth or sixth to arrive at the rectory porch on Wednesday. Sonny Boy Lovejoy was already there, mopping his brown curls, and overdelighted to see her. Dugdale Winthrop unfolded his long body from the five steps of the porch along which he had draped it, and led her up the steps to a seat at the top beside Ellen Terra, who looked rosy and cozy in the summer heat. Mark came out of the rectory carrying iced Coca-Cola, with Angela, thin and cool, and good-looking Logan Knight helping him. Mark greeted Hope casually, together with Carrie and Mary Newcombe, who were just then coming up the walk with Morton Hadley and three or four others among the young people of the parish. They were all pleased with the idea that, with Mark Barbee as their rector and their youthful ally, they could make a new amusement center for themselves at St. James's.

The Cotillion Club functioned only twice a year and was heavily weighted with the old. The Oaks was never entirely theirs. It operated for profit and most of the profit came from wealthy northerners who filled it from late summer through the fall. They had all plenty of time and energy. They offered these to Mark in full measure as long as he could keep the balance between exuberance and effort.

Hope, filled with nervousness and enthusiasm, made her two suggestions hastily, before they were all properly settled on the porch, the jackets and sweaters they had brought in case the evening should grow cool used as pillows to sit on.

"Why don't we have an extra cotillion?" she suggested briskly as soon as the greeting chatter had faded and her bell-like voice could be clearly heard by all. There was an instant of silence and then a brief babble of formless objections.

No one voiced the objection that all the rest of them took for granted. Anything done in the name of religion, no matter how limited its patrons, must admit anyone who knocked at the door. The Episcopal Church was formally open to all sinners and social climbers. The function of the cotillions was to distinguish the elect, but not necessarily of the Lord. To open a cotillion to cash customers would be like exchanging the social register for the telephone book in towns where it was vulgarly necessary to print the names of people who were somebody and not just anybody. Mark did not protest the decision nor join the protest. He was aware what the real objection was, but he sympathized with Hope, who could not seem to learn the difference between theory and practice, in religion or anything else.

Disgruntled and flustered, she promptly made her other suggestion, without stopping to consider the different objections to this. "A treasure hunt, then," she said, raising her voice above the babble.

This time, the others did not even bother to object. The treasure hunt had acquired a special function in Andalusia, and its practitioners had no intention of going back to the simple form of hunt, suitable for a large and heterogeneous group, in which some bright couple merely won the treasure. Paying no attention to Hope, they immediately began to argue the relative merits of a fish fry by the river or an ordinary, evening-dress-optional Friday-night dance.

69

While Hope sat sullen and silent, they decided, quite promptly, vociferously talking down Mary Newcombe and Logan Knight, on the dance. The rest of the evening, while they drank Coca-Cola, which some of the men spiked from pints or hip flasks of corn whiskey, they discussed details.

It would be held two weeks from Friday night, in the parish house, which was big enough and convenient and free. If this one was successful, it could become an institution and they could hold these dances regularly. In order to give it conventional gaiety, stags would be admitted for 50¢ and couples for $1.50. It might be cruel, but it was necessary that in a town where the girls outnumbered the boys a certain number of girls be left at home.

The proceeds would go to Mark's most cherished among St. James's charities, the nursery school for the children of working mothers, which during weekdays occupied the parish house rooms that harbored Sunday school on Sundays and Boy Scouts and the Ladies Aid on week nights.

Mark was pleased. He had spent a good deal of energy on the nursery school and he dreamed of hiring a full-time, trained teacher for its small, gay pupils instead of having to depend on volunteer help. A series of such dances might take care of this. He also loved to dance.

Mr. Matthew Dugdale Winthrop, Mr. "Sonny Boy" Lovejoy, whose given name was presumably known to his parents, Miss Ellen Terra Rook, and Miss Caroline Gregory were formally named the committee in charge of arrangements. The four immediately started arguing about chaperones. Sonny Boy, with his salesman's shrewdness, said no chaperones should be admitted free, any more than they themselves would admit themselves free. Mary Newcombe said the committee was being too arbitrary, but they finally all agreed to Sonny Boy's suggestion, provided the committee made sure that a contingent of respectable chaperones agreed to pay to come. Sonny Boy, who loved festivity and was in his element arranging it, pulled at his brown curls and, turning to Carrie, suggested that she and he go up to Oglethorpe and spread the good word there, so as to get a contingent to come down to Andalusia for the fun.

Hope, still moping, but wanting to be back in the group, said she had a couple of friends in Marianna who would adore it.

"That's fine," said Dugdale, whose long, lean body lounged below hers, "honey." He looked up at her pretty blonde face, petulant now, approvingly. "But we don't want too many from Marianna. Too much money, too few manners."

It was a mild enough remark, and Dugdale, for all his ostentatiously broken heart carefully preserved from a college jilting, was openly an admirer of Hope's, but together with the other snubs she had received, it rankled. Besides, Mark was impartial again. He had not even acknowledged their intimacy with his eyes. Also, she was uncomfortable, sitting on the top step, with her back against a post, her arm stiffly withdrawn from contact with Ellen Terra's warm round arm. Her body was not as well-padded as it looked, for it was stocky rather than plump, and she could feel the bones of her bottom and her spine. The night was close and she began to feel miserable in the heat.

Mark, apparently uncomfortable, too, got up and stretched himself. "You-all sure have hot weather for April," he remarked, this time to them all, ignoring the fact that she was not one of them, as he was not. "Unusual or not."

Hope remembered that he had promised his answer to her father and the other vestrymen by the twenty-ninth of April. She calculated quickly that this was the Sunday after the dance. They must make it a success, she thought in a prickly panic, for he *must not* go away to Mobile.

"My father said," she stated, lying deliberately, but sure that she could underwrite her lie, "that he'd love to make a special contribution. Buy the orchestra, or something."

"Good Lord," said Sonny Boy, "that's terrific. I know a honey, a lamb, a peachie pie of an outfit we can get from Atlanta if we have enough of what it takes." Sonny Boy was an authority on jazz and the others immediately deferred to him and Hope.

"I must go home. We'll talk about it," said Hope, nervous with their sudden approval. She had planned to outstay the others.

Sonny Boy immediately jumped to his feet. "I'll take you, honey."

She left on a wave of approval and gratitude. But when she

71

reached home her momentary triumph was dissipated, despite Sonny Boy's flattering and easily acquired attention. She could wheedle the money from her father, or she had some of her own. That was no problem. It was the knowledge that if she lived in Andalusia a hundred years she would still be capable of making suggestions that would be automatically dismissed by her fellow citizens. Her memory scarcely included the few years she had not lived in Andalusia, but the others seemed to have memories bequeathed to them by former generations. They always seemed to know and remember things that she did not know or remember.

In the semi-darkness of the porch, under the cover of the general conversation around them, Ellen Terra had said to her, without directly referring to her first suggestion, that an open cotillion had once been given, during the Spanish-American War, for patriotic purposes. This had resulted in a broken chandelier at the Andalusia House—this was long before the first Oaks had been built —and a clear understanding that such a thing would never happen again. Ellen Terra said, exactly as if she had been there, that it was awful. Now Ellen Terra was still on the rectory porch with Mark, and Hope was at home in bed.

Sticky with resentment and heat, lying in bed and unable to sleep, Hope decided that she would give a treasure hunt herself. They could not object if she gave one herself! She would arrange for the winners to donate the treasure that she would provide to the church. That should please Mark and at a real Andalusia treasure hunt, for which she herself selected the guests, something was sure to happen. She had reached a point where she cared less what happened than that something should. Every time she saw Mark Barbee she was tortured by his idleness. If he had looked at her as he had looked at her that Thursday morning, if they had shared the intimate understanding of Holy Saturday, he had no right to ignore her publicly as he had done this night. She could bear him to break her heart, just so it was definite and forever. She could not understand how Angela and Ellen Terra could be so relaxed, so casual, so gay. As if it did not matter how long things took. Hope felt that her energy, her love, and the heat would drive her crazy. She must find some outlet, even in tragedy. The treasure hunt would use her energy and it must surely precipitate something, something, something. Planning vigorously, she fell asleep at last.

The treasure hunt, comparatively new among the town's social functions, had already been sanctified by custom and had grown its own set of local rules, like the local moss that festooned the simplest trees. It ranked now with the cotillions and the post-wedding chivarees as both significant and glorified.

It had become the automobile-and-prohibition form for general courting, sometimes supplementing and often preceding the declared courting of selective dating. It replaced, as such, the parlor kissing games of earlier periods and the hay rides and house parties of still earlier. The way it had evolved in Andalusia was complicated, meticulous, and almost cynical in design, inviting as it did each boy and girl to sample one another, together and alone, without any previous commitment of declared interest. It went like this:

An even number of members of the opposing sexes gathered at the starting place, the house of the hostess or host. They drew the numbers by which they were paired and the slips of paper that gave the clue to the hiding place of the next clue. The first couple to arrive at this hiding place, selected for privacy, picked up, without opening them, their copies of the second clue and waited for the second couple to find them. The two couples then changed partners and the first boy departed with the second girl to look for the hiding place indicated in the second clue. The other two waited for the third couple. The first girl then left with the third boy. And so and so and so, in rigid relay, until the chances of each having a turn, and more than one, with each of the others of the opposite sex, either while looking for or while finding the places where the clues were hidden, were mathematically most excellent. A young and uncritical married couple was always asked to supervise the affair, to invent and plant the clues. They also provided telephone information to any couple that found one of the clues baffling and might thus be lost to the pattern and the game for more than the allotted limit of half an hour to a clue. The winning of the treasure was unimportant. The dalliance of the hunt was what mattered. More than one romance had begun with such an opportunity to sample freely—and the rector himself, to whom the treasure chest would be given by the winners, was well aware that this time he was himself first prize if he could be won.

There were six young men, six young women and seven clues for that night the following week, and a gigantic full moon to light these latter-day sex rites.

Angela stood beside the burdened camellia bush in front of her house. The Madison yard was fully carpeted now in rough green and bordered with the bright, rough thickets of Bailey's favorite zinnias. Carefully she selected and detached two wide, tender blossoms from the bush, one for her hair and one for the neck of her dress. Her white dress, her hands, the white camellias, and her pale brown hair and pale face caught the incandescent light of the moon, and shimmered under its cold, pervasive beauty. The soft green sweater, arranged carefully over her shoulders, its sleeves swinging coyly and correctly useless, the bright new green of the grass, the harsh, gay colors of the zinnias were as dim and meaningless as was the color of her lightly rouged mouth and the expressive color of her brown eyes. She looked up at the moon, which was making the night something thrown on a screen, larger than life, mechanically brilliant in grays and silvers so compelling that color seemed never to have existed, making a moving picture of life and love. She felt like a wraith. She was tall on the outsize screen, with a head the size and weight of a mammoth pumpkin. Putting one hand up to support the sudden weight of her tilting head, she wrinkled her nose as she smelled something sweet, stronger than the faint smell of the summer earth which had been diminished by the empty splendor of the moonlight. The green linen handkerchief she had borrowed from her mother was in her hand and her mother's expensive and indelicate perfume lingered in its folds. Angela tossed the handkerchief onto the bush, where it hung black against the hard black leaves of the camellia bush in the moonlight. She hated smells except those drawn by the sun from the warm and undefiled earth. She loved camellias, which bruised like gardenias but did not smell.

Walking down to her car standing ready beside the curb, she held her too heavy head, garnished with its bright, perfumeless flower, high. She knew that this night Mark Barbee would kiss her because he was a gentleman and she was a lady, and a gentleman did not refuse to kiss a lady who held her face up to him in the proper way at the proper time in this ritual wooing of their time. She felt neither excitement nor reluctance, only regret. This was not how it should be, but there was no other way for it to be. If she did not lift her face, he would not bend his head, because he was the pursued and she the pursuer. In this kiss lay her faint hopes. This was not how it should be, but it was how it was. There was no escape for either of them from either of their roles.

She got coolly and steadily into her car, her head high, and started the instantly responding and softly purring engine. Driving down the street toward Hope's house, where the hunt would begin, she looked far and straight ahead of her down the long street that led to the horizon, feeling the way with her tires as if they were feet, knowing the way as surely and almost as minutely as if she had walked there in bare feet the thousand times. Looking at the illusory curve the flat, southern earth made upward toward the horizon, she thought that all carefully acquired knowledge was wrong. If she were to drive straight on up to the visible horizon, without slackening or speeding her motor, she could drive straight over the edge of the gently upcurving platter of the earth, and she would tumble, together with her car, into infinity, falling in endless, leisurely spirals through the bright and endless night.

There was a light in front of Hope's porchless front door and the door was open. Angela drew up quietly to the curb, behind the several cars already there, and sat with her hand on the ignition key. As long as she did not turn it, she was still in control of her own destiny, able to flee the inexorable fatefulness of this night. The power of the motor was her own power, idle, subject to her will. Once she had stilled it, she was helpless. It was the men who would drive the cars that moved through the night in search of hidden treasure.

Expertly, without conscious thought, she tabulated the cars, recognizing by their cars the other human beings who would share the night. "Li'l ol'" Sonny Boy Lovejoy's ubiquitous, shiny salesman's Chevvy was next to Carrie's long, red, custom-built roadster. "Pretty Boy" Logan Knight's Model T was still marked with "Hello Honey" and "Excuse My Dust" and "Pax Vobiscum," having returned from college with its owner. It still wore the silver radiator cap of a lady, superbly sculpted, that Logan had stolen from the Dean's LaSalle in an escapade that had brought him intercollegiate honor as an undergraduate. Funny that Logan had done such a thing. She had been what she thought was in love with Logan off and on for quite a bit of her life, Angela thought ruefully. She had sighed at him periodically from the water cooler, over the edge of her paper cup, in grammar school. She had written passionate, and secret, verse to him in high school. His snapshot had grown curly in her mirror at Miss Luttrell's—and she had bought her gasoline, gallon by gallon, from the filling station that hired him during his summer vacations from college. He had always been kind to her, dreamy-eyed and courtly and kind, even to the tomboyish bag of bones with twin hanks of pigtails who had skated up and down his block in the hopes of seeing him. Twice, promising that the gap of four years in their ages would one day diminish between them, he had called her "my little Angela." She had cherished the sound of the possessive pronoun until it was echoless and meaningless. She had waited for him the past summer, after he graduated from college, in nervous anticipation, but he had gone to some camp as diving instructor. She had waited again, in the fall, but he had gone to New York to work for an advertising agency so that he could study art at night. When he came home, dreamy-eyed and reticent about sacrificing his career as an artist to take care of his mother, Mr. Stone had given him a job in the bank. Everybody had felt proud of him and sorry for him, including Angela. It was then, when it was too late, that the town had rewarded her long devotion. They had made a match between them in their minds, between the grown-up Angela, vaguely labeled as an intellectual, and Logan, the town's own artist. He dated her now, too, regularly, though not exclusively. In his high, dreamy way he had hinted at the promise of a transcendent love that might find them both at last. But Mark—Mark—Mark—was there, and Logan seemed to her never to have existed in her full heart at all. Not even to the extent that Morton Hadley existed, whom she had, at least, experimentally kissed. It seemed so feebly inconclusive, to have wanted something so much and then not to want it. Her eyes closed as if in weariness, opened and changed focus.

Morton's car was there, or rather, his father's car, four doors and a capacious back seat. Morton must have brought "dear" Mary Newcombe with him, since he had been going pretty steady with her for several months and she had no car.

Bill Bloodgood's two-seater was parked just ahead of her, jaunty and sleek with care beneath the dust of its sixty-mile trip down from Oglethorpe that night. Angela giggled faintly, squeezing her ignition key tight between her thumb and forefinger, as she reminded herself that William Shy Bloodgood, from Oglethorpe, was the only man in the whole wide world she was specifically forbidden to date, to kiss, or to marry. Not, sensibly, because Bill was no mother's ideal, wild as he was and casual about things like money and jobs and nice girls' reputations, but because Angela's great-uncle, Ed Miller, had owned the saloon in Oglethorpe and sold the whiskey that Bill's maternal grandfather, Wild Willy Shy (Squire William to you, Ed Miller) had drunk for forty-two years until it had driven him raving crazy and finally dead. Up your kilts, ghosts, thought Angela Lord Madison, Hannah Miller's daughter, impudently. But the challenge was empty. She wanted none of Bill Bloodgood, who reminded her of a rampant stallion, furious with fences only because they were fences, kicking his heels at the blue sky. "Missy" Maidenstone would fix him, she thought, when he got through proving to the whole county that he needn't and married her at the cathedral in Oglethorpe. Bridled and broken, gaited and guided by the Prettiest Girl in the South, with her steely fingers in white kid gloves, he was the kind that jumped through hoops instead of over fences, she thought, with something like regret. She was afraid of horses, but she resented them docile. Why did Bill always remind her of horses? It was the way he carried his head.

She heard the sound of another motor and then saw in her rear-view mirror that Dugdale Winthrop's touring car was sliding in behind hers. Horses, again, she thought. Dugdale did not remind her of horses, but he made horses seem in the offing. He looked lost, long and thin and lost, down from a horse. He rode—like a centaur. Horses carried his long, drooping body as if it were inevitable that he was upon them and that they should do his sad will. Everyone said he would be Master of the Oakland Hunt in time.

Bowing her head as if to fate, she switched off her motor at

77

last and waited submissively. Mark would be with Dugdale; he had no car. Mark—Mark was there. She felt her heart both swelling and heavy.

Dugdale appeared beside her alone, walking awkwardly with his ridiculous height, his shoulders held forward and hunched slightly upward. He looked down at her silently, with hurt eyes in his long, mournful face. Curving over her, he said plaintively, "Let me sit here a minute with you, Angela, darling."

She shifted her buttocks slightly on the seat and nodded her willingness. She was afraid to speak, fearing that her voice would match his, as cooing doves mourn antiphonally in the moonlight. He was all the sad young men in the South and in this moment he found her kin.

Lord, she prayed, feeling her knees melt and her hands lift within themselves, Good Lord, deliver me from sweet sorrow. . . . Dugdale climbed in beside her and gently lifted the hand that lay idle beside her where she had dropped it from the key to her car.

"You're sweet, Angela," he said.

She heard the melancholy longing in his voice and looked into his dark, thirsting eyes. It was her sadness he longed for, her frustration, her tears he thirsted to drink. She threw back her head in a gesture like a pony's, rejecting even comfort for her sorrow. *Lord, make Mark love me!* she prayed, commanding God instead of supplicating. Her hand clenched slightly, and Dugdale relinquished it instantly. Leaning back, he put his clasped hands behind his head.

"It should be good," he said, conversationally. "I was out riding and saw a dee-vine clue. Don't tell."

The young married couple Hope had selected to do the clues for the hunt, who were now doubtless waiting in Oakland, at the other end of the chase, for the night to begin, to proceed and to end, were good at games.

"Yes," she agreed, briskly.

"Who-all's coming?" he asked. "Besides you four girls, and Mark—and me and Logan . . ." He looked at her expectantly. Next to the soul's sad confidences, he loved gossip. "Sonny Boy?"

"And Morton and Mary," said Angela.

"They'll have five children—in, let's see—eight years. All

with runny noses," said Dugdale. "A house full of little toidies and Pablum for breakfast!" He shuddered, affecting a distaste for domesticity that he did not feel. He was Uncle Duggie to half a dozen nieces and nephews and present-lavishing godfather to half the younger marrieds' first-borns.

"I thought Morton was looking for out," said Angela with mild, uncontrollable spite. "He had a date with Hope last week."

"Hmmm. Ten'll get you five on Mary. Is Rachel coming?"

"I think so," said Angela. "Yes, of course. There's her car." She had not checked Rachel in because the conservative coupe was facing the other way, across the street. Rachel was born with a racial sadness, she thought, with the slight surprise any realization of Rachel Mirimar's Jewishness always gave her, as Dugdale had been born with an already broken heart. It was the reason she had never been close to Rachel, whom she liked. "And Bill Bloodgood," the name faintly delicious only for being forbidden, "and Mark," she added, self-consciously aware that Dugdale had already mentioned Mark, but unable to help herself in her desire to speak his name. "Didn't you bring him?" she asked hurriedly and foolishly.

Dugdale peered at her, alert to the nuance. "No-o-o-o," he drawled. "Ellen Terra's picking him up. . . ."

"Hi!" called Angela too loudly. Sonny Boy was standing in the lighted doorway, shading his eyes and looking out into the night.

"Hi, there," he replied, swinging the screen door wide and prancing through it. "Don't you two know better than to sit out here? Uncoil, monster, and come out of there with my girl!" He addressed Dugdale, whose height was an offense to his cheerfully belligerent shortness.

"Okay, half-pint," said Dugdale.

Sonny Boy opened the door for Angela and helped her out of the car. The three of them stood on the sidewalk together for an instant, adjusting themselves to each other, to a party.

"I'll get off my knees if you'll come off that ladder," offered Sonny Boy, looking at Dugdale's stretching shadow cast by the moonlight. He turned and winked broadly at Angela, with whom he stood exactly eye to eye. Angela grinned back at his cocky, cheerful bulldog face and restrained an impulse to pull affectionately at his tousled brown curls. Another car was coming around the corner. That would be Mark and Ellen Terra. . . . Sonny Boy took Angela's arm and squeezed her elbow as he guided her up the sidewalk, while Dugdale hung back to greet the newcomers.

"Honey, I've got it all fixed for you and me to draw the first lap together," Sonny Boy said in her ear. "You're the prettiest thing I ever saw, with that white flower in your hair."

"I just came to this party on a chance of seeing you," said Angela absently, almost mimicking his manner.

Hope said, in a high, excited, hostessy voice, "*Sweetie*, what a pretty dress! Come on in and Morton will help you to a drink."

The radio was playing "My Blue Heaven" and the ritual had begun.

No one of the women later forgot this evening, or ever remembered it consecutively or whole. Only Rachel Mirimar, tall, dark and lovely, remembered its electric-lit, crowded beginning in the living room at Hope Stone's house in Andalusia, or its electric-lit, confused finale at the hunting lodge that belonged to the Stones in Oakland. Her perspective was different. It was the friendship of women and the intimacy of a group that she wanted and sought and needed, not the intimacy of male and female, to which she was preordained and which she could have for the asking when she was ready.

Rachel Mirimar knew that she would not marry in Andalusia, where she had been born and lived all of her quite happy life. She could, if she wanted to, but she would not. She would marry in Oglethorpe because there she could choose among her own kind. It was as if her life were lived on two planes. From one, contented and temporary, she sought only a little more than she had, to be a little more completely part of it, to draw its normal course around her like a good, warm daily cloak. The other plane had existed for thousands of years and she would give the hostage of her marriage to its future. There was no prejudice against Jews in Andalusia. There were two families, like the Mirimars, who "belonged" and others who didn't, but the belonging was based on family distinctions indistinguishable from those made among gentiles. A number of aristocratic Spanish Jews had settled in Oglethorpe County before the Civil War and were as much part of the county tradition as the Knights, the Bloodgoods, or the Madisons. What fear or kinship out of the past for the future kept the Jewish families intermarrying, as they did, instead of scattering their seed and their identity, Rachel did not know. She only knew that she would marry one of them in Oglethorpe. It meant that you had nothing whatever to explain.

Meantime, looking with intent approval around the tasteful, mahogany-furnished living room that Hope hated because it was different from the other living rooms in Andalusia, Rachel felt little tendrils of feeling attaching her to these pleasantly known and daily encountered people. She loved them all.

So pretty hostess Hope said to her, touching her arm with a light, seemingly affectionate gesture, "Watch Morton or he'll slug you. It's very strong corn, although we've had it aging for a month!" Carrie crossed the room to her, her signature of a walk drawing attention to this fact, and chided her for not coming over to see the Gregorys. "It's been a coon's age," said Carrie, her saturnine face openly pleasant, "and do tell me how your mother is. I adore your mother." Ellen Terra, arriving last, bounced into the room ahead of Mark and Dugdale dispensing unapologetic apologies. She plumped herself down beside Rachel and whispered to her. Her warm, clean, kinelike breath agreeably tickled Rachel's thin, narrow ears. Her lavishly applied perfume pleased Rachel's high, curved nostrils. "Would you believe it, but mama and papa had an argument about whether I should wear a girdle!" "Did you?" asked Rachel. "Of course not! Papa said I looked nakeder than the day I was born." Rachel, who wore one, giggled and agreed with Ellen Terra that parents were impossible. Angela pulled her into a quartet that was starting in opposition to the radio. "*Rachel* can carry a tune," she said, as if proudly, her arm through Rachel's, while Sonny Boy and Bill Bloodgood dropped fraternal arms around the girls' shoulders and they all sang, "A-around her neck she wore a yellow ribbon. . . ." Even Mary Newcombe, absorbed in her great age of twenty-three, was casual enough to imply a perfect understanding between herself and the younger Rachel. Rachel felt contented, a cheerful brick in a sturdy wall, a house in a row on a street, a link in a daisy chain, and no longer a great, awkward, lonely, isolated ego.

81

Under the radiant chandelier, against the dark hangings and darker furniture, in contrast to the many-colored bouquet of girls, the men, divested indoors of their dark jackets, gleamed masculine, muscular, and clean in their white flannels and white linen shirts. Looking at them from the cozy center of her identification with the women, Rachel found them an adequate background for the precious, linked friendship of women. She bestowed on them, as a whole, her grateful approval. Sonny Boy was indeed amusing, Bill Bloodgood was dramatically handsome despite the sparseness of the dark hair that formed a thinning widow's peak, Morton Hadley had boyish charm. Logan Knight was a "dreamboat," a knight errant from a more gallant era. Dugdale Winthrop no longer seemed to look down his thin nose from the inordinate height of his long body, but to be purposefully tall in order to make her feel small and female despite her own height, which was considerably greater than Sonny Boy's and Morton's and that of the other women. She was pleased when the charming young Episcopal minister, Mark Barbee, whom she scarcely knew, eagerly accepted the offer of her car. It was the males who were expected to drive in the Hunt and he had no car. She was unaware that he accepted hers so quickly because he could thus avoid making even this faintest hint of preference by taking Carrie's or Hope's or Ellen Terra's or Angela's. She felt it was the seal of his immediate acceptance of her as entirely one of them. It was part of the male group's concomitant approval of the female.

Logan Knight was assigned to Hope's car, because his old model T would put him at an unfair disadvantage, and the group became a cluster around the hat full of different numbers and the hat full of identical clues.

Rachel was sad because now they would be no more a homogeneous group, but only solitary, lonely couples streaming away from each other into the gigantic night.

For the others, the important moments and the things they remembered and the things that it mattered for them to forget came now. The moments they remembered were lit by violent flashes of moonlight, like lightning. The moments they later forgot were as deeply forgotten as the night's shadows were black.

The clues they followed through the night were neither clever nor difficult—ditties that led up to or away from the intervals between them.

Where the Young Lambs learn the Glory of the finest days of yore
You will find at least a hundred Keys that never locked a door.

In the musty room, the littlest and whitest fleeced lambs of the town were gathered together on Sundays to learn that Jesus suffered them to come unto Him. On weekdays, the poorer and more motley lambs whose mothers discarded them daily in order to earn their bread gathered to learn to play and sing. Now, as the moonlight forced its brilliant way through the carelessly washed windows of the parish house into this nursery room, Ellen Terra made mock protest as Bill Bloodgood, down from Oglethorpe to kiss the mouths of Andalusia's maidens, caught her waist with mock force and tucked one of her shoulders under his armpit and swung his face down to hers. The mild, stimulating struggle between light, exploratory kisses brought her firm, ungirdled posterior up against the hundred keys and two octaves in the bass descended together with scarcely a note missing. The resounding *whump* detached a thumb tack, and a colored print of the three wise men fell to the floor.

"Stop playing the piano, baby," said Bill, catching her chin in his hand. "Ellen Terra, you're so cute and pretty, I just don't know what to do about you. . . ."

The voices of the second couple to find the parish house nursery caused them to draw quickly apart. Bill wiped his lips with a handkerchief and Ellen Terra patted her short dark hair as the door was fumbled open and Angela said, "Hello there," in the sweet, self-conscious voice she used around Logan Knight. Logan's tenor, light-bodied and seeming as disconnected from his thoughts as the back of his eyes seemed disconnected from the objects of his regard, said humorously, "What's going on here? A piano lesson?"

Bill and Angela left Logan and Ellen Terra together. They paused outside to examine the next clue by flashlight before climbing into Bill's car. Bill did not even try to kiss Angela, which might have provided her with at least the warmth of temptation to temper her determined, chilly purity. His lively attention, both promiscuous and catholic, was elsewhere, divided among the near-desperate charms of twenty-three-year-old Mary Newcombe, the exquisite, precise prettiness of his blonde hostess, and the provocative, wanton virginity of *that* Ellen Terra.

Ellen Terra, in the parish house, generous and unreluctant, kissed Logan Knight twice, before Morton Hadley and Hope came in. For all that she rarely lost a scrap from the cluttered rag bag of her memory, she could never afterwards remember whether she had ever in her life kissed Logan Knight or not.

Morton was rudely in advance of Hope and when he drew deep on his cigarette, Ellen Terra saw the imprint of Hope's hand on his pink, sullen face. She felt both surprised and sympathetic to Morton. They left Hope in the nursery with Logan and went off into the night together.

In the summer, busy, bouncing I,
In the winter, lonesome, high and dry.

The next box of neatly lettered clues was perched on the top of the diving tower above the swimming pool at The Oaks. Morton was made antic by the deflation of his masculine ego because Hope had turned on him and, instead of maidenly refusing him, which was fair and within the rules, had hauled off and hit him as if he had insulted her. It was as if she found him personally undesirable. He tiptoed out to the end of the high diving board and bounced furiously above the half-empty swimming pool. With an impulse to redeem himself by valor, he bounced high and higher on the creaking board until Ellen Terra squealed in only partially simulated alarm.

"Pooh," said Morton, responding to her alarm. "Look!" He spread his arms as for a swan dive, bouncing still on the stiff, long unused board.

"Don't, *don't*," cried Ellen Terra as he nearly toppled, betrayed by the stiff resistance of the board and by a look at the water, which was suddenly very cold, very far away, and very shallow in the dazzling moonlight.

"Come *back*," she called, as if to a child. With a child's shaken bravado he came, to be warmed into almost manhood again by her warmth, generated partly by the titillation of mild alarm.

So Ellen Terra kissed and fondled and cozened them all this night. She was kissed and fondled in return, but not rudely or importunately this night, because there was a purity of purpose and a remoteness of design in her lavishness that imposed spontaneous limits on her partners. She was almost less than remote with Dugdale Winthrop, enchanted momentarily beyond her purpose by his lean, supercilious, somehow wistful body, but he smelled the aura of her virginity, which was very strong this night, and was only affectionate and wistful with her. So, when she met Mark, in the fifth shuffling of partners, she was warm as toast and aching and ready. Since he was her purpose and her design, there was no limit imposed by her on his spontaneity. Already carefully kindled, she flamed now, vivid and unashamed, offering herself without stint in the moonlight.

Neither Ellen Terra nor Mark remembered exactly where this happened or how long this, their one kiss, lasted. It was as if in dry midsummer an already flaming dry pine had leaned into another dry pine, fat with resin and vulnerable with heat, and they were both instantly ablaze from tip to root.

Hope's clear, loud voice was like a gust of wind that blew them inexorably, still blazing, apart. Shaken and blazing, they obeyed the pattern that forced them to separate, which gave Ellen Terra into the short grasping arms of Sonny Boy Lovejoy, while Mark stumbled quickly away with Hope and into the waiting car.

When Hope said, the clearer and the more bell-like for her nervousness, "Stop the car, Mark," he obeyed without thought and turned to her, still trembling and still ablaze. Her mouth gave way instantly. Preserved for him, it was his. It became the mouth he had just kissed, yielding without stint, soft and part of his mouth. The perfume strong in his pulsing nostrils was the same. The blue eyes were closed in ecstasy as the black had been. The body he touched now with his frantic fingers was not the same body. It was harder and stockier, but it was equally his, yielding, too, and catching immediate fire. He could not seem to get enough of it or of kissing, frantic and violent in the moonlight, hurting and bruising her to her passionately responding delight.

It was Hope who heard the other car coming and urged him to move on. Trembling and sweating, Mark abruptly let her go and jerked the car into motion. Tearing through the moonlight toward the next trysting place, which he had already guessed, he could not yet stop to think.

Flail tails, fill pails,
Where I am, no males!

He swung the car into the courtyard and stopped it with an abruptness that threw Hope rudely forward. There was already a car in the courtyard and they could hear the voices inside the dairy, where a couple were waiting for them. They stepped out quietly into the courtyard and stopped urgently once. There was a strong, acrid smell all about them and Hope remembered ever after that she had all but laid herself down on a dung heap to give herself to this man in the moonlight. She started to speak in a harsh, dazed whisper.

"Darling Mark, darling, please . . ."

But he stopped her. "Don't say anything," he implored, whispering, too. "There's nothing to talk about." Then he kissed her once more, hard and hotly, catching her face in both hands and holding his body away from her stocky body, which was on tip-toe reaching up and toward him.

Mary Newcombe called "Who's there?" and they moved together past the dung heap and into the shed that sheltered the pragmatic and antiseptic-smelling apparatus for milking the kine that supplied Hope's still daily drunk milk.

Fools will find, given time,
Hidden in another rhyme
Where human foot has often trod
A poem made by only God.

A large indentation in the muddy bank on the Andalusia side of the sluggish, curling river formed a natural swimming pool. It was shaded by willows and oaks, and full of lazy, pleasant, muddy currents. Nearby grew a mammoth oak tree with lower limbs so massive and so straight as to make the construction of a tree house inevitable. It had been built and rebuilt through the generations. It had been roofed and was now roofless, had served as a dressing place by day and a trysting place by night. It was here that Mary Newcombe and Mark Barbee climbed the solid enough ladder to find Morton Hadley and Angela Madison dawdling and desultory in each other's company as they waited to be relieved. Mary handed Morton a folded clue from the tin box in the tree and scampered down the ladder again, briefly buoyant as a child, without a backward glance, knowing that Morton must follow her now at least as far as the next clue led.

Mark and Angela sat down together on the bench built rustically around three sides of the thick-planked platform that rested on the great limbs of the tree. Their movements were deliberate, graceful and rhythmic, as if they were performing a formal dance, a ballet, for which they had composed neither the music nor the steps.

Angela was cool and calm. She was remotely, but not intensely, aware that this, her moment, was ill-chosen. As the middle couple in the complicated routine of the Andalusia treasure hunt, they could not even stretch nor shorten the time they had together, as they might have done in the elastic intervals of the hunt. They could only be there, subject to the haste or the lack of it of another couple. She was cool with her painstaking refusal to touch or to be touched in the almost playful tribal ritual of the hunt before she should come to Mark. She could summon now only a surge of knowledge that she loved this man. She had no infectious warmth to challenge his complementary coolness. She was calm because she felt that she was not quite truly alive by the light of the moon.

She felt him as cool and as calm, and wondered fleetingly what had been the shape and progress of his evening. She knew and guessed that, good at games, he had contrived by calculation and by playing his luck to spend most of his previous time with Mary, with Rachel, and with Carrie. These three would demand nothing of him. She was also sure that he had been once with Ellen Terra. Ellen Terra must surely have destroyed any illusion that he could play this, Andalusia's game, by his own rules, or for its own sake. If it was his intention now only to keep the score even, she must play with him even at this.

She lifted her pale face to him, as she must, her light brown hair like darkened moonlight in the shadow of the tree, and closed her eyes that had neither luster nor sparkle nor intelligence in the white light that filtered through the tree's great, open branches. Mark bent his head and kissed her coolly, feeling for her a cool regret.

His brain was back in furious, determined ascendancy over his aroused body, his already aching loins. The interval with Mary, whose desperate interest was elsewhere and who attracted him not at all, had doused the raging fire lit by Ellen Terra and fed by Hope. No kiss could disturb the embers again this night. Reaction and reflection had produced a thick fright and a rigorous, disciplined calmness. He had too nearly destroyed the hard-won fruits of his long celibacy. He had not even kissed a girl since the nurse from the hospital in Sewanee had celebrated with him the end of his freedom when he had graduated from the University Divinity School into the unmarried priesthood. For this, he had won special respect within himself for the profession he had chosen, which demanded such sacrifice. He had won also the precious right and proper perspective from which to choose him a wife with his heart and mind and not only with his body. This right and perspective had been momentarily lost and, until he regained it, he must protect himself thrice over from all women.

He knew, remotely and thus protected, that he might just possibly have loved this lean, clean-smelling and unfinished girl. If he had had the freedom to know Angela easily and alone. If she had not loved him first. If Ellen Terra had never kissed him and he had not responded so instantly and so completely to her voluptuous perfection, her soft and magnificent body. If Hope had not offered him so devastatingly and so honestly the compact devotion of her completed self. If Angela had been the only woman in the world, he would have felt no sense of loss.

Angela kissed him as coolly, knowing that her heart was too tough to break, and concentrated on the need to refuse herself the ugly and youthful release of tears.

When Bill Bloodgood claimed her, she went with him jauntily. She drank deep of the bottle in the side pocket of Bill's car and refused to kiss him, too, when he politely bent to her this time, as she had refused all but Mark—this time out of purity, perversity, and the fear of tears.

Where the thicket is the thickest, in the thickest of the thickets
You will find me with the leader of a ragged band of pickets.

Mark, having picked up Carrie again in the relentless shuffle, drove her in the car loaned him by Rachel Mirimar toward the deserted house in the bamboo thicket to the east of The Oaks. The Negroes called the house haunted. Like Miss Sis's nearby house, it was buried in wildly growing, voracious, tree tall bamboo. Unlike hers, it was unprotected by human vigilance against the bamboo that pushed at its empty windows, prodded the slanting floor, oppressed the crazy roof, and shoved the surrounding fence into mad shapelessness. Mark thought of Miss Sis and the waste of fine women and stopped the car near the house and lifted Carrie's dark, well-defended face to his own. It was then that he imparted to her the knowledge that he admired and liked her as it was balm and healing to be admired and liked. He also conveyed to her raw and certain instinct that, with all this admiration, he could not touch her misshapen body with unself-conscious pleasure. She stirred against the muscular envelope of his fine strength and opened her heart without protest and in deep privacy to this bitterness that no balm could soothe.

At 18 I am happier far
Than the other ages are.
Next you find the place to drink.
It is later than you think.

89

By the time Morton Hadley reached the eighteenth hole of The Oaks golf course, a hole he enjoyed and habitually played under par, he considered himself at last engaged to Mary Newcombe. Therefore he made no attempt to dally further with Ellen Terra, who was again beside him.

On his previous way from the house in the tree to the haunted house in the bamboo thicket, he had turned off into a pine grove beside a field and had stopped his car. In the back seat of his father's car, he had discovered that he was unmistakably ploughing hitherto unbroken and fallow ground. He had refrained from investigating this possibility before, during three months of regular dating with Mary, because he had not been sure whether it would make him more pleased than not. It did make him more pleased than not, and, being an honorable young man in the position of having despoiled not a woman but a lady, he considered the obligation to marry her. He allowed himself a few qualms and some consideration of not doing so on their accelerated way to the haunted house, which the treasure seekers would soon leave to the bamboo and its ghosts.

During this interval, while she repaired the visible damage to her face, Mary Newcombe permitted herself to be frightened. Not having quite dared to use the opposite tactic of refusing his ultimate demands, she had gambled on Morton's sense of honor and had hastily and painfully yielded him her pearl of some price. If this proved insufficient, and he failed now to propose, the alternatives for her were unpleasant. Her father was unfortunately far too civilized to flourish a shotgun on her behalf. He was sufficiently old-fashioned to wield the equivalent of a horsewhip in the privacy of their home and she could even visualize herself melodramatically outside the door in the southern equivalent of a snowstorm. More likely, she might well remain indoors and spend the rest of her life as a not quite old maid. She was twenty-three and Morton was the first man to date her steadily for three months on end for some time. Bill Bloodgood's past desultory attentions were patently selfish and patently temporary, based on the supposition that at twenty-three she might be no longer virgin and therefore fair game for dalliance. She was pretty enough and capable enough, but Andalusia was undeniably short of young men. Two tears marred the powder she was replacing.

Morton, having disposed of his qualms and feeling tired and unlike a scene, patted her hand affectionately with a hand he removed from the wheel. "Cheer up, honey child," he said cheerfully. "It doesn't hurt the second time, they tell me, and it's lots more fun in a double bed."

Engaged now, except for the ring, Mary was able to remember the night for the rest of her life with benign and amused sentimentality.

> *Amphibious forever more,*
> *One foot on water, one on shore.*

The boathouse nestled by the wide, muddy, sluggish river that abounded in fish. The hunters piled into it, on each other's heels. They were hungry, thirsty, and tired and had settled almost everything that could be settled in an evening.

> *Scissors and snails and puppy dogs' tails, all three*
> *Add U in and You have Me.*

Rachel and Bill Bloodgood reached the buoy first and won the right to present the treasure to the rector of St. James's. Rowing awkwardly because he had not rowed since the previous summer, Bill caught a crab and got Rachel thoroughly wet. He behaved gallantly and she gaily, but the incident was more annoying than amusing since they were engaged in no sex play that could give it piquancy. The incident ended the hunt, and Rachel returned eagerly to electric-lit identification with the group straggling into the lodge that the Stones had built near the boathouse.

Rachel reached eager hands again for the friendship of Angela, Carrie, Ellen Terra and Hope. It had not occurred to her to speculate on whether one or the other of them was in love with one or another man. It seemed both natural that they might be and un-important if they were. The important thing to her was the friend-ship they gave each other. This friendship, she believed, was the most precious stuff in life. Without the reservations raised between human beings by differences of age, sex and background, she be-lieved it must be finally intimate with myriad exact and unconflict-ing interests. She was baffled and rebuffed, finding them now bristling with strangeness under the light of the lamps, in the shiny, loud gaiety of the regathered group. They seemed to avoid both her and each other.

Hope cast a small, bright radiance from her great blue eyes impartially over them all. She gabbled precisely and flitted ably as a hostess, meticulously making answer to every remark, urging food and drink and happiness on her guests. In the future, she remem-bered none of this, remembering only of this evening the clear in-stant in the moonlit courtyard, the words she had not said, and that she had all but laid herself down on a dung heap.

Angela stayed by the victrola, choosing records to play as if with passionate and intent discernment. For no reason, she played several times over a sentimental arrangement of "Among my Sou-venirs," singing tunelessly along with the music. She was thus in the future able to relegate this night to a place among many other nights and to remember it out of the final past in connection with yesterday's sentimental music. She paid no attention to Rachel, but permitted Logan Knight and Dugdale Winthrop to help select other sad records for her to play.

Carrie created a late diversion by getting quietly drunk and indulging in an aimless quarrel with Bill Bloodgood, who was hot-tempered as well as handsome. Their quarrel began over the rela-tive merits of two makes of shotgun, proceeded acrimoniously to dogs, and would have become unpleasantly personal if Bill had not remembered with an effort that he was a gentleman.

Ellen Terra alone was effortless and natural, although bone-less and vague. She was clung to by Sonny Boy, who, having inad-vertently received the passionate residue of the kisses meant for Mark, was assiduously trying to arrange for more. He reminded her of a puppy in heat, his brown curls dewy and his hot breath pant-ing. If she had been less vague, she might have been sorry for him and gone with him alone. Later she remembered the evening in enormous, moonlit detail, forgetting only that she had kissed Logan Knight. It was she who, yawning enormously, suggested that it had been a fine party and that it was now over.

Mark Barbee, who looked like a marble statue in his rigid exhaustion, and danced rather like one when he was called upon to dance, left first. He took Rachel with him, offering to leave her with her car at her home not far from the rectory.

He said the polite things to his hostess, Hope, thanking her for inviting him to his first treasure hunt in Andalusia. It was unique, he remarked formally. Hope could make no protest at his leaving. She, the hostess, must stay and see them all away. She could not suggest that he stay, too. She smiled him a direct and secret farewell, to which he replied with a marble smile.

Ellen Terra gathered up Logan Knight to return with her and Sonny Boy to pick up his car. She paid no attention to Sonny Boy's sullen and audible *sotto voce* objections to Logan's company. She had no more use for Sonny Boy. She was wholly and wonderfully sleepy.

Since it was easier for him to go back to Oglethorpe straight from Oakland, thus saving himself five out of sixty miles, Bill Bloodgood left alone after an inconclusive evening. He offered first with some warmth to take Hope home, but she refused. Morton Hadley and Mary Newcombe departed together, both quite pale now, after Mary had fervently and significantly thanked Hope for a wonderful evening. Dugdale Winthrop took Angela and Carrie home, stopping with them for a drink at Carrie's house. Hope had insisted, after Mark left with Rachel, that she would go home alone, since she wanted to close the lodge behind them all. The married couple would follow her in to see that she was safe.

The married couple thanked Hope and said they had been much entertained. She thanked them for their trouble, their cleverness with the clues and their patience. Together they muddled the dishes from the late supper into a pile, emptied ash trays, and turned out lights, commenting that the treasure had pleased Barbee and that it was amusing that Bill, from Oglethorpe, and Rachel, who was not an Episcopalian, should have won and presented the treasure to St. James's church.

On the way home, trailing Hope's swift car, the married couple discussed the hunt and the observations they had made with bright, expert, experienced small-town eyes. During the course of the evening, Sonny Boy had switched his eager attention from Hope to Ellen Terra. Ellen Terra—in this they were intuitive and premature—seemed to find the tall, supercilious, horsy Dugdale Winthrop the next best choice after Mark Barbee. Dugdale, with his usual perversity, seemed to have suspended himself around Angela, like half a parenthesis. He always fell for girls who were madly in love with somebody else. Angela looked as if she were about to float off down the river with a lily in her hand. In the opinion of the couple, spontaneous and sure of itself, Angela and Logan Knight were a natural. They were both the dreamy, intellectual type. Pausing to regard their arbitrary matchmaking, the husband moodily and incautiously remarked that there was something about Angela Madison that really did it to a man, got right to first base, though he could not for the life of him say how or why, she was skinny and no terrific looker and not much of a flirt, but there it was. In revenge, his wife revealed that she considered Logan Knight on a diving board the most divine sight in the world and besides he had that wonderful look in his eyes that made you feel like he was bringing you red roses, and *besides*, for a last word, he was such a catch, well-born and good-looking and so sweet to his mother and doing so well at the bank that even old button-mouthed Mr. Stone spoke of him as a fine young man. Even-stephen, and more, their glances said, and they exchanged a truce in a further glance, reverting practically to the theory that Angela and Logan Knight would suit each other. That almighty Bill Bloodgood, down from Oglethorpe, had not got so far, they went on with local pride. He had not diverted Mary Newcombe, fortunately for Mary, or picked up Hope or Ellen Terra. Mary and Morton, they were sure, were finally a thing. Unless they missed their expert guess! They would be young marrieds by June, unless they missed their guess, and would leave the next treasure hunt to the still hunting. Mary was lucky, at that. Rachel, now, there was an odd girl. She never seemed to have anybody really, male or female, she cared much of a hoot about. Like Mark Barbee. Equally friendly to everybody.

With quickened interest, they discussed Mark Barbee at some

length. The young clergyman had certainly taken his wolf toll of sinful hearts. Why Angela and Hope and Ellen Terra and even Carrie were plain nuts about him. They hoped he would pick one and stay in Andalusia. He was an addition. But he certainly had not shown any preferences. He was letting the girls stew in their own juice. They laughed with the cruel amusement of the settled, and the husband wondered privately what Mark did for tail. His wife opined that Mark seemed to prefer Carrie in a way, but of course it was his business to be kind. . . .

Mark walked rapidly back to the rectory after leaving Rachel in polite haste. He went quickly to bed at the rectory, making certain that his house showed no gleam of light. When he finally went to sleep, it was to dream that he was running a relay around a gigantic asphalt track, alone, his hands full of batons. A vast, high-voiced cheering section roared incessantly at him, led by a cavorting, cartwheeling foursome, in nurses' uniforms, whose faces were the size of the moon.

8. Mothers of Women

Ellen Terra sat on the side porch in the sun-warmed shade of the striped awnings. The canvas couch on which she sat was attached by chains to an iron frame, and the chains creaked faintly as she stirred the couch to uneasy action with the tip of her toe on the floor. She was recalling Mark Barbee's kiss and following her response to the memory through her body with concentrated, repetitious pleasure. She was as warm as a kitten on a hearth and contented as a cow in a green pasture, chewing for the moment the cud of last night's wonderful sensations.

"Ellen TERra," called her mother. Ellen Terra could never tell where her mother's voice came from. It had a round, resonant quality that filled more space with less volume than other voices. It was considered a beautiful voice, but it was so carrying, penetrating and pervasive that her mother had had to develop a sibilant whisper for private conversational purposes.

Moving as if to get up, Ellen Terra sniffed as if her mother's voice might trail her mother's perfume and she could thus tell by smell where to find the source of the voice.

"Ellen TERra!"

It would never do to irritate her mother on this of all mornings. Ellen Terra bounced out of the swing and went quickly around to the front door, letting herself in and banging the screen door purposefully so that her mother would know she was coming. Mattie was setting the table in the dining room on the left.

"Yo mama callin yuh, Miss Ellen Terra," said Mattie, as if anyone in the house would not know this.

"Where is she?" asked Ellen Terra.

"In thuh settin room upstahs," said Mattie, who always knew. It was this knowledge and her acceptance of it that made Mattie permanent in the Rook household. She was none of the things Mrs. Rook valued in a servant. She was never trim nor impeccable. She was not deft and expert like her Pinckney. She was not a fabulous cook such as Nanine was, who had come from New Orleans with Clementine Terra Rook when she was a bride and who had left the Rooks within a month. Mattie was like a lightning rod, content to receive the full force of Mrs. Rook's wrath and to conduct it quietly through herself into the ground, while she went on quietly performing her heavy daily duties. Because she could do this, she stayed, and Mrs. Rook gradually forgave her sins.

"Mad?" Ellen Terra asked anxiously.

"Nawm. She feelin real sweet this mawnin."

Ellen Terra opened the sitting-room door and stood near it. Her mother's sibilant whisperings at close quarters distressed her so that she always tried to keep a distance sufficient to command her mother's normal, melodious, enveloping voice.

"There you are! Go by the rectory before lunch, dear, and ask Mr. Barbee to dinner with us tomorrow night, will you? Your father and I want to encourage him not to go away to Mobile. Right away, Ellen Terra!" as her daughter did not move. Mrs. Rook was painting her nails by the window and was intent on her work. "Poor boy," she added, for no reason that Ellen Terra could think of.

In deference to this unexpected piece of luck, Ellen Terra crossed the fingers of one hand behind her back. This was a way to look at Mark again by daylight, while the memory of his incompleted kiss stayed vivid on her lips. Then she frowned, remembering a hindrance, and hugged her fingers together.

"He's going to the old Lovejoys tomorrow night, mama. The Judge went and asked him Sunday."

"Well, make it for this Sunday, then," said Mrs. Rook absently, holding one hand away from her face and squinting at the nails.

"Oh, mama, Mark *never* goes out on Sundays. It's his hard working day."

Her mother looked in her general direction. "Mark?"

"We all call him Mark, silly," said Ellen Terra. She giggled at the absurd thought of calling Mark Mr. Barbee. "You can't call a guy mister just because he turns his silly collar around." He had not worn his clerical collar to the treasure hunt, she remembered with faint surprise.

"You could," said Mrs. Rook indifferently, bending back over her nails and dragging her hair forward as she did so. Her hair hung over the back of her chair, abundant and black, five feet long by actual measurement from the crown of her head.

"Let's do Monday," said Ellen Terra. She had promised Sonny Boy Lovejoy a date for Monday, but she could break it.

"Fix the day to suit yourself, then," said her mother, "but go *on*."

"Why not ask Angela and Dugdale Winthrop and the Madisons? Then Pinckney could dress up and help Mattie and make it a real pleasure party," said Ellen Terra. She paused. She had preferred the quick vision of a gala evening to that of Mark alone with her two parents, and herself in relation to her parents alone, and possibly even her little sister and brother, who were so tiresome at the table. Perhaps, though, she had been hasty to seat Angela there. She crossed the fingers of her other hand.

"Good Lord, I should think you saw enough of Angela!" Mrs. Rook looked straight at her daughter, divorcing her mind from her nails, from the notion of replacing the chintz on the big chairs by the sitting-room fireplace, from the problem of the yard man she must hire to replace that no-account Randolph, from the idea of once more tackling Mattie on the subject of starched uniforms for afternoon. She was having the young minister to dinner primarily for the sake of her stupid daughter. If Ellen Terra had not brains enough to know that the tall, slender, false-sweet-faced Angela, with whom she had wasted so much time, was a dangerous rival, her daughter was a fool. If she did not realize that Mark Barbee was not only attractive but an exceedingly eligible young man, she was an even bigger fool than her mother suspected her of being. Mark Barbee would be a bishop almost as sure as he was ordained—with his charm and breeding and, probably, brains—a southern bishop. It was one thing to marry a minister, poor pickings at best these days, but a bishop's mother-in-law had something to be charming about. "Ellen Terra," said her mother ominously, "come here!"

Ellen Terra stirred and came slowly over to her mother, her feet leaden and her spirits plummeting. She could feel the rising of the scalding breeze, feel and fear the threatening tempest. She wondered wildly what she had said or done to arouse her mother. She almost never knew. Nice mother, handsome and loving, don't be mad, she pleaded in her mind. Her mother was so dreadful when she was angry and Ellen Terra had learned no protection against anger or even against love

"WHAT have you been doing with yourself?" her mother whispered.

"Me? Nothing!" said Ellen Terra, penitent, her mind nervously numbering a hundred sins.

"You haven't been using that cream I gave you! Your skin is a mess. WILL you learn that skin like ours must be cared for?" She paused and Ellen Terra signified her overwhelming willingness to use the cream by massaging her face with the fingers of one hand that she released from behind her back. "And *what* may I ask, made you put on that hideous blouse and skirt when you got up?"

"I was—I was . . ." said Ellen Terra, mistaking this attack for the real attack, as she always did, crossing her still hidden fingers on the other hand so hard that they hurt, and hoping that she would say the right thing before her mother's anger grew swifter and more devastating. She could think of nothing to say. She heard herself saying, "I was going to get lankety Dugdale and Rachel and make a foursome with Mark maybe to play some golf this afternoon, it's such a bliss-making day. . . ."

Miraculously her mother's brow cleared, the storm warnings dropped and the winds of her temper died and retired to nothing in the subterranean caves from which they had sprung. Ellen Terra found it difficult to believe, as she always did, that the pleasant mouth and harmlessly, vaguely wrinkled brow her mother turned to her now could ever distort themselves. "Your game is certainly improving, dear. All right, then. Run along and play with Mr.—er—Mark and ask him to dinner. Did you have a good time last night?"

"Wonderful," breathed Ellen Terra with thankful relief. "I'll ask Mark to dinner Monday. Family dinner."

"You ready, Angela?"

Her mother stood outside Angela's bedroom door, calling through the door. She had agreed, considering herself rational and good-natured, never to enter her daughter's room without her daughter's permission.

"Am I going to drive, Mama?"

"What, darling?"

"Am I going to DRIVE? Come IN!"

Mrs. Madison opened the door and surveyed the room. "What a pigpen, baby! Didn't Pinckney clean you up this morning?"

"I didn't get up until time for lunch."

"Well, you do look nice," said Mrs. Madison.

She did, too. It was not unpleasing to don her only black afternoon dress, the most expensive dress she owned. (If black was not good, it was tacky.) She wore, too, her pearls, including earrings, her highest heeled black pumps, and thinnest gunmetal stockings. On her head she was even now adjusting a hat woven of fine black straw. It made her face look small and lightened her hair. Perhaps it was quaint to dress one's self up like this and to go a-calling, leaving cards on the Gregorys and the Stones, as if she did not see them almost daily. Only her mother and Mrs. Rook, among the younger matrons, observed this old-fashioned ritual. The year before, home finally and duly finished from two years in Oglethorpe at Miss Luttrell's, back from her brief trip to Europe, she had refused to go. She had been full of restless and ill-defined revolt. Despite this, and earlier protests, she actually enjoyed calling. She liked form. She was glad to observe such a ritual with her mother this day. It was easier to behave well if you knew exactly what was expected of you. It was easy to discipline yourself by time-honored rules. If anything could make graceful the renewal of her daytime relations with Hope, Ellen Terra, Carrie and even perhaps Mark, it would be to meet them thus, armored in white gloves, renewing the identification of herself as Miss Angela Lord Madison with engraved cards from her black leather card case.

"Pinckney's going to drive," added Mrs. Madison.

Angela nodded, and picked up the spotless kid gloves, symbol of the occasion. She began to work them onto her fingers, reserving her thumbs until last.

"You look nice, too, Mama," said Angela. "I enjoy you all dressed up and laced into your stays with that prunes and prisms expression on your pan."

Her mother still had a neat figure, when its pudginess was duly tucked into elastic, and her legs were slim to the point of seeming inadequate to support the body above them. Her ankles were slender and fine and her face smooth and round.

"I ought to wear a girdle every day, but it gives me indigestion," said Mrs. Madison placidly, wrenching her body slightly to ease a roll of flesh gathered around her waist.

"You have a most ladylike burp," said Angela, teasing her. "You should wear corsets and cultivate indigestion."

"Now, Angela," said her mother.

Standing beside her, Angela reached down to squeeze her mother lightly around the waist, as she had once reached up to do the same thing. She felt very fond of her mother and could not remember why she had hated her the year before. She was far more akin to her father, who was nervous, restless, disciplined and sensitive, but closer to her mother, from whose slumberous vitality her own vitality came. She and her father were both dependent on her mother in this house, she thought, as well as fond. It had been dissatisfaction with her changing self that had made her so dissatisfied with her mother, who did not change. Life with Mother was predictable and simple, thought Angela, grateful for this. There were very few things that changed her comfortable mother from a featherbed into a feather wall. If she was blankly, unalterably, detestably stubborn in opposition, and even occasionally shrill and vituperative, she was seldom opposed to anything. Finally opposed, she had become twice in Angela's shrinking memory, not a human being but a Thing, transparent-eyed and beyond communication,

IOI

unendurable to live beside. These two periods were like nightmares, from which she awoke to the endurable reality of her mother's mild tempers and only occasional stubbornness, to her usual placid, pervasive, agreeable presence, the nightmare already half-forgotten because it was over. By yielding quickly, and seldom, she could live such a pleasant life with mama.

She would hate to live, as Ellen Terra did, perched precariously on the maternal bosom of a volcano. You could neither predict nor mollify nor relate to their cause Clementine Rook's eruptions. Perhaps that was why Ellen Terra was so stupidly sweet-tempered. There was no nook or cranny left in the Rook household for anyone else to possess his own anger when Mrs. Rook was angry. Only little Tiny still howled into her mother's tempests. Mr. Rook had long since retired behind veiled, if often twinkling, eyes and into the ice-blue guest room with the single bed.

"You do look pretty, Angela," said her mother.

Not pretty enough, thought Angela, without reproach to her mother, but anyway fine-boned and clear-eyed.

Angela stepped back with natural deference to let her mother precede her into the hall and down the wide staircase.

"PinckNEY!" called her mother, but he was already outside in the car. He dearly loved to drive.

They called first on the Eckford Winthrops, who were not only blue-ribbon, highly pedigreed, Old Southern Stock, but most politely rich again, after a proper interval of southern penury. This gave them ten social points out of ten. They called on the Misses Minor, who ate insufficiently from silver plate they could not bring themselves to sell, and on the Judge Lovejoys, who had produced Sonny Boy, to their mutual surprise, at the end of a trying period originally diagnosed by Dr. Dandridge as Mrs. Lovejoy's change of life.

Sonny Boy actually joined them in the drawing room. He had a job selling cars, having rejected the law or having been rejected by it, but he was too natural born a salesman to have to spend much time at that. He conversed with Angela, neatly and without laughter, in the tone and context of the social call, which was different from a visit. Like his compliments, his social behavior was exaggerated to the point of parody, but it was impossible to tell whether he himself was aware of this.

They called on Miss Lucy and Mrs. Cranborne. Miss Lucy had been not only the belle of the town, in the days when Angela's mother was young, but the last great belle of the state. There was scarcely a middle-aged husband in Andalusia or in Oglethorpe who had not once laid an unaccepted proposal at her feet as they might have sent flowers to a popular corpse. Angela examined her with renewed curiosity, seeking in her buxom, faded gentleness the secret of her once famous charm. She would be Miss Lucy until she died, so thought Angela with pity. Her invalid older sister and her omnipresent mother with the omnivisible wens would never die. She would not even become Miss Cranborne before she died. Angela wondered why on earth this woman had never married, if only to escape her mother.

They called on the Hadleys and the Newcombes, both business families with more claim to income than to ancestors, and on the Widow Knight, who lived in an apartment over a cousin's garage, having sold the Knight house for a business property in order to send Logan to college. The Newcombes and Mrs. Knight were out and they left cards.

Retired Dr. Dandridge, who had brought both Mrs. Madison and Angela into the world, did not recognize them, but his wife thanked them sweetly for coming to cheer his dotage.

They did not call on the Mirimars, who were moving today, early in the season, bag and baggage, out to their hunting lodge in Oakland for the rest of the year. Nor on the Misses Laskwell and their mother, who led such queer lives now that they had turned their old plantation into a dairy which the daughters ran themselves. They went next to see the Stones. They would go afterwards to the Gregorys and last of all they would go to the Rooks, who were partners with them in business and therefore practically kin.

"My daughter certainly sounds happy this afternoon," said Mrs. Stone, peering suspiciously around the door in a way she had, as if looking before she leapt into a room. Having reassured herself that it was the room she had supposed it to be, she came in with a firm, heavy tread and blindly regarded Hope, who stood in the middle of her bedroom dressed only in peach-colored glove-silk panties and a flat, tight, glove-silk brassiere. "I like to hear my girl sing. She's very musical," Mrs. Stone nodded twice, in firm approval.

Hope, who had stopped her spirited, moderately well-trained caroling when her mother spoke, wished for a brief, clarified second, in all dreadful honesty, that her mother did not exist. Her mother had the inevitability and structure of a brick mausoleum. When she was there, you could not imagine that she had not always been where she was, fixed and immutable, housing in the present the whole of the long dead past. When she was not there, she was entirely not there. It was a characteristic of the dead. Hope felt that way about her dead younger sister, Anne, who existed only in the momentary memory of the emotion she had once felt for her. Except in the mausoleum that was her mother . . . there Anne was as real, as alive, and as changeless as Hope herself.

Hope told herself quickly, and with equal honesty, that she adored her mother. She had so much to be grateful for, including the indulgence with which her mother granted her every dictatorial whim. The other girls envied her her mother, sweet, efficient, uncritical, indulgent, and undemanding. After either refusing to notice, or failing to notice, the snubs and reservations accorded her by the members of the enclosed southern society into which the Stones had moved from their native New England, Mrs. Stone had won an impeccable place for herself in the life of the town, if not in its inmost heart. For this her daughter, Hope, was passionately grateful, and with reason. Her mother was both accepted and admired. As a housekeeper, she was flawless. She had even managed to keep and to control the ancient Cajun Negro woman, Nanine, who had come from New Orleans with Clementine Terra Rook and who was the best cook in town. Nanine had left successively and stormily the employ of the Rooks, the Madisons, and the Winthrops. If Mrs. Stone had no taste for her seasoned and highly complicated food, she had recognized Nanine as an invaluable asset to a successful hostess and had utilized her firmly for fifteen years. In this she was conceded to have beaten the southerners at their own game: the use and control of black talent. Mrs. Stone was also an unusually accomplished amateur pianist, a ladylike and much appreciated talent. No one in

Andalusia would ever say, as the Stones' old friends did to Hope in her summer visits to Cape Cod, that Anne Peck had obviously sacrificed a concert career to be such a fine wife and mother. It was not considered an alternative in Andalusia.

In deepest truth, which she refused to penetrate, what Hope wanted was to have loved her mother. Her mother, present and indulgent, and well-behaved, filled her with what she did not define as fear. Her mother was so dreadfully ugly and yet they looked so much alike.

Mrs. Stone looked around the frilled and feminine room. "Mattie's cousin certainly does up those organdy curtains nicely," she remarked with satisfaction. "It's remarkable how some of them respond to a little teaching. I really wonder at Clementine sometimes, the way she lets Mattie slack off."

To Hope's irritation, Mrs. Stone sat down heavily, sideways on the chaise longue near the window.

"Ellen Terra says Mattie's expecting again," said Hope.

"Oh, well . . ." Mrs. Stone was charitable with Negroes. "But couldn't anybody speak to Pinckney? Mattie's not young any more."

"What would you *say*?" asked Hope speculatively.

"One of the men, I mean," said Mrs. Stone.

Hope began to dress, pulling a severe one-piece knee-length cotton frock on over her short blonde hair.

"Are you going to play tennis?" asked Mrs. Stone, peering dimly at the dress.

"I thought I would," said Hope, stepping into matching shorts. "I think I'll get Mark Barbee to come out and play with me." She was always honest with her mother, and believed her mother utterly honest with her. There was no reason not to be, with Mother, so uncritical and so uninterfering. You did not have to ask Mother. You told her.

"Such a nice young man," said Mrs. Stone frankly. She had no need to say anything ever that she did not mean because she said so little that she did. No amount of southern garrulousness had broken her lifetime habit of reticence, which had no connection in her mind with dishonesty. None whatever. "I was very nearly opposed to your father and my joining the Episcopal church when we came here, since we were both brought up as Methodists, but I said just the other day that if the Episcopal church is attracting such good young preachers, I am glad you have been brought up in it."

"So'm I," said Hope. She pulled on stockings and a pair of brown oxfords. "Oh, Mother, do get my racquet and tennis shoes out of the closet downstairs or wherever they are. Please."

Mrs. Stone rose and moved firmly toward the door. "I'll leave them in the downstairs hall for you."

She went out, leaving the door half-closed, since Hope was dressed. Hope waited a second and then tiptoed over and closed it tightly. She knew that theoretically, according to Andalusia, she should not telephone Mark. Still, logically, she felt entitled to do so. He was, being southern and male, too capable of slow movement. Naturally, after last night, she must see him. In deference to convention, she would merely ask him to play tennis with her at The Oaks, where she was a member of the tennis club and he was not. She must get to him as soon as possible and he would, of course, do the rest. It was not possible to sit around idle, living in the however glorious past. The night was over. The present was here. The future was coming, and should come quickly. It was five o'clock in the afternoon and she could wait no longer for her slow love.

She had an ivory-colored extension telephone in her room, of special French design. Her friends also envied her this indulgence of her mother's. The other girls in town had promptly demanded them, admiring hers. So convenient for chatting on rainy days when they would not see each other for a matter of hours, so private and cozy. But the other mothers had indignantly refused them such nonsense. A telephone was a family affair, for public and restricted use.

Lifting the graceful one-piece instrument from its cream-colored cradle, she asked the operator softly for the rectory number.

"Why he gone out tuh play he some goluf, ma'am," said Madeleine's rough voice, answering at the other end. Why did Mark have that no-account old Madeleine for a cook? She would take no proper care of him. "Will I tells him who call?"

"No," said Hope. "Yes. Ask him to call Miss Stone."

Nanine came into the room and Hope hung up, surprised that she was blushing.

"Yuh wanna change yo dress or yuh wanna go down now jus

lak yuh is?" asked Nanine, puckering her thousand wrinkles at Hope.

"For heaven's sake, *why?*" asked Hope. Nanine's habit of leaving out the key to her communications was insanely irritating.

"Miss Angela an Missus Madison dey downstahs all dressed up lak Christmas mawnin, come to call. I gonna pass em out some uh muh pasties. Missus Madison ain't had no pasties lak dat since she trew me out. I fix huh so she's sorry yit."

"Pinckney makes a good cake," said Hope truthfully. Nanine scowled at her and she added, also truthfully, "Not as good as yours. I'll come down like I am."

Carrie clumped down the flagstone path to where Mrs. Gregory was pruning a bed of dahlias. She waited, withdrawn and a little sullen, while her mother straightened her large back with an audible creak and pushed back the gardening hat that flopped over her beet-red face. Her mother took off one glove and rummaged in a large pocket for her handkerchief.

"What, darling?" she inquired mildly into Carrie's silence.

"When I came home three sheets to the wind . . ."

"Three what to the what?" asked her mother, mild and puzzled.

"When I came home drunk," said Carrie bluntly, "the other day before lunch, I promised you I would not take a drink before six P.M. for a year. It is—" she checked the diamond wrist watch her father had given her for her nineteenth birthday, keeping her eyes from meeting her mother's—"five-twenty-three and one-half and I would like a drink. A small one."

"Is anything the matter?" asked Mrs. Gregory. It had been a long time, years, since she had been able to say to her daughter, does it hurt, darling, tell Mother where it hurts. It had been years since Carrie would admit that anything hurt. Too much had hurt during the operations and the treatments that had failed adequately to lengthen or straighten her leg.

"No," said Carrie. "Not a damn thing. I just want a drink. Okay?"

"Of course. I want one myself, actually. I declare it's *hot* this year. Fix one for me, too, Carrie. A Scotch and soda—lots of soda."

"Do you really want one?" asked Carrie, remotely, affectionately. "Or did the books tell you that it's bad for growing girls to drink alone?"

Mrs. Gregory sighed. She had read many books and consulted several specialists. She had tried to follow their instructions, their often conflicting instructions, so that she could help Carrie, so that she could bring her tragically handicapped child to normal maturity. She had learned the anatomy of much childish behavior. She had learned to call Carrie's naughtiness "behavior difficulty." She had found that she had made a number of mistakes in raising her older son. She had, it was true, successfully kept her daughter from remaining in the dark womb of her illness, too sheltered by maternal pity, or overwhelmed by the dangerous maternal love for the weak. She had insisted that her daughter live the life of the other girls her age, even sending her one year to Miss Luttrell's in Oglethorpe, where the young ladies of Andalusia were traditionally finished. She had been intelligent and "wonderful" and had exercised the most rigid self-control. But it was Carrie alone who had hardened herself so that she would let no one near her pain. She had developed the fierce and lonely pride which defied pity and love equally. Nothing in the books so diligently perused had taught Tracy Buford Gregory how to keep her daughter, Caroline, whom she so loved, near enough to ask for, to accept, such maternal comfort as she might need. Mrs. Gregory had no idea whatever what Carrie thought of her now, how much she loved or did not love her. She did not know to what extent she was an influence in Carrie's life. Her daughter treated her almost as if she were the fond parent and her mother the well-meaning, but often misguided child.

"I *want* a drink," said Mrs. Gregory, sighing again, and with weary honesty, "but not a big one. A long, cold, little one. I've been struggling with these dahlias all afternoon. That Frank is irresponsible as a baby. I almost wish I had Bailey."

"No, you don't," said Carrie. "Bailey's garden belongs to *him*. I'll fix your drink." She turned and made her dissonant way on the flagstone path that echoed to her heels, hitting unequally loud on the echoing stones as the normal leg saved the twisted one.

They were sitting in comfortable silence on the glass-enclosed porch that opened off their big living room when Annie announced Mrs. Madison and Miss Angela.

"Ask them to come out here, please, Annie," said Mrs. Gregory. "I'm too comfortable to move."

"Yes'm," said Annie, and lumbered away, tightening her white apron strings over her neat but ponderous rear as she went. She was a big, fleshy, handsome Negro woman who switched her starched uniforms elegantly and was spare with her carefully enunciated speech. Carrie said she was obviously a Scotch black, or a colored Gregory.

"I do think Hannah is silly the way she keeps up this calling business," said Mrs. Gregory to Carrie. "I never do it any more except on strangers."

"Oh, well, you're *you*," said Carrie, and her mother did not know whether this was intended as a compliment or not.

"Don't get up, Carrie. . . . Hello, Tracy, dear!" Mrs. Madison pecked at Mrs. Gregory's cheek. Carrie was already on her feet.

"Howdoyoudo, Mrs. Gregory? Hi, Carrie . . ." Angela was tired now and ready to relax from her formal behavior. She was invariably rigid around Mrs. Stone, whom she would have said she liked very much. She was more comfortable with Mrs. Gregory, of whom she stood slightly in awe. Only at the Rooks could she relax completely. For some reason, she had no fear or respect for Mrs. Rook, only for Alton Rook, who would not be there.

"Would you like a drink, Hannah?" asked Mrs. Gregory. "Carrie and I were just cooling ourselves off."

"Lord, no, thanks just the same, Tracy," said Mrs. Madison, sinking into a chair. "Nanine absolutely stuffed me with those marvelous little cakes of hers at Anne's. She knows I can't resist them, the she-devil."

"And you all bound around with your best corset," said Angela.

Mrs. Madison looked disapproving. Of course, the Gregorys were not like lesser friends, but this was still a call.

Carrie turned to Angela before she could sit down. "Let's leave the girls to their chatter," she said impudently. "Mamas never let their hair down when the younger generation is around. Come on upstairs with me."

"But . . ." said Mrs. Madison, protesting, but Mrs. Gregory nodded approval.

"Run along, children," said Mrs. Gregory. She turned to Mrs. Madison. "It's Nanine's diabolical form of revenge because you and I couldn't take her black temper. She feeds them to me every time I go over there. You know, sometimes I miss that old reprobate, and I certainly miss her crab gumbo. Anne Stone is a wonder to have kept her!" They had said this to each other a thousand times in fifteen years.

Carrie stopped to pick up a bottle and two glasses from the sideboard in the dining room and stuck one foot in the swinging door to the kitchen to open it enough for Annie to hear her. "Bring ice and soda up to my room, Annie."

Angela stretched herself gratefully on the chaise longue in Carrie's high-ceilinged, big-windowed bedroom on the second floor, humped herself up and smoothed the short skirt under her so that it would not wrinkle, and put her hat aside.

"I don't think I want a drink," she said.

"As you like," said Carrie. "But you've time if you do. Your maw will forget she's supposed to leave when she and my maw get to chewing the fat. What do they find to chew? Such a disgusting expression, chewing the fat."

"Isn't it?" agreed Angela lazily, watching Carrie pour whiskey into one glass while she waited for Annie.

"I've got the yellow-dog blues, Angela, and I feel like a bitch. Do you mind if I come out all over bitch, like spots? I don't mind being a bitch with you. Why is that?"

"Like to like," said Angela without much conviction.

"No. You aren't a bitch. Yet. You may become one, but you aren't one. However, I don't feel analytical, I feel bitchy. And I am anti-mother."

"In particular," asked Angela without much interest, "or in general?"

"Both. Mine's well-meaning. Such a nasty virtue. She acts as if I were made of eggshells and were balanced on a tight wire. She is so aware of my so-called sensibilities that she makes me think I have some. Actually my character resembles a keg of nails and my balance is like a coal barge on the river."

"Smoking like a tug," said Angela, laughing at her.

"Children should be forcibly removed from their mothers at the age of fifteen and not permitted to see them again until they are forty-five," went on Carrie, stumping out her cigarette angrily and indicating to the neat, silent Annie that she leave the tray on a table within easy reach.

"What got you on this twig?" asked Angela. "You usually get on fine with your mother."

"That's not the point," said Carrie. "I do. I shouldn't, though. That's the point. But I'm not going to leave home. I'm just talking. I am merely irritated by the unbecoming spectacle of four middle-aged mothers half in love with their minister."

"Oh, nonsense," said Angela, aroused at last and shifting uncomfortably on the chaise longue.

"Of course they are! Yours and mine and Ellen Terra's and even that lump of too, too solid flesh, Mrs. Stone. They want us to get him so they can have him vicariously."

"Oh, shut up, Carrie," said Angela gently. "Mix me a drink. I will have one. You're nuts. You don't think straight." She wrinkled her brow and waited until the drink was in her hand. There was an answer somewhere to everything if you could find it. Carrie was merely hungover and cross. "Mothers get nervous in the mating season. That's all. They flutter. I probably will when my daughter takes down the movie stars and starts mooning at traveling salesmen or itinerant soul savers."

"I won't have a daughter unless I am damn sure I can let her the hell alone," said Carrie. "I probably won't anyway," she added. "Even my mother thinks the chances of my marrying are dim. Let's be old maids. It's the only dignified thing to be."

"All right," said Angela. "Suits me." Miss Sis and Miss Lucy had dignity. That they did have. "You know, I think I'll go to business school."

"You're nuts," said Carrie succinctly. "There's no possible point in working unless you have to work or unless you're really good at something. It would be worse drudgery than being a two-buck whore, if you will permit me the expression. Besides, your mother wouldn't let you."

"I want to get away from here," said Angela. "Sometimes."

III

"You could just take a train," said Carrie.

"I like Andalusia," said Angela contrarily. "I belong here."

"We're stuck here, you mean," said Carrie. "It's ours and we're its." They were both perfectly sober, but they had a feeling of talking to each other from a great distance, over a thin, silver wire. "Well, we're in it together. That's something."

"Thanks," said Angela.

"Sorry I was rude about the old ladies. They just want us to have what they want and think we want and haven't got sense enough to let us alone. Ellen Terra's the only one that'll get what she wants because she wants what she gets."

"I wouldn't trade mothers with Ellen Terra," said Angela, shuddering slightly.

They were both silent for a moment. Carrie contemplated her mother, wanting for her daughter the things you got if you had Ellen Terra's minutely perfect, inviting, desirable body, wanting for Carrie the things Carrie wanted herself too deeply to let herself hope for them. Angela thought of Ellen Terra as she had once seen her, facing her mother's erupting, lavalike wrath, cowed and shaking.

Her own mother's voice, sounding sweet and reasonable for all its high pitch as it was lifted to reach up the stairs, called her name.

She took a last swallow of her drink and got up, smoothing her skirt and putting on her hat.

" 'Bye now, Carrie," she said. "See you tomorrow."

"What rubbish we talk, you and I," said Carrie.

"Fun, though," said Angela.

Angela went down to join her mother at the foot of the stairs, to say good-bye to Mrs. Gregory.

As they went out into the late sunshine, her mother remarked, "I want to stop by the rectory and ask young Barbee for dinner next week."

"Oh, not now, Mother," said Angela, almost petulant. "Telephone him."

"As you like, dear," said her mother reasonably.

They got into the car and Mrs. Madison told Pinckney to drive to the Rooks'.

There, Mrs. Rook told them blandly enough that Ellen

Terra was out playing golf with Mark Barbee and another couple and that she had no idea when Ellen Terra would be home.

"Young people often get home so late these days," said Mrs. Rook with satisfaction.

So Ellen Terra was the first to see Mark again, having the most enterprising and uninhibited of the mothers. Angela stared at Mrs. Rook's white face with the lines like that of old china on her petal-like skin, her hair unnaturally black and piled high in a style long past, her expression avid and cunning. She hated her and turned with relief to look at her own mother's pleasant, ordinary, unenterprising face.

9. Party

The form and formula of the treasure hunt had precipitated contact and crisis between the man and the four women who loved him. So the form and formula for the next ten days gave him respite.

Lent was over and it was the season for sports. Games were taken seriously where so much of the time was summertime and where no one worked too hard. The girls, muscular enough and well-trained, played as they were expected to and had learned to play games, intently and sexlessly. Even Hope accepted that after a game was over absorption in it continued. Ellen Terra did not expect to be kissed after an afternoon of golf.

The preparations for the dance were also taken seriously. These involved groups and included another dozen young and youngish people besides themselves.

In their homes, to which their parents successively invited Mark, the girls were well-behaved as children are well-behaved. They were not permitted to monopolize the minister who came for the evening. They did not resent the insistent background of their childhood which lingered in their treatment at home.

Thus Mark was able, with deceptive simplicity, to reduce the four women to girls, to consider them as one problem and to simplify the problem. If he did not want to become the victim instead of the master of his maleness, or to become less a man, he felt he must control and direct not only his body and his heart but his thoughts. Taking pride in the difficult restrictions of his profession, he rediscovered, in an old-fashioned manner, God.

He saw his life now simply. He would stay in Andalusia for at least two years. He would work to help men become Christians. It was up to the men to make Christians of their women. On the women he shed a new benevolence, cold as starlight.

The four impatient women translated his benevolence and filled their hearts' enforced idleness according to the different resources of their natures.

Angela, understanding it best, tried to match his renunciation. Finding herself inept at austerity, she became merely cross. Crossly she decided that her affections, and even her love, were qualified and therefore valueless. Her friendships had only the patina of intimacy. Her face was too long. To total the sum of her happiness was to add, like Alice at the behest of the White Queen, one and one and one and one, and her sorrows added nothing to nothing to nothing. By the end of the ten days, she had retained only the virtue of a cross-grained dignity and had lost even the pleasure of sun on her face.

Carrie, having felt this one man flinch to touch her body and watching him now wary of her spirit, was glad that she had been prepared always to lose what she most wanted and to live with losing it. Curiously, she relaxed and gradually, through the ten days, she let herself be both as mean and as kind as she felt like being, which was very mean and very kind.

Hope, her imagination limited and her optimism interminable, considered herself engaged to Mark. Because he was a preacher, his kiss was her promise. Being southern, he was slow. Awaiting further demonstration from him, she filled in the interminable time making concrete plans for their future.

Ellen Terra merely considered herself Mark's. She was thus made blissful and was perfectly willing to prolong the bliss just as it was. Waiting for Mark to take her, she very nearly yielded to the importunities of Sonny Boy. Only the still unbroken habit of not-quite and not-yet guarded her as angels might. Once she belonged to Mark, the possibility of infidelity was beyond her conception.

These five attitudes collided and collapsed at the dance.

The night of the dance was clear, starlit, and warm. Mark emerged conventionally arrayed in his dinner coat, with which he wore a neat black tie instead of the neat black dicky that proclaimed his profession. The girls were minutely prepared and carefully gar-landed. Their luxurious, newly old-fashioned dresses touched the floor and were shaped once again to display and not to flatten and disparage their female bodies as their daytime clothes did. Their burnished heads were duly self-conscious on their powdered and sweet-smelling necks.

Carrie took her place early with a serious Dugdale Winthrop by the side of the door where the two of them collected entrance fees from a gratifying number of townspeople. Mark greeted friend and stranger alike with a personal welcome. Angela worked hard with ebullient Sonny Boy to supervise the refreshment booth and to shepherd the band that Hope had paid for. Ellen Terra and Hope stood together in the middle of the freshly waxed floor, gathering the dance around them, waiting to fulfill their obvious destiny as the belles of the night's ball.

For Hope and Ellen Terra, their ten days flowed into the night for a breathless hour of almost unbearable delight. They reached, on this night, after their short, sharp, vertical climb, the summit of their lives. It was indeed the summit of their youth, and they had learned to value nothing else so greatly. It was also the summit of their lives in the eyes of the world they lived in.

Small, both, they were as alike as peaches, ripe for the pluck-ing as only sun-ripened fruit can be ripe. Brunette and blonde, they were equally delightful to see, to smell, to taste, to touch. The lively, small, and slumberous black eyes and the huge, clear blue ones reflected the same bliss. The tea-kettle purr and the ringing silver bell of their two essentially domestic voices sang siren songs. They were perfect and successful. Success has its own separate charm, and the young men, the boys, the older men swarmed to touch them for luck as well as love.

Mark could no more help dancing with them than he could have helped swimming if he had fallen into a river. He could no more help competing for them than he could help trying to win at tennis. He could no more help wanting their small, lovely and separate bodies than he could help wanting water when he was made thirsty by the sight of it. He smiled down into their confident eyes and could not resist the flattery of knowing they were his, while tall, wistful and mannerly Dugdale Winthrop, gay, cocky little Sonny Boy Lovejoy, dreamily handsome Logan Knight and the violent visitor, Bill Bloodgood, strove with him for their favors. He was also aware that they were dangerous. Danger added its own charm to attraction. The priest in the man regarded the situation with almost pleased alarm.

It was when Ellen Terra and Hope met face to face, full tilt, at the end of a dance in which both had had a dozen partners and each had danced, yielding and certain, in Mark's arms, that they measured each other in an instant of calm and knew that something was wrong. Ellen Terra possessed only one incompleted kiss on a moonlit night and Hope had only completed a kiss that was Ellen Terra's.

Excusing themselves, they made their way together to the "powder" room. Here they took turns repairing the minute damage heat had done to their singularly pretty faces.

"Isn't it bliss?" asked Ellen Terra, doubtful now.

"Wonderful," muttered Hope between lips stretched taut while she applied lipstick.

"Sonny Boy's the best dancer I ever . . ." said Ellen Terra judiciously.

"I would rather dance with Mark," said Hope, looking at Ellen Terra.

"Oh, so would I. Or with Bill. He attacks you so. But that's personal. Like kissing. I mean as a dancer," said Ellen Terra. If she lost Mark, it was her mother who would be inconsolable and furious. Her mother did daily and terrible battle with life instead of letting it happen to her. Ellen Terra saw herself, arms wide, yielding while torrents of life poured over her, delighting and battering her.

"Mark is *quite* the best dancer," said Hope, stubborn and upright, yielding at nothing. She was unwilling to bend, preferring to break. She obliterated the knowledge that Mark had also kissed

117

Ellen Terra in the moment of knowing it. She must marry Mark now or die. She could not go on and on and on.

Ellen Terra took her arm. "The music's beginning again. It's a tickle-toe band, Hope. Let's dance. You look right off the top of a Christmas tree. Let's go out and dance."

They went out to be claimed by innumerable partners, slipping only a little on the incline that was leading them down now from the summit of their lives, down on the other side.

Hope tiptoed up as they danced again together and said urgently in his ear, "Mark, *do you love me?*" Mark replied gravely, feeling her sturdy and honest warmth, "Of course," and then added quickly, "everybody does." He forgot that, not having been born one of them, she might not understand that this was a complete qualification.

Ellen Terra said to him lightly, "Don't you want to go outside with me, Mark? The moon's coming up." He answered lightly, "Naturally. But I can't. I'm host." Ellen Terra knew that this was nothing which could be something. There was nothing to do but wait, gathering popularity like bouquets either to offer him or with which to comfort herself. She only wanted really now just to kiss him again, once if no more.

Mark knew that tomorrow he must do the hard, clear, sensible thinking he had postponed for ten days. He must set for himself a course of practical conduct in order to stay in Andalusia. He must disentangle himself not so much from the situation he was in as from the one he had obviously permitted Hope, at least, to think he was in. He was quite entitled, he thought stubbornly, clergyman or no, to conduct properly limited investigations among marriageable young women until he found the one he wanted. Tonight they were so lovely that he had quite easily fallen a little in love again with them both. Even, a little, with them all. He had danced with Angela and found her light and almost absent in his arms, silent and faraway. On the floor, in the crowd, he had watched her, gawky, lanky, and almost unattractive, despite the distinction with which she wore her silver gown, unsure and young. He had sat for one brief moment beside Carrie before Dugdale's father had lumbered up to take her away from him. She looked saturnine and old, her shoulders rising powerful and bony above the severe black dress that covered her legs. He was touched by them both.

It was when he went to pay his respects to the mothers that he realized that what he had felt to be mild and on the whole pleasantly exciting danger was unpleasant and alarming. The mothers sat, huddled and hovering, on the sidelines. They were no longer gracious mistresses of houses inhabited by charming children who were not expected to monopolize the dinner table. They were not enjoying themselves, as older people in this town made a business of enjoying themselves. They were duennas of the open market place, eagle-eyed, expectant, ready with dowry and contract. Ostensibly they were entertaining themselves separately from the young, gossiping, drinking, dancing occasionally, fanning themselves in the heat. But these four at least were serving a more time-honored purpose than the pursuit of middle-aged pleasure.

Mrs. Gregory said merely, being mother of the least marketable daughter, as well as the greatest lady, "Carrie tells me you shoot well. Indispensable in hunting country like this."

Mrs. Madison said, as if absent-mindedly, "Angela looks so pale! I think she's been working too hard to make this a success. She wants to help your mission. She cares so about these things. . . ."

Mrs. Rook, formidable, her black hair piled high above her abnormally white face, which she had ill-advisedly rouged in conformity with current styles, her eyes small and suddenly focused, said, "Ellen Terra is quite changed these days. So serious. Quite a woman. We do, Mark, think you are doing well here and we hope, her father and I, that you will stay a long time in Andalusia. There was some argument about calling you because of your—well, you're young. But we are glad we did. We expect you to dinner again, next week."

Mrs. Stone said only, "They marry so young in the South, don't they?"

Alton Rook, sitting next to the women, beside Cecil Madison, watched everything with curiosity concealed only by an ingrained habit of concealment and with compassion tempered by his habitual, humorous, private fury. Indulging his humor at the expense of his sympathy, he regarded the four fleshy fisherwomen, one of whom was his wife, dangling the hooks baited with the wriggling bodies of their daughters, one of whom was his daughter. Mark looked rather like an agitated trout, he thought. Mattie said the clergyman resembled the movie lover, John Gilbert. He did not. It was his charm that made him give an illusion of good looks. He'd show up homely soon enough. Poor pious fish, he had better bite while he had at least a choice of bait. Did he actually think he was a better man than his elders because he was young and could still swim a long way before getting caught?

He turned to Cecil Madison with a mild, unkind gleam in his eye. "Unless he buttons his pants like he does his collars, he'd better go ahead and marry yours or mine."

"Who? What?" asked Cecil Madison, blinking at him in a startled reproachful fashion.

What the hell? He and Cecil had known each other, man and boy, for damn near fifty years, he thought, and Cecil still shied like a silly ass if you mentioned sex in connection with white folks. He talked pretty shocking about his nigras, when you considered it. But mention a white man and sex and he acted as if you had insulted his mother.

Alton went on, with a mild notion of making a little trouble. "Looks like your girl has it as bad as mine," he said.

Cecil looked at his daughter, who was dancing with Logan Knight and grinning passionately up into his handsome face.

"Been crazy about Logan since she was fourteen, about," said Cecil Madison, blinking. "Think he's just waiting until his mother's taken care of to pop question. Don't mind. Fine young man. Looks a bit dreamy, but that's what Angela likes. Girls don't like fellows they can't handle. Angela's pretty gentle."

Thunder and revelation, thought Alton Rook, regarding Angela's father. How can anybody be so blind, deaf and plain dumb?

Alton eyed Mark's back, retreating now to the dance floor. What was a young male like that one doing in the ministry anyway? Any mother's son who could give wholesale credence to Christian theology nowadays was a womb-crawler by nature. Mark would end up bringing his wife's breakfast and letting her take him to bed. Hell's bells, his little, black Ellen Terra needed a MAN to beat her.

"Alton!" said Clementine Rook.

"Yes, dear," said Alton Rook, mocking himself privately. It took more than skepticism or humor or muscle to make a wife-beater.

His wife waved an empty glass and an unlit cigarette at him, mock-pleadingly cocking her head. Meekly he served her and with the corner of his eye watched Mark cut in on Angela. In the light of the preceding scene, it looked as if Mark were making his choice. Alton sighed. He felt heavy with liking for the young man, all the same, and he wanted him for his own little girl.

Mark was not making his choice. He needed help and he knew that Angela, if she would, could help him.

Angela, publicly unpopular at a public dance, had lost even her dignity. She took several hasty and sizable drinks of corn whiskey and redid her face four or five times in an effort to increase her animation, improve her looks, change her luck. The whiskey seemed like water. The powder caked with sweat. She found herself slobbering with gratitude because Logan Knight danced with her long and often, ignoring her high-handed indifference to him since Mark had come to town. She blamed Mark viciously both for her feeling of desperate unattractiveness and for the impartiality of his favors.

"Having fun?" she asked him furiously.

"It's a fine dance," he replied, warned by her tone and wondering how to ask her help.

"I saw the mamas giving you the workout," said Angela recklessly. "Why, you're the mamas' pet. The latest catch."

"Clergymen aren't catches," he said evasively, further alarmed by her words and still wanting her help.

"Oh, *you* are," said Angela.

"Don't be like this!" said Mark sharply.

"Why not?" asked Angela, completely at sixes and sevens with herself. So much for renunciation, so much for dignity. Love and misery all but engulfed her and she wanted to weep. She took refuge in anger.

"You're too nice," said Mark, knowing that the words were meaningless.

"I'm not," said Angela, adding vigor to anger. "I'm sick and tired of pretending to be. Everybody knows that in a 'nice' way, we four 'nice' girls . . ." Her voice had risen.

"Come outside," said Mark coldly. "I want to talk to you."

"You mean you don't want anybody to hear what I'm saying," said Angela, feeling detestable.

"All right," said Mark. "But I want to talk to you, too."

He stopped dancing and took her arm.

"They'll think . . ."

"They think already!"

He hurried her out the front door, past Carrie. Neither of them noticed the panicky dismay with which Hope saw them leave. He went with her, without guiding her, to the shadow of the oak tree that grew between the parish house and the church and that was older than the church.

"Now what were you saying?" Mark asked her.

The words were still there and she said them now, tumbling them out with embarrassment.

"Well, we four 'nice' girls have gone and fallen for our 'nice' young rector and our 'nice' mothers are all for it and there's nothing 'nice' about it!" Having said it, she was chagrined and appalled. In place of anger, came thought, welcome, refreshing, disturbing and rapid. "I spoke without thinking," said Angela apologetically. "I was babbling. I'm sorry."

"Don't be sorry, but please think. Tell me honestly what you do think. I'm all muddled up, Angela. I can't think straight myself. Listen, what shall I do?"

"I don't know," said Angela. "What do you want to do, Mark? You know how it is, don't you?"

"I suppose so, but it sounds so conceited to admit—well, that anybody has—does—like you more than you bargain for."

"It's no use being gallant," said Angela, "darling. We all fell for you and that's all there is to it. You know it."

"It's a responsibility, if somebody cares more for you than you've gotten around to caring for them," said Mark, staring at her.

"It's not your responsibility," said Angela coolly. It was bliss to think. She was doing honor and justice to thinking. She was thinking for herself. She offered him the honesty of her thoughts. "You know as well as I do that girls are just as apt to fall in love as men. More so. They have more time for it. If they do, and the man doesn't, they'll get over it. Anybody can take care of unrequited love. It's different from being loved and losing. It must be. It's less important. The whole point is, you're a preacher."

"Yes, that's the trouble, isn't it?" said Mark reluctantly. "Listen, Angela, I don't want to marry anybody. I want to stay here and do my job." He pushed his nervous fingers through his thick, brown hair. "I've been drifting and not working hard enough. I've been—careless. Now, tell me, can I stay?"

"I don't think so," said Angela. "I think it's too late." She did not want him to go away. It would be much worse than his staying. Loving him hopelessly was more rewarding than never to see him again. She thought carefully, honoring thought and repressing her rising, confusing emotions.

"Why not?" asked Mark, momentarily angry. "Just because you girls like me and I'm a bachelor. I don't see what that's got to do with it, really. Say what you mean!"

"It's too late," Angela repeated. "I think. You see, you're southern born."

"What's that got to do with it!" Mark glared at her, making it hard for her to tell him what she meant. Stay! she wanted to say to him. Only that.

"You know there's an awful lot of loving that isn't love and a lot of liking that's close to love and a lot of kissing that's not for keeps and all that. You haven't done a single thing that Dugdale or Bill or Sonny Boy couldn't do."

"Not half of it," said Mark, clenching his teeth and thinking angrily of answers to what she was saying.

". . . but the trouble is, you forget you're not a southern boy any longer, but a—man of God?" She hesitated, feeling pretentious, and then hurried on so that he could answer her and explain why she was wrong. "It's as if you had your hand on the Bible when you do anything. That's why Hope and Ellen Terra probably believe you meant it. Though we would all of us know better about anybody else. So, you see, they think you've promised."

Mark looked down at Angela soberly. "I'm sorry. I've been careless, or stupid, but I don't think I've done anything too terrible, even for a preacher. I want to do the job I set out to do. A man can't run away."

"Yes, he can," said Angela, nodding her head mournfully. "This is a small, small town and they won't let you forget you stole an apple when you were twelve years old if you live to be a hundred and get to be District Judge. You know that. You're tied to everything you ever said or did or thought in a town like this. It takes tough characters to live themselves down and not be just a collection of what they were in a town like this."

"Look here," said Mark earnestly. "I've tried to wear my collar two ways and I got in trouble. Unless you four send me away, I want to stay and do my job. What about it, Angela? I'm tough enough!" He was boasting, his lower lip thrust forward, and Angela loved him so, she thought she would burst. "What about it?" he repeated.

"You stay," said Angela, "if you're tough. And don't worry about us. We're tough, too, I reckon. At least, Ellen Terra and I are. And we'll all behave pretty well. You'll see."

"I'd like to kiss you right this minute," said Mark, ruefully and frankly.

"Don't," said Angela, shaken.

"What about Hope?"

"You'll have to disillusion Hope, but she can take it. She'll run up to Cape Cod and find a Yankee. Hope's practical. And so pretty. You'll see."

"And Carrie?" said Mark.

"You can ask Carrie," said Angela. With thought had come generosity. With generosity came pain and real renunciation. Angela learned as she stood there that you can stand anything if you think about it clearly with the separate and exciting brain.

"I'll ask Carrie," said Mark, after a pause. "And I'll stay! Angela, this job of mine needs everything a man's got, if he is one, and I've been holding out, see? It's not easy, but who wants it easy? It wasn't easy to go into it. I tried to be anything but a—a man of God. I even tried to be an atheist. I tried hard. My grandfather was a whole man, a wonderful old ruffian, dirty as a goat and a preacher that could make you know angels. But my father wasn't anything. Went to sleep in his mind and stopped thinking and made parrot noises and motions. He was beautiful, saintly-looking, silver hair and all that, and the church ladies adored him. I couldn't stand being like that, so I've tried to keep on being a normal guy. That's not the way. You've got to be better than that, whole hog, like my grandfather." He had never spoken to anyone quite like this and he looked at Angela, anxious and exultant.

"You can stay," said Angela, listening to him and loving him and feeling his dedication and knowing that she could never share it. It was too far away from her and he was going away from her, too, although this was the moment of their real intimacy.

"Thank you, Angela," said Mark, rubbing his hair.

"Thank me for nothing," said Angela vigorously, lifting her head. "Thank yourself. I believe in God again, if you don't mind." She was saying this for Mark. She knew that it would comfort him. She knew it because she loved him. It was not true. If anything, she believed less in God than ever before in her life. She admired God, she thought oddly. That was what she did. Because of Mark, she admired Him and the Episcopal religion through which He had manifested Himself to her. She admired Him because He gave her the freedom to doubt Him. "It's a good, tough religion, ours," she said wonderingly. "It's so beautiful. If you can stand its—freedom." It comforted your doubts with beauty. It permitted you to doubt. She wanted impulsively to go away and think about this, but she could not violate the form of the dance.

They stood for a moment, immeasurably separated. Mark's head was thrown back and he felt once again strong and happy and sure. Angela had done this for him.

Angela, aware that she had lost the simplicity of her childhood faith as well as her first true love, and that she might never again find the equal of either, took comfort because, in love and pain and deliberation, she had said exactly the right thing to comfort Mark. She had taken care of her man. For this, she believed in herself again.

They turned wordlessly, went back into the parish house without touching each other, and joined the dancers on the floor. They danced quietly, Angela following where Mark led, one hand lightly resting on his shoulder and one clasped gently in his. He relinquished her before many minutes had passed to Logan Knight and went over and touched Morton Hadley on the shoulder. Morton was sitting beside Carrie in one of two chairs placed near the door by a potted palm. It was a graceful convention in Andalusia that one sat with Carrie exactly as one danced with the others. It was neither chore nor charity because she was an amusing and restful conversationalist. Mark was puzzled by the sullen alacrity with which Morton yielded the chair as if he were escaping from punishment. Mark sat down by Carrie.

"Hello, lady," he said, smiling at her with new assurance.

"Hello, Reverend Mister Don Juan," said Carrie. "I was wondering when you would come around and shed a little more charm on baby." There was no humor in her voice, only a thin social tone, as if this were banter. It did not hide the desire to hurt him. Carrie had discovered in herself a remarkable agility in meanness. Perversely, she was enjoying it.

"I want to talk to you," said Mark, ignoring deliberately both her remark and his quick anger as she spoke. "If you'll let me."

"I'm tired of hearing about you," said Carrie. "Dugdale sat over here and sang your praises. I told him you were okay—but not to trust you. *Not to trust you* for a minute."

Mark was stung at once in his touchiest pride among men, as she knew he would be. He was too angry for caution or for manners or for the denigrating charity due a cripple. She challenged him too nearly. To her amazement, he rose to leave her. She knew better than he did that this was worse than hitting her, worse than anything he could say to her. To leave Carrie alone in her chair was like leaving another girl on the floor in the middle of a dance. It was a social crime. Carrie was the town's own and the town would rally to protect her, the more quickly from any but their own. This was something that would not be forgiven him nor forgotten. She looked at him, seeing his clear intention, and said urgently, "Get me a drink and come back here quick."

"Why?" he said, standing over her, rigid with anger.

"Because I want you to. Because I *trust* you to. Please!"

He turned and left her. She was not sure that he would come back.

Alton Rook, seeing her alone, came over to her quickly. He

wished that he knew more about what the young people were up to. He felt as if the young were fooling him.

"I'm saving this chair for Mark," said Carrie apologetically, praying that Mark would return. "He's gone to get me a drink." Mr. Rook was so much shrewder than the rest of his generation. "I hope you-all have managed to persuade him to stay in Andalusia," she added primly.

"I hope so, too," said Alton. "Say, Carrie, I have an historical theory I'm working on."

Carrie jerked her shoulders impatiently, not wanting to pay any attention to this old man at all. "How interesting," she said in an edged voice.

Alton persisted, wondering at himself. "You know, I think the Civil War killed off so many men and so murdered the spirit of the rest that it turned the South into a matriarchy." He was about to go on, expounding the idea that this, her generation, would right things and the South would again take its place in the nation.

Carrie looked at him with surprised and acrid interest. Matriarchy! That's a fine simile for henpecked, she thought. "That's right!" she exclaimed. "Blame everything on the Civil War!"

There was not even the pretense of respect in her voice. Tracy Gregory wore the pants in her family, too, though Tracy concealed that fact better than most beneath a solicitous manner and her uneven, rump-sprung skirts. Carrie knew the score, but, like most young people, he thought, only the total, not the intolerable pluses and minuses that added up to middle age. What was he doing, trying to talk to this ferocious young woman? If you can't fight 'em, flee 'em, Mark, he had advised the young man. "It's too hot for a dance," he complained formally.

Mark came back with two Coca-Colas and stood with Alton Rook politely until the older man moved away. Then he sat down again beside Carrie.

"Did you put any corn in it?" she asked, taking the glass.

"Yes," he said, "in both of them. Now, for God's sake, Carrie, tell me why you said that."

"I didn't say it to Dugdale. I was being nasty to you," said Carrie. She sighed. "I like being entirely nasty. It's so damn much simpler than messing about being halfway decent." She sounded both wry and plaintive.

"It's not simple," said Mark sternly. "You can't help being decent. You're built on the bones of decency. Now tell me, because I have to decide tomorrow, whether I should stay in Andalusia."

"Will what I say make the difference?" asked Carrie.

"No. I have to decide for myself."

"Then," said Carrie, "for my part, stay. You are most welcome." She said it sweetly, with quaint formality, her head high and her eyes calm and a little cynical. What a pretentious notion she had cherished of herself, she thought. She was no she-devil, mean or kind by whim. She was only a minor-league lady with one bad leg.

Ellen Terra and Hope passed them among the dancers, whirling and swirling and bedecked with popularity like flowers.

"Damn it," said Carrie impatiently, turning to Mark. "What a tempest in our teapot. Stay if you want to! Leave if you don't! It's as simple as that."

10. **Flight from Women**

In the particolored dawn, Hope turned her sodden pillow and determinedly renewed her weeping. She had sobbed so vastly and so unreasonably into what had been left of the night when the dance was over that she had seemed to dissolve and to die slowly with the dying-down moon that still hung forlornly in the sky, while the sun rose quietly and the birds sang in the alley behind her house. Now she wept reasonably. As day came, lively and miserable, she searched her mind for things to cry about. She shed a few tears for the little boy who had teased her when she first came to Andalusia because she said "wa-ter-r-r," instead of "wawtuh," for a puppy dog who had run from the lawn out into Egmont Street under the wheels of a Packard car. She cried because Bill Bloodgood had not asked her for a date at the dance. Perhaps she was not worth a trip all the way from Oglethorpe and even her popularity was only a dream. She wept for her youth. Then she squeezed out a few final tears, bitter ones, remembering again that she was humiliated. She had accepted a proposal that had not been given.

This thought brought her bolt upright, sniffling and humiliated.

As the sun rose higher and a breeze blew into her window from across the land, smelling of pine, she got up and padded in her blue, frilled nightgown to her white desk. Taking out a sheet of dark blue notepaper, she sat down, pen in hand.

Dear Mark, she wrote slowly, bearing down on the pen. Twice she retraced the name. She could tell him that she was going to the Cape this summer with her family. She did not want to go to the Cape. She wanted to stay and dance forever, cut in on many and many a time during each dance, in Andalusia. She wanted to live in her own house here in the warm South and to live in it forever. She could tell him that she would join the choir as he had suggested, but that might convey the opposite of the renunciation she intended. Her bare toes curled. She turned the paper over, face downward. She was hungry.

Getting back into bed, she rang the buzzer at the head of her bed, deciding to breakfast there, and then to sleep.

It was her mother who came in, instead of Nanine. Hope half-closed her eyes and pretended to be still almost sleeping, in case her mother should notice that her eyes were red.

"Ah, you young people," said her mother, "after dancing all night long. Carrie's downstairs, Hope. She says she's going out to shoot skeet at the Oaks and do you want to go? I was about to say you were asleep when I heard you ring."

"Tell her I'll be dressed in two seconds," said Hope, immediately relieved. "Tell Nanine to pour me some coffee, quick."

"Yes, dear," said her mother. "It's a lovely day."

As they drove off, Hope said to Carrie, "I couldn't sleep."

"I couldn't either. It's too fine a day to wallow around in bed. Glad you were up."

"I hope Mark stays," said Hope, only a little dolefully, as they crossed Gloucester and went toward the Oakland road without passing the rectory.

"Sure," said Carrie. "It's better if he stays. I warn you, Andalusia can be very dull."

"Why warn me?" asked Hope, instantly annoyed. "I live here."

"You've got an out up yonder," said Carrie. "You've never stayed here the whole long, long, long summer."

"I think I'll stay this year," said Hope, "even though it got hot so soon."

"It always does, almost," said Carrie. "We forget. Stay if you can stand it."

"To prove it, I think I will," said Hope.

"You'll make a southerner yet, my pet," said Carrie, having seen that the big blue eyes had cried throughout the dawn. She stepped on the accelerator, grateful for the speed of her swift car that carried her only a little way and back again. She felt her hands on the polished steering wheel as they would feel on the smooth wood of her new gun. She was glad that pine trees smelled as they did when the sun shone, as they did the summer long. She lit a cigarette with the lighter that was built into the dashboard of her car and breathed the smoke in deeply. Familiarity was the greatest of boons. It was no effort to use only one leg instead of two when you were used to it. Hope had two homes, two choices, but Carrie had only one. And Hope was part of it. "Stick around," Carrie said.

Angela pummeled her pillow angrily, squeezed her face shut, and tucked her head down on her hands, drawing up her knees until they touched her elbows. A few minutes later, she straightened out, clasped her hands under her small bosom and closed her eyes again in her back-tilted head. Finally she sat up, made a face at the curtains she had so carefully drawn and around which the sunlight was seeping into the room, and threw back the muddled sheet. Thought was like strong coffee and kept you awake long after you were tired of being awake.

Pulling back the curtains, she saw the full glory of the day.

She decided abruptly to go to Marianna and buy herself some red shoes. She had been putting off a shopping trip there for a month, for no better reason than that each day in Andalusia held the possibility of beholding Mark Barbee's body and face. Today she would relinquish him by leaving him.

She hesitated at the telephone and then shrugged, picked it up, and asked for the Rooks' number.

"For heaven's sake, Angela," said Mrs. Rook's vibrant and

carrying voice, "the poor child's sleeping and I should think you would be, too."

"If that's Angela—" said Ellen Terra's throaty purr at a distance from the telephone. . . . She must be leaning over the bannisters, in her nightgown, and speaking to her mother "—tell her to hang on."

"Hang on, Angela. The little idiot seems to be awake after all!"

Angela passed the rectory on her way to pick up Ellen Terra, who would go to Marianna with her. She saw Mark coming out of his front door to get his mail and waved to him cheerfully without slowing the car or calling a greeting.

"It's the funniest *thing*," said Ellen Terra, installed in the car beside Angela and leaning her head back on the seat, "I couldn't *sleep* after I got home last night. I was wide awake as a fluffy hoot owl. Imagine that."

She had lain in her bed, re-creating the incompleted kiss that Mark Barbee had given her so long ago until it was as brown and tattered as a fingered camellia and no longer produced any feeling within her. She had lost even the immediate longing to complete it.

"We look like the wrath of God," said Angela, "both of us."

"It won't last," said Ellen Terra comfortably. "A night's sleep and presto! I think I'll get some bright red shoes, too. With heels like stilts. And a red ribbony straw hat."

"Nice with your black hair," said Angela.

Mark, pacing his study floor in the bright morning after sleeping very little and badly, had no way of knowing that he was forsworn and that each of them in a different way could be counted on now for a different kind of dignity. He faced his problem as he had left it the night before. He had no measure for judging these women. He did not know why, in Andalusia, desperation was added to the normal heart, why it seemed impossible to counter, refuse or ignore them.

The doorbell rang and he went to answer it. Madeleine, cleaning upstairs, would wait to hear whether he went himself before she would make her reluctant and rheumatic way down the high stairs.

Alton Rook stood quietly before the rectory door, in the strained immobility of the controlled and nervous man. Grateful for the interruption, Mark wondered whether the two overwhelming women, his wife and his daughter Ellen Terra, had squeezed the juice from this man between them. He seemed more bloodless than ever, only his eyes warily alive with wit. He and Mark had been embarrassed together since the night after the vestry meeting when Mr. Rook had come to the rectory. Now he refused Mark's cordial invitation to come in.

"A professional call," said Mr. Rook apologetically, "I want you to tell me, if you will, what you have decided. I go to press tonight, you know, and you're a big story. I won't tell anybody and my typesetter is deaf and dumb."

"It's not that," said Mark helplessly. "I haven't decided."

"Give me a ring when you do, eh?"

"Sure," said Mark. "Do come in."

"You don't need me," said Alton Rook unexpectedly. "I'll call you at the last minute, if you don't mind."

"Certainly not."

"And I hope you stay," said Mr. Rook, looking at him directly with a quick, frank look. "Montana was made for men, but where we need 'em is around here."

He left with this and Mark went back into the study. Nothing seemed to bring him the final courage to say irrevocably that he would stay.

When Dugdale Winthrop telephoned and asked him to have lunch and play some singles, he accepted with a sense of escape. He could think better in the dark, that night, after an afternoon of exercise and a long, cold shower.

That night, Hope and Ellen Terra did what girls did in Andalusia when they spent an evening together. Having refused half a dozen dates for this Saturday night, the night after the dance, they had none. They had both hoped that Mark would ask them. He had not. They could not be with him to ask him to stay, stay, stay in Andalusia. They could only be two dateless girls, together on the town.

They drove downtown for Cokes together, drove up and down Main Street, exchanging conversation with their horns with other cars, drove around the other streets and remarked on the cars that were or were not in front of other doors. Morton's car was at Mary's door, and so was Logan Knight's, who had Carrie with him. He dated Carrie routinely, once a month, one-fourth as often as he dated Angela. The four were playing bridge and drinking in the Newcombe living room.

Sonny Boy had gone for Angela, early that evening, and had subsequently taken her downtown to the movies. Dugdale Winthrop had disappeared in the direction of Oakland, presumably to Rachel Mirimar. They passed and repassed the rectory during these peregrinations, and watched in the instant they passed, without changing their deliberate speed, Mark pacing the study floor. They both felt ordinary, tired and a little cross.

"You don't suppose he will decide to go away?" asked Hope, experimentally feeling her calm pulse.

"If he does, he does," said Ellen Terra calmly, feeling stuffed with calm.

"But it would be dull," said Hope, confidently echoing Carrie.

"It isn't important," said Ellen Terra. "I reckon nothing is. It's how you are when what happens and not what happens that matters." The words pleased her, seeming profoundly chosen to express something profound.

"I don't know what you mean," said Hope irritably.

"I don't either," said Ellen Terra and laughed. "I just go on being old me, no matter what."

"I'm going to be what I want to be," said Hope firmly.

"Swell," said Ellen Terra.

When they passed the rectory again, an hour later, they were on their way home. The evening had been exactly like any evening spent thus before Mark Barbee had ever come to Andalusia, before they had reached the high, dizzy summit of youth and popularity at the dance, as such evenings would be after they had come far down from the summit, unless something changed for them.

They saw that the lights in the rectory study were still on, but they did not see Mark in the room. Hope, peering into the night with wide, blue eyes, discerned him sitting in the swing on the rectory porch.

"Hi," she called, seeing him.

Ellen Terra stopped the car. She had nothing in mind. They were on their way home. Since he was there, they would say good night to Mark. She heard the swing creak as he got up from it, heard him say "Hi . . ."

She got out of the car and Hope perforce followed her. Ellen Terra's light, thin dress swung at her knees as she moved up the walk, her breasts tugged and bobbled beneath the low-cut neck. Hope walked firmly without wobbling.

Mark met them at the steps, lounging above them in perfunctory welcome.

Now that they were there, they felt slightly foolish. This was a girlish thing to do, to join a man sitting alone on his front porch, without his invitation to do so, girlish and daring in a giggly sort of way. Having acted girlishly, they proceeded without volition to behave girlishly and meaninglessly.

As if nudging and daring each other, they made their way together to the swing in answer to Mark's formal and unenthusiastic invitation, now that they were here, to join him.

"It's so hot," said Hope, foolishly.

"We were ridin' and ridin' around," said Ellen Terra in a little-girl voice.

"May I offer you a dope?" asked Mark. "It's all I have."

"I'd *love* one," said Hope.

"Me, too," said Ellen Terra, and giggled.

As he went in the door to get it for them, the girls turned to each other.

"What did we do this for?" asked Hope.

"I don't know," said Ellen Terra. "I feel silly silly."

"I do too."

The tension under which they had lived and behaved for so many days had gone entirely in the languid, relaxed and wasted evening. They were unable to stiffen even to the level of their normal manners. Either one alone might have told Mark, with charm and dignity, that she had forsworn him and that if she loved him still she would keep it quietly to herself and it need never occur to him or disturb him unless he wished it to. Together, they were caught with a gesture that looked like the ugliest kind of flagrant pursuit. They felt inert and helpless.

Helplessly, they carried on a cross conversation in clichés which irritated Mark visibly. Trapped in their unbearable foolishness, their conventional stupidity, they stayed on and on. They wanted nothing but somehow to make an exit so graceful that it would wipe out these continuing and embarrassing moments. Unable to find a way to leave thus gracefully, they were unable to leave. The moments passed, sticky with giggles and cheap with false gaiety.

Hope, caught in a further embarrassing predicament, made it worse by coyly underlining it. As she went inside to go upstairs to use the rectory bathroom, Ellen Terra turned to Mark.

Something in his face, looking down at her with frank distaste and disapproval, moved her to tears. There was nothing left to do but cry. She had forgotten how nice it was to cry.

"Don't cry," he said. And because these, at least, were honest tears, his voice expressed compassion.

Obediently as a child, she stopped.

"Better," he said.

"Oh, Mark, darling," said Ellen Terra, her voice purring with a child's utter distress, "we meant to be so extra-nice and you would want to stay and not be bothered by us and all, and then we were just nasty. Like silly little monkeys. Everybody behaves like monkeys sometime. It's awful. I'm so sorry."

"It's all right," said Mark, looking at her childishly puckered face, finding her at once exasperating and very touching. The idea that he had very nearly considered marrying this round bundle of charm and brainlessness amused while it frightened him. In some ways she was as destructive as her mother, although she was unutterably sweet, he thought.

"You're very nice," she said formally and stood up, fumbling for her handkerchief to wipe her damp face. It dropped out of her lap and he bent down and picked it up and handed it to her. She moved to him like a fresh-washed child and tiptoed up to kiss him, as a child does, asking forgiveness, promising to be good, wanting to be forgiven even for this childishness.

He touched her lips with his and then his arms were around

her and her body was tight against his. It was his doing and not hers and he seemed no more able to help it than to help the fact that he had been born male. He kissed her with rising passion and he kneaded her body with his amorous hands. He wrenched his mouth away and took her astounding, beautiful bosom in his two hands, hurting her while she yielded to pain and passion with complete and instant and perfect submission.

"If you want me," she purred breathlessly, gasping a little, "you can have me, Mark. You don't have to *marry* me or anything."

"Oh God," he said and stepped back from her with an effort that shook him. He gritted his teeth and looked at her and knew that there was nothing for him to do but go away. In the wilderness, he might learn to possess himself and to be something more than he was now. He hated himself and all four of them with irrational disgust. He wanted her ripe body so much that it was agony.

Inside the house the telephone rang.

"Excuse me," he said formally to Ellen Terra.

"It's Daddy," said Ellen Terra mournfully. "The edition goes to press about now. Don't tell him I'm here."

There would probably be no need to tell him. Anyone passing could have seen the three of them on the porch in the shadows. They had noticed no one in the still night, but probably the car had been spotted from somewhere by someone. By their cars ye knew them in Andalusia.

The screen door slammed behind him. Upstairs, he heard the sound of flushing water as Hope presumably completed what she had so specifically announced she was going to do.

He picked up the telephone and said, "Hello!" more fiercely than he intended to.

Hope appeared at the head of the stairs, trim and neat and freshly washed of the tears she, too, had shed. She bore only the smallest resemblance to the girl who had been giggling on the porch so short a time before as Ellen Terra, all repentant child and then all passionate woman, had borne as little.

"Oh," said Mr. Rook's voice. "Sorry if I woke you or anything . . ."

"No, sir," said Mark, "I'm still up."

"I just thought—hoped—you might have a word. Sorry to be

such a pest of a newspaperman, but I sure would like to run the story if . . ."

"Certainly," said Mark. "It's cowboys and Indians for me, Mr. Rook."

"Well," said Alton Rook, "I'm sorry, of course, but God bless you, son, I think you're wise. Every man needs a couple of years like that. Too bad we don't all get it."

"I don't know," said Mark.

He hung up slowly. He would get rid of the girls and go to bed and to sleep. His decision was made, and it was probably the best one. He was too irked to care. They had each one brought him face to face with himself in a different way and he had found himself lacking. He would go out among men, among tough men, and become what he had so confidently thought he already was. They had honored him by offering him the best they were, and he had not had even the decency to refuse them with honor to himself as well as to them.

Angela, Carrie, Ellen Terra and Hope were all there to see Mark off on the afternoon train. Of their mothers, Mrs. Gregory was there and of their fathers, Alton Rook.

The crowd at the station was restless, with the twin restlessness of a farewell and of a cocktail party. The interval seemed both unduly prolonged and too short for the effort that had gone into dressing up and getting there. The movement within the group was jerky and aimless, except for the young people, tentatively pairing up in order to extend and transmute the occasion.

Standing on the edge of the crowd, his thumbs in the side pockets of his seersucker trousers and his hat pushed to the very back of his head, Alton Rook surveyed the scene with narrowed eyes. He was scowling protectively and he felt neither witty nor wise. His feeling toward Mark was one of dismissal compounded with affection and regret. It had been a good thing to have the young man around. It had stirred everybody up. It had stirred him up and reminded him of his youth when he had wrestled with the accepted patterns of love and faith, revolted against both, succumbed to both, and lost both. It had forced him to realize again what he had lost, a not unpainful process, but an enlivening one. He wished Mark luck in running away from a situation the young man might never better.

Fathers Gregory and Stone, he reflected sardonically, had refused to lend even their outward approval to Mark's defection by saying good-bye. The vice president of the oil company and the president of the bank were fuming in their offices, not because Mark had refused their daughters, but because Mark was going rambunctiously off to be a missionary instead of taking the pulpit in Mobile. Successful men were so sensitive to slights. Cecil Madison was not absent for any reason. He was really busy at The Place, where any success he might have accrued to his owner-wife. When Cecil was away, his nigras got out of hand. Besides, Alton doubted whether poor old Cecil ever thought of a white person, even his daughter, in human terms any more, or cared if they came or went.

The mothers were not there because they were lurking in their large houses nursing the fury that hell had no like of, thought Alton Rook, remembering his wife's face that morning. Scorned through their daughters, only Tracy Gregory among them had the gumption and the resignation to pretend she was not.

The kids were all there. Looking into the crowd and searching out the four girls with his eyes, he wanted to pat their unsuccessfully disguised faces and their sweet, solid, undisguised rumps. Good kids, they were taking it on the lifted little chins they had stuck out so far. Gallant, they were gallantly supported, rallied to by the very boys to whom they had preferred Mark. Boys and girls alike, these young people were behaving with gallantry. The girls, one of whom was his own girl, publicly wounded, were publicly proud, like tapped pines, their feathery heads high, ignoring the sap that visibly dripped from the cut in their tender bark. . . .

His heart opened suddenly and his old optimism and belief in human happiness welled up again for the new generation. Dark Carrie asked nothing in compensation for her affliction. Hope was pretty and prim and sturdily competent enough to fill even his own generation's dream of a virgin princess who would make a fine wife. Angela, a restive colt, needed only handling to make her a sleek, fine filly. And his darling, black, absurd little Ellen Terra was a cupful of honey ready to spill over with the gathered sweetness of her youth and sex.

His eyes moistened as he regarded these children. Their youth touched him unbearably. They were so much younger than he remembered youth. Looking at them, he was painfully hopeful for them.

Generations were like crops, he thought, diverting himself from sentimental tears, but indulging his vision. Every now and then the earth loosened and the rain and sunshine fell in proper balance and the labor of men and women bore abundant and goodly fruit.

His own generation, he thought, diverting himself again from sentimental and rhetorical tribute to youth, stank. The petticoat revolution of his time had carried its triumph into excess. Women, not content with victory, wanted revenge. And were well revenged, he added with oblique commiseration. Which their daughters, in natal wisdom, must know. So, he concluded cheerily, as the train came lurching and snorting around the long bend in the tracks that paralleled the bend in the river on the other side of town, these touching, gallant, newly alive children, these sweet-faced, proud, free children, sought each other to love fairly. The four girls, one of whom was his daughter, had loved a man openly and lost him sadly and, seeking further, would find and, finding, would cherish and, cherishing, would make happy and, making happy, would be happy. Their world would be a better place, with men and women in proper relation to each other, and the new generation would recapture the art of living together in happiness.

Pooh pooh for us, he said to himself as he had heard them say to each other, hoo-ray for you.

Mattie, before the birth of her third child, prevailed upon Fate Pinckney to marry her.

"When ah got me uh man," said Mattie, arguing peacefully, "ah doan wants nobody thinkin ah ain't got um."

"Ain't nobody gonna think you ain't had none an just carryin you aroun a barrel uh moonshine under that dress," said Fate, resisting to the last.

The marriage was an occasion for delighted amusement

among the circle of their white employers, and for commensurate generosity. Miss Angela Madison presented the groom, to his nearly frantic delight, with a shined-up second-hand Model T Ford. Miss Ellen Terra Rook gave the bride not one but two wedding dresses, the first designed to cover her current girth and the second for her matronly future.

The narrow alley between and behind the white folks' streets of houses gradually quieted after the excitement. Under the thick archway of oak limbs, the dust settled down. From the gray, close cabins came only the sounds of crowded sleeping. When Amanda Church was away, as she often was with some man or other, the alley was a self-consciously respectable place, the Egmont Street of black Andalusia, presided over by its own formidable dowager, Georgianna Church.

Sitting on the quivering steps of their home, the skirt of wedding dress number one pulled out from under her weighty rump, Mattie voiced her only mild complaint. "Ah had me kinda uh hankerin tuh be married by duh white preachuh he look like Mistuh Gilbut," said Mattie, "but he gone."

"No white preacher for me," said Fate from the dusty little yard into which he had crowded his car. He was polishing the hood of the Model T, as he stood there beside it, with the sleeve of his wedding jacket. "I's glad to be married by black. I don't mind white people one *at* a time, but I can't stand em in bunches."

"Vanity an foolishness, oh Lawd, in duh churn uh duh Lawd," said Mattie's mother, rocking on the porch next door in the endless rhythm that seemed nightly to renew her tireless heart. Georgianna often sat there until dawn, the creak of her chair mingling with the mighty snores of her daughter, Mercy, who slept within, with the chittering of the dawn sparrows.

"He ain no bunch, Miss Ellen Terra's revund," argued Mattie. "Gone an lef dem po weepin ladies uh-pinin on duh vine."

"Peakin an pinin, sin an sufferin," said Georgianna.

"Aint pining sos you could notice it none," said Fate. "And if your Ellen Terra ain't lost her cherry, I's wrong."

"Tuh who?" asked Georgianna indignantly.

"To that old long-laigged Dugdale Winthrop, that's who," said Fate.

"Gwan," said Mattie. "Mistuh Lovejoy, he's duh one dat's been sniffin aroun . . ."

"Ah use tuh wash huh sweet lil face when she no biggirn uh baby angel, mah Lawd, ain it awful?" said Georgianna.

Their three-part laughter filled the night with music proclaiming the joyous brotherhood of man.

"Whut next?" asked Mattie, wiping the laughter from her face with her petticoat.

"You mean, who next," said Fate. "Miss Anglah, I reckon."

"She so skinny," objected Mattie.

"In the summertime, she ain't too skinny," said Fate. "And if she fix em, I bet she fix em up good."

"She gonna marry Mistuh Logan?" asked Georgianna, her voice querulous. "Everybody say she gonna marry Mistuh Logan."

"Nanine say Miss Hope she done set huhself aroun tuh love Mistuh Logan," said Mattie. "Miss Hope she right putty, she mo putty dan Miss Anglah."

"Dunno nothing about Hope and dunno nothing about Carrie," said Fate. "Cain't anybody tell about Yankees and crippled gals. But they is one thing for sure. Ain't none of em got nobody and somebody is plenty for anybody."

"Naw he ain't," said Mattie immobilely.

Georgianna said, "Somepns betterirn nothin an sometimes its mohn plenty."

2

Done and

Left Undone

1931

11.   Miss Lucy Miss Lucy

It was late in the summer of 1931 before the town of Andalusia realized in its collective consciousness, below the level of titillation and speculation, that Lucy Lee Cranborne had murdered her mother. Nobody had minded in the least when Mrs. Cranborne died. It was difficult at first to mind, several months later, because her daughter had killed her. It was also very, very hot, and had been very hot for some time, which made it hard to find the immediate energy necessary to transfer theoretical horror into horror over the fact.

The reappearance of Miss Lucy, in deep mourning, on the streets of the town, bringing books to and removing them from the library, marketing, conscientiously taking her mother's bad-tempered, still youthful Scottie to walk, made it difficult to believe the fact. Accepted, it finally took on the public aspect of Miss Lucy's placid, unchanged and private countenance.

In the interval between knowledge and acceptance, when Miss Lucy's fate hung in skittish balance, the townspeople felt queasy rather than either curious or vengeful. The conception that to understand all was to forgive all, the psychology of forgiveness by explanation, was not theirs. There were always reasons why people did what they did. Punishment was for the commission of sin and murder was sin. Yet no one actually wished Miss Lucy pilloried in the public square. As one of the last great southern belles, her name, a fine old name, too, was still fragrant as a pressed rose in the annals of her class, the town and her state.

Nor was there the necessary leadership for punishment by general disapproval. The middle-aged matrons of the town, who normally provided such leadership, had reason to be grateful to Miss Lucy, who had refused to marry their husbands. Their husbands felt for her an old affection for the quality of her refusal, which, including all supplicants, had wounded no male pride. This affection had never been either rearoused or entirely destroyed by her pleasant-faced, self-contained, fattening and fading presence.

Yet the decision, in effect, to ignore Miss Lucy's unexpected, single, middle-aged crime was curiously incomplete. If anyone had either defended or attacked her with conviction, publicly or private-ly, there would have been a nervous stampede and scant mercy for Miss Lucy. As it was, the residue of feeling about her was one of resentment, not for having taken the life of her unattractive mother, nor for having gotten away with it, but for some deeper reason which those who felt it failed to understand. Only two people under-stood it. One was Arabella White, wife of the new rector at St. James's Episcopal Church, and the other was black Georgianna Church. The only person who ever suffered for Miss Lucy's crime was the only person who never once thought about whether she had or had not committed it, the Reverend Mr. Robert White.

Among those who had to settle with his own conscience on the subject was the town coroner, who was legally responsible for listing Mrs. Cranborne's death as caused by acute indigestion and heart complications. He would have said that what drove him to see Dr. Dandridge the day after an American Legion meeting in early August was the pricking of his conscience. Not even in that particular group of men, among egos still touchy from the remote, kindly snubbing not they but their fathers had received at the hands of such as Miss Lucy, was there any suggestion that he do anything about Miss Lucy. She belonged to the new poor, for one thing, which took the edge from the half-remembered past. To cover any embarrassment they may have felt in possession of such knowledge about her, and any milder resentment they also felt about her, they made a rough, midsummer joke of the murder, remarking that they wished their wives would do the same for their mothers-in-law.

Oliver Jarvis, the coroner, would have made a good judge. He had a nice instinct for truth, for justice and for clemency. Son of a farm laborer, he had become an officer in the army by a process of survival on the Marne and had made an excellent public servant in various small capacities since then. He was accustomed to rely on his own judgment when there was no higher authority, but now he felt the definite need to shrug his small responsibility off on other shoulders, even those of a madman.

The doctor, a tall, stooped man with a corrugated face and a mouth that had all but disappeared inward, opened the door. Oliver Jarvis peered in and was relieved to see that Mrs. Dandridge was not there, behind her husband, ready to carry on the doctor's conversations for him and to refuse or grant the visitor his admittance, depending on her judgment of his errand.

"Hello, Doctor," said Oliver Jarvis, shaking hands. He pushed his way past the doctor into the narrow hall as the doctor looked at him with a vague, passive welcome in his inward-looking eyes. After hanging his panama hat carefully on the rack, Oliver Jarvis made his way into the doctor's consulting room. He waited politely while the doctor followed him in and obediently settled himself behind his desk, motioning Oliver Jarvis to the leather chair on the other side of it.

"Well, and what seems to be the matter, Colonel?" asked Dr. Dandridge, pushing a six-months-old medical journal aside and resting his bony elbows on the desk. He called all men "Colonel" and all women "My Dear," just as he called all female children Miss Merryweather and all male children Mister Humpty Dumpty, to the delight of the children. It was a system designed to conceal the fact that he no longer saw their faces or recognized their clothed bodies.

Oliver Jarvis raised himself slightly and pulled at the seersucker trousers and cotton-knit shorts that made his crotch uncomfortable in the heat, and then settled back down again. Everything took time and there was plenty of time.

"That was a fine job you did for me, Doctor, when I had that infected appendix and then got pneumonia. Drains and adhesions, you remember. Haven't had anything worse than a bad cold since." The appendix had been removed when he was fourteen years old, and since he had returned from the war he had gone to one of the younger doctors.

He saw recognition dawning, as he had hoped, in the old, lightly leaking eyes as the heavy, lowered lids raised themselves.

"Well, well, I am glad to hear it. I *am* glad to hear it!" said the doctor, with a passionate concern he never had to pretend. He had tortured himself into early senility by constantly rediagnosing every case he had ever lost, and he comforted himself a little still, as best he could, with those he had saved.

"I'm the coroner now," offered Oliver Jarvis cautiously. "The town coroner."

"Of course, of course," said Dr. Dandridge. "D'you know something? I'd like to perform an autopsy every time. *Every single time.*"

"Good idea, I tell you. What's worrying me is old Mrs. Cranborne. A lot of people are saying she died of arsenic poisoning."

"Of course she did," said Dr. Dandridge testily. "Any fool would know that. Plain as a carbuncle on the end of your nose. The question is—oh my God! If I had injected . . ."

Oliver Jarvis waited patiently, fanning himself with a newspaper, while the old doctor talked and talked. The doctor finally put his hands over his eyes and said in a despairing whisper, "I just don't know. I'll never be sure. In this case, I don't think so. I don't think Dr. God Almighty could have done any good. It was a question . . ."

Oliver Jarvis interrupted him before he could start over again. He saw that he would have to jar the old man into sanity if he were to unload his responsibility. The old man could still handle responsibility when it was thrust at him. A good many of the town's poorest, to whom he never sent bills, and some of the town's other tradition-bound families, like the Cranbornes, who had refused to relinquish his tender, concerned, frantic and indecisive care, could attest to that.

"They say Miss Cranborne—Miss Lucy—killed her, *murdered* her." He leaned forward and looked up under the lids of the doctor's eyes.

"So she did," said Dr. Dandridge. "Or at least," he said, looking at Oliver Jarvis with his eyes suddenly lit by the vast residue of his intelligence, his mouth folding even tighter into lines that indicated inward laughter, "she did, if I didn't by not giving her that second injection. So, Mr. Humpty Dumpty . . ." Oliver Jarvis did not know whether he had been reduced to the status of child because of his appendix or his last statement. ". . . so, what, Coroner? Miss Lucy is a fine, healthy woman, with a good many years to live, unless she takes to drink. She won't take to drink."

"No, she won't," said Oliver Jarvis, puzzled because this statement annoyed him. "What would you do, Doctor, if I reopened the case? You attended her. It's my duty, you know, to reopen it." It *was* his duty. There was no way around that.

"In a pig's ass and your duty be damned," said Dr. Dandridge, fully alive now that life was threatened. "I'll swear upside down and crosswise and on the Bible of my blessed mother that Mrs. Cranborne died of spoiled crabmeat and that you are Miss Lucy's paramour trying to make trouble for poor Miss Lucy. I am too old to tell the truth all the time."

Oliver Jarvis laughed. He laughed until his face was beet-red and the sweat trembled off his chin. Miss Lucy and he . . . The doctor was a card. He felt good all the way down to his toes.

"Have a drink," said the doctor.

"You've talked me into it, Doc. Thanks a lot. Thanks a whole hell of a lot."

They eyed each other in comradely understanding as they each drained half of a small glass of neat bourbon. Before they had finished the whiskey in their glasses, the doctor was up from behind the desk and pacing the floor. He turned on Jarvis, remembering even a name in his state of revitalization, his determination to protect any life that he could protect. "Did Black send you, Coroner?"

Black was the Chief of Police. Oliver Jarvis smiled, recalling his one conversation with Francis Black on the subject of Miss

Lucy. "If you have a murder to report to me, damn it, Ollie, report it officially. If you haven't, leave a lady's name out of anything you say." Black understood the law, both written and unwritten. He had a sense of duty toward both, but no discernible conscience. Jarvis admired and envied Black, but could not emulate him. He shook his head at Dr. Dandridge, and the doctor resumed his pacing.

"If I had," he said, "given the second injection sooner . . ."

Oliver Jarvis said earnestly, "Don't fret yourself, Doc." He got up, with a decisive bounce, adding, "Well, now . . ." and went out of the consulting room into the hallway to retrieve his hat.

"Glad you're all right," called the doctor after him. "Very, very glad."

"Bob White's not here," said Arabella White, wiping her hands briskly on her apron and then pushing open the screen door to greet the two visitors. "Come on in anyway, do come on in anyway." She untied her apron as further invitation and indication that she was through doing whatever she was doing that required an apron. With one hand she reached out and grasped Ellen Terra's plump, naked arm. "Do come in out of all that heat!"

She resembled a red terrier chivvying two charming, woolly sheep, thought Arabella, as she amiably, with words and gestures, urged Ellen Terra Rook and Hope Stone Knight into the high-ceilinged living room across the hall from the rector's study. The room was cool, with the green outside blinds closed across the open screened windows and an electric fan with rubber leaves whirring and turning softly from a low table. The two girls sank gratefully together onto a chintz-covered couch and sighed in unison.

"So cool . . ." baaed the black sheep, Ellen Terra. Her small, round, dark eyes were solid as ink spots, and as expressionless, in her round face under the shorn black bangs.

"How do you do it, Mrs. White?" baa-baaed the white sheep. Hope tossed her blonde hair back over her thick shoulders with an accustomed gesture. Then she lifted her hair away from the back of her round, white neck and bent her head to the breeze from the fan. "Keep it so cool, this room, I mean."

"Windows and blinds open all night," said Arabella briskly.

"Blinds closed at dawn, but at *dawn,* fan on when the sun's high. Nice, isn't it?"

The two girls nodded appreciatively, in unison.

"But," said Ellen Terra plaintively, "dawn . . ."

"Also," said Arabella, chivvying them still in her role of terrier, "I have a pitcher of fresh-squeezed orange juice in the ice box . . ."

"Wonderful," they said, "heavenly."

Arabella bustled away, five feet and three and a half inches, in her heels, of terrier-housewife. Her wiry, clipped red hair, with fibers of gray which proved that she did *not* dye it, rose on her head like a grass fire in short, dead grass. Her wiry body, on the determined heels, moved purposefully along the wide, newly waxed hall. She went on through the back door and along the trellised, covered passageway that led to the kitchen and dining room, thus separated from the house as they had been for ninety-five years. Practically, she deplored this arrangement and was sure that it would never have survived in any house but a rectory into the practical, labor-saving present. As a housewife, which she had become for two months, pushed into housewifery by the obscene, accumulated filth in the old rectory and an epidemic of cockroaches, by the lazy sloppiness of the first two servants she had tried, and by the incurable, tobacco-shedding sloppiness of the husband whom she would never leave nor could induce to leave her, she deplored it. A flourishing, thick-limbed wisteria vine blessed, beautified and darkened it. If there were, at the other end of it, a cook who could plan meals as well as prepare them, she would never need to know beforehand what she would eat. The passageway would provide a separation between the eating part of life and the speculative. Bliss and enchantment! She should run into the street, crying for a cook, however indifferent to dirt, who would materialize food at the end of the dark, wisteria-shaded passageway, calling her with a silver bell only when it was ready. She could live in the cool front room, where the two girls now awaited their housewife-hostess, and speak in a vocabulary far removed from the one she was currently employing.

Her heels clicked her rapidly into the small dining room at the end of the passageway, through it, and into the almost burnished kitchen where even the cobwebs spun by the ineradicable inhabitants were new ones. She stared vacantly around at the achieved cleanliness and then, spotting the ice box, remembered her objective. It would never do to get in a readin' and thinkin' mood right now.

Because readin' and thinkin' would only separate her from her real quest. The lady was in search of herself.

Abruptly she pulled the pitcher out of the ice box, setting it on a tray she had recently repainted and decorated with a flower pattern cut from a woman's magazine. Putting her forefinger to her temple, she stared momentarily at the tray and then put a fresh green linen doily under the pitcher and under the tall, polished crystal glasses which she was almost sure she really loved. She had her pride, whoever she was. And her rewards. If she did not love the pots and pans she served as housewife, look how they loved her. The copper ones, especially, radiated content on their gilded hooks patterned beside the stove, their very bottoms glistening with the steel wool of her well-simulated affection for them. As for this tray, it was charming, as in the slick-paper magazines that fed the misty longings of the lower middle class. The lost Arabella must have had a knack for decorating the obvious.

The blonde head and the black head pulled slightly apart as she entered the living room, and Hope's bell-like voice vibrated with an interrupted note.

"Were you talking about me?" asked Arabella, hearing the slight hoarseness in her own voice which came from smoking too much. You could always amuse the young by being direct. It always surprised them, coming from the old. "Or about Miss Lucy Cranborne?"

Ellen Terra giggled nervously and got up, helping Arabella to settle the tray and passing a glass of orange juice to Hope when Arabella poured it.

Hope said, "Oh, do you *know* about Miss Lucy?" Opening her huge, blue eyes, her mouth hanging open a little after she had spoken.

"No," said Arabella promptly, "and I don't want to, hear? Not one word."

"Mrs. Dandridge told my mother and Ellen Terra's mother

months ago," said Hope uncomfortably, "but *we* didn't find out for ages."

"Good for your mothers, keeping it from you. As for me, nobody tells me anything and I don't intend they shall!" She was ridiculously emphatic and Ellen Terra giggled again, purringly, her sweet plump body bouncing a little as she giggled. Arabella looked at her with sharp interest. There was a childishness about her body, despite its excessive bloom, and an innocence in her round painted mouth and small round eyes, in her almost perfectly round painted face, that belied her reputation.

"Nobody's mad at Miss Lucy," said Ellen Terra softly, wounded and puzzled.

"That's Carrie," said Hope quickly, welcoming the interruption as a horn sounded outside the house. "She's meeting us here."

"I'll go, Mrs. White," said Ellen Terra, as Arabella started toward the door.

"Thank you." Arabella turned to Hope, watching her slither down a little further on the sofa, her face vacant and her stocky body inert. She felt in Hope energy gone sour and transmuted into a lethargy that was as exhausting as energy. "How's your little girl?" she asked Hope brightly. "She's a beauty, a real beauty. I love little girls, especially good-looking ones. I get on with 'em, too. Bring her over."

"She's pretty," acknowledged Hope, the clear voice bespeaking the energy. "Spoiled, though. They spoil them so." Her heavy-armed gesture included the whole race of Negroes and the whole world of grandparents. "Logan does, too. Their father should do something about making them mind or something, don't you think?"

"I suppose he should," said Arabella, laughing, although she was not amused. She liked children in theory, and often in practice, and resented the selfishness of grownups who left them without the protection of clear discipline. Logan Knight's features wavered in her mind as she tried to think critically of him in this connection. She could not summon a face for him. It was curious about Hope's husband. When she was around him, she found him so charming a young man. She liked his gentle manners and precise speech, and she was partial to good looks. She had felt mildly sorry for him,

153

thinking Hope must be a drag on any man, with her lethargy alternating with the unpredictable stimulation of drink. Arabella had watched sympathetically as he dealt gently with that lethargy, prodding Hope into the action necessary to take leave of a room. But when he was not there, she could never remember him at all. He vaporized out of her mind. "Fathers are such soft-hearted saps about little girls," she theorized vaguely, not thinking this especially about Logan Knight, but finding it an appropriate remark.

Carrie came in ahead of Ellen Terra, her foreshortened leg thumping across the wide, raised doorsill into the darkened room.

"Hello, Mrs. White! Ellen Terra says I'm invited for orange juice. I do thank you."

Arabella looked with surprise at the enlivened face greeting her. She had not seen Carrie Gregory for a month. The girl looked ten years younger. There was a spring in her awkward step and a glow in her face that had been a drawn-down mask in her mother's house the month before. She must be in love, thought Arabella, with the quick, sympathetic pleasure automatically felt for the handicapped. No woman ever changed that much except for love of a man. She almost said, "I'm so glad, my dear."

"I don't know when Bob White will be back," she said, realizing anew that they had come, not to see her, but her husband. "He went out calling an hour ago and I expect him before lunch, but Lord knows what time. He's a most unpunctual man." She said it proudly, as if this were a special virtue. She always talked thus about Bob White, maintaining to the world that even his habit of spilling tobacco from a smelly pipe was the most admirable of male traits. She suspected that he had gone to call, among others, on Miss Lucy Cranborne again. He was a fool, the biggest that God had ever called to His precarious service.

"This is nice," said Ellen Terra, her impeccable manners like those of a well-trained child. Spontaneously, and without hope of gain in her innocence, she added, *"You're* nice!"

"Thanks," said Arabella. If people, in all innocence, liked you, you must be there to be liked. Nobody could like a Housewife, or a Hostess, or a Rector's Wife.

She felt the pangs of friendliness and the distressing stir of curiosity. They said of these three girls sitting in her living room and the one, Angela, who was not there, of these four variously good-looking, unfunctional women supported by cheap labor and modest family fortunes, these pleasant-mannered, pleasant-looking girls living in the shadows of their firmly fleshed mothers, about whom she felt no curiosity whatever, they said: That Ellen Terra could be had for the asking, and not in marriage, and that her kisses were passed around like a big paper bag of lollypops. They said no one would marry her now because no one had already. They said that Hope adored and neglected her child, adored and neglected her husband, Logan Knight, and that she was drinking too much. They said that her mother, Mrs. Stone, adored them all and that her son-in-law adored Mrs. Stone and that it was a good thing for all of them that they lived together, since Hope was drinking too much. They said that Angela Madison and Bill Bloodgood would never marry because obviously what kept them apart was what kept them together. Angela's natural taste, they said, ran to ministers or to dreamy, gentle men like Logan Knight, while as for Wild Bill Bloodgood, look at the glamorous girls who fell for him. He should have married Missy Maidenstone, in Oglethorpe, they said, a beautiful, high-handed, high-spirited young woman who could handle both him and his mother, and Angela should have married Logan, naturally. If Mrs. Madison and Mrs. Bloodgood had not proclaimed their unalterable opposition, it was doubtful that Bill and Angela would have seen anything in each other. Pity all around, they said, wasting everybody's time and tempers, and if they did not look out, their mothers would have to support them forever. They would never marry each other, anyway, Bill and Angela. So they thought and said. And Carrie, they said, would never marry at all, naturally, poor girl, was she not brave and her mother was a saint. They said that Miss Lucy Lee Cranborne had murdered her mother, and so she undoubtedly had. "They" were often right, deducing the fires from the never invisible smoke, and, if they were wrong, they often imposed what they thought on the people about whom they thought it. The bastard truth of their assumptions became stronger than the real truth, which one could only hope, in time, to find out about oneself.

There was something more to these girls than the things they said about them. There was a certainty in their relaxed triendship that made her optimistic. She considered their mothers merely disposable. These girls were not yet disposable. What did these girls with disposable mothers think of the woman who had disposed of her mother?

"We do think Mr. White is fine, Mrs. White," Hope was saying to her.

"He's a good man," said Arabella, tucking away this bit of knowledge, for there was something to be learned from any human being's reaction to her husband.

The three began to chatter lightly, weaving a pattern of soft sound and explanation. It seemed that when a certain Mark Barbee was rector, they had had Friday night dances in the parish hall, for the benefit of the day nursery. It seemed that the Reverend Mr. Luke Cox, who had replaced Barbee and whom Bob White had replaced, disapproved of the dances. Perhaps Mr. White would like to start them again, with them to help him?

Arabella listened with her outer ears, grimacing semi-intelligently in agreement. Their voices charmed her, in a town of arid voices, and she was susceptible to voices. Ellen Terra's purr was a kitten's and Hope's voice was a bell, with the ring of good glass, and Carrie had a dark voice, unslurred. She could not remember Angela's voice exactly, except that it was infinitely shaded.

"Talk to Bob White," she said finally, cutting across their conversation. "I know he'll approve. Wait for him to come, do wait for him to come."

Having silenced them, she asked them, wanting their reactions to something more vital, "What was Mrs. Cranborne like? Do tell me what she was like. She died before we had time to call on her."

Their reaction enlightened her. They squirmed. That's what they did. Even Carrie, whose misshapen body was rigidly disciplined. They squirmed and they were downcast and puzzled at the thought of Lucy Lee Cranborne, who had murdered her mother. They were thinking of their own disposable mothers. They were troubled in the night, she thought. She was interested because they were troubled.

"What was she like?" she insisted, prodding them.

"Why, she was—old," said Hope doubtfully, miserably.

"And fat," contributed Carrie shortly. "And a fearful gossip."

Ellen Terra, whose memory, like her thinking, was in visual images, suddenly recalled her inescapably. "She had moles on her face and wattles like a turkey," she said, "and she planted her feet when she walked. Like this." Without getting up, Ellen Terra uncrossed her legs and spaced her two small feet, in their bright red sandals, her plump, bare legs parallel to each other, setting them firmly in such a way as to convey the impression of groundgripper shoes and thick stockings. "And she said puh-puh-puh before she said anything." Ellen Terra's mouth puckered on the puh-puh-puh, which was almost soundless.

"Ugh," said Arabella.

"She was a bore," said Carrie, sulkily. "A quite dreadful bore. A mean gossip and a bore."

"Oh, but lots of people are," said Arabella, as the other two nodded agreement.

"She was special," said Carrie, "because she forced you—but forced you—to gossip, too, and bore her back."

Arabella was pleased. Carrie was amusing. "Miss Lucy . . ." she prompted.

Carrie looked at Arabella in rebellious discomfort. "What does Mr. White think?" she asked, frankly, at last. There was a challenge in her voice and belittlement of Arabella.

"He doesn't make judgments," said Arabella, protecting Bob White and concealing the crossness she felt from her voice. "Ever!" she added emphatically.

"Oh?" said Carrie. "No?" She was frowning.

You are coming to Bob White with your troubled consciences, thought Arabella. Much good that will do you. He is only good. Just plain good. No use to anybody. Go on and kill your own mothers, he won't care. Or don't. He won't care either. But he will reciprocate your love and trust because he loves and trusts everybody. You'll have that, for what it's worth.

Ellen Terra said plaintively, "Miss Lucy is just like she always was. *Just exactly.*"

Intuitively Arabella, who was very intuitive when interested and remarkably obtuse when either bored or prejudiced, understood then what they did not understand. Oh, the dear, humid South which demanded that sin be punished in the heart of the sinner! She felt then truly that she had returned home, after all these years, thirty and more, of living in the West, the North, the fringe along the Mason and Dixon. She was rediscovering, at last, the South of her birth, and the rediscovery would go much deeper than the knowledge in her bred and born bones. She had been distracted by the indistinguishable country-club atmosphere of the town's well-to-do surface and had failed to realize where she was. In Texas, where she and Bob White had settled for ten years on the vast land that was floor to a vaster sky, man was punished that other men might not sin. In the sophisticated, newly intellectual North, sin had been reasoned away and punishment was desultory, anachronistic, cruel and accidental. In Andalusia, they wanted of Miss Lucy that she should punish herself. The pinched nostril, the shadow of midnight tears. This was the least that Miss Lucy could do for them. Otherwise murder was not sin and there was no barrier thereto. But Miss Lucy was exactly as she had been. Unforgivable Miss Lucy!

The front steps shook and the front porch creaked and the screen door slammed. Bob White was back. The girls rose, instantly and naturally, to greet him. In deference, thought Arabella, not to his age, which was fifty-five, nor to his gray hair, of which he had only wisps, directly behind his ears, nor to his girth, which was perfectly round, nor to his height, which was brief, nor to his intellect, which was dormant, nor to his fortune, which was nonexistent, not even to his collar, which was turned the other way around, but to his goodness, which was infinite. She nodded at them appreciatively.

"Well," said Bob White, in his wavering tenor, "am I invited, or is this only for ladies?"

They urged him into the room, surrounding him prettily, flirting with him to the verge of outrage, albeit innocently. She never understood why women invariably flirted with Bob White when he never knew it. She herself could not bear to be unresponded to in anything, even in hate. You might as well flirt with a sandpile as flirt with Bob White. Which was too bad, she thought, because a clergyman had as much to gain as a doctor, a lawyer, or a salesman by the most infinitesimal recourses to the charm of his masculinity. And for all his roundness, for all his funny face, he was a man.

"I am late," he said without apology to his wife, "I think. But I went by to see Miss Cranborne and she insisted that I have coffee. She had some real French coffee." He smacked his lips.

The three girls stirred and sighed almost in unison. Their faces lightened and cleared. They handed to Bob White all that troubled them. They gave Miss Lucy to Bob White, leaving the murder in his stainless hands, relieving themselves of the burden which he so absently and innocently accepted. He could not protect them from her, did they not know that? Nor they him, when he was crucified for their sins, or Miss Lucy's.

Arabella was so angry that she got up and left the room, murmuring an excuse to which the young women vaguely assented, concentrated as they were now on Bob White. After the momentary pause while they sighed their relief and sloughed off Miss Lucy, they had plunged into a repetition of the pretty patter about the parish house dances. Even Hope was animated, and animated, was pretty. Unthinkingly and cheerfully he gave his immediate consent.

When they had gone, she came in on high, clicking heels to find him scattering ashes in her living room, which seemed no longer cool.

She herded him, scolding him, into the study across the hall and then she attacked him, arms akimbo, unable to understand after thirty years of being his wife that it was still and always useless. "You should not go every day to see Miss Lucy Cranborne," she said, "you should not."

"She's a lonely lady," said Bob White, waving his pipe, his homely, bulldog face contented as he loosened the belt that bound his billiken belly. "Her mother died just before we came, you know."

"Oh Lord," said Arabella. "Bob White! She poisoned her mother."

"Arabella," said Bob White in the semi-stern tone he used very rarely, "you should not say things like that, dear."

Arabella glared at him and sighed an expiring sigh. "You are the only person in all Andalusia who doesn't know it," she said tartly.

"Would you like to come with me?" he asked equably. "She seems to like company. Her sister died, too, you know. She was an invalid."

"I don't think she killed her sister," said Arabella. "No. I don't want to come with you."

She might go out of curiosity, which in this case was a lewd reason. He went out of his ridiculous innocence, his sublime and bottomless motivelessness, his blundering and unconscious response to human need, his complete himselfness. Let him go, then. If he was misunderstood, it would not be the first time. Clever as she was, aware of it as she was, wary as she was, she could seldom avoid trouble. He was often in trouble and out of it again without ever knowing it at all.

"Do you go on principle?" she asked him hopefully, even after thirty years. This she must condone. This she would fight for, her head provocatively high. "She must need a priest, even a confessor, I should think."

"No," he said, tamping his pipe. "I just go."

"Little Lamb, who made thee?" she quoted fiercely, clenching her fists. For such gestures was Christ crucified, in the small towns of Israel, in Galilee and Jerusalem. But He was crucified on purpose. If they said of Bob White that he offered the stainless mantle of purity to an unpunished murderess, he would not even know what they were saying.

"What, dear?" he said, picking up but politely refraining from opening a copy of Science Stories, which he liked to read for a little while before lunch. "Have you any more of that orange juice? It tasted mighty good."

"All right," she said, and turned her back on him.

When she came back with a glass of orange juice for him, she said forcibly, "What's the unforgivable sin?"

He looked up and blinked at her. "Nonrepentance," he said obediently.

"Of course!" After thirty years, she was still trying to provoke him. "Don't forget even you can't forgive the unforgivable, Bob White."

"I wasn't trying," he said, mildly humorous, his sweet, round mouth tucking a smile around the stem of his pipe. "I'm not supposed to forgive anybody, Arabella. I only tell 'em God will. You exaggerate my function."

This place, this Andalusia, she wanted to tell him, is a dangerous place. It's a violent place. It's an implacable place. It's an unpredictable place. I want to stay here, in this place, discovering at last what I am. We have lived too long among strangers, Bob White. I want to lay my bones among my kind, and eat round, brown, juicy, ripe scuppernongs off the vine. Scuppernongs won't travel. You have to stay where they ripen on the vine.

She wanted to bargain with him. I will be The Rector's Wife, she wanted to offer him. I will be it from Easter to Whitsun to Christmas to Good Friday, through Advent and Epiphany and Lent. I will. That will make it easy for you, and not put such a burden on your goodness, which is too pure. I will do that, if you will be careful. I want to stay here, because I think I can find myself here. But you could not bargain with him.

"Let's stay here," she urged.

"Fine," he said. "I like it here. It's a happy town."

It is not a happy town, she wanted to say. It is just a town where people amuse themselves ably. Perhaps the best way to deal with him when he walked in danger was to ignore him. He strayed casually among the poisoned tongues of the world, unconscious of death-dealing gossip, undisturbed by the lightning flashes of misunderstanding that sometimes falsely lighted his motives. So he ambled among these dangers and, more often than not, out again, untouched. She must eat her scuppernongs greedily and seek herself hard, until he was made invulnerable by time. The mantle of habit would shroud his goodness and make it bearable because it would be taken for granted and therefore dimmed. If he became the town's own, they would never disown him. They would not disown their own, neither good man nor murderess.

She had better take up gardening, which was safe. She was too bored to remain a housewife, and if she became too interested in those four girls she would become a meddler and not all of his innocence could save him. She would get a cook and she would garden. Poppies, she thought, all colors, and with petals like thin, thin paper. They would grow in this substandard soil. She would ask Bob White to ask Miss Lucy to recommend a cook who would soothe her spirit and feed her body. Miss Lucy would know best about Negroes. She knew who she herself was, did Miss Lucy. You had to know who you were in order to murder your mother. You had to be very, very sure.

In a moment of silence, during which she forgot Bill Bloodgood sitting in the chair beside her on the Madison's front porch, it occurred to Angela Madison that Miss Lucy's life had gained nothing from murder, not even money. If you had anything to gain by it, you could not do it, she thought, obscurely relieved. You could do it for pity, of course, but Mrs. Cranborne had been aggressively well. It was the sister who had suffered, lingered, and then died. Nobody had ever suggested that Miss Lucy killed her sister.

You certainly could not kill your mother in order to marry the man you loved, Angela thought before she stopped herself. Not that she, Angela Madison, had ever wanted to kill her own mother, she hastily amended her thoughts. Of course not, she assured herself. At least, she thought further, with the slow fairness that kept her most extravagant or her primmest thinking from ultimately deceiving her, not quite. At least, she thought, relaxing further into the prickling relief of honesty, not very often.

Having admitted to them, Angela tried to retrace her matricidal moments. They were curiously irrational. The night her mother had so arbitrarily dismissed her defensive announcement that she was in love with, in fact engaged to, Bill Bloodgood, Angela had felt merely testy. Her mother's attitude was not only predictable, it had been predictable since before Angela was born—before her mother was born, when her mother's uncle, Ed Miller, had opened a saloon: before Bill was born, when his grandfather had the first of the drinks in Ed Miller's saloon, the first of a total that sent him ultimately to his grave, drunk and crazy. Everybody was disgraced and they had no intention of mingling disgraces. The saloonkeeper's niece could never condone the drunkard's grandson—such was the retaliatory snobbishness that sought to protect itself from snubs. Nobody ever forgave anybody for anything, thought Angela, until they were well revenged. It was provoking to be the revenged upon, but it did not provoke to murder. Her mother's further and continued attitude that Bill was a wayward young man, anyway, with an unstable reputation and too much charm, was merely conventional. So much for that. But the day Bill had lost his job again, the one with the Oglethorpe Lumber Company, she had wanted to kill her mother. And the night Bill had been out with Ellen Terra . . .

She turned hastily toward Bill and said, "Why do you suppose she did it?"

"Why do I suppose who did what?" asked Bill, who had dropped Miss Lucy from his thoughts after the mention of her name that preceded the silence between them. His mind was solely preoccupied these days with his new job and with the man who was his boss. There was a shade of irritation in his voice that had seldom been absent from it when he spoke to Angela during the past several days. He emphasized his irritation by keeping his profile turned to her.

Angela sighed. The attained rhythm of their long, unannounced engagement was broken. The slow harmony of their latter days, which had included even their moments of anger, was gone. They were braced away from each other, waiting for either marriage or disaster. Meantime they must talk about something, preferably something besides Schuyler VanDyck Ball who was going to make Oakland into the smartest resort in the South, who was the man who held their future in the hollow of his curiously curling, small hands.

"Why Miss Lucy did away with her maw," she said disconsolately, feeling their disharmony in her tightening solar plexus.

Bill took out a cigarette and made a business of lighting it. In the flare of the lighter she had given him, Angela watched the skin pucker and tighten along his jaw as he sucked in his breath to draw smoke into his lungs. The cleft in his chin had deepened lately, she thought, and he was very nearly unbearably beautiful.

"*Darling,*" said Angela, leaning toward him, seeing his profile as if it were in the light that had flared and subsided. She felt infinitely more tender toward him, now that she had no more fear of losing him. Lose him she might very well, still and always. But the gnawing fear of it had gone at last when she realized that she had nothing more with which to keep him. He had demanded from her in the arrogance of his maleness, coaxed from her with the charm of his lordly appreciation of her, supplicated from her, all

163

unknowingly, in support of his wild, shaky pride, and received from her, finally, all that she had to give.

Each time he had drawn from her a deeper loving, she had realized with surprise how much she had withheld from him, reserving this for herself, or that for her friends, or something for her family. Now, to lose him would be like death.

"Darling," she repeated, helpless and tender.

He responded a little to her now, but unable to match her in tenderness, he reached over and patted her cheek with two fingers.

"Ugly old lady," he said.

"Me?" asked Angela, unfailingly seeking from him the one gallant lie he consistently refused to tell her.

"You, too," said Bill, "long-puss."

Long in the jaw and the nose, and he would never tell her she was pretty, although she knew that she still often gave the illusion of being pretty, when her hair was brightly brushed and her skin was almost as brown as her eyes.

"Mrs. Cranborne," said Bill, suddenly yielding to her diversion and concentrating his imaginative and often malicious memory on this woman whom he had met not more than twice, "was one of the most re-mark-ably homely old ladies . . ."

"Wasn't she?" said Angela too eagerly, unable to stop herself from interrupting him midsentence, scolding herself as she did so for the nervousness of her tongue. It was all right when they were babbling together, as they so often were, with shared thoughts and sure foreknowledge of what the other one would say, or repeating an old conversation for the pleasure of its repetition, playing a kind of conversational hopscotch on clearly chalked squares . . .

Bill hitched one shoulder in resentment, but acknowledged the interruption only by repeating his last three words. ". . . homely old ladies that ever stayed alive so long. She had wens, Angela. *Do you remember her wens?*"

She half shook and half nodded her head. Surely this job was *the* job and luck was with them. Let them look away from S. V. Ball, who meant their foreseeable future. Let them turn with relief to the contemplation of murder.

"Those wens," he said absorbedly, "had a life of their own. They lived on that ugly pan of hers and leered at people. They had eyes and mustaches, those wens, and there was one on the back of her neck to look at you from behind. Just imagine that poor Miss Lucy, living with those wens!"

Angela shuddered, remembering for the first time the dead woman's face, with a large brown mole on the right cheek and one on her chin, and undoubtedly one on the back of her neck.

"Miss Lucy didn't kill her mother," said Bill judiciously. "She murdered those four wens."

"Four?" said Angela. "That makes everything all right, of course."

"Of course," said Bill. "But naturally. One murder is rude and personal, but four is merely slaughter."

She felt his withdrawal in the sensitive nerves of her solar plexus.

"What?" she asked cautiously, reaching for him.

"What do you really think of him?" asked Bill. "Really, I mean."

"Oh," she said, and paused. She curbed her impulse to answer angrily that Van Ball was a two-bit Yankee with a million bucks who was incomparably lucky since William Shy Bloodgood had consented to work for him. "Why, he wants to be nice," she said. "I reckon he is nice, really."

"Possibly," said Bill. "I wish he wouldn't keep saying 'I have to trust the men who work for me' and then looking around the corner. Damn it, what did he make me his manager for, if he doesn't trust me? That's not something you talk about. You either trust a man or you don't."

"It's a funny thing. They don't trust anybody, really," offered Angela vaguely, meaning the rich who came down to Oakland from the North, as well as this very rich one who had bought The Oaks. "Still, they must know a bargain when they get one. How can you get rich if you don't know that much?"

"He didn't get rich," said Bill. "He just got born. Sure, I'm a bargain. Why not? This is the job I want. We'll never be rich."

"I don't care about that," said Angela. Only just rich enough to cut the umbilical purse strings. Only just rich enough to buy off the obdurate disapproval of their mothers. Then she could murder her mother if she wished. She would have nothing more to gain. Still . . . She frowned. Perhaps Bill had been too easy, too eager. Maybe a man like Van could not value anything he paid too little for. He was already inclined to take credit to himself for Bill's idea of the hunting lodge in the swamp, for the Hunt Club Room and the paneled gun room that Bill had so enthusiastically planned. "Maybe you should ask for a raise."

"Don't rush me," said Bill. "I'm having fun."

Bill was a natural-born host, thought Angela. He could make each guest who came to The Oaks feel that the birds flew and the ducks swam and the gun barrels glistened in his particular honor. S. V. Ball must understand that much about his new manager.

"You should hear him," said Bill, laughing suddenly. "He talks about that fancy firm of lawyers he's got in New York like my grandmother used to talk about niggers. He talks like he thinks they 'tote' with his money. He calls them 'my trustees' just like my grandmother said 'my niggers.' Wonder how those guys like that, from a kid."

"He's just spoiled," said Angela.

"He says he's got to go back to New York and keep an eye on them. Then your ever loving William will be the boss man and we'll get that funny, little fat minister of yours to marry us."

"He will, too," said Angela. She was moved to devotion by Bob White as she had only twice been moved by men, once by Mark and forever by Bill. Her feeling for Bob White was different. It was simple and joyful. He was alive and so she was less fearful of everything. He was her luck. With him had come luck: Van Ball and *the* job, the job that would enable Bill proudly to demand her hand in marriage, brooking no tenacious refusal. She was stronger, with Bob White in town, as she was stronger in the sunshine, when the weather was hot. He looked at her and took her for granted, took her love for Bill for granted. Like her feeling for the other two men she had loved, her love for Bob White was unqualified. "He's a candy lamb," she said. He's good luck, she thought. You needed luck, whatever else you had.

Bill regarded her quizzically and winked at her, in a sort of conspiratorial agreement. He went on, "We'll move to Oakland, Missus Bloodgood, dear, and buy a long, red bloodhound and train him to bite your mother and mine if they ever come near the place."

Angela regarded him joyfully.

"My," said Angela, "what a beautiful plan."

"In the meantime, 'my' Mr. Ball is a damned early riser and tomorrow is my early day at The Oaks." He leaned back and blew a gray, shadowy smoke ring, which curled out over the railing into the smoky black shadows of the night. "Oh, he's a nice enough little bastard." He heaved himself out of the chair with a sudden movement and took a restless step or two.

Angela moved her hands languidly, gathering into them her purse and the cigarettes from the table beside her. She was about to pick up the two glasses from which they had been drinking when Bill stopped her with his hand.

"If anything happens to *this* job . . ." he said gaily.

Angela got up and stood close to him, facing him.

"It won't," she said.

"Please ma'am find out what Miss Lucy used before I see your mother again? Huh? You'd do just that one little thing?"

"Sure," said Angela. "Any little thing for you, honey."

"Then we can live in ever loving peace with your sweet pappy and sleep forever in a double bed." His half-seen face in the night, so near hers, was grinning.

"Lovely," said Angela fervently. "Lovely."

He tipped up her chin with one finger and kissed her, rolling his mouth lightly across hers with a movement that came from his whole body. His hand slipped down her throat and she thought for a moment that he was going to ask her to come with him, for an hour, into the night. She responded to him with the familiar, so easily aroused now, sensations of desire and of fear. She wanted him, almost always she wanted him, for the quick satisfaction that came now to her bony, lively, affectionate body, even more for the deeper satisfaction of satisfying his slumberous, restless, demanding vitality. And she was terrified.

The ragged flag of their mutual pride flew high because the town did not know. For all it knew about them, for everything it knew about them, for all its prying eyes and animal ears, this it did not know.

One person knew, Angela reminded herself, harsh with herself. Logan would never betray her, but he knew. He had to know because he alone knew that she had nothing to lose. She wished, diverted from fear, that she might have been simple and strong and patient, when Mark Barbee had left her heart empty. Instead, she had sought to escape the austerity of her emotionlessness by seeking to fulfill her old love for Logan Knight. The town had insisted so that she and he were "made for each other"! People nodded at them and beamed. . . . She had yielded to him finally in the hope that the very act, toward which she felt both awe and half-innocent, half-knowledgeable curiosity, would fill the stellar space between the fine words they said to each other and the graceless little sexual thrills she felt when he kissed or petted her. But the act had been as incomplete as all the rest of it. She had felt, she thought, the more purely virgin when she came to Bill than if she had been still virgin.

Angela still wore an aura of thin, nervous, frequently, ill-tempered virginity, more convincing than many a virgin's. Bill was quaint and cavalier enough, for all his lusty vigor, to have insisted upon taking his bride virgin to bed, seeking his necessary pleasures meantime in a gentleman's gutter. The town did not know. Perhaps it would have been better, thought Angela fleetingly, feeling her fear. There was degradation in furtiveness, even in the service of pride. Fear canceled out desire, sometimes, so that she looked at him, as now, with almost empty eyes. Still, it would not have been better. She nuzzled her chin into his hand.

He took his hand away. "I'd make a pass at you, honey," he said coolly, "if I weren't too damn tired to lift the back seat out of the car."

"Never mind," she said edgily, unable to reconcile her relief and her disappointment.

"Just a little arsenic for your mother," said Bill, "if anything happens this time."

"It won't," said Angela. Luck was with them now. Bob White had brought them luck.

"Good night, baby," said Bill.

"Good night."

They hesitated, standing close to each other. Bill reached over and squeezed her arm and she patted his hand with her free hand.

"It's a promise."

Angela nodded.

He walked down the steps and along the walk past the camellia bush, walking with the light, tiptoeing tread which belied the powerful body. He turned, silhouetted against the pale light shed by the street lamp on the corner, and raised his arm. Climbing into the car, he raced the engine he tended with such exquisite care and drove off into the night, the quick, noisy acceleration a mark of his driving.

You can't, darling, she thought, not if you have anything to gain by it. Miss Lucy could not have done it if she had had anything to gain.

"Sho I know *why* she done it," said Georgianna Church to her daughter, Mercy. "Ain't I raised an bred in dat house?"

"Well, I don't," said Mercy. "Miss Lucy, she so gentle-like."

"It's duh wild-tempuhed an duh mild-tempuhed dat does tings, Mercy. It's duh onreasonable and duh *tow* reasonable. It's duh quick-sufferin an duh long-sufferin. Tain't duh everyday us like." Georgianna's ancient skin moved along the sharply visible bones of her face to create a smile.

"I still dunno howcome Miss Lucy . . ." said Mercy, her calm, high, brown brow puckered above her soft, brown, inquiring eyes.

"If yuh wants tuh know all ah knows, you is gotta live uh lot mo yeahs, Mercy, daughter." Georgianna's one vanity was her age, to which she added two years every birthday. Her wisdom was her humblest pride.

"Yessum," said Mercy, looking at her mother with slow, temperate affection.

"Ah tells yuh, cause you is muh honey lamb baby," said Georgianna, "an cause you has uh understandin heart. Den ah gots somepn ah wants yuh tuh do."

"Yessum," said Mercy.

Georgianna leaned back in the overstuffed chair that had once sat in Mr. Madison's office at the Miller and Rook Pecan Company, where she had worked now for twenty-five years. She closed her eyes and in a moment she started to pat her knees, stopped, and in another moment began to speak.

"Ever *time* Miss Lucy she went into uh room . . ." The left hand pat-patted Miss Lucy tripping into a room. ". . . ol Mizzuz Cranbohn she went in too." The right hand slapped the bony knee with the heavy tread of a heavy woman. Both hands stopped. "Ever time," said Georgianna. She paused.

"Ever *time* Miss Lucy say uh livin word . . ." The left hand tapped. ". . . ol Mizzuz Cranbohn she say three . . . puh puh puh . . . and den ten mo. Ever time." She paused.

"Ever *time* Miss Lucy git uh leas lil lettah fum uh *ol* frien . . ." Georgianna swayed lightly and her two hands patted a complicated rhythm on her thin, wide-held knees, the left hand light as if it were handling biscuit dough, the right hand heavy as a hammer. ". . . ol Mizzuz Cranbohn she read it, she read it now, she read it right ovah Miss Lucy shoulduh, she read it. Ever time."

The rhythmic patting gradually stopped and there was silence in the small, crowded room where the three black women lived when the third, the troublemaker, Amanda, was at home. Mercy was breathing deeply, one long breath to her mother's even two. The voice began again, perceptibly higher.

"When Miss Lucy wuz uh little gul, she go an climb duh apple tree. Mizzuz Cranbohn she cain't climb no apple tree!"

Mercy laughed and her mother opened her eyes. Mercy Church could follow her mother just so far and then her practical humor got the best of her. Georgianna huffily clasped her hands and said complainingly, "How kin ah tells yuh nothin when you is jus uh gigglin gul? Well, anyway, Miss Lucy she grew up and she had uh hundred an fifty beaus. An Gawd knows how many wanted tuh marry huh, but she didn't want tuh marry no man an share huh bed wid um. She got so she didn't want nuthin but tuh be lef alone and dey lef huh alone af-while, all except huh maw. An one day she fix it so she be lef all alone. Dat's all. Dat's all ah gonna tell yuh anyway."

"Whut you say to her, Mama?" asked Mercy with practical inquisitiveness.

"Nothin," said Georgianna, lying. "Nothin at all."

"Whut yuh say tuh huh, Mama?" asked Mercy, coaxing.

"She say she wunt yuh should go an cook fuh duh Revrund White an Mizzuz White," said Georgianna flatly.

"Me?" said Mercy, astonished.

"Yeh, you. An yuh got tuh go. Cause you kin comfort em wid vittles when duh trouble comes. Somebody got tuh suffuh. Somebody. Cause Miss Lucy she won't."

"Whut yuh say tuh huh, Mama?" asked Mercy, coaxing.

"Ah say 'Miss Lucy, Miss Lucy, yuh gotta be sorry.' An she doan say nuthin. An ah say 'Miss Lucy, Miss Lucy, yuh got tuh *try* tuh be sorry.' Miss Lucy she laugh and she say 'Georgianna, when I burn in hell you gonna come down from heaven all the way to bring me some cool lemonade? You gonna bring me some juicy scuppernongs offen yo vine? Yuh gonna do that, Georgianna?' An ah says, 'Sho Miss Lucy, ah do dat. Yuh knows ah do dat.'"

12.   **The Affianced**

"And this is our dear friend, Angela Madison," said Mrs. Bloodgood, grasping Angela's elbow with her muscular hand and pulling
her forward to meet the twins, who had been invited to come in,
after dinner, for coffee.

And this, thought Angela, is progress. Last year she would
have said "my son's friend." Last year she would not have invited
the twins at all if Angela was there.

"Yes, Cousin Alicia," murmured the twins. "Howdedo, Miss
Madison."

Thus introduced, Angela spoke becomingly to the elderly
women who were second cousins of Bill's. The twins, withdrawing
their rag-doll hands one after the other from the light pressure of
her handclasp, regarded her in an open ecstasy of curiosity. Their
four identical eyes bulged and their two identical mouths worked
a little in unison.

"And now," said Mrs. Bloodgood, her hand tightening on
Angela's elbow, "I am going to ask you to pour the coffee."

She guided Angela across the room, pushing her slightly
ahead, twisting and turning her minutely, as if Angela could not

otherwise find her way among the scattered, dangerous rugs, the myriad chairs, the fragile-legged tables loaded with accumulated whatnots and hand-me-downs that must never be permitted to exercise their natural perishability. The course set for her was diagonally across the perfectly square surface of the floor. There was a fractional pause as she was guided past the rigid, hugely high-backed chair, covered in faded but still ravishing pink velour, which was almost, but not quite, incongruously frivolous. It was Mrs. Bloodgood's chair, centered obliquely so as to command, but graciously, the room. Bob White looked up at them, twinkling in its rosy glow, a sublime pink Buddha, benignly unaware of the failings of his human companions, equally unimpressed with their virtues or their pretensions. He was also unaware that Mrs. Bloodgood wanted her chair, which he had appropriated after dinner and to which he had immediately returned after his introduction to the twins. He had been equally unaware of Arabella's attempt to deflect him. From a round-bottomed, round-backed straight chair by his side, Arabella frowned into the fractional pause and then smiled directly and conspiratorially at Angela. Bill looked from across the room and dropped Angela a slow, triumphant wink.

The handle of the heavy silver pot was so hot that Angela very nearly dropped it with a small screech of pain. She saw Mrs. Bloodgood's eyes narrow and she grasped it again, firmly, and poured the steaming coffee neatly into one of the thin, elegant cups. Trial by fire, she thought submissively, remembering her early feeling against the tyranny of things. All her life, she thought, astonished, she had refused to cherish anything except the small and battered, which could be tucked under the arm or left behind in case of flight. Admiring its beauty, she had promptly rejected this coffee pot as a possession, a trouble, a tie, a trap. It was odd that, so carefully unencumbered and poised for flight, she had never come near to fleeing.

Mr. White said, "Now what is pleasanter than good coffee served by a pretty girl?" and Angela rewarded him with her love.

"William is working so hard he rarely has much time for his poor old mother these days," said Mrs. Bloodgood to the twins. "It isn't as if Andalusia were very far."

173

"Not the way he drives, it isn't," said Arabella. Mrs. Bloodgood ignored her.

"I really do not complain," said Mrs. Bloodgood, settling her thin buttocks with an air of resignation on the sober secondary cushion to which Bob White had so innocently and insolently relegated her. "Besides, Mr. Ball has taken the trouble several times to tell me that he is entirely dependent on William. He simply cannot get on without William." She put down her coffee cup and patted her wig. Typhoid had left her without hair or teeth so many years before that she was no longer conscious of the left-handed gesture with which she reassured herself that the thick, black false hair, cut and curled to reach below her ears and banged over her forehead, was there, of the right-handed gesture with which she habitually covered her full-lipped mouth when she talked, hiding the lumpy china teeth. "Is he an Episcopalian, Mr. White?"

"Who? Mr. Ball? Yes, indeed," said Bob White. "The regular old-fashioned kind you don't often meet among young men these days."

"Dollar in the plate man," murmured Arabella White, so that only Angela heard her.

"Ah," said Mrs. Bloodgood. "One can always tell. General Bloodgood used to say . . ."

There was never any response sufficient unto the former remarks of the worthy dead. Even the twins knew this, and, acknowledging themselves inadequate, they opened paper fans and began industriously waving them in front of their long, ludicrous faces. Bill suppressed a yawn and recrossed his legs. Angela felt her eyes cross slightly in the effort she made to look respectfully attentive. Arabella White pushed a finger up behind her ear and into her rough upgrowing red and gray hair.

Into the pause that Mrs. Bloodgood reverently employed to bracket a quotation from the late General Bloodgood, Bob White, wiping his sweating face and bald head with vigor, said reminiscently, "That was the best steak!"

Mrs. Bloodgood said, with reproof and vexation in her voice, as well as responsive pride, "I was raised to know meat, Mr. White. I always select my own. That's one of the things I believe one should do oneself. The General . . ."

"I could tell that, ma'am," said Mr. White. "We lived in Texas a long time, you know, and I say it takes a cowboy or a southern lady to choose a steak."

The twins said "teeee" on a shrill, rising note, then turned to the arms of the sofa on which they sat and began to trace the carving with scurrying, pointed nails.

Bill said, "If you're good, Mr. White will let you come to his church."

"Oh," said the twins, and folded their hands in their laps, folding and clutching the fans as they did so. "Will you take us, William? Will you?"

"Of course he will," said Mrs. Bloodgood.

"That will be *lovely*," said Arabella, and then grinned at Angela.

Bill stood up and stretched, emphasizing the height of the room, its upward oblongness. His white jacket was patched with sweat across the shoulders and as he stretched it clung damply, dragging at his soaked white shirt. This house had been built soundly against the heat, thought Angela. For summers on end, for the three earlier summers when she had been its occasional and unwelcome guest, this house alone had been impervious and impenetrable to the heat. This drawing room had been cool as chilled cucumbers, under its shadowy ceiling, within its thick walls, while people sweltered in lesser houses like her own, while the street outside steamed even at night, its asphalt soft as gumbo mud. This summer the prolonged and record-shattering heat had finally seeped into this room, like silt, filling it slowly and solidly, and now, in September, the room still held the heat against the cooler air of the September evening. Angela gasped lightly in the thick air.

Arabella White looked at her watch and visibly prepared an astonished exclamation at the time. Angela turned to Mrs. Bloodgood, placatingly, turning away from Mrs. White.

Bill said, "How about a brandy, Mother? One for the road, before we start home?"

"Home is here, William," said Mrs. Bloodgood.

"Sure, but I'm a working man these days."

The twins said "teeee," a falling scale of appalling sound. The sound had the ugly, half-innocence of female puberty, the impersonal malice of twin sibyls prophesying the horrid and inevitable. Mrs. Bloodgood frowned at them and they quickly drew down their long faces, hiding them behind the paper fans.

"If Mr. White approves of liqueurs," said Mrs. Bloodgood, turning almost archly to the clergyman.

"I love brandy," said Bob White.

Arabella White said, "Oh, *apricot* brandy," with an infinitesimal trace of disparagement in her voice, when the bottle was offered to her. The twins moaned softly and dribbled with pleasure as they were each handed a glass. Bill touched Angela's fingers as he poured her glass. Angela was very glad she had made no alliance with Arabella when alliance had been offered her. Contented, she sat back and cuddled her glass between sips. She was almost a Bloodgood and she owed them her almost loyalty, twins and all.

"Delicious!" said Bob White, tasting his brandy at once.

"It comes from my grandmother's cellar," said Mrs. Bloodgood.

"Very superior home brew," said Arabella White, sipping daintily.

At a cue from Mrs. Bloodgood, the twins obediently got up in tremulous haste and started backing around the sofa, pushing aside the heavy red portieres at the window behind the sofa. Bill caught them and guided them back into the room, warning them gently to say good night. His manner was wry and gentle and in no way apologetic, even when they bowed nervously to the motionless grandfather clock in the corner whose hands were set at some long past eight-twenty, in a permanent expression of disapprobation of any later hour. The twins might have been shy, awkward children, the way he handled them, thought Angela lovingly, as she rose in deference to their age.

The twins caught sight of Mr. White, then, and pushing in front of him, regarded him urgently.

"He'll let you come," said Bill.

Bob White was on his feet, smiling at them and nodding.

"Certainly," said Arabella. The twins regarded her with alarm, and backed away.

To Angela they said, "It's-so-nice-to-meet-you-at-last-Miss-Madison," and then rustled docilely out the tall door, their bony skeletons, inside the dark draperies with which they were covered, noisy but quite controlled.

Angela stood beside Mrs. Bloodgood to say good-bye to the Whites. She felt grateful to them for being there this evening, which was a milestone in the long, painful retreat Mrs. General Bloodgood had made from her prepared position that her William must not, should not, marry Angela Madison, Hannah Miller's daughter. She was grateful to Bob White for his accepting the evening without giving it significance, and to Arabella for offering her an alliance which she had refused.

Tall and tense, Mrs. Bloodgood turned away from the party thus ended and toward her son, including, however unwillingly, the woman her son had remained so determined to marry.

"Come in for a minute, children," said Mrs. Bloodgood. "You know I am unable to sleep before midnight."

They followed her back into the house and sat on either side of her when she seated herself in her faded but impressive chair, which disposed her height in dignity and cast a rosy glow that softened her terrible face. She put one hand on Angela's wrist as if to quiet her until she was ready for her, and turned to Bill.

"Now tell me," she said to Bill, "everything you have been up to."

This was the weekly payment Mrs. Bloodgood exacted for taking care of her bachelor son in the so hardly maintained, still exquisite luxury to which he had been accustomed since birth. How she did it, now that the money was so certainly inadequate, Angela did not know. She wondered if there were naked rooms upstairs, closed and locked on the absence of their treasures, which had been sold. She wondered if Mrs. Bloodgood got down on her own papershell kneecaps and stretched the long bones of her body over the gleaming polish of the living-room floor. How else was this polish attained? There was no patent polish, produced by science, that would make such a mirror of that floor and such jewels of the ancient tables. Surely the dying Negro woman in the kitchen, with the eyes that had died already, would not be able to do more than sit by the gaunt kitchen stove and cook and cook and cook the dishes that nightly covered the varying length of the exquisite dining room table. (The two kinds of potatoes and two kinds of rice, the amazing choice of vegetables, the fowl and the meat . . .) Somehow, tall, fragile, yet immeasurably strong, Mrs. Bloodgood must do this herself. For Bill was expected only to accept it as his due, and to relate to his mother the life he led apart from her—while she never questioned him to discover whether or not he lied, which he often did, nor berated him for any escapade, nor failed to blame fortune and not himself for failure or disaster. She was capable of using anything he told her obliquely against him later, but the time of telling was a time of truce. They both enjoyed it. Bill felt it incumbent upon him to amuse his mother, as part of the fair price, and she was an irresistible audience when she chose to be. Angela had listened several times, admiring his talent for narration and the subtle distortion of facts with which he mirrored his life for his mother. Tonight the distortions, magnified by his mother's further distortions in accepting them, distressed her unreasonably. Lying seemed to her a clean and decent thing compared with this corroding of the truth.

Angela tried to slip her wrist from Mrs. Bloodgood's touch, but the relaxed hand instantly tightened. Gently she insisted, and immediately Mrs. Bloodgood let go. Angela lit a cigarette and leaned back, ceasing to listen to Bill, content with the knowledge that she could bargain with Bill's mother. She knew at last in this moment that her future mother-in-law's implacable opposition to herself as a daughter-in-law had nothing whatever to do with herself. It was not because she was Hannah Miller's daughter and because Hannah Miller's daughter was not worthy to marry Alicia Shy's son. Alicia Shy was not ashamed because her father had died disreputably drunk in Ed Miller's saloon, as Hannah Miller was ashamed because her uncle had owned the respectable saloon. Gentlemen died drunk. Gentlemen also married beneath them, and this was forgiven and permitted them. Angela had never thought of this, defensive of her mother's deep, hidden shame and resentful of the shaky pattern that called itself aristocracy in Andalusia. Alicia Bloodgood, nee Shy, would snub forever Hannah Miller, nonetheless accepting Hannah Miller's daughter, who was also, thank goodness, Cecil Lord Madison's daughter. This was not the reason for Bill's mother's painful opposition. It was only that Mrs. Bloodgood could accept with pleasure no woman whom her son would take to

wife. Not even Missy Maidenstone. Especially not Missy Maidenstone, who had a high-handed will of her own and no humility. Mrs.
Bloodgood must be grateful, at least, for Angela's humility. She did
not possess her son, she only clung to him, perhaps pitifully, but,
be it said for her, scorning pity. Angela had looked at Bill's mother
during dinner, sitting at the head of her elaborate board, unbeauti-
fied by the flattering light from the tall, silver-supported candles,
holding her hand over her ruined mouth, saying at times a gracious
thing, and had known this much. Now she was immediately so
certain of the rest that she could not understand why she had not
known it earlier. The knowledge both released and defeated her.
In place of the warm, almost craven desire to be liked, to be forgiven, to be loved, by this formidable and frequently charming
widow who was mother to her man, Angela was at last able to
arrive at terms with her. Marry Bill she would. Relinquishing all
demands for affection, she would bargain with Bill's mother for
peace. If she could not bear to live in disharmony with any part
of her life, she could manage to live in false harmony.

"And what do you think of your new rector, Angela?" asked
Mrs. Bloodgood, turning to Angela and demanding her attention.

"I love him!" said Angela fervently, with the unprotected
natural candor that could always be surprised out of her by an unexpected question when she was thinking of something else.

"Oh!" said Mrs. Bloodgood, raising her eyebrows. "Dear me.
Such fervor. I must say I don't find him very lovable. What do you
love about him? His table manners? His *face?*" She laughed.

To Angela's surprise, ire rose within her and a brief violence
of anger blinded, deafened, and shook her. She would bargain away
no part of love or luck. "Because he's him!" she said furiously, un-
grammatically. She felt her lower lip swell and push out as it had
done when she was an angry child.

"Oh!" said Mrs. Bloodgood. "Well, I daresay I am just unduly prejudiced against people who spill gravy on my mother's tablecloth." She spoke with a lack of rancor that again took Angela by
surprise.

"He likes to eat," said Angela, still belligerent, thinking of
Bob White's careless gusto, which had indeed resulted in spots on

179

the heavy tablecloth and on his black vest and on the white linen lapels of his suit.

"It's always a pleasure to feed a man who likes to eat," said Mrs. Bloodgood, as if she had reflected and changed her mind.

"And," said Angela, liking her anger and insisting on complete defense of her love, "you can't think he is homely if you really look at him. There's nothing mean in his face. Nothing! Not the least little thing that wants to hurt anybody. He has a lovely face!"

"I can't go quite that far, my dear," said Mrs. Bloodgood, lifting her hands in humorous surrender, "but, come, I give you your Mr. White. I expect it was that wife of his who really annoyed me. I do hate to attack wives because I usually get on so much better with their husbands."

This was one of Mrs. Bloodgood's small vanities, and one that Angela did not begrudge her. She was more than willing to bargain away Mrs. White, who was visibly able to fight her own battles, in return for Mr. White, whom she loved.

"Mrs. White's cute," said Bill provocatively, with raised eyebrows, watching the two women. "She's almost a match for you, Mother."

Mrs. Bloodgood bridled. "I must admit that *Mr.* White is very well connected," she said, capitulating finally.

"Did you hear what Mrs. White said when you were prying into the reverend's ancestry?" asked Bill.

"I did," said Mrs. Bloodgood, straightening her long back rigidly.

Bill laughed and Angela suppressed a smile. Mrs. White had remarked in a carrying aside that *her* father was a Georgia Cracker preacher and her mother a Limey who ran a livery stable. She had not explained what Angela knew: that the Cracker preacher had been the Right Reverend William Eckford, D.D., Bishop of Georgia, and the Limey a British-born lady who had discreetly rented her horses in the summer in order to pay for keeping them brilliantly sleek for fall hunting.

"It may be witty," said Mrs. Bloodgood, "but I consider it tacky."

Angela understood well enough how far Mrs. Bloodgood had yielded in yielding her Bob White. She understood also, her anger receding, that Mrs. Bloodgood could not possibly like Mr. White, whom she could neither impress, intimidate, nor irritate. Mrs. Bloodgood was not used to anyone who treated her as the exact equal of other people. Angela, cheerful in her first bargain with her future mother-in-law, tossed her Arabella White whole, to appease and thank her. "I don't know why Bob White married her," she said deliberately. "Arabella is a bit of a bitch."

"Angela!" said Mrs. Bloodgood, pretending to shock, smiling at her in a very nearly friendly fashion.

"You know you agree!" said Angela daringly, almost intimate. From now on, she thought, it would be different. One part of their struggle was over. Once Bill had proved that he could support his wife, Mrs. Bloodgood would bestow on them the rigid formula of benediction. She would make her private reservations graciously and Angela would counter them with kindness because his mother had worn her paper-shell kneecaps to her bony knees for Bill. They would the saloon keeper's plump niece, could yield as graciously. Feeling bargain together for peace in Bill's house. If only her own mother, momentarily disloyal, she shied from thinking of her mother.

"Well . . ." said Mrs. Bloodgood, bridling, almost gaily, "there *are* words we never used in our day!" Then she added slowly, her voice grating a little, "I expect I shall be seeing the Whites again in the future, so I must practice my Christian charity."

The admission that her son's wedding might take place at St. James's made Angela's heart thump with passionate hope.

"Mr. White's services are so beautiful," Angela said, leaning forward, her eyes soft and beseeching.

"No doubt," said Mrs. Bloodgood, expressing doubt, but friendlily. "Of course, I think there's no one at all like dear Dean Withers at the Cathedral, but maybe you and your Mr. White will have more influence with William than the Dean and I have had. He is the most heathen sinner, isn't he?" She spoke of Bill, with a gesture in his direction, as if he were not there, inviting Angela, in the immemorial fashion of women who have declared a truce in their undying enmity, to disparage together the man they both love.

"I like him the way he is," said Angela, flatly, stubbornly.

In the momentary silence, the ancient dour silence of the grandfather clock was like death in a quiet room. The woman took the girl's final measure with exhausted eyes. She was losing her son and she was losing him whole. There was a look like the mourner of death in her eyes, and Angela, implacable, was full of pity.

"Let's have one more for the road," said Bill grinning impartially at them both. He wiped his forehead with a big linen handkerchief and moved impatiently.

"I think you should take this child home," said Mrs. Bloodgood austerely, with an inflection that reduced Angela in status from a female ally or opponent to a foolish and inconsequential virgin.

"Come on, child," said Bill. "Besides, I'm a responsible working man, remember, ladies, and I have to get up mornings."

"So you are," said Mrs. Bloodgood, conceding the point as if temporarily. "Well, you may bring Angela next Tuesday," she added, making it a queen's command.

"I'd love to come," said Angela warmly, submissively. "I'd truly love to come." Even if she were Miss Lucy, she would now let Bill's mother live. Bill's mother could stay in the world with herself and Bill and Bob White. She need murder only her own mother, under Bob White's benign, unseeing, and all-forgiving eyes. She pulled down the corners of her mouth in humorous refutation of her absurd and inexcusable thoughts, and then turned them up again in a smile at Bill's mother. The smile was reciprocated on the surface of the withered, half-destroyed face, over the badly constructed china teeth.

As they left, Mrs. Bloodgood hesitated and then bent stiffly from her inordinate height and pecked at Angela's cheek. Angela, surprised again, and this time into warmth, kissed her truly on the dry cheek that lay against hers. She pretended not to notice when Mrs. Bloodgood, with a gesture of repudiation, wiped off the lipstick she had thus left against the elderly and lightly rouged flesh. She reminded herself that she must never return the substance when she was only offered the form.

Bill drove back to Andalusia at a furious speed, heedless of the scrub kine that strayed at will on the open highway. One small cow emerging just in front of them, a shadow detaching itself with wayward swiftness from the shadow of a huge oak tree, caused Bill to brake and swerve so abruptly that Angela bruised her forehead against the windshield.

"Sorry," he said solicitously. "Want me to slow down?"

"It's up to you," said Angela shakily. "You're driving."

"God, I love you," said Bill, holding the headlong speed.

They did no other talking until they were established in a booth at their favorite roadside speakeasy, boldly half-hidden beside the road halfway between Oglethorpe and Andalusia. Touching glasses, they sipped experimentally and nodded simultaneously.

"Out of the proper bottle," said Bill with satisfaction.

"Good," said Angela. "Joe shows proper respect for you."

"That's almost real, old-fashioned bourbon, like Old Grand Dad used to make," he said enthusiastically. "Drink up, honey. I can do with several of these."

She lifted her glass, looking at him over the rim with brightening, brown eyes.

"I'm so damn happy," he said. "You don't mind?"

"Mind!" Her love for him was a flock of birds, rising within her on buoyant wings.

"My mother," he said in such a tone that Angela held her breath, wondering what he could be going to say, "is my mother and I admire and like her. She is also a cantankerous old bitch who thinks I hung up the moon, only I hung it up wrong. I'm wonderful and everything I do is wonderful, only it would be more wonderful if it were different. Now you, my angel Angela, when you love a man, you love him whole. When you said you loved that roly-poly, funny-looking clergyman because he was him—that's a reason. Furthermore, I admire your choice in men. Nice guys, both of us."

"So you are," said Angela softly, breathing lightly so that she would not disturb the look in his eyes staring at her as if he had not seen her for a long, long time. "So you are."

"Do you realize that you have never once, not once, in all this time, said to me, 'William, don't you think you've had enough?' What a woman! I'm the luckiest man alive. Joe, bring me a drink. To drink to my bride."

When the second drink arrived, he leaned back, took off his

tie, folded it neatly, put it into his shirt pocket, and rolled up his sleeves.

She did not speak, feeling that he had something to say.

"Despite my mother's shortcomings," he said formally, winking at her as he said it, "I am right pleased that she has finally got the sense to like you."

Oh, but she doesn't, Angela refrained from saying. She has only decided to get along with me because she stands to lose more of you if she doesn't. . . . She realized that men have little interest in the arrangements women make with each other, only caring for the effect of these arrangements on themselves.

"You've been so patient and so sweet, Angela."

Thank you for appreciating it, she thought. Only there wasn't anything else to be when his mother and hers were standing pat on such very firm grounds, with the whole ethics of a civilization behind them. He could marry her, all right, if and when he could support her in the style to which they had accustomed them. Then he could, anyway. But they had not put it that way. They had made it the test of his manhood.

"You've been patient, too," she said, "and sweet."

"Can you take the twins?" he asked merrily.

"Naturally," she said. "Why not?"

"Thank the Lord you're a southern gal," he said. "Everybody's got to have somebody crazy in the family."

"Mine was a great-aunt," said Angela. "Only she was really wacky. She's dead."

"Lucky you," he said. "Mine are only cousins and only mentally retarded, but it's the duplication. You remember that terribly pretty girl from Connecticut I got engaged to in Oakland in 1929?"

Angela nodded. She felt an unwarranted twinge of jealousy, not because he had been engaged before he became engaged to her, but because the girl had been so extraordinarily pretty.

"She nearly died when she met the twins. I took her around there myself when I got bored one night. I stirred them up a little, too. Then, I pretended I thought they were perfectly normal."

Angela shuddered. "Poor girl! Why didn't you ever take me there, Bill?"

"I didn't think they were funny any more. By the way, I suppose you know what mother's asking them to come tonight means?" He smiled jubilantly.

Angela knew. It was the seal of her acceptance. Marry the family, you marry it, overweening pride, crazy cousins, and all. "But why did she ask them when the Whites were there?" asked Angela. "I thought that was odd."

"Mother always lets the twins come when a clergyman is there. I think she thinks clergymen are partly responsible, as representatives of God, and that anyway they are good for the twins. Mother's rather gallant about the twins." He looked at her quizzically.

"She is," said Angela.

"You'll make a wonderful Bloodgood," he said. "My dear, dear love."

He was looking at her with a luminous expression of rediscovery that bemused her with joy.

"And you'll never get together with them to whittle me down. Not you! When you love a man, you love him whole. You don't pick at him, do you? If you stopped loving me whole, you'd stop altogether, wouldn't you? You won't stop, will you?"

"Yes," she said, bedazzled and adoring, radiant. "No."

"Oh God, I love you." He put his hand down on the table, palm up, and she put her hand into his. The communication of their bodies through their fingers made her dizzy. "Let's have another drink and get out of here. Listen, Angela!"

"What?" she said.

"There's that little hotel the other side of Marianna. I don't think anybody could possibly find out. Just this once. Call your family and tell them Mother has invited you for the night. They'll never check on you there. Will you? Will you?"

She nodded dizzily. She could refuse him nothing in the world he demanded of her.

While he negotiated at the bar for a bottle of whiskey, she put in a call for her house. As central impersonally repeated the Andalusia number, Angela felt a moment of panic. She was asking her mother to face, finally, her daughter's intimacy in the house of her mortal enemy. It was too sudden. It had taken her weeks to prepare her mother for her first dinner invitation to the Bloodgood house. Her right to dine there was long established. But this was different. She could only hope that her father would come to the telephone. But it was her mother's voice, thick and high with sleep, that answered the persistent ring. She could see her mother at the other end of the telephone, half asleep, her blonde-gray hair hanging in thick, untidy ropes down her thick, bare back, the deep lace V in her thin nightgown pulled wide by the heavy breasts.

"Mama . . ." said Angela cautiously. "Mama . . ."

"What's the matter, Angela?" asked her mother, alarmed. Her voice had the instinctive night's-middle protectiveness with which she had always risen to her children's nighttime demands—when they were sick, when they were dreaming unhappily.

Angela warmed with remembered affection and gratitude. "Darling," she said, "it's nothing. Bill's car won't start and it's too late to get it fixed or anything. Mrs. Bloodgood wants me to spend the night. So don't worry."

Her mother's sleepy, aggrieved protests were self-acknowledged as ineffectual.

"Well, what do you want me to do?" asked Angela, pressing the advantage gained by her double lie. "Go to a hotel, for heaven's sake?"

That settled that. "Of course not!" said Mrs. Madison, aroused. "I suppose you'll have to stay with her. Without even a toothbrush! Really, I think it's very, very careless of Bill to put you in such a position."

Angela held the receiver a little way from her ear and let her mother's protests diminish of their own futility. She could scarcely forbid her daughter to spend the night under the Widow Bloodgood's roof, under such circumstances. She could only bitterly resent the necessity, adding it to the other resentments she had felt since the first time Bill Bloodgood had turned up at the house, Angela's suitor.

In a final flurry of frustration, affection and annoyance, Mrs. Madison said in a mild wail, "Well, be careful, then!"

"Careful of *what*?" asked Angela, believing herself for the moment that she would actually spend the night in one of the peaceful, polished bedrooms upstairs in the Bloodgood house.

"Oh, ghosts or bedbugs!" said her mother, pettishly.

Angela suppressed a giggle, her humor restored. "Good night, darling," she said fondly and hung up.

Nevertheless, it would make her mother broody, if not angry. Angela would have to spend some time tomorrow soothing her mother's ruffled crankiness, restoring her mother to her usual placid good humor. She could do this. She could always handle her mother except when nightmare descended over their house, as it had only three times in her memory. Then her mother was mad. Not cross, but mad—inhuman and monstrous. This would not happen. Angela always believed that it could never happen again. It was too unbelievable, when her mother was like that, too unendurable. Tomorrow Angela would only have to spend a little time soothing her mother. She shrugged her shoulders, putting the future from her. She was free, through a little simple, not too painful lying, to spend the night with Bill. She was going to spend the whole night with her love.

On their way to Marianna, by a devious route, which included many miles of rough, dirt road, but which avoided both Oakland and Andalusia, their mood was one of light-minded hilarity. They chattered and gossipped and reminisced, more like old friends than lovers. They sang snatches of song, insisting on exactitude in the lyrics, since neither of them was accurate as to tune. Bill made puns at which Angela groaned and jokes at which she laughed disproportionately. They teased each other, calling each other "Horse Face" and "Pretty Boy." They drank occasional sips, straight from the bottle he had bought, but he did not get drunk, and she almost never did get drunk, having a fine-drawn sense of grace and having acquired, through occasional disaster, an exact knowledge of when to stop.

Only three times did they touch on anything that mattered to them, while beneath the casual gaiety of their behavior, the exciting tension of their bodies grew and grew.

Once she said, "Tell me, good-looking, did you ever sleep with Ellen Terra?"

The question came up like a hiccup, unwilling and unbecoming. They both moved slightly away from each other, equally annoyed. There was a point in her passion for him when her jealousy interrupted her. Before that, it was submerged. After that, it was gone. For that moment, it separated them.

She did not really care because he had made love to many women. She had expected to care, and wanted to care, but she had not. It was part of him, like the beautiful, arrogant way he moved. Her jealousy, like her curiosity, was for lesser feelings, not for passion itself. It was for the after-friendliness, which made affection as sweet as love. It was for his vulnerability when he had been made happy. She did not want anyone else to know, to have known, his vulnerability, to have uncovered it and touched the final gentleness that he had hidden there. Her jealous questions, never answered, betrayed only her curiosity and not her true jealousy.

"Certainly not!" he answered her reprovingly. "What in the world if I had?"

It made her sulky, suspecting that he had. She pouted, turned away from him.

He might at least satisfy her curiosity, if he could not allay her deeper jealousy. She shook herself, aware that she was petty. It had cost him a wrenching effort to forgive her her lack of virginity, and it had cost her nothing to forgive him many women. That was the way it was. She wanted to explain to him again, because he had suffered, how little it had meant when Logan Knight had penetrated her body in the name of high, poetic love. She had striven to invest the act, then, the motions of coupling, with the meaning of love. She had believed the high-flown words with which Logan excused himself and her for satisfying his physical needs. It had been a literary surrender, an empty expression of the aching wish to love, as Logan talked of love. Her body had received Logan, but never accepted him. She had been confused between words and the deed and had felt a mild distaste combined with a lingering, conventional guilt. Afterward, she had felt a strong revulsion and a longing for purity that made her long hesitant with Bill. But gradually, wanting Bill honestly, her body had learned from him. Oh, it was sweet, sometimes, when you were free of fear, the things you could share in the act of love, the revealingness of it, the extra feelings and small sensations, the emotion that welled and subsided, and what remained after.

"I was only curious," she apologized humbly.

"Well, don't be!" he scolded.

Once she asked him, "How's Van?"

"The Ball is fine," he said overheartily. "Just fine. Theoretically, he's one of the nicest guys I know. And if he keeps his word to go back way up North and leave little sonny boy here in charge, I shall be a happy man. Job I want, girl I love. What more does a man want? Except whiskey to drink."

Once he said, puzzled, "Now why do you suppose exactly Mother decided to invite your Mr. and Mrs. White tonight?"

"Oh, I know that one," said Angela, lightly cynical. "She was getting in her claim to him so my maw can't own him at the wedding."

"That's too complicated for me," said Bill. "You women!"

It would make her mother furious, thought Angela uncomfortably, when she found out that Bob White had been there. Bob White was her own clergyman, and she would resent the fact that he had unwittingly permitted Mrs. Bloodgood to lay mild claim to him. She put the thought from her. This was no time to be thinking of their mothers.

As they neared Marianna, they grew quieter and Angela moved very close to Bill on the seat and put her hand lightly on his thigh, feeling the muscles that tightened and loosened with the changes he made in his acceleration.

"We haven't a suitcase!" she exclaimed, feeling for a moment shy.

"Yes, we have," he said. "Trust your old man. There's one in the back."

"No!" said Angela. "You think of everything. What's in it?"

"Ten boxes of cartridges and some hip boots," he said.

They rocked with laughter as the car jounced rapidly over the rough back road.

"Just the very things you need on a honeymoon," said Angela.

"The boots are absolutely brand new," he assured her.

At the hotel, which was small and modern, the clerk accepted it without question when Bill signed them in as Mr. and

Mrs. Walter Bly, the name they had agreed upon after an excursion into absurdity in considering possible choices.

They went decorously up to the double room on the second floor, thanked and tipped the clerk who set down the suitcase with a "Whew!"

"Books," said Bill gravely. "Makes it heavy. My wife and I are great readers."

'My wife' repeated Angela silently, taking a long, deep breath.

"I never was much of a reader," said the clerk, and left them with the faintly condescending air of superior ignorance.

Angela moved about the nondescript room as if trying to find something. Embarrassed by the aimlessness of her movements, she changed a china ash tray from the writing table to the little table beside the bed, and then, extraordinarily, blushed. Bill said, "Be right back," and disappeared into the adjoining bathroom. Angela sat down on the side of the large bed and then got up again, smoothing the spot behind her. She frowned. It was ridiculous to feel so awkward. They had not been awkward in the essentially unbecoming circumstances of most of their love-making.

She went into the bathroom when he came out, passing him without touching him, smiling at him with stiff self-consciousness. He had half a glass of water in his hand.

"If you want a drink, I'll share this with you," he said.

"I've had enough," she said, and closed the door.

She hesitated behind the closed door before she came out again. She wore only a slip and she felt grotesque. At her age, after all this time, she should be so easy and natural. She stood with clasped hands, in an attitude of prayer, and begged that this night, of all nights, should be memorable. With a hasty gesture, she took off the slip, smoothed her hair and opened the door. It was stifling hot in the room, as if it were August and not September. It was not hot, as Mrs. Bloodgood's house had been hot, in defeat, but in ill-built lack of protection against the southern summer.

She stood now just inside the room, her arms placed in formal modesty across her thin body, looking at him with helpless, almost virginal radiance. Turning, he put down the glass from which he had been drinking, deliberately stamped out his cigarette, and, with a wordless exclamation that tore at her heart and caused her ears to sing, came over and reached out for her.

A sheet covered them lightly, not for warmth, but for protection from the several flies that buzzed in the screened room. Angela lay awake, tense and almost perfectly happy. In her utter absorption in Bill, she had forgotten herself entirely. He had given himself to her, in the end, in an arrogant glory of giving that was new to them both. He had withheld nothing of himself and had subsided against her in complete contentment and trust. And she had received him with a deep acceptance that was both immeasurably humble and immeasurably proud. He reached for her through the night, grumbling in his sleep if she moved away from him. She knew, tremulous and tense, that this was a final proof of his love. Toward morning, he woke up and made sleepy, slow-moving love to her. She held back her own night-long eagerness to match the lazy rhythm of his awakening, and afterward she slept deeply.

When they awoke together, the sun streamed through the windows and they were sweating in the heat. They knew that they had waked late, that the gossiping world of day was awake before them, that he was overdue at work and she at home. Defiantly they clung to the privileged privacy of the impersonal, cheaply furnished room. They made love bawdily and daringly, exposing their pleasure to the sun. Then leisurely they dressed and decorously they descended into the hot, ugly dining room at the hotel where they were Mr. and Mrs. Walter Bly. Still defiant, they refused to hurry, ordering huge breakfasts for the satisfaction of ravenous, late-morning appetites for food.

While they ate the pancakes for which they twice demanded more syrup and more butter, they made occasional desultory remarks intended to reflect a settled matrimony, designed for the inattentive ears of the colored waiter. Replete and calm, they finished final cigarettes and commanded the bill. The waiter accepted the excessive tip blandly. The small bellboy heaved the nonsensically heavy suitcase down the steps from the room that had been theirs and out into the sunshine. The clerk accepted payment for the bill and invited them cordially to return when they passed this way again. With prim connubial nods of farewell to the impersonally gathered staff that waved them off, they set out again on the devious route that would take them back to the Oglethorpe road and thence home.

They were both faintly grumpy on the way back, resenting the retracing of the rough roads, having eaten too much in their gusty hunger. They did not speak of the interval just spent nor hope aloud that it could be repeated. Bill remembered with irritation that he was very late and that Van disliked waiting for him. Angela felt a renewal of fear in the exposure of the car and themselves on the roads at high morning, and encouraged him crossly to hurry.

Still, there was a new closeness between them, very near to the core of their beings, which their petty fractiousness did not disturb. Love is like peeling an onion, thought Angela, pulling down the corners of her mouth, as she habitually did when she objected to her own mental similes. You uncovered layer after translucent layer of feeling inside yourself. . . . She wondered if, when you got down to the last, last fragile, exquisite skin, there would be nothing left, or whether the very center of love, if it could be reached, was as solid as stone. Bill had already forgotten, she knew, details that she would never forget of the night just spent. She truly did not know whether they were more likely or less likely to part some day because they had had such joy. Joy was as hard to live with as sorrow. But it was so infinitely much more worth it.

As they turned into the Oglethorpe highway and headed for Andalusia, she squeezed his arm tentatively and he reached over and gently patted her cheek.

With half-furtive bravado, they drove into the town, glancing secretly from rigid profiles at the streets to know who might see them. No one they knew did see them. In the high morning, the housewives and the cooks had returned from marketing and were back indoors to avoid the heat, the ladies were still indoors, and the men were gone from the residential streets.

Only Bob White, at the corner of Gloucester, was in his yard, having chosen capriciously to mow the rectory lawn in the hot sunshine, between paragraphs of the sermon he was writing inside. Uncle Jimmy, the sexton, whose duty it was to mow it, must be drunk again, thought Angela. As they exchanged comfortable, unself-conscious greetings, Angela felt a return of her buoyant breakfast spirits. There was no curiosity, suspicion, or even approval in Bob White's cordial gesture and his squeaky "Hi, there!"—only his benevolent pleasure at seeing them. She felt blessed, as if his wave was benediction. She felt lucky.

"He's a good guy," said Angela radiantly to Bill.

"M . . . m . . . m . . ." said Bill, cheerful, too, and flicked his finger at her uncovered knee.

The block farther down, Bill dropped her in front of her house, blowing a two-fingered kiss at her together with a puff of smoke from his cigarette, and drove off without looking backward, driving fast, as if fleeing. Walking up to and into her house, her heels weighted with reluctance, Angela found herself hastily and childishly inventing corroborative details with which to embroider the lie she had told her mother. She was no longer the woman who had gloriously fulfilled her lover and been fulfilled by him. She was no longer even the girl who had come to subtle terms with her lover's mother. She was losing stature with each step. By the time she reached her mother's room, she would be no better than a child, placating with wide-eyed fibs the mother-being, anxious only to cut short the scolding and dispel the air of plaintive disapproval. Be your age, baby, she told herself sternly. Be your age, Angela Madison, almost-Bloodgood, for the Lord's sake, all twenty-four years of it.

She entered her mother's room with assumed sprightliness, clutching the sum total of her years in her mind. Her mother was lying in bed, propped up on feather pillows, matching Angela's lie of spending the night as a guest of Mrs. Bloodgood with the lie of a headache which would impose on her daughter a double burden of guilt. Angela felt a curling wave of humorous tenderness for the plump, petulant, usually placid woman. For the moment she was the stronger of the two.

"Poor mama," she said without mockery. "The old head! You haven't had one in such ages. Can I give you a massage? Or get you something?"

"Just stop bouncing around," said Mrs. Madison morosely. "Really, you do walk on your heels, Angela!"

"Sorry, darling," said Angela, tiptoeing over to the arm chair from which she could face her mother. Sitting silent, in her new-felt strength, she reflected newly on the situation. It was hard on her mother, really hard, she realized compassionately. Her mother was one of the few people in the world who lived content with her own achievements. That her mother's mild round of social activity represented solid achievement and not a natural heritage was easy to forget. Her mother betrayed herself only in the extra avidity with which she sought her name in the society notes of the Andalusia *Banner*, by the fading cotillion invitations stuck triumphantly in the edge of her dressing-table mirror. Her placid contentedness was a pleasant thing to live with, good daily bread to nibble. It was classic and ironic—as well as unbelievably petty—that Bill's mother, Alicia Shy Bloodgood, was the one woman in the county who still cared to snub Hannah Miller Madison and who was capable of snubbing her without reservation or trepidation, with undiminished malice, and with absolute assurance.

"It isn't true, is it?" asked her mother querulously, disbelieving, "that the *Whites* were there last night?"

"Why, yes," said Angela reluctantly, cautioned by her mother's tone.

"Do—you—mean—to—say," said Mrs. Madison in an ominous, dead-level voice, firing each word separately at her daughter as if she were reloading her tongue each time, "that—that—man—went—to—dinner?"

"Well, why not?" asked Angela nervously. "Mrs. B. invited him last week."

"Why not?" asked her mother, her voice entirely devoid of inflection. "Why not? Please leave the room, Angela." She looked at her daughter with bleak, wholly transparent blue eyes, then closed them and heaved her heavy, white body over on its side so that her back was to Angela.

Angela walked automatically from the room and went blindly down the hall and down the back stairs, ignoring Pinckney, who spoke to her from the kitchen, holding her tears within her trembling eyelids. She went out across the back yard and opened the garage and got into her car. Sitting behind the wheel, she took a few deep breaths to stop the trembling in her stomach, holding her eyes to stop the tears. The heat in the garage made sweat start all over her body. The trembling lessened and she lit a cigarette.

She was still bemused by the strawlike cause, but she recognized the beginning of nightmare. So it had begun the third time in her life, two years before, when her father had refused to fire Georgianna Church. So it had begun the second time when her oldest brother had run away to sea. So it would go on, like living asleep bound between feather mattresses, until it was over.

Why had she let it happen? Mrs. Bloodgood's invitation to the Whites had even seemed to her cause for rejoicing. It was part and parcel of Mrs. Bloodgood's slow, painful acceptance of her son's love. The evening was a milestone, and Bob White's presence had blessed it and made it valid. His blessing had seemed to follow her and Bill through the night. . . . But she should have realized that her mother would hate it. She would hate to have her clergyman going to the home of her enemy, all unwittingly blessing the union she opposed. But Angela could not have known, however wise she had been, that it would make her mother mad. Not angry—mad.

She could not endure it. She would be driven to madness herself, to murder. (Move over, Miss Lucy!) To suicide. To flight . . .

It could be endured, she reminded herself sternly. They had all endured it, except her brother, when her brother had run away to sea. (He had come home to forgiveness and the fatted calf.) Her father had endured it for the sake of Georgianna Church. For the endless time after Georgianna had made some chance remark—whatever had she said?—that had precipitated the mutual black-and-white minor malice of a lifetime into nightmare, her father had endured it. And Georgianna Church still worked at The Place, and her mother had apparently forgotten even her early malice toward the malicious old colored woman.

But Angela could not endure it now.

Slowly she backed out of the garage and on out into the street. Deliberately, with painstaking care in each separate motion of driving, she drove down Gloucester Street to the blue rectory at the corner.

"He jus lak Gawd," said Georgianna. "He jus be. Ain no use tuh nobody."

"Lessen they help themselves," said Mercy.

"Gawd don hep nobody heps theyselves," said Georgianna. "Gawd let um hep theyselves if they wants tuh hep theyselves. Everbody got Gawd wrong. He doan do nothin. He doan even listen. He jus be. He jus be good. If he done things, he couldn't stay good. If yuh wants tuh be good, go look at Gawd and go be good. That's all."

Mercy said comfortably, "I dunno so much about Gawd, Mama. Mistuh White is the only person this side of Gawd don't seem to know if you is black or white, let alone care. He don't seem to care is you good or bad, neither."

"Dat's Gawd all ovuh," said Georgianna triumphantly. "Duh devil's duh only one cares uh hoot."

Mercy said, "Miss Angela came around yestiddy and asked um if he'd marry her and Mistuh Bill th'out bothering they parents."

Georgianna sucked in her breath. There was no smallest piece of gossip about black or white that she did not dote on and embroider with her oblique understanding. "Whut he say?"

"He say, sure if they got a legal license and is responsible and over twenty-one. That's what he's for, he say. Missus White she brown him up and brown him down after Miss Angela gone. 'You is jus asking for trouble, Bob White,' she say."

"He ain't askin fo it or not askin fo it," said Georgianna. "Trouble is trouble, an tuh Gawd it doan make no nevuh mind. Marry um or doan marry um. Tain't up tuh Gawd."

13. A Good Man

"What are the stakes?" asked Carrie, tearing the cellophane from the twin packs of new cards. "Before we start and it gets complicated."

"Tenth? Fortieth? Twentieth? None. I don't care," said Hope. "It's your choice, Angela. It's your house."

"Twentieth," said Angela promptly. "I get grabby at a tenth and careless at a fortieth." She meant that Hope was avaricious when the stakes were high and that Ellen Terra overbid when they were low. Her own game was relatively unaffected.

"You *can't* play for nothing," said Ellen Terra. "That makes it flimsy jackstraws."

Carrie fanned out one of the decks, blind side up, and the three others who were standing by the table made their choices of single cards.

Flipping hers over, Hope exclaimed, "The jack of spades. Lucky for me. Who else is high?"

"I am," said Carrie, "unless somebody beats the king."

Angela and Ellen Terra had drawn low cards and they sat down opposite each other on either side of Carrie. There was no choice of place. The luck of the night had not been established.

"Mind if I put another piece of ice in my drink?" asked Hope.

Angela shook her head. "Help yourself."

"It's odd," complained Hope as she sat down, "but I can't drink very much after dinner any more. It makes me sleepy."

Ellen Terra said, "It's the only thing that keeps me awake. I get sleepy hearing people talk."

"Cocktails do me in," said Angela. "Not highballs. Martinis especially. They taste so delicious I forget to stop."

"One heart," said Carrie. "Do you really like the *taste* of liquor, Angela?"

"One spade," said Ellen Terra.

Angela frowned at her hand. "Oh, Lord, yes. Since Papa got some real imported stuff, I learned to love it. Don't you? The good, I mean."

"No," said Carrie. "I drink solely for the effect. I think you do, too."

"I don't," said Angela. "I never did. It was always for some other reason. Now I like it." She would have gone on, but Hope said, "Two clubs," and she paused again to re-examine her hand, then said, "Pass," reluctantly.

"Three clubs," said Carrie from the side of her mouth, closing one eye against the smoke from the stub of her cigarette. She was the only one of them who smoked without removing the cigarette from her mouth and she had developed a set of slight facial contortions accommodating this habit.

Ellen Terra shrugged and passed and Hope said hesitantly, "Three hearts." Angela knocked lightly twice on the wooden rim of the table, indicating that she had nothing more to say. Carrie exclaimed, "Four!" as she put out her cigarette and lit another. Angela knew that she was counting on Hope's inability ever quite to bid the full value of her hand.

After Ellen Terra led, Hope laid out her hand, neatly and exactly, a little slowly, as if titillating her partner with the unveiling of a hand better than her bids had indicated, and then leaned back, waiting for an expression of gratitude. She accepted as thanks

Carrie's grunt which was, actually, a tribute to Carrie's own astuteness.

Hope's inborn New England caution caused her to underbid, decided Angela, but what was it that made her demand appreciation for her very faults? Did excessive self-esteem or too little produce this insatiable appetite for thanks? You never did get thanked for the best you had, thought Angela. But Logan was the kind of man who thanked you for everything.

She marked a game in hearts to her opponents and gathered up the cards and began to shuffle absent-mindedly, as Ellen Terra started to deal the other pack.

"Revenge, partner," said Ellen Terra, slewing the cards carelessly around the table. "Say, did you know my mother's got her war paint on?"

"No," said Angela indifferently. "What about now?"

"She's mad as seventeen wet furious guinea hens at Bob White," said Ellen Terra.

Carrie looked up. "You tell her to let the man I love alone!" she said sharply.

"He's the man I love," said Angela, alert. I do, she thought, I love him truly. More than I loved Mark, in a way. But not like I love Bill. That's different.

"I do, too," said Ellen Terra. Bob White made her feel good. That is, Bob White made her feel like a good girl. He made her feel that God approved of her, just as she was, and not as she had been told she should be. It was a restful feeling.

"How can anybody ever be mad at Bob White?" asked Hope. "He's so sweet and so nice."

"Mama can get mad at anybody," said Ellen Terra with a kind of rueful pride, "even with a sugar candy lamb like Bob White."

"Well, tell her to lay off," said Carrie. "Bid, for heaven's sake."

"Two diamonds," said Ellen Terra, indicating, according to Culbertson, an exceptionally powerful hand. The card table immediately tensed and the rest of this game was played with entire attention. Ellen Terra and Angela arrived at a slam bid, and went down one when a dramatic finesse failed of its purpose.

"Gallant try, partner," said Angela to Ellen Terra. "Well worth the risk."

"Magnificent defense, partner," said Carrie jubilantly to Hope.

Angela's thoughts returned uneasily to Ellen Terra's statement. She asked petulantly, "Why is your mother mad at Bob White?" If the two formidable women, their mothers, got mad together, she thought, frowning, God help the innocent man at whom they were angry. Clementine Rook was violent and active in anger, as her own mother, inert, was implacable, was mad.

Angela's stomach quivered faintly as she considered her mother's so rare and so oppressive, her pervasive, inescapable feather-wall obstinacy, once her anger was not so much aroused as settled. Once she was mad. Angela sent a shivery little thanksgiving upward with a quick puff of smoke from her cigarette for the random ease with which that anger had been recently averted. She had been lucky. You needed luck, whatever else you had. At the rectory, in Bob White's presence, accepting his casual assurance that it was his duty and pleasure to marry her whenever she soberly and sincerely wished it, everything had seemed simple. She could even believe that it was simple and possible to marry without your parents' consent. Sensible, even. But Arabella, clicking down the stairs on five-inch heels to say good-bye to Angela in the hall, had whispered with bitter, comradely knowingness, "Bet your maw was damn cross because we went to Mrs. Bloodgood's party," and her illusion of simplicity was gone. Her fingertips had flinched from the roughened bannister post at the top of the rectory steps and then lifted in a gesture of appeal and greeting as Dugdale Winthrop drove around the corner in his car. That was luck. Dugdale had stopped his car and spoken, and, speaking, knew her mood, and, knowing, stayed with her. He had come home with her, paying court to her. Courting, thought Angela, not her, but her unease, her fear, her unhappiness, her need. Her mother, seeing him suitor, was diverted.

Thank the Lord for the diversion that had released her from nightmare. She had even let her mother think that she was, perhaps a little, seriously interested in Dugdale Winthrop. Now that Logan was married to Hope, her mother would be very happy if only Angela were going to marry Dugdale. Logan Knight and Dugdale Winthrop, instead of Bill, thought Angela with amazement and momentary disgust. How could a loving mother be so cruel and so blind? But she was thankful for diversion. Diverted, her mother was reasonable. Reasonable, she had agreed that Bob White had gone to the Bloodgood dinner table as innocent in social intent as a hungry, fresh-whelped puppy. Reasonable, she could be brought around again to the slow-growing knowledge that Bill and Angela were going to marry. If Bill were a success—not a Bloodgood, but a success on his own—her mother would yield. You did not refuse to let your daughter marry successful young men, even though you hated their mothers. Successful young men were prizes. Her mother loved to win prizes, even the pink, ruffled tea cozies that Mrs. Lovejoy always gave for high score at bridge.

"Why?" repeated Ellen Terra, as if she had just heard Angela's question. "Why, mother's been dithering away like a beheaded chick for six months over a memorial to the ghost of Grandma," said Ellen Terra, who was just out of dead black clothes and permitted to wear black and white, or all white, six months after the death of her maternal grandmother. "And she met that architect at Oakland, the yummy one, and then she decided to build a chapel and he designed it."

"St. James's has a chapel," said Angela.

"This will be a large chapel," said Ellen Terra.

"What use is that?" asked Hope.

"None," said Carrie. "None whatever."

"Anyway," said Ellen Terra, "Mama had her mouth all puckered and Bob White turned her down and Mama's in a green-striped yellow-tiger rage."

"I do hope she doesn't make trouble," said Angela, with a quick wrinkling of her forehead. "Bob White's the first nice thing that's happened to Andalusia since Mark."

Their light, unembarrassed laugh rose like music from the touched chord of their shared memory, their shared love which had left no scars, only temporary empty places in their several hearts and a vacant pulpit at St. James's.

"We shouldn't make a habit of loving our clergymen," said Carrie. "It's too old maidish."

"Nobody could have loved that dismal pansy 'Father' Byrd," said Angela. "Thank the Lord he only stayed eighteen months."

"Was he a pansy, do you suppose?" asked Carrie.

"Just a skinny eunuch," said Angela.

"How you talk!" said Ellen Terra, genuinely shocked.

"Sometimes you really are disgusting," said Hope, primly and honestly. Then she added pacifically, "Why do you love Bob White? I like him very much, but I don't *love* him."

"Bridge," said Carrie acidly, "requires a small amount of attention."

Good old Carrie, thought Angela. She loved the flowering briar patch that was Carrie's spirit. God bless you, Carrie, thought Angela. God bless us all, thought Angela expansively. In this year of our Lord and our lives, 1931: the year of Bob White and S. V. Ball and David Bradford, the thin schoolmaster who loved Carrie, or at least who looked at her as if he had never seen another woman in all his life.

"Your mother told my mother she was furious with Bob White," said Hope to Ellen Terra, when the uninteresting hand had been played. "I didn't really pay attention. I was—sleepy. But mother was awfully sympathetic. Mother said it was a shame that Mr. White had hurt your mother's deepest feelings for the dead and that Mr. White was really *not* very discriminating and that he was behaving like a dictator."

"Nuts," said Angela. "He's about as dictatorial as a three-year-old baby."

"*They're* frightful dictators," said Hope.

Angela shrugged impatiently. "Well, Bob White isn't."

"*I* know he isn't," said Hope.

"If the old gals start ganging up on him," said Carrie darkly, dropping her hands which had been hovering over the cards Angela was absently dealing, "it'll be murder."

"Why didn't he let her have her chapel?" asked Angela.

"Well," said Ellen Terra, with a certain relish, "it goes like this." She paused. "Your mother's not lurking, is she, honey?" she asked Angela, lowering her voice.

"No. No. Out," said Angela impatiently, waving her hand toward the door. "Both of 'em."

"Good," said Ellen Terra. "Well, the chapel—see?—would be where the Sunday school building is now and the Sunday school would be moved over next to Miss Lucy's hedge and that would be okay except there wouldn't be any place for the nursery school playground during the week, just after the town helped put up all that money for new playground equipment. Bob White said he just hated to refuse, but the children needed the playground, and Mama said she did not approve of the town being charitable with tax money, especially these days, and Arabella White said private charity was a lovely thing which did the giver no end of good and what about giving a new school building instead of a chapel, and Bob White said, now Arabella, and Mama said Grandma was a great lady and a great Episcopalian and a chapel was most worthy of her memory, and Bob White said it was very suitable, but that, of course, children were the inheritors of the earth and nobody could want to deprive them, and Mama said certainly not. Then Mama said she had a wonderful idea and that she was sure Miss Lucy, if tactfully approached, would be willing to turn that big back garden of hers, with those two beautiful oaks and the grass and flowers, over to the school, since she was all alone now and didn't even have a yard man to keep it up properly . . ."

"Oh, God," said Carrie.

"And Arabella said maybe Miss Lucy was a more noble person, but that she herself would not have a bunch of children yelling and trampling in her garden all day for all the world, and Mama said of such is the Kingdom of Heaven, and Arabella said for her part she thought the Kingdom of Heaven would be better looking if you did *not* add Doric chapels onto Gothic churches, and Mama said she felt that Arabella was disrespectful to a very fine architect as well as to Grandma's memory, and Arabella said not for the world would she be disrespectful to Grandma's memory, but that the architect was a plumber, and Bob White said Arabella!"

"*That* Arabella!" said Angela.

"She was trying to draw the fire, or I miss my guess," said Carrie.

"She nearly did," said Ellen Terra, who had got her breath again. "Mama felt so sorry sympathetic for Bob White being married to her, she forgave him for not getting excited about Grandma's chapel and he promised to speak to Miss Lucy and Mama told Papa that night that she might have misjudged Bob White when she had found him so cold and unsympathetic and inattentive when she tried to get spiritual help from him."

"Oh," said Carrie. "Oh, Lord."

"Anyway, she saw him alone the next time and he was very sweet, I guess, but stubborn. He kept acting so sympathetic, Mama thought she had him, but she never got close. He said he had talked to Miss Lucy and that Miss Lucy said she valued her privacy more than she did life itself and that while she lived that hedge would grow taller and thicker every day of her life and that when she died the whole thing, garden, house, and lot, would go to St. James's in the name of Bob White."

"Oh, *God*," said Carrie.

". . . and Bob White said he had refused to accept it in his name, but not in the name of the church. *Then* he proceeded, ever so mealy-mouthed, Mama said, to refuse the chapel in the name *of* the church *and* himself as rector, and even, Mama said, had the nerve to suggest a scholarship fund for the nursery-school children or even a puky little stained-glass window as a memorial. Mama blew up and said she really could not talk to a man who could accept a gift from Lucy Cranborne and refuse one from *her* and that it was high-handed officious and unchristian of him, and Bob White said it was not the giver but the gift he was refusing or accepting and he could not justify to himself in the name of God the chapel instead of the playground, and Mama said he was putting physical values before spiritual ones, and he said not at all, and had, said Mama, the gall to laugh and say that the church body itself hardly seemed crowded to overflowing these hot Sundays and that the little chapel was still big enough for him and Miss Sis Whittle all by themselves on Thursdays and that if this situation changed, happily, he would be delighted to reconsider. Then Mama said, really, if he had the interest of his parishioners and his church at heart he could make Miss Lucy see that she would do very well to give over her garden, it was the least she could do, if her rector considered it a proper penance for her sins, and Mama said Bob White looked as if he were as innocent as a child and started talking about theological differences between the Anglican conception of the priesthood and the Roman Catholic, and Mama said she got so mad she just walked out on him. And Papa said, well, really, dear, perhaps Bob White doesn't know about Miss Lucy, and Mama said well, then, he's stupid as well as horrible and that makes it worse and anyway I can't abide the awful little man and I don't see how I can take communion from his disgusting hands and what are you going to DO? And Papa said, 'nothing' and Mama said yes he was, too—and there she is, cross as black pepper on a rainy day."

"It's a mess," said Carrie.

"If Miss Lucy weren't in it!" said Hope. "That's what upset my mother."

"It'll blow over," said Angela. "Won't it?" She added daringly, "What's so awful about murdering Mrs. Cranborne?"

Carrie laughed with surprised amusement.

"Don't talk like that," begged Hope. "I don't think it's funny. It makes me feel quite sick. You're joking."

"No, I'm not," said Angela.

"Pooh," said Carrie. "Angela's right. She was a horrid, useless woman who was no good to anybody and bad for everybody. I'm glad she's dead. She was an unholy bore. If I'm glad she's dead, why should I quibble over how she died?"

"She was a speckled old rotten mushroom," said Ellen Terra, "but nobody ought to kill anybody. It isn't fair."

"You kill me, Ellen Terra," said Carrie affectionately.

"Anyway," said Angela, "nobody wants Miss Lucy to get hanged, do they? And everybody likes Bob White. It'll blow over. Things do."

"I hope so," said Carrie. "Let's play bridge, if we're going to play." Before the hand was half-played she said, "I won't have them pick at Bob White, those bitches."

Hope said indignantly, "Don't call . . ."

"Your mother a bitch? All right. Sorry. I'm just nervous.

You see—" she paused, and smiled with unusual sweetness, with an air that was close to being maidenly shy—"David's mother is coming down. To look me over."

"Carrie!" exclaimed Angela, thinking, oh my dear, and how you hate strangers, with your leg and all.

"Anybody want another drink besides me?" asked Hope. She fixed herself one and sat down.

"What are you going to wear?" asked Ellen Terra.

"Let's don't talk," begged Carrie. "Let's finish the rubber." Play bridge, she admonished herself, play and do not look at or speak of or otherwise disturb the fragile substance of your lovely luck, your sad pleasure that is almost happiness, your timid hopes. Angela may grasp joy firmly in her two hands and hold it, may speak of it in a loud voice, and even fight for it, lose and regain it. She knows a strong joy. She, Carrie, must leave hers swaddled in sadness and sharpness, protected from glance or sound that might disturb it.

They did play, commenting only on the cards, holding friendly and occasionally acrid post-mortems over the hands, playing as they had been taught to play, as their mothers and fathers played: respectfully, thoughtfully and quite well. Carrie and Hope won, by a narrow margin. Angela mixed fresh drinks for them all while the scores were finally added and rechecked and while they decided whether to play a return rubber.

"Why don't you marry Van?" asked Angela unexpectedly of Ellen Terra, who sat back now, blinking like a sleepy kitten.

"All right," said Ellen Terra amiably. "I think he's a lovely, snobby little darling, all over pink and white. Tell him to ask me."

"You can't marry a Yankee," said Hope, opening her eyes so wide that her face seemed to disappear behind them.

"Why ever not?" said Ellen Terra. "Besides, I'm so lazy and he's so rich and kind of touching. I feel so sorry for him."

"That's absurd," said Hope. Then she looked quickly at Angela and as quickly away again.

"Let's play one more," said Angela. "I don't feel sleepy. I feel good." She felt optimistic, that was what she felt.

Carrie looked at her luminously and said almost gently, "It's good to feel good."

Hope said eagerly, determinedly, "I feel good, too." She put her hands out toward them, reaching for them. She was the only married woman among them, and that made her somehow lost to them. And now she was twice lost because her husband was away. Logan was in Marianna, foreclosing some mortgage or something like that, for the bank. She was frantic for fear he would never, never return and then she would be nowhere. He seemed so gone, when he was gone. He was so handsome. She remembered how he was handsome. There were so many girls in the world, such pretty, pretty southern girls. She was losing her looks. She was getting old and he had not aged a day. Babies did that to you, darling as they were. They were, of course, darling. And so pretty. They could be fat and still be pretty. She was getting fat. She must not get fat. She must do her hair again. Tonight. Logan swore he would love her when all her endearing young charms—but she could not trust to that.

"If Bob White," said Angela to Carrie, "would just stop going to see Miss Lucy . . ."

"Well, he won't stop," said Carrie.

Hope put her head down on her hands without warning and began to weep, tears slithering between her fingers and dropping on the deck of cards in front of her. "He's so sweet, Bob White," she moaned. "I can't bear for him to go away. He's so go-o-od."

"For God's sweet sake," said Carrie, "he's not going."

"Calm down," said Angela. "We won't let anything happen to him."

"Won't we?" said Hope. She dried her eyes and reached for her drink.

"Do you need any more of that?" asked Angela.

"Just a wee nippie," said Hope. "Do you mind?"

"Well, no," said Angela.

"I'm going home," said Ellen Terra, stretching like a cat and yawning. "I promised Van I'd go fishing tomorrow."

"One more rubber," said Carrie, restlessly shuffling the cards.

There were footsteps on the porch and then a voice from the open door at the end of the hall.

"Hi . . ." said a male voice, tentatively.

"Hey," said Angela. "Who's there?"

"Nobody but us chickens," said Sonny Boy's voice cheerfully. "Are you home?"

"Come on in," called Angela, too lazy to get up.

The screen door squeaked and the footsteps entered the hall, and then Dugdale Winthrop and Sonny Boy Lovejoy emerged into the lighted living room.

"We peered into your window and we decided that you girls were just longing for company," said Sonny Boy.

"We surely are," said Ellen Terra. "You're in the very nick. I was about to go home." She wiggled in her chair, looking up at them bright-eyed.

"Don't go home," said Dugdale. "The evening's a pup."

"How about some liquid refreshments," asked Sonny Boy, "now we're here?"

"Help yourself," said Angela. "It's for free."

She could not decide whether she was glad they had come. It tidied up an evening to have males in it. Women alone grew sloppy and Hope was on the verge of a crying jag. On the other hand, their coming had revived the evening, prolonged it. Otherwise she might soon have forgotten it in sleep. She loved to sleep. Lately she had snuggled into sleep as if it were cold in the room and she was snuggling under blankets. It must be that fall was coming, although the September heat was unabated. It was strong, the heat, but weary, like a strong man tiring. Cold, or the knowledge that it would grow cold, made her sleepy. She yawned.

Sonny Boy said, "Lovely bridgework, Angela."

" 'Scuse me," said Angela carelessly. "It's the heat." It was not the heat. It was the forecast of cold.

There had been a perking up in the room, but no excitement at the advent of the young men. Sonny Boy pulled up the other chair to the bridge table, content to divide his well-worn attentions among Carrie and Angela and Ellen Terra, parceling out his gay, bedraggled compliments among them. All but wagging his tail, thought Angela.

Dugdale had ambled into the room and circled it, his long nose quivering in his hound-dog face, his eyes sliding away from the eyes he met until they met Hope's. He found what he sought in the wide blue eyes and drew her into the corner beside him. Hope was the only one of them in whom he had never displayed his sad, self-defeated interest until now. When Hope was unhappy, it was always with a brusque, practical unhappiness from which he could draw no sustenance. Had Logan actually broken Hope's heart that Dugdale was going to comfort her? If Dugdale told Hope that he loved her, Hope would believe him. She was Logan's wife, faithful and safe. Still, how safe was any woman if she believed in comfort?

Hope's voice rose over the desultory conversation at the bridge table. "Make them *stop*," she begged. "Make them let him alo-o-one."

"I was telling Hope," said Dugdale, with the funereal avidity with which he could not help dispensing gossip, "that Mrs. Rook is really out for blood. She's got a mad on at Bob White, did you know?"

"We know," said Carrie. "Now what? Damn it, everybody else likes the man!"

"I do," said Dugdale, "very much. And I would hate to have Mrs. Rook mad at me."

"He's muh friend," said Sonnny Boy sentimentally.

"Mrs. Rook doesn't own the town or St. James's," said Carrie, "for God's sake." She looked at Hope, who was swaying a very little in her chair, tears swaying on the edge of the blonde lashes that fringed the enormous eyes. "Come on, Hope. Snap out of it. Let's go out to Joe's and get some air and a nightcap."

"I'll take her home," said Dugdale solicitously.

And drink her tears and present your shoulder for her to dampen agreeably and then kiss her to comfort her, thought Angela. And confess your hopeless love for her? Watch out, my friend. Hope's safe in a way, but she's dangerous. She might be betrayed into believing you all the way. You can handle any horse in the world except one that trusts you more than it trusts itself.

"I'm going with you," said Carrie, with harsh firmness.

Carrie would not let Logan come back to find that his wife had been taken home weeping drunk by Dugdale Winthrop. Good old Carrie.

"Let's all go," said Sonny Boy. "Come on, Angela, honey."

"Not me," said Angela. "Thanks all the same. I'm going to stay home and say my prayers for Bob White!"

Angela stretched up and Dugdale bent down from his sorrowful height and seemed to promise that, thin reed that he was, he was both gentleman and friend to Bob White. His wan support would be given to the clergyman. He would gallop slowly to his aid. Sonny Boy bounced, his eyes jiggling on the level of her own, reminding her cheerfully with a double squeeze of his little, suggestive hands, that he was loyal to his loyalties, spread thin as they were, loyal to the whole legion of his friends and to all the girls he had professed to love. Hope, wobbling and blind-eyed, needed only to find where Logan stood, to stand stockily herself, steadied on her stocky legs. Angela did not know where Logan would stand.

Ellen Terra hugged her, breathing kinelike in her ear banal thanks for the charming evening. It was a vague warmth, not really a communication. Even when these familiar young men were there, Ellen Terra was with men and no longer one with women.

Carrie said harshly, "Stop worrying, idiot. You dither so. Take it easy, and keep your pistol handy."

When they were gone, Angela went back into the living room and picked up her half-empty glass. Restlessly, she took two rapid gulps and surveyed the disorder, the glasses and cigarette butts, the cards untidy on the table. She could straighten it up, leaving the room behind her comfortable and renewed, or she could go up to her neat room, leaving this one for Pinckney in the morning. There was nothing more she must do except to go to bed and then to sleep.

She dropped her hands and set down her glass among the others. Leaving the room, she started up the wide, dark polished stairs.

When her light was off she lay quietly, drifting swiftly into deep, cool sleep. In the oak tree outside her window a mocking bird was singing. We will go out and eat ripe scuppernongs at Miss Sis's in the morning, she thought vaguely. We will bring, Bill and I, a big bag of ripe scuppernongs to Bob White in the morning.

14.   **The Married**

Hope gave a smothered yelp and hit out at whatever it was that crawled on her arm. Her wrist struck flesh and the blow unleashed a scream like that of an animal in pain. Bemused and dreadfully distressed, she opened her eyes wide and stared into a child's pink mouth, with its two rows of small, perfect teeth stretched wide apart.

The distress that was all that was left of the dream she had been dreaming, and the horror and distress of the moment of her awakening, yielded to immediate simple solicitude for her daughter.

"Oh, Cecelia, darling!" Hope sat up heavily and reached her arms for the little figure. The child was still on all fours, arrested in the position of crawling across the wide bed to her mother, who had been sleeping crowded into the far edge of the bed, against the wall.

"You hurt me," said Cecelia, sullenly. Pulling back on her haunches, avoiding her mother's arms, she deliberately opened her mouth again and recommenced her screaming.

From the quality of the sound Hope knew that no physical damage had been done. "Oh, hush, hush, hush, Cecelia!" she said, covering her assaulted ears.

"No!" said the child, pausing to insert the negative in the middle of a scream. Trying to kick out at her mother, she succeeded in unbalancing herself and toppled backward off the moderately high bed. The thud of her body was dulled by the rug at the edge of the bed. In her immediately redoubled shrieks, pain, justification, surprise, fear and a kind of triumph were mingled. Hope scrambled across the bed and swung her legs down to one side of the child. The bedroom door opened wide and Mrs. Stone and Nanine forced themselves through simultaneously.

"Cecelia!" crescendoed their voices as they raced across the polished floor, thick white legs in silk and skinny black ones in gray cotton churning in unison. Together they gained the rug. Nanine, folding her bones downward like a Lazy Tongs, gathered the squirming, kicking, howling little girl to the bones of her concave breast. Rocking back and forth, she began a shrill wavering singsong in Cajun French designed to comfort and soothe the persecuted and afflicted.

Mrs. Stone straightened from her thick waist and turned on Hope. She folded her arms across the ample bosom that descended downward in a single curve and raised her voice above the combined tumult on the floor beside her.

"Hope, how *can* you BE SO CARELESS . . ."

Hope sat rigid, her legs hanging over the edge of the bed. She had not looked at the women, fearful of finding their figures as monstrous as their voices, their faces as grotesque and outsize as the face of her child when she had awakened, as monstrous as the faces in her fading dream.

"What a racket you-all are making," said the male voice gently. It penetrated the noise in the room, as a bass note can be heard among the shrillest treble. "Hope!" exclaimed the voice, in mild reproof.

Hope opened her great eyes and blinked at the wavy, unfocused lines of the doorway. Logan lounged in the door, never monstrous, proportioned gracefully against the jamb. Still, something was wrong. He should not be there so early in the afternoon. He should not be reproving her for anything that happened on a weekday afternoon. If only the world she had waked into would come into focus. If it made sense and were not so noisy, she could cope with the world. She clapped her hands and blinked away her rising, frantic tears.

Nanine was still crooning, but by this time almost inaudibly. Cecelia shoved against the bones so barely covered with dark flesh and released herself ruthlessly. With a single, fluid motion, not so much graceful as flawless, she was on her feet. This perfection of movement, available only to a child, was gone as she imitated the provocative grace of a young woman in a mincing walk toward her father. Her face was innocent of any marks of tears and her smile was provocative and sunny.

"I'm Daddy's brave girl," she announced in her precocious voice, melodiously reminiscent of Hope's, "and I had a *terrible* tumble."

"That's a good girl. That's a poor baby," said Logan.

"Mummy pushed me," said Cecelia, turning the smile downward into a pout and peering upward, under her lashes, at her father.

"Mummy didn't mean to," said Mrs. Stone.

Nanine glowered up at Hope, black incontinent rage on her ravaged black face.

"I waked Mummy," said Cecelia virtuously. "Just like you said, Daddy."

"You'd have waked the dead, honey," said Logan. "Now, run along with Nanine and Nanine will give you a big cookie. That's Daddy's angelface."

"Two cookies," said Cecelia, as Nanine began the deliberate motions of rising. "No, three. No, *ten hundred* million cookies."

"I was so startled to see you, son," said Mrs. Stone, panting, her hand on—or near—her heart. "It's Wednesday."

"I didn't mean to startle you, Maw, dear," said Logan in the light, bantering tone he used with his mother-in-law. "Aren't I welcome on Wednesdays?"

"Of course," said Mrs. Stone, wanting to be playful, but unable to achieve lightness. "Certainly. I just thought . . ."

"I won't be here tomorrow, if that's what you want," said Logan, teasing her. Then he explained, before his teasing could bother his humorless mother-in-law. "I have to go to New York, on business for Paw. It's an awful nuisance, being away so much right now, with the golf tournament opening, too. Anyway, I want Hope to help me get my things ready, if she's not too tired. Are you, darling?"

"Oh, no," said Hope, heavily. "But I wish you didn't have to."

"Can I help you, dear?" asked Mrs. Stone. Logan shook his head. "Do tell me. . . ."

Cecelia grabbed her grandmother's mottled white hand and the black one Nanine held outstretched to her. "One—two—three . . ." she counted imperiously and flung herself upwards.

"Heavy!" the two voices complained, acquiescent and proud. The thin arm and the thick one crooked as they took the weight of the child's sleek, rounded body.

"One—two—*three* . . ." counted Cecelia.

Propelling the child thus from the room, Mrs. Stone said breathlessly, "I'll see you later, dear."

Behind them, Logan closed the door, letting the knob turn slowly so that the firm click of the latch should not rudely shut Hope's mother out. He turned to Hope with gentle reproach in the surface of his eyes. Hope lowered the lids of her great eyes to hide the look from herself, unable to bear reproach just yet. She struggled with the impulse to roll back across the bed, to push herself against the wall, to try to scramble back into sleep as into a dark hiding place. She could not bear reproach just yet, nor the knowledge that Logan was going away again. Resolutely she set about tidying the house of her mind and making it ready to receive reproach and knowledge. Scurrying and pattering about her mind like a good housewife, she did away with the lingering traces of her nap, her dream, making the disordered mental bed in which she had slept and covering it with a bright, presentable daytime spread. Methodically she picked up the pieces of shattered calm that the child had left behind her and swept up the dust of resentment that had settled in the wake of the two women, white and black, the one so temperately, irrationally critical of her, the other blackly, incontinently angry with her. Turning then to Logan, she waited, ready for his reproach and his news.

"You shouldn't let Cecelia scream like that," he said gently. "It's not good for her."

She put away the reproach neatly, without bothering to dispute her responsibility. Justice was abstract, reasonable, and attainable to her in concept, but she found it hardly worth the bother any more. Logan disliked argument.

Reproach left the surface of his eyes. She looked closely up at him, trying to see into the second layer of expression that was occasionally uncovered in his eyes. He had brown eyes, light and clear and dreamy on the surface, and dark underneath. She never could read his deeper eyes, like muddy water visible under clear, and believed him spiritual and deep. Only when he read poetry to her did she feel hopeful that she was close to his inner self.

"I have to go to New York," he repeated. "Isn't that a stupid bore this weather? Damn it, anyway. The bank has no more soul than a pig. Taking a man from his family, and his golf, and the books he wants to read . . ."

"I'm so sorry," she said, "and I'll be so lonesome."

"You'll have the family," he said, kissing her. "And it won't be very long, I hope."

She put away the knowledge of his absence, the emptiness of the future, as she had tidied away his reproach. If the house of her mind was straight, she could go out into the sunlit garden of activity. He had said he needed her help.

"I have a secret to tell you," said Logan, sitting on the bed beside her. "It's a real secret, honey baby, no fooling. Can little blonde Yankees keep secrets?"

When he called her a little blonde Yankee, it was gentle warning that she could really displease him if she did some certain thing. Displease and disappoint him.

"It means a lot more work for your man, sweetie, but I can't pass it up. Damn it, I owe it to Mother."

He would take no money from Hope for the support of the chipper, inexhaustible widow who had managed through multitudinous expressions of her energy to support him inadequately through school and college. She was an admirable woman, in the town's eyes, left ladylike, tiny, and penniless when Logan was a child. He was an admirable son who had come home to take care of her, gallant in his appreciation of her gallantry. With his salary at the bank, he was buying her a house and paying for a maid. He

had promised, disapproval tempered with indulgence, to invest in
a hat shop for her when he could afford it. "I want a hat shop that
will *lose* money," his mother had begged. Meantime she did no
more dressmaking, hating it, but contentedly made hats for herself
and several for Hope. Hope wore them loyally, flowers and all,
though her personal tastes were severe. And hung her mother-in-
law's gift water colors on her bedroom walls, and went to see her
when she indulged her weekly headaches. "I never had time for
them before," Mrs. Knight would explain happily, when Hope
found her in bed with iced cloths on her head. Hope was fond of
her and admired her, but was, for some reason, fearful of her. Logan
adored her.

"There's Mother," Logan went on, "and it's what they all
call a remarkable opportunity. You *can* keep a secret, baby?"

"Oh, yes," said Hope. "Honestly."

"Van Ball wants me to take over the Andalusia end of the
finances at The Oaks!"

"For the bank?" asked Hope.

"I won't bother your silly head with the details," said Logan,
pinching her arm. "The bank's in it. And a couple of New York
banks. It's big, sweetheart, bigger than Bill Bloodgood has any idea.
Van needs somebody he can trust, so he picked on me." Logan
sighed. He discounted himself as a businessman, although Hope's
father said pridefully that he was amazingly shrewd. No one had
ever accused Mr. Stone of nepotism when his son-in-law made rapid
advancement in the bank. No one had even accused Logan of marrying Hope for that purpose. "Of course, he's been pretty daring, Van
has, starting such a thing in a depression. If it flops, he's a fool. If
it goes over, he's foresighted. If it goes over, it'll go over big. It
would be funny if I got rich, wouldn't it, darling?"

"We could have a house of our own," said Hope spontaneously. "In Oakland."

Logan said gently, "You always jump so far ahead. We'll
have our own house, honey, when I can give you one as good as
the one you have. And a cook as good as Nanine, and everything
else you want. I won't have two women sacrifice themselves for me,
because they love me. You know I don't mind living here because
I know Maw and Paw are wild to keep you and Cecelia with them.

Lord knows it doesn't matter how I live—Mother and I made out on hot dogs at Miss Mary's for a long enough time—but you . . . And your snow-princess hands!" He picked up one of Hope's square, well-tended, perfectly manicured hands and patted her fingers. "Can I use 'em to help me pack? I'd ask Alice to help, or Maw, but you do make a suitcase look like a Christmas present from Cartier's."

Hope started happily to slide from the bed, to go quickly into the garden of activity as he invited her, but her mind made her pause.

"What about Bill?" she asked. "I thought he was Andalusia manager."

"He doesn't know yet," warned Logan, "and it may make his position a little bit less important, but his—ability—isn't financial. I've had to learn caution the hard way, but Bill just hasn't any and it's worried Van. Now, don't you talk to Angela . . ."

"Of course not," said Hope. "You ask Paw." She had picked up his affectionate, humorous terms of address for her parents. "He knows I can keep secrets."

"Angela thinks she's a whole lot brighter than she is, and she wouldn't understand the arrangements. Any more than you would, honey baby. Bill's all right. He's just a bit wild. He's useful when he's curbed. Van knows that well enough." Logan smoothed the combed waves of his light brown hair. "Bill lacks discretion, that's all. It's not only money. Take this Bob White affair . . ."

Hope padded over to the chair where she had left her fresh clothes neatly folded. She was cuddling the words to herself: "Angela thinks she's a whole lot brighter than she is." For all her devotion to Angela, she had always felt *that*. When she felt him elusive, she had often feared that Logan, in his hidden heart, longed for the companionship of Angela, his intellectual companion, the girl of his first devotion. She felt infinitely reassured. Picking up the panties edged with lace and the brassiere new and cupped in outline from the chair, she trotted briskly toward the bathroom.

"Just one second, Logan," she begged, going in to wash away the last traces of her nap. When she emerged, Logan was draped on the chaise longue, smoking a cigarette.

"Did you say something about Bob White?" she asked, her

voice muffled in the dress she was pulling on over her head. "What about him?"

"Nothing much," said Logan casually. "Only Bill insisted on inviting him and Mrs. White as our guests for the Saturday night dinner-dances. It's an old tradition at The Oaks. The Episcopal divine for free. I went along with Bill, I admit. But (a) we can't afford any pretty gestures just yet, really. And (b) we are going to be pretty dependent on local patronage for a long time. The out-of-town people have got out of the habit of coming, with The Oaks run down the way it was. Now, it seems as though Mrs. Rook has a mad on Bob White. Did you hear she refused to go to the Lovejoy bridge party because the Whites were coming? Got Mrs. Lovejoy in an uproar."

"Mrs. Rook's a holy terror," said Hope.

"Just autocratic," said Logan judiciously. "But she gets away with it. Mr. White's a nice guy. I like him. But not smart. I hate this woman-thing myself. But hotels and churches have to please the ladies. I'm in business, and it isn't good business for The Oaks to annoy Mrs. R. That's what Van says. He's the boss, not me, thank the Lord. And while I'm at home, I can stop thinking about it, can't I? I can think about you in your step-ins." He stood up, stretching his still slim, still muscular body languidly, and walked over to her. He did not touch her, merely smiling with the surface of his eyes a promise for the night. He went over to her dressing table and, picking up her brush, smoothed the waves of his hair absently. "There are drawbacks," he said ruefully. "It's not my idea of fun to go to New York as a businessman."

New York had been the goal of his dreams as an artist. She had begged him, even now, to leave the bank and go still in search of his dreams. She had even planned the comfortable attic that they could afford on her money alone. He would not have it that way. A man could not live on his wife's money. An artist was also a man. With a mother. And, now, a child as well as a wife. He sighed, and she echoed him.

"I've got to go and see Mother this afternoon. The train goes pretty early in the morning."

"I'll pack for you," she said eagerly.

"You're an angel," he said. "Now, let's see. New York in September . . ."

Hope went over to her desk and took from one pigeonhole a pad with her name printed in blue ink at the top of each page. From the drawer, she removed two sharp pencils and, picking up one, tapped the eraser against the end of her chin.

"Shall I put in some whiskey?" she asked, calm and happy, enjoying the busy surface of the hour. "And a couple of good mystery stories for the train? I know they're trash," she added as he looked at her dreamily, "but you mustn't try to really read on the train. It's too exhausting. Just to pass the time."

"All right, then," he said, humoring her. "And I suppose a pint of whiskey—no, make it a quart. Or two. I wouldn't trust a New York bootlegger. 'Bye now."

She heard him calling Cecelia as he went down the stairs. Taking the pad, she turned to a second page and began making a separate list of the small things she would buy for him. Tearing off the two pages, she weighted them side by side on the desk and went over to her dressing table to brush her hair and make up her face.

Cecelia was sitting on the back steps, nibbling daintily and alternately at the cookies she held in each hand, when her mother came down. The skirt of Cecelia's fresh dress was hiked up behind so that she would not wrinkle it nor soil by contact with the steps anything but the cotton-knit shorts she wore under the dress. The sun-tinted skin of her round bare arms and sturdy back was so delectable and the face that tilted upward toward Hope so irresistibly round that Hope plumped down beside her and hugged and kissed her. The child accepted the caress with the bored affability of the surfeited.

"You mustn't muss me," she admonished her mother, wriggling to free her arms so that she could continue to carry the diminishing cookies alternately to her mouth. "I'm new." She finished eating, licked the crumbs from her fingers and smoothed the short skirt down so that it reached her knees. "You're new, too." She inspected her mother's linen suit with an air of qualified approval. "Where you going?"

"Downtown to buy some things. Do you want to come with

me?" Hope found her daughter immeasurably charming when she chose to be, and if the choice of being so was deliberate, the charm itself was genuine.

"Toys?" asked Cecelia.

"No. Things for Daddy. On his trip."

Cecelia considered the alternatives. Nanine was busy in the kitchen and Mrs. Stone was talking interminably on the telephone in the living room. Cecelia was in the midst of a feud with her best-friend-of-the-moment, who lived down the block. For answer, she jumped up and began to pull her mother up by the hand.

Moving briskly and competently through the hot afternoon, Hope found the whole town a garden, bright with surface colors. Parking space opened to her, beneath her tires, marked by cool white lines, seemingly reserved for her in the moment she wanted it, in front of the places she had checked as likely to have the things she was seeking. She blew, like a cool, brisk breeze, into the fetid air of the nearly empty stores and received from the desultory clerks a special service almost as competent as her demands. Like fresh-picked posies, they offered her also the easy flattery that always seemed so eager, so sincere, and so spontaneous on the lips of the fragile-skinned, fragile-boned southern clerks. "Mrs. Knight, I declare you get younger every time I see you . . ." And "pretty . . . pretty . . . pretty" applied to her daughter, applied to them both, with astonished exclamations over the fact that there was, if you looked with willing and informed eyes, a resemblance between mother and daughter. Cecelia, trotting agreeably beside Hope, respected her intentness and made no attempt to command her attention. Cecelia accepted her own compliments with airy, avid grace, as one accustomed to flattery, but she was less than impertinent. The concoctions served to them at the curb in front of the Central Drug Store were bouquets of sweetness, and a tall Frankie, serving them, flirted equally and almost fervently with both mother and daughter.

When the last item had been crossed from the neat list, they started with the last small parcel to the car, still fresh and purposeful in the wilted afternoon.

"We did such a *lot* of *things*," said Cecelia.

"Didn't we, though?" said Hope. "You were a great help."

"Yes!" said Cecelia. Then she giggled. "Look. The funny man."

The Reverend Robert White was coming out of a store with an awkward mass of bundles clutched in his arms. He tried to tip his battered panama hat that was set anyhow above the fringe of his hair and, dislodging the hat, also dropped two of his packages. Cecelia laughed with delighted malice.

Hope helped Bob White retrieve his bundles and said to Cecelia, "Say hello to Mr. White."

"Won't," said Cecelia loudly.

"Don't," said Bob White cheerfully, but Cecelia only frowned at him and put her hands behind her back.

Most children loved Bob White, thought Hope fleetingly, but she did not have time to consider this, feeling a rush of self-conscious guilt in his presence. She wanted to warn him, standing there so pink and cheerful and sublimely innocent in the sunshine, that he should, he must, placate Mrs. Rook. They all placated Mrs. Rook. It was a perfectly neat and possible procedure, following naturally on Mrs. Rook's periodic bursts of anger. It would make it so much easier for them all, for Logan, who hated such women-things.

"I've been buying some things for the nursery," said Bob White cheerfully. "One of the littlest ones has a birthday tomorrow."

He did look rather like a cherubic, summertime, messy, birthday-party Santa Claus, thought Hope, irritated. A clergyman had to remember his dignity, just as a businessman did. It was part of the job.

"Can I help you?" asked Hope solicitously, reaching for two of the packages that looked in danger of falling again.

"No, thank you, Hope. Unless you could tell me your secret of staying so cool when you shop. My, I'm hot. Tell your Maw I might drop in for a glass of iced tea later. Eh?"

He trotted off, and Hope was unable to tell him even that her mother had never been able to reconcile herself to the southern manner of dropping in; that Mrs. Stone was also his potential enemy because Mrs. Rook had long ago ruled that Mrs. Stone was to be accepted in Andalusia on very nearly equal terms as herself. Maybe she could tell Arabella, if she could bring herself to make the awkward effort. Bob White trotted off with his packages to his car, jutting carelessly from the curb in a "No Parking" space near the post office. No policeman in Andalusia would even speak sharply to the clergyman. Hope walked quickly and resolutely to her own car, trying to shrug away all thought of him.

Cecelia said, "He's funny."

"Nice funny," said Hope.

"Ha-ha funny," said Cecelia, slyly. "I wanta nother icecream-soda."

"No, indeed, baby," said Hope. "We'll go home now."

They wrangled all the way home, Cecelia stopping short of a tantrum because she did not really want another icecreamsoda, being replete. Hope turned her over to Nanine at the door, disregarding Nanine's furious scolding because she had not informed her that Cecelia was going downtown. She called Alice, the housemaid, to bring up the bundles to her room, and instructed her to saddlesoap Mr. Logan's suitcases, the big one and the smallest, and bring them to her.

Absorbed and precise, she packed the bags she had selected for her husband from among the suitcases she had bought for him two Christmases ago. She chose impersonally and exactly from among his possessions the shirts, the socks, the underwear, and the shoes, the suits and the ties, the tools of cleanliness, that would serve him on his trip. When the job was done, she knew that it had been perfectly done. The tingling in her fingers died. She looked at her watch. Logan would not be home for an hour, or an hour and a half. Then he would be going away. He would be gone in the morning. The time loomed ahead of her, empty and strange.

She stood still, in the middle of her bedroom, to which she had restored final order, so that it might never have been slept in, or packed in, or even lived in, except for the evidence of the firmly closed suitcases and the dress laid out on the bed, to which she would change when she had bathed.

Hope heard the sound of splashing water and the crow of the child who was still a baby. Nanine was ministering to the sweet perfection of her daughter's body. Nanine would prolong the ministrations beyond their purpose, beyond a rite and routine and a brisk pleasure, into a game requiring the patience of a Negro to play.

Hope would be unwelcome if she joined them, if she took away the bony, slow-moving black hands and substituted her own capable ones on the child's delightful body, if she foreshortened into a bath the game in which cleanliness was a by-product. She turned and went into her own bathroom, turning on the shower as hard as it would go.

Dressed and ready for the evening, she stood again in the middle of the floor. There was still a long time before Logan could possibly come home, before it was time to walk in the garden at sunset. She loved the suitable rituals of the sunset hour, the agreeable activity of greeting her husband and her father, of bidding her daughter good night. She was expert and content, making cocktails for them all in the big, heavily furnished, comfortably furnished living room. She enjoyed their recapitulation of their sex-separated day, as if the differences of one day from another were greater than the sameness. It was a splendid time of day, and it would not be the same with Logan away.

Hope looked quickly at the closed door of her room. She moved quickly and went to the closet and opened the door. Stretching, she reached up toward the hats listing slightly on their row of velvet stands. Reaching between a white straw with a rose-colored band and a helmet knitted from gold thread, she drew out from behind the hats a bottle. Tiptoeing into the bathroom and closing its door behind her, she took a glass from a holder over the basin and poured herself a drink. Folding down the top of the toilet, she sat down and took a rapid series of sips.

The house of her mind was in disorder again, littered with old, unhappy thoughts. Cautiously she began to clear and clean and straighten it, until it was neat as a dream house. She took a quick, housekeeper's glance around and was satisfied. Her thoughts were shining and presentable. She was thinking of Logan and how happy she was.

She got up and poured the last spoonful from the glass down the basin drain, clucking as she did so. This was the last time she would nip alone in this fashion. One needed a nip, of course, when one was so rudely awakened. . . . She washed the glass and brushed her teeth, rinsing her mouth from the rinsed glass. She tiptoed out of the bathroom and replaced the bottle on the shelf, behind the hats. One of the velvet stands rocked as her hand brushed it and she steadied it quickly, settling the wide-brimmed hat thereon at an exact, very exact, parallel with the high shelf. She closed the closet door and went to the door of her bedroom. Opening it, she stood there quietly, for a long time, almost immobile, until she heard her mother's bedroom door open and an instant later the front door downstairs.

"There you are!" she exclaimed cheerfully. Now, she thought, I must go down and fix their drinks. Purposefully she walked down the stairs and into the garden that was the hour before dinner. She hoped anxiously that Bob White would stay away. She wanted everything to be nice.

15. The Unmarried

Sprinklers whirled slowly in waltz time, showering the new acres of grass with perishable diamonds. In the middle distance, a Negro man raked smooth the gravel of the curved driveway, moving not quite lackadaisically enough to be graceful. A small black boy with the face of an impish gargoyle was spitting on the rag with which he was polishing the brass knobs and ornate locks on the open double doors at the entrance. The massive doorman stopped watching the boy and turned, with the effect of a low bow, toward Alton Rook.

"Mawnin, Mistuh Rook," said the imp, rolling his eyes sideways and pausing in his work.

Alton Rook recognized him as offspring to Pinckney and Mattie, but could not remember which one he was. "Morning, young un," he said ambiguously.

The doorman, light-colored and tremendous of frame, was a stranger to Alton. He achieved the very nearly impossible, in Alton's opinion, by reprimanding the boy with one eye while with the other he greeted the visitor.

"Can I help you, sir?" he asked, in a colorless accent.

"Did Mrs. Rook leave any word where I could find her?" Alton asked. His wife had telephoned him to meet her at The Oaks. To pick her up, as she put it. Alton, alert to all the absurdities of the language, had an immediate vision of himself struggling to hoist his wife from her feet. She had explained why, but it had not mattered why, and so he had not listened. Something about having driven out with Hannah, who was staying for lunch, and something about Ellen Terra on an errand. Grumpily he had put aside his Sunday by-lined column on which he was working. Being interrupted when you were writing was like being interrupted in the middle of a meal. It was disconcerting. It also gave you literary indigestion.

"It might be she left a message at the desk, sir," said the doorman. "There're lots of ladies here. Some is watching the tennis, sir."

The "is" is the first slip he's made, thought Alton. He looked up and around the man at the newly carpeted hallway leading in to the hotel. He felt a reluctance to enter it. It was too new for him. He had liked it the old way better, the wide wooden hall that echoed to his heels. He was an old-fashioned fogey and must admit that Van Ball was doing a bang-up job on The Oaks. Southern charm plus Statler comfort, thought Alton Rook, and plenty of dignity about both. The young man knew what he was doing. He had excellent taste. Alton should be grateful that the old Oaks was being refurbished with taste.

He decided to try the courts before entering the hotel, although Clementine rarely exposed her porcelain complexion to the sun. It was not the sun that had made it crack into myriad tiny lines, as porcelain did when it was badly baked. Nodding to the doorman and to the imp, he went along the path between the huge canna beds that led to the tennis courts. He was early, anyway. Unable to go back to his column, with departure too imminent for its completion, he had left the office. He could write anything else under any kind of pressure, he thought, like a good newspaper man, but he was tizzy as a poet about his column.

On the first court, his daughter, Ellen Terra, partnered with Dugdale Winthrop, was playing mixed doubles against Mary and Morton Hadley. Alton stopped and watched them, his head nodding back and forth in courteous attention to the play, although he was primarily interested in looking at Ellen Terra. When he saw her thus, not as a child in his house, but as a person among people, outside himself, he was always attracted to her in the queerest way. It was not exactly sex, although Lord knew she was a sexy baggage, but a warm, faintly shocking feeling. If she had been a young lady from, say, Oglethorpe, he would have made an excuse to sit next to her at some point, to talk to her, mock-paternally, to think secret little thoughts about pinching her in plump and tender places. He was, he thought, without condemning himself, an old goat. He was at the age where the tenderer the flesh the more appealing. It was doubtless reprehensible, especially when it verged on mild incest, but there was no point in denying his unguessable thoughts. He was free, of course, to pinch his daughter in the plump and tactilely delightful places that demanded it, as he had been free to do so, and had done so, since she was a sexy little baggage of three. But in the act, he was freed of goatishness. He was still pinching his own baby child, even if she was twenty-three—or twenty-four? He could never remember. In repetition, in habit, there was safety. Funny, he had never been tempted by Tiny, the little one, who was a plump, unattractive thirteen now. Not even when she was a round-bottomed baby. He had never cared to pinch Ellen Terra's sister, only caressing her conscientiously, at decent intervals. He looked at Ellen Terra, forgetting to turn his head when the ball crossed the net away from her. She was rose-pink with exertion and her black bangs clung to her forehead and her face was merry.

"Get your cotton-pickin' fingers off my ball!" she cried to Dugdale, who could never help trying to cover the whole court, as if covering a polo field from the back of a trained pony, stretching his long length behind and before his partner, as if determined to commit suicide rather than let a ball go by him. Ellen Terra made a wild shot, having deflected Dugdale, and the game went to the young Hadleys.

"Why didn't you let me have it?" asked Dugdale mournfully in the pause. "That's five-four."

"'Cause I won't stand here like an old moldy moth-eaten statue," said Ellen Terra.

Where did his brainless child get her way of talking?, wondered Alton for the hundredth time. Then she saw him. "Hi, Pop," she called.

He waved, indicating that they should go on playing and take no time out for amenities in the direction of his elderly presence.

Morton prepared to serve and Mary stood planted at the net, her head twisted so that she could frown back at him. They had been married three years now, reflected Alton, and it could be a hundred. Even his Clementine had not begun to bully him quite so thoroughly quite so soon. And Clementine had kept the powerful charms of her immense sexuality for quite a long time, too, he reflected. Mary had been married and had scarcely allotted enough time for a honeymoon before she was pregnant, sick, unattractive and domineering. So much for his theory that this was a better generation! Mary did not even pretend to be sexually deferent, which the older women, even Clementine, had the grace to do. She had taken Morton's meager ego right out in front of the whole town and murdered it, stone dead. His Ellen Terra had never so much as teased a man over the tenderness of his ego. Not even her father, he thought suddenly. And yet no man had appreciated her enough to take her to wife. Men wanted women to be insufferably hard to get, for the satisfaction of their egos, and then let them become merely insufferable without protest. Men and women together were conniving to destroy men, to make them into edible spiders, serving as procreators and meals! "Nize babies, itt opp all de gemmun," he thought, paraphrasing Milt Gross, and walked hastily away.

He considered sending Ellen Terra away, if Clementine would let him. He would miss her tactile presence, her purring voice, the non sequiturs and the adjectives of her speech—but there must be somewhere in the world where men outnumbered women. There must be somewhere in the world where a large humility of spirit was a virtue. And anywhere else his poor child would not be condemned, by rote, for the simple-minded enthusiasm with which she gave away everything she had—free. Anywhere else they would not know how much she had given away, since she still had so much to give. The record of her philanthropy had been kept from birth, in the town of her birth, in the minute, parsimonious bookkeeping that went on in small towns.

Pausing again at the second court, where a number of people were watching the game from the side, he pretended to look for Clementine, but again grew interested in the contestants.

Logan Knight and Bill Bloodgood were fighting out the end of a game. While Alton stood watching, the score returned twice to deuce. The points were lengthily achieved. Bill was a powerful player, driving for the baseline, his shoulders behind each shot. Logan took each one on his ubiquitous racquet, seemingly languid, putting no power into his returns, but always, somehow, getting them back, usually getting them back though they came like bullets, though they touched the farthest edge of the line farthest away from the place where he was. He won a point when Bill finally drove out, or when Logan patted a return gently enough so that Bill could not drive and he could cunningly cut the returned ball away from Bill's racquet. He lost when one of Bill's drives came too fast and too accurately for him. It was an interesting match, irritating in a way, because Bill was the more attractive and the better player, but Logan would win. Alton was sure that Logan would win.

Unable to leave the game until it was decided, he went over and sat down beside Van Ball, who sat apart from the other spectators. He felt, subconsciously, that he was being kind to the stranger from New York to go and sit beside him. Van acknowledged him with a quick nod, a turning up of his thin, well-cut, drooping mouth into the simulation of a smile, and both men settled into watchfulness, their heads metronomes of attention to the game. Alton was momentarily caught up in pleasure at the classic beauty of the two players. He was always affected by human beauty or ugliness. The young men were of a good height and age and were both at the peak of their well-cared-for physical maturity. It was, to Alton, a handsomer thing than the unfinished beauty of youth. Bill was stockily proportioned, broad-shouldered and sturdily thighed. His hair sprung away from his big head, the fact that it would thin already apparent, but the process not yet far along. His face was strongly featured, the cleft giving no weakness yet to the chin, and his eyes were a wild, bright blue. Logan was slim and almost fragile in appearance, narrow-hipped and clean-limbed. He had a narrow, sweet-featured face and the air of an other-worldling.

The game went to Logan when he patted one back that Bill hit ferociously into the net. There was applause from the small group of spectators who sat down the way from Alton and Van Ball. It was the sympathetic applause that goes to the winner who is obviously the less equipped to win. Logan made no claim to be an athlete. Bill played a much better game than Logan. Or so it looked. Bill, mopping his ruddy forehead, tied a handkerchief around it over his eyes to protect them from sweat. Logan murmured apologetically, as if he had won by luck and not by rights. He looked over once at the spectators, his light brown eyes expressing his rueful apologetic gratitude for their applause. Logan prepared to serve.

"What's the score, Van?" Alton asked Van Ball. He was still unwilling to leave.

"Six-five," said Van, adding, "Mr. Rook." His voice expressed no sense of an inequality in their ages, despite the term of his address. "That Logan Knight is a son of a gun, isn't he? Never misses a return. It's amazing."

"I'd hate to play him," Alton surprised himself by saying. "Spoils the game."

Van looked faintly contemptuous. "He wins," he said. "Isn't that what counts in a game?"

"Is it?" asked Alton mildly. It was years since he had bothered to argue anything more subtle than the price of newsprint.

"I'm no sportsman," said Van, offering information about himself with an air of offering something of necessary interest to the listener. "I admit it." It was a boast, not an apology. "I'll tell you a secret, Mr. Rook. I fish with worms." He leaned back and laughed secretly.

"So do I," said Alton, chuckling, not unamused. "I never saw the sense in being fair to fish."

Van laughed again, this time offering his laughter to be shared, taking it for granted that Alton meant more, instead of just exactly what he had said. "Look at that," he said admiringly, as Logan barely retrieved a smashing ball and floated it back to Bill. "Bill's a fish for those."

Alton looked and was unreasonably glad when Bill managed to drive the ball back, although he drove it straight at Logan for an easy return.

"By the way," said Van, an introduction that warned Alton that he had something of direct importance to say, "it's under that old hat still, but I want *you* to know. I've hired Logan to work for me. I haven't figured out the title yet—don't want to hurt Bill's feelings, as you can understand—but Logan will be the financial manager here and in charge when I'm gone. I'll have an announcement for your paper, and we'll have some kind of party."

"Thanks for telling me," said Alton formally. "A newspaperman always likes to know these things first. Makes him feel wise, y'know, and gives him time to tell everybody else. Good for the paper. But," he went on, thinking of Logan, whom he had known all these years as a dreamy child, a stringy adolescent for whom his better teachers had high, poetic hopes, a beautiful young man who had won an art scholarship at a good university because character counted high and he had made excellent grades while waiting on table to ease the burden on his mother, "I'm kind of surprised."

"Listen," said Van, in his nasal, rhythmic voice. "*You* shouldn't be."

Van paused after the implied compliment and Alton Rook waited, expectant and somewhat puzzled.

Van turned toward him with a hesitant air. "I was raised on Rembrandt and Tschaikowsky and Latin," he said surprisingly.

The digression seemed important to him. Alton nodded vigorously in encouragement, and offered him his listening face.

"I'm cultured as hell," said Van, his color rising, and went on, with nasal belligerence, to say in a tumble of words something that had obviously been on his mind for some time, "I enjoy it. But who bought the Rembrandts and had Paderewski play in our drawing room and paid for the tutors? Grandfather Ball, who couldn't write when he died, except his name on checks. This is corny, Mr. Rook, but it's still true! You southerners forget it. I love it down here. I'm a man who can appreciate the biggest art of all. Gracious living! My uncle, Schuyler VanDyck, on Manhattan Island, knew all about it, and he ran his hotel that way. But nobody's got time for it any more in New York. That's why I came down here to build *my* hotel. But you can't confuse gracious living today with yesterday's. That's why I like Andalusia better than Oglethorpe. It's still alive. But there's still the Oglethorpe attitude, I call it. I get bloody well sick of it! I don't like people to want me to thank *them* because *I* do them a favor. You know what I mean, Mr. Rook. A couple of the old gals even told me I was desecrating this tumble-down old mess of a hotel because I'm fixing it up for people to live in graciously again. For crying out loud!"

He's right to resent our attitude toward him, thought Alton. But he is a fish, just the same. He's fallen for Southern Culture. He's fallen for Gracious Living in the Old South.

"You'll bring us your prosperity," he said, curtailing his self-entertainment and turning to tease the young man. The Yankee myth of permanent prosperity was as unsubstantial as the southern myth of culture. "And we'll give you culture . . ."

Van turned on him defensively, suspicious, and then no longer suspicious as he looked into the crinkly, mock-candid blue eyes in the thin, worn, bland face. He was intended to share the joke. "I knew I could talk to you," he said, hiding his eagerness beneath his pride in his sophistication. "This place will prosper, all right. I know what I'm doing. I know what I want. I'm a realist."

Alton looked back at the court. Any loud claim to realism bored him.

"Some people will think I'm wrong about Logan, just like they thought I was wrong about buying The Oaks. It's the same thing. That dreamy air—wonderful for doing business. It intrigues people. Makes 'em think they're getting poetry for their money. Stuff you can't buy. Nuts! You can buy anything. Logan wants to paint, and everybody admires him because he's an artist. He'll have enough money to retire and paint if he really wants to by the time he's fifty. I tell you, he's the shrewdest businessman in town. Don't tell me! But he doesn't offend people with it. He's the one for me. I know how to pick 'em."

Still bored by Van's truculent attitude, Alton nonetheless

was again stimulated by what he said. He considered Logan, under the guise of watching the game again. By golly, Van, the self-professed realist, was right this time. That was the mysterious secret of Logan's two-depth eyes! Always had been. He was playing it both ways. The town accepted the young man as they had the boy. As a boy, he had sacrificed his dream of idleness to work at school, so that he could try for the scholarships that would ease the burden on his mother. Everybody had fallen for that. As a young man, he had come home. He was sacrificing his artist's career to support his mother. And then he had fallen in love with pretty Hope, although everybody had put him down as Angela's natural mate. Ah, but he could never be accused of marrying the boss's daughter, which was just exactly what he had done. And no matter what happened to him, he was protected. He was an artist, poor boy, who had left his art in the name of honor for the sake of his mother, then his wife, and his child. Nor could anybody say he was not an artist. They would never know. He would be forgiven for anything he painted at fifty, if he did. He had sacrificed the best years of his artistic life. . . . Alton wished with all his heart that Bill would win the game he was watching. Bill was a bundle of absurd faults, but Bill was what he was. He stood or fell by the awkward open standards he set up for himself.

Alton rose, saying that he must fetch his wife before it rained, as the oppressive air indicated that it would do. He looked and saw clouds gathering at the edges of the sky, although the sky overhead was clear and perfect. It was really of no importance to him that Bill Bloodgood, an erratic and often overbearing player, an erratic and ill-disciplined and often overbearing human being, should lose a game of tennis. But he did not want to see Logan win. He did not want to see Logan deprecate his winning, as though he brooded behind his artist's eyes because tennis was only a game, not worth the winning.

As Alton ambled back to the hotel, he heard, in a kind of second take, what Van was saying as he left him. Deferential greetings to Mrs. Rook—that was the hotel keeper speaking—and a smart suggestion for enlivening the announcement about Logan so that it would get space in the metropolitan papers. Alton threw assent back to Van over his shoulder, nodding at him briskly in an attempt to be friendly.

He entered the card room at the hotel in time to hear his wife's penetrating voice, not loud, but inescapable, projected from some special acoustical arrangement in her china white throat. "I never was so furious in all my life. That nasty little man is literally being *rude* to my *dear*, dead mother. . . ."

Alton Rook felt his spirit turn stone-still inside him and then turn and run like a rabbit down some dark, inner hole. Clementine saw him and murmured parenthetically in her carrying murmur, "So *sweet* of you to come for me, darling," before she finished her other sentence. Bob White was a completely honest man, he thought. He made no compromises at all with what he was. But nobody could treat the universe as his house, the world as his equal, women in human terms, and get away with it.

Ellen Terra came up behind him and pinched his ear. He jumped, as if she had hurt him.

"Don't fidgety," she admonished him.

He wished his daughter, expressive as she was, would obey a few grammatical rules. He noticed that her brief shock of coarse black hair sparkled as though she had been under one of the whirling sprinklers.

"It's started to rain," she replied as if he had asked her. "Just in time to save me and Dugdale from defeat."

He noticed the other tennis players and the spectators drifting their several ways along the corridor outside the card room. Some of them were going to the "Hunt Club," a room that served as a speakeasy. Others were dividing to leave by the front or the side entrance of the hotel and several were headed for the spacious dining room. He noticed Dugdale Winthrop, walking as if he had just climbed down from his horse, and Sonny Boy Lovejoy, trotting like a puppy, beside him. They had linked arms in what they called their Mutt and Jeff pose. He saw the schoolmaster, David Bradford, who had brought his mother all the way from Louisville to see Carrie and who would now undoubtedly marry Carrie. A thin, undistinguished-looking fellow, carrying a balloonlike head on the stalk of his neck, he had a way with children, and no doubt, with women. He had managed to get Alton's own young wooden-headed hellion, Agrippa, to learn something, thought Alton charitably. Clementine was wholly pleased with him. The Oakland Tutoring School would flourish, no doubt, if The Oaks flourished. God knew it was better than the sloppy Andalusia P. S. And David, as its headmaster, would be an addition to the community, especially as Carrie's husband. Still, David seemed inadequate to Carrie. Alton liked Carrie.

Alton made a face. What difference did it all make? So this was the way things went. To hell with it, he thought. Get out of here, Ellen Terra, for God's sake, go away! You need something tougher than the breed around here. You've given too many bits of yourself to these lesser men. Go out to California and marry a truck driver, for God's sake. Go to Texas and marry a self-made millionaire. Go to Pennsylvania and find a coal miner. He had once said to her—it was when Dugdale and Sonny Boy were alternating at the house, boring him to death by being so polite to her father before going out to seduce Ellen Terra, or to accept her seduction—you need somebody to beat you black and blue. He had said that to her, and she had laughed.

He reached out and pinched Ellen Terra's cheek, her downy, hard-rubber cheek, until she let out a startled "Ouch." He let go, and patted her on the plump, irresistible buttock nearest him.

"Run along," he said to his daughter, "and don't bother me."

He was very tired. Middle-aged, he thought, was a wearisome thing to be. You still had your energy without the faith to expend it. You had lost your optimism, but had not gained resignation. "Ah youth," he quoted to himself, looking at his child. "Pass the bottle."

They came to the thin edge of the lessening rain and crossed through it and out into torrential sunshine. The end of the rain was marked across the road with a dotted line, like a county line on a map. The dust eddied under the front tires on the dry road and rose behind the car in a high, thick stream that lengthened as they moved, ending at the edge of the rain.

"I like rain," said Ellen Terra. "I like sunshine better."

"What don't you like?" asked Carrie without turning her

head, steering the car skillfully to straddle the rough, worn ruts, which trapped most of the road's traffic.

"Hail," said Ellen Terra. "I hate hail."

"Poor hail," said Carrie. "Why?"

"It's so inconsiderate," said Ellen Terra.

"We're late," said Carrie.

"Doesn't matter," said Ellen Terra. "Uncle Peter's always there with the key and he'll know where the package is. It's only some cans of the new gumbo they're making at The Place. For mother to try at home. It won't be too heavy for Peter to lift. I like gumbo."

"What don't you like?" asked Carrie.

"Okra," said Ellen Terra. "Okra by itself. It looks so naked and nasty and green and it spits."

"Put in a nickel and you always get a candy bar," said Carrie. "Ellen Terra, you're priceless."

"I can't ever tell when you're making fun of me," complained Ellen Terra.

"Never!" said Carrie. "Oh, God damn it to hell."

"What's the matter?"

"We're overheating. Look." The red column on the register had risen above the line marked "danger." "If I stop, we'll boil over. How far is The Place now, do you think?"

"About five miles, I reckon," said Ellen Terra. "Can we make it?"

"Maybe. Oops. No!" The column rose abruptly to the top edge of the glass.

Still functioning coolly, although she felt a half-irrational fear for the car, Carrie spotted a break, farther down the road, in the sliverlike pines that lined the road and offered no shade in the fierce noonday. Heading for the break without changing her speed, she turned into the break when she reached it, bouncing across a shallow ditch and a dusty hummock into the cleared space in front of a gray board cabin. She wrenched the car abruptly under the umbrella-shaped canopy of a chinaberry tree that stood in the space. The drooping branches at the edge of the umbrella scraped the top of the windshield and the nose of the car touched the thick trunk of the tree as she pulled on the brake.

"Get out!" she commanded Ellen Terra, putting the car in neutral and leaving the motor running. "And get away!"

Ellen Terra scrambled out of her side of the car and ran across the clearing. Sticky and trembling with the necessity for controlling her imperfect body with deliberation, Carrie opened the door beside the steering wheel, thumped to the ground and moved with awkward rapidity to the other side of the tree. The car rumbled and burbled ominously. The hood shook and the dignified silver figure of Diana in flight that decorated the radiator cap shimmied in an incongruous, Little Egypt dance. The two women watched the car, preparing to duck if the boiling water should geyser. In a minute, the sounds and the shaking began to diminish slightly.

"We might find some water here," said Carrie, her voice normal and calm. "Hey!" she called. Her voice seemed to catch along the pines that encircled the clearing, like a stick lightly rubbing a picket fence, and then to return to die at her feet. Looking at the cabin, she saw that it leaned precariously to one side and that the beam that had propped up one wall on the outside had fallen to the ground. The steps to the porch were broken and the porch rested on three sawed-off tree roots, the fourth having rotted away so that there were inches of space between it and the sagging corner of the porch.

"Shall we go in and see if there's a faucet inside?" asked Ellen Terra, regarding the house dubiously. "It looks like the old black witch's house."

"Oh, it wouldn't have running water," said Carrie. "Don't be silly. It's just deserted. Lots of them from around here moved into town. To be nearer the soup kitchen, I reckon. There might be a pump out back. Ouch!" As she moved, several dry sandspurs from one of the clumps that matted the clearing caught in her ankle. "You'd think these things were alive," she said, bending down to remove the fierce little balls that clung to her skin by half a dozen minute hooks each. "Ouch, damn it."

"Want me to turn the motor off now?" asked Ellen Terra.

"Not yet. Come on." Gingerly Carrie picked her way among the sandspur clumps and around the cabin. There was a well with a long-handled iron pump at the back of the house. Carrie raised and lowered the rusty handle twice, screwing up her face at the dry screeches emitted by the ancient pump. "It would need a bucket of water to prime it, if there's any water in the well, anyway. And if we had a bucket of water, we wouldn't need the pump," she said.

"Now what?" said Ellen Terra, stopping about two yards from Carrie. "Nobody ever uses this lonesome road this time of day or anyway much."

"I know that," said Carrie, annoyed. She sat down on the smooth-topped oak stump that had previously been used as a back-yard chair and got up again when the gnats swirled up to her and surrounded her in hundreds. Waving her arms through the cloud of insects, she said angrily, "You'll have to go for help, Ellen Terra. And I'll have to wait for you in this minor-league hell hole."

"Five miles!" said Ellen Terra dolefully.

"Oh, hush. You could do it on the golf course and not even notice. I'd rather go than stay, but I'd only slow things up. Besides, you'll probably find a nigra on the way and he can tote you a bucket of water back here. If anybody comes in this direction, I'll come on down the road and pick you up."

"All right," said Ellen Terra, deftly murdering a mosquito that had lit on her arm.

"And *hurry*."

"In this heat?"

"It's better than sitting still. Get going."

"Yas'm," drawled Ellen Terra in the tone of a reluctant Negro girl, but she started to move with comparative briskness.

"Go *on!*" shouted Carrie after her when Ellen Terra turned to wave at the bend in the road. The thin pines closed behind Ellen Terra. The little clouds of dust raised by her heels subsided. Carrie was alone.

She went over to the car, climbed in, and turned off the motor. The radiator thumped violently in brief reaction and then there was silence except for the Lilliputian roar and whine of the high-powered insect world to which the clearing now belonged. Carrie pulled down the sleeves of her blouse and drew her legs up under her pleated skirt to diminish the areas of exposed skin. Taking the pillow she habitually used behind her back, she adjusted it under her head. A lifetime of discomfort had made her adept in the art of relaxing purposefully to counter discomfort.

Gradually her body grew somnolent, the insects took her for granted, and her thoughts took the shape of a dialogue with Angela. The dialogue took on the reality of a dream dreamed just before waking and she could hear her own voice and Angela's. They spoke of a fact of which they had never spoken and then they talked of the few things of which they had never talked, or had spoken of only in the elliptical, euphemistic speaking that concealed more than it revealed. There was a delicately defined area of reticence among them all and it was this area that Carrie and Angela invaded now.

. . . you see, darling, i knew david had asked you and then ellen terra to go with him to the cotillion before he asked me, but both of you had dates.

. . . you did know? said angela, surprised. i never told you. ellen terra didn't tell you.

. . . no, but david did and then he gave me this lighter to make up for that. he's sweet.

angela merely nodded.

. . . do you like david, angela?

. . . i told you i did. he's rather formal, don't you think? and louisville sounds like a mean, dirty kind of place. still kentucky's south and i suppose those stiff collars are because he's a schoolteacher. sure, i like him.

. . . he's sweet. sweet and foolish and he reads poetry—like a poet.

. . . sounds fascinating, said angela in a dry voice.

. . . it's sheer southern barbarism to think a man should not read poetry!

. . . don't be touchy, carrie, said angela sharply. Then, unexpectedly, do you love him, carrie?

. . . he looks at me as if he could not believe i exist because i am so wonderful.

. . . that's not what i asked you, said angela.

. . . well, how would I know for sure? i've only had practice in not loving men so far. of course i love him.

. . . will you be happy, carrie? asked angela persistently.

239

. . . what the hell does it matter? you talk such bunk. you can be happy if you like, if you can. i don't even mind your happiness. you have a nice kind of happiness, like a song singing, when you are happy. why aren't you happy more often since you have such a charming, inoffensive way of being happy?

. . . let's don't talk about me, said angela.

. . . i can't stand most people when they are happy. not ellen terra because she gets so soft and goddamn silly and not hope because she wants everybody to clap hands and make a circle when she's happy and it makes me want to spit in her eye and go off and mope. or else she boasts about it as if she invented it. and not my mother when she gets cooing over her damn roses. and not your bill bloodgood when he goes on a rampage of happiness because he hurts my eyes and ears. bob white can be happy if he likes because he just goes around like a walking sun. but not anybody else. not around me. except children. everything is except children.

. . . didn't know you liked children so much, said angela. always thought you couldn't stand them.

. . . a lot you know about me, for all you know about me.

. . . nobody knows anything about anybody except themselves, said angela. well, what do you want, carrie gregory, if you don't want to be happy?

. . . unhappy people belong together.

. . . like sick people? asked angela.

. . . I'M NOT SICK.

. . . of course you're not! angela was indignant. she spoke soothingly. he's a gentleman, there's that. she added hastily, seeing carrie frown. besides i do like him. i even flirted with him to make bill mad and ellen terra did flirt with him seriously, for all the good it did her.

. . . he wasn't interested.

. . . only in you, said angela obligingly.

. . . it hurt so when it happened.

. . . it always does, said angela.

. . . how do you know? have you and bill . . . ?

. . . so I've heard, said angela, smiling her virginal smile and carrie had to admit that she had almost, but not quite, trapped her and that she still did not know whether angela and bill had.

. . . it hurt inside, terribly, and it hurt my leg. he seemed to lie so heavy on my leg and it was the only part of me he caressed, over and over, so tenderly, and it hurt so dreadfully. i don't mind pain, you know. this is something you learn. to move into it. to meet it and take it on, to welcome it in a way. if you shrink from it, if you are scared of it, if you try to get out of it, it's no good. you have to move to meet it and make it belong to you, or else you belong to it. but that is something you learn after a long time. so i didn't mind that it hurt me. but it seemed to hurt him, too. I don't understand that. can it hurt them, too?

. . . i don't know, said angela, smiling enigmatically.

. . . he said carrie, carrie, carrie, when it was over, and he was glad. not happy. glad. and then he said good night very formally and kissed me on the forehead—on the forehead—and went away. the next day he came and took me out to oakland to his school. he didn't say anything the way one might expect, but he took me out to see his boys. angela, you don't know about little boys. i never knew any, since they stopped pulling my braids at school. they are so nice, so decent and so nice. he has six now to tutor. and there will be lots more when more people come to oakland when van and bill get oakland really going. he's going to make it a boarding school when he can. he used to teach in a boarding school in kentucky.

. . . i know all that, said angela.

. . . he's so sweet with them, angela. to see him walking down the path with his arm around a shoulder and a damn little brat's beautiful face looking up at him. you know how david looks, like an overgrown kid, an ichabod crane, gawky and all legs and arms and his neck's sort of thin and young and those medieval manners of his. but when he's with one of them, he looks sad and broody beautiful.

. . . i can hardly believe it, said angela.

. . . oh shut up! and one of them said to me, the snub nose from new york, miss carrie, where'd you get the game leg? no guff. no not looking. just where'd you get the game leg, miss carrie? i said i had infantile paralysis and this one, his name's jimmy and he comes from new york, said, gee, miss carrie, just like governor roosevelt. gee. do you know what that did to me? and david just smiled at us both.

241

. . . very touching. then what? said angela, sounding like carrie talking to angela instead of angela talking to carrie.

. . . you met his mother, said carrie.

. . . of course i did. charming lady. if you can stand all that junk jewelry, said angela.

. . . she was wonderful to me, said carrie, honestly, angela. i thought it was gush at first, but she means it. she couldn't be happier if she'd picked me out and arranged the whole thing. it was pretty nice for me. i'm not exactly the wife mothers dream about, you know, am i? it was a little bit embarrassing because david hadn't asked me yet, but it made me feel good, too. and she gave me a really beautiful pin, just before she left.

. . . a beautiful pin? asked angela derisively.

. . . *yes*. david's great-grandmother's, damn you. and i didn't dare wear it until last night when david asked me to marry him. he told me i was the only woman in the world for him, the only one there had been or would be, all his life long. and that's all i'll tell you about that, angela madison. it sounds absurd in the telling, but it was—wonderful. and he begged me to forgive him, too, for being a beast. if you laugh, i'll kill you. and me, i'd been wondering why he didn't make any more passes at me and why i wasn't pregnant, which i wasn't. he wanted to have waited, he said, but he couldn't.

. . . it's not as easy as that to get pregnant, said angela. fortunately, and it's not easy to wait.

. . . so i find. but some day i will have one of those wonderful, bright-faced brats for mine.

. . . like cecelia, said angela.

. . . not like cecelia! she's a girl and anyway it's not her fault. it's never their fault when they're babies.

. . . are you going to marry him? asked angela.

. . . this morning i got a letter from him saying that no matter what happened he would be a better man because i existed. he's so sweet.

. . . are you going to marry him? asked angela.

. . . do you want me to be an old maid because you and everybody else thought i was stuck with it?

. . . don't be nasty, said angela. with all my heart, i wish you well. you know that much, you suspicious bitch.

. . . he thinks i'm the most wonderful thing in the world. oh, he's sweet. maybe he has never even kissed another woman. go on and giggle, damn you, you and your bill bloodgood who has kissed at least fifty women to my certain knowledge.

   . . . lay off bill!

   . . . sorry. but my david is sweet, and sad, and i cherish him tenderly. you hear? tough old carrie gregory, how i do go on. *yes*, i'm going to marry him and tonight i'll tell him so. that's long enough to wait, isn't it? even for the victorians? he's an early victorian, that's what he is, angela. and i like it.

   . . . that's fine, said angela. if you like it.

   . . . i do!

   . . . you can have it, said angela.

   . . . go to hell.

Carrie drowsed off gradually, angry with Angela for being so unsympathetic. To hell with Angela.

Ellen Terra had a blister on her left heel before she had gone half a mile. Slowing her pace to accommodate a painful limp, she pouted and fumed. It's all very well on a golf course, she thought, but she'd have worn comfortable oxfords on a golf course.

Trying to protect her left heel, she came down too heavily on the right. The high spike on which she balanced turned and she almost fell. Now her right ankle was distinctly sore. She stopped walking. The sun promptly focused on her unprotected head and the sweat began to roll from the sensitive glands of her body, under her arms, behind her knees, from under the black bang of her hair. She took a handkerchief from the damp cleft between her breasts and wiped the sweat from her forehead and her upper lip. There was a wet, dirty mark on the handkerchief where she had wiped off the dust with the sweat. Insects materialized and multiplied around her. Frantically she began to move forward again.

There was no use going back the half-mile to the car where Carrie was waiting in the chinaberry's shade. Beyond Carrie, in that direction, lay six or eight miles of road, along which they had just passed, through telephoneless, waterless pine country, not only deserted, but never inhabited by anybody. She did not dare go into the thin woods around her for their shade. The woods were full of chiggers and probably snakes. Ellen Terra had never wanted to investigate the properties of any snake. They were all equally alarming to her. If she and Carrie had only taken the familiar road leading from farther along the highway, someone would have picked them up or some farmer brought them water. This cut-off from Oakland was a track through a desert of second-growth pine, through a skinny wilderness of miserable, short-needled trees that did not even smell pleasant. Still, nearer The Place, she must find some cabins in which Negroes lived.

Ellen Terra stopped again and took off her shoes. She had an impulse to sling them petulantly into the dry depression beside the road and to leave them there, but they looked so inadequate and dainty and fragile in her hand that she crooked her finger into the narrow strips of leather that ran from the thin ankle straps to the fretwork at the toes and prepared to carry them. The dust squidged through her toes and her feet felt better. A few steps demonstrated that there was caked dirt with sharp edges under the dust and pebbles from which even the thinnest of leather soles had protected her. Her feet shrank tenderly from every further step.

It was then that she heard the noise. In a panic of hope, she listened with held breath and forward-tnrust head. The noise grew louder and there could be no mistaking the smooth functioning of a powerful, properly cooled engine. Flinging brief thanks in the direction of God, Ellen Terra began a hobbled running down the road. When the car came into sight far down between the pines, she ran into the middle of the road and waved her arms over her head.

The car approached at an alarming speed, its driver contesting the right of the rutted, piny woods wagon track to slow the highway pace of his powerful machine. Ellen Terra leaped, alarmed, to the side of the road, waving her shoes at the car.

Heavy brakes brought the long, low monster to an abrupt halt, and Van Ball said, "Why, Ellen Terra Rook!"

The dust caught up with the car and eddied and settled around them and over the car.

"Hi!" said Ellen Terra breathlessly, indignant and importunate, and then hushed.

They contemplated each other for a wordless instant. Ellen

Terra's mouth, bitten formless and pink and free of lipstick, hung slightly open. Van's compressed and chiseled mouth relaxed into a smile and then into a wide grin.

"Get in!" he ordered her spontaneously.

Obediently she trotted around the car and opened the door on the other side and climbed into the seat. Both of them were immediately self-conscious because he had not performed the ceremony of getting out and helping her into the car. Ellen Terra squirmed and wiggled her bare, dusty toes, and then brought one foot up over her knee and inspected it tenderly.

"You have pretty feet," exclaimed Van involuntarily.

"I got a blister," said Ellen Terra, hastily putting her foot back down and touching her face with her free hand. Her shoes were clutched in the other.

"Nobody has pretty feet," said Van, frowning. Then he demanded, "What *are* you doing like this?"

"Carrie's down the road," said Ellen Terra. "We boiled over. I'm so thankful you came along."

"I was looking for you," said Van. "Your mother said you had gone to The Place. I went there and they said you came by this fearful road. . . . Damn it, I was going to ask you to lunch."

"Not like this," said Ellen Terra.

Van's face resumed its habitual expression of touchy sophistication. "My, you're dirty," he said, mocking her.

"You just try walking miles and miles in the stinky hot sun," said Ellen Terra.

Van put the car into gear and started off. "Ball to the rescue," he said. "You were born out of your class, Ellen Terra. You look adorable dirty. I feel like a City Slicker in a Grade B movie."

"You talk so funny," said Ellen Terra, suddenly peaceful. "I just love to hear you talk."

"Don't give me that southern sweet-talk, you-all," said Van.

Ellen Terra pouted. It was right mean of fate to let him, of all people, catch her like this, bare and dirty of face, with a blister on her heel, even odorous from her noontime ordeal. "I want to go home," she said childishly.

"I'll take you home," he said, "dirty face. Don't worry."

The car was rocking and rocketing along the rough track. Ellen Terra averted her face. Clutching her shoes, she kept herself from swaying in his direction. It was no distance at all in the car to the cabin where Carrie's car stood under the chinaberry tree.

Carrie heard the car coming as if in a dream and then too real to be a dream. She sat up and reaching into her bag brought out a compact and a comb and refreshed her sleep-crumpled appearance. She heard Ellen Terra call "Hi . . ."

Van helped Ellen Terra out of his car and they came toward Carrie.

"Good God, Ellen Terra, you're a sight," exclaimed Carrie. "How in heaven's name did you get that filthy?"

Ellen Terra wiped her dusty face with her soiled hand. She wanted to cry. "I don't know what in the little old world I'd have done if Van hadn't come along," she offered.

"It's wonderful that you did, Van," said Carrie graciously.

Ellen Terra resented Carrie's pure-boned, pure-bred, high-held face. She resented the clear poise of the low voice. Carrie would never get disheveled merely from walking a bit in the sun.

"Could you take us home? Then we'll come back with water later, in Ellen Terra's car."

Carrie, in her decisive way, was making the suggestion least likely to cause their rescuer embarrassment or trouble. She was getting Ellen Terra by the most direct route to the bathtub. Ellen Terra ceased to feel resentment and was grateful. She turned with gratitude to Van, lifting up to him her dirty face.

"You were sweet," she said humbly. "I'm sorry about lunch, hear?"

"I'll call you next time," said Van. He sounded derisive. But he always sounded derisive. "Tomorrow, maybe," he added.

In the morning, when Angela came for her, Ellen Terra went on out with Angela in the car. She was sure it was bad luck to stay at home waiting for the telephone to ring. It never rang when you listened for it. But riding with Angela toward the drug store where they would stop for a Coke, she was miserably restless.

"What's the matter?" asked Angela.

"I've got the blues," said Ellen Terra. "Don't drive so fast. I found a gray hair this morning. Right here." She touched her black bang.

"One gray hair in hair like yours doesn't mean a thing," said Angela. "Look at your mother's."

"She dyes it," said Ellen Terra. "We streak. I can't stand it. I pulled mine out with tweezers. I'd love to be a little old lady," she added, "in a shawl, squeaking at my deaf husband. Wouldn't you? But I sure do buckety loathe getting old." She wanted to get married. You could go right ahead and get old, once you got married. She did not really want just to get married. She only wanted to be married before she was old. Otherwise the pictures did not fit. She fitted herself, as a round-faced, black-eyed, white-haired little old lady, in a shawl, next to a cheery, tired little fat man with a white fringe who looked like Bob White and stamped into a shiny kitchen at the end of a wisteria passageway, looking for a glass of orange juice—next to a cranky, crotchety, meager-bodied Van, tapping his gold-headed cane and sipping port by a giant hearth. . . . She could not imagine being married to Bob White, of course, but she could imagine pampering someone who grew to look like Bob White and then who grew sweeter and sweeter and older and older. She could imagine being angelically patient with Van when he was at least ninety years old. . . . It was a sign that you really loved someone if you could imagine loving them old.

"I saw Van yesterday," said Ellen Terra. "He's . . ."

"He's up to something," said Angela cheerfully. "I feel it in my bones. Ellen Terra, I wish you'd find out what it is."

"Oh, he's always up to something," said Ellen Terra. "He can't help it, poor sweetie. He just can't sit still and be up to nothing. He admires you greatly," she added pleasantly.

"Good," said Angela. "He's still up to something. Bill thinks so, too. You find out."

"I'll tell you if I do," said Ellen Terra. "He said he might call me up this morning."

"Why didn't you say so?" said Angela. "Let's go have something at your house. He's not the type that keeps on calling."

"That's a good idea," said Ellen Terra, immensely relieved.

Angela let go of the wheel for a brief instant, stretching her arms upward over her head, and then caught the wheel, preparing to turn the car around. "I feel so good!" she said joyously. "This summer's going on forever!"

16.   Marry Me Do

There was a hunter's moon, pomegranate-colored and pumpkin-sized, in a wild muscadine-colored sky.

Ellen Terra paused between Schuyler VanDyck Ball's car and his house, the night whole and beautiful and huge around her, now that they had ceased to hack it to pieces with noise and movement.

"It's the loveliest, stillest, *biggest* night," whispered Ellen Terra. She turned her hands outward from the wrists and lifted her round head and her round bosom toward the round moon. The tall pine trees stood like royal sentinels, having laid a thick carpet for their feet and scented the world around them.

"Are you waiting—for me to kiss you?" asked Van, touching his light, clipped mustache, defending himself against the obvious night and the obvious girl. His voice reassured him, as it always did, of his invincible sophistication. It was the very best voice that the best metropolitan money could buy. It spoke in rushing little phrases, pronounced as single words, with pauses between the phrases, like two-beat rests. The timbre was half-drawl, half-snarl, the cadence rhythmic and unmusical, the accent half-discarded-British and half-early-American-gutter.

Ellen Terra turned to him. "I just *love* to hear you talk," she said.

He grasped her elbow and she moved with him pliantly, as if they were dancing. He shook her arm and pulled a little. Feeling what it was he wanted, she let her heels hold her back. He intended to seduce this seductive girl, but he did not intend to be seduced by her. Nor by the soft, deeply colored night, nor by the scented and carpeted world prepared and guarded by the pines, nor by the sweet, unseasonable weather, nor by the South itself, nor by gaiety, gallantry, pride, friendship, gentleness, admiration, pliancy, or pleasure, nor by love. You must be the investor, not the invested in. You must live on the interest and never touch the principal of your life. So he had been taught.

Ellen Terra came with him into his house, making no protest beyond the obedient dragging of her heels. So she had come with him into his car after dinner, asking no questions as to where he was taking her. So she had come with him through the night, making no comment when they arrived at the brusquely placarded, well-fenced boundary of the property he had bought for himself, a dozen miles from the hotel in which he had invested. She had driven the car through the gate for him, as he called for her to do, waiting for him tranquilly on the other side while he padlocked the gate again securely behind him, moving over when he climbed back under the wheel. She had been comfortably silent while they drove along the winding private road through his acres of pines, past the roused kennels where his hounds bayed and the unaroused Negro shacks where his servants lived, and finally along the slow, exquisite curve of the muddy river beside which he had built his house. Placidly she stood at the edge of the room while he turned on the lamps, and contentedly she overpraised the room by their light. She went, unhurried, to the big, fat-cushioned couch in front of the cold fireplace and settled herself at one end of it, in her own kind of comfort, half-inviting, half-self-sufficient. She watched him while he drew the heavy curtains across the plate-glass window, shutting out the night and the view of the moonlit river and the sound of the mocking birds in the trees outside. Alone with him on his own terms, in the house he had built, on the night he had selected, at the hour he wished, she waited for his own good time, feeling no volition and no self-consciousness, only the nether tingling of the knowledge that he must have brought her here to make love to her. She ached a little, enjoyably, from the wielding of rod and line beside him in the boat that had taken them down the wide, slow-moving river below the town, in the late-lasting summer afternoon that should have been fall. She knew that she would be happy when he made love to her, because he was so querulous and demanding. Composedly she understood that he must make elaborate preparations before making love to her. Completely comfortable on the wide, accommodating couch, she was as natural as a cloud, a tree, a bird, a cat. Everything she said to him had the bewildering shape and ring of golden truth, not because she maintained any relations with the truth, but because what she said was effortless, a breeze blowing, a bird singing, a cat purring.

She took the drink he mixed for her and drank with him as he sat, restless as she was relaxed, across from her, in an armchair of despotic proportions. While he endeavored to establish for her the evaluation he put upon himself, she responded to him quite simply by falling in love with him.

He was a small man, delicately proportioned, with thin, pale skin that turned pink but did not tan. He held himself unnaturally erect, which had the effect of making him seem slightly shorter than he was, just as his clipped, blonde mustache made him look slightly younger than he would have looked clean-shaven. He was cleanly muscled and well co-ordinated, his body having been as carefully tended and trained as a Japanese garden of flowers, and fastidious in a choosy manner of his own. He had a family portrait of a face, each feature defined and inherited from the positive faces of his ancestors. It would have been a striking face, even a magnificent one, if it had been full scale, instead of almost in miniature.

He had inherited likewise, together with his names, his share of the family character traits and his share of three family fortunes, all still impressive, but diminished. His inherited ego had been as carefully cultivated as his thin, small body, and was as unnaturally erect.

From the accumulated confusion of his anomalous upbringing, he had learned to honor his money, acknowledge his social equals, suspect his fellow man, and protect himself. He knew that by running very hard in the same place he could maintain himself there, and that this was a credit to his intelligence and his balance and no small accomplishment in a swiftly changing world. He was neither especially frivolous nor particularly moral, and he felt no need either to expend lavishly or to justify socially his share of worldly wealth. He was immoderately stubborn, and it was this trait that characterized him and set him apart as an individual.

Consciously he did not understand or value his stubbornness, calling it by other names, such as perspicacity, intuition, determination, perversity, contrariness, high temper, or reason. The pictures he drew of himself for Ellen Terra did not include it.

Submissively she listened and admired him in turn as scion, sophisticate, man of the world and man of business, builder of hotels, defier of depressions. She admired and even accepted the pictures, but she did not fall in love with them.

She fell in love with the little man in the big chair, scrubbed clean and tightly buttoned into his clothes and his manners, thin and white and querulous, who had decided to own and perfect The Oaks, not because he believed in it and in himself, but because he had inadvertently one day folded in his small, well-cut, drooping mouth. There he sat, explanatory and boastful, terrified and worried to death, because by so doing he had challenged a whole host of powerful things: the decay of this part of the South and its pride in decay, which made it violently ungrateful for help and unhelpful to its helpers; the depression in the money markets where his fortunes were harbored, which made his trustees shudder with horror at his petulant, inexhaustible insistence that he invest in a luxury hotel at this time; the law of the land that men could not drink; the weather, which had been worse for hunting than at any time since her father's paper had printed its first issue; the shade of his uncle Schuyler VanDyck, who had owned the Schuyler and defied posterity ever to run a good hotel again, the way he had run one. . . . Van had challenged them all, shaking his small, curling fists at the universe, all because he had so inadvertently folded in his small, well-cut, drooping mouth the first time he had seen The Oaks, two years ago.

The rest was accident, or mere corollary, such as his buying this pretty piece of land nearby and building a house on it, because he fancied himself as a hunter, a poker player, a whimsical man of privacy, a seducer of women. . . .

Lazily, loving him, she compared him to the other men she had or might have loved as much, or nearly as much, the ones to whom she had offered herself without stint, understanding their strength and their touchy maleness in her very heart, desiring to yield to it. This was how she was, and it was only fleetingly and afterward that she reminded herself that this was not how she should be. Still, the thought crossed her mind and even surprised her, no man had ever asked her to marry him. . . . The thought was lost in her continuing, growing delight in the man who sat opposite her. There he was, puny, testy, fractious and frightened, a little silly, but purely and wonderfully stubborn.

She summed up her unutterable delight and her love by exclaiming, "You are just plain, old ornery stubborn as a cross-eyed, bow-legged nigger mule."

He frowned briefly and did not pause to realize, even if he could have realized, that this woman, of all women, loved him truly for what made him a man. Feeling her warmth, he turned wary at once and desisted from evaluating himself, trying now to establish for himself the value he must put on her, determined as he was to buy with the coin of seduction what was already his for nothing.

He set traps to catch her, to put a price on her, and to make the price low. He looked at her with derogatory eyes, deliberately aware that the so comfortable body on his couch was too plump, that the round face looked like that of a gingerbread girl, that the black eyes were too small.

"You would look good in furs," he conceded. She would, too, he considered coolly, bundled in ermine, her gingerbread face and black bangs peeping from an ermine cap that matched a muff for her plump little hands. She would look good in them, and he was determined to find her avaricious.

"Not *now*," said Ellen Terra. "It's too hot."

"Do you like diamonds, this weather?" He derided her, insisting that she was avaricious.

"Oh, yes," said Ellen Terra. "They sparkle."

"So they do. So does sand," he replied.

"I like sand, too," said Ellen Terra, blinking at him.

"You're stupid," he said, exasperated.

"Not really," said Ellen Terra. "I don't bother to think a lot. It doesn't get you anywhere."

"Doesn't it, indeed?" asked Van. "Think about this. Do you love me?" He waited for her answer cynically, expecting her to counter with the question he would refuse to answer.

"Oh, yes," said Ellen Terra, sighing. "I do."

She disconcerted him because her answers rang with truth. If she loved him, it was surely a trap. He knew how to avoid such traps.

"Would you love me if I were poor?" he asked in a tone intended to indicate his disbelief, his uncatchability, his sophistication.

"Why, I can't imagine you poor," said Ellen Terra, wriggling and wishing that he would not talk quite such nonsense. "You're such a gold-plated sort of man. I could love a raggedy poor man, though, if that's what you mean," she added casually. "I have."

"Oh, so I am not the first man you ever loved," he said, triumphant, feeling that he had caught her out.

"Of course not," she said. "How can anybody love anybody unless they practice whenever they possibly can?"

"Damn you, anyway," he said crossly. "I wonder if you are just plain dumb. Listen, stupid, put your pea brain to work for me a minute. I have other things on my mind these days, cute as you are. Give me one of those ouija board answers of yours to this one. What am I going to do about Bill Bloodgood?"

"What do you need to do about him?" asked Ellen Terra, wishing that he would hush and come over and kiss her.

"I don't trust him," said Van uncertainly.

"Oh, but you should do that," admonished Ellen Terra. "He's wild and all that, but he's trustworthy, you know. He's an old-fashioned, ruffled-bosomed gentleman, for all he's wild."

"Southern poppycock," said Van, irritated. "He's a spendthrift. I need somebody like Logan Knight to watch him and hold him down."

"Logan can't hold Bill," said Ellen Terra. "Bill's a big. Logan's really a little. You could get Logan to count the money, very carefully, you know, and then give it to Bill, just so much and no more, to spend. Don't let Logan worry about spending it. He's not good at that. He doesn't have enough fun."

"You make it sound so easy," complained Van. "So easy. You make everything sound easy, Ellen Terra. Nothing's easy. Don't you know that? Nothing is *easy* like that."

"Poor darling," said Ellen Terra. "Poor darling."

Then she held him in her arms and felt him weeping within himself for all the unbearable complication that was life. She knew with gladdened and sorrowful heart that he was indeed a poor, terrified darling and that he could be her own. She poured out for him all the unbounded pity she had never lavished before on anyone, pouring it over his tortured, hog-tied, frightened, untrusting soul. No one had ever purely pitied him before: there was too much envy for what he had, or exasperation for what he had not, to permit pity for him to make more than a sticky emotional paste in any other heart he had ever touched. Her pity was mixed only with respect for the twisted, overriding stubbornness that was what made him a man. She did not want him to yield to her pity. She did not want to devour him or mother him or dominate him or possess him. She wanted only to comfort him and to admire him, thus fulfilling them both. Nothing had ever happened to him before that prepared him for this. He had sought to seduce a hick-town girl, and he found himself snaring a bird, capturing a cloud, and holding a breeze in his arms, immeasurably comforted by a woman's natural and transcendent pity, warm with her humble admiration, taking miraculously what was already his.

"Ellen Terra, Ellen Terra, Ellen Terra!" He tested her name and his need for her, nuzzling at her bosom, kneading her warm thighs with demanding fingers. He was overwhelmed by her and almost trusted her. Yet he was still wary with all the thousand lessons in caution his money had bought for him. "Funny, funny, funny little darling," he said, his words almost unchecked, very nearly uncounted and unconsidered. "Sweet, sweet, sweet."

It was then that it occurred in Ellen Terra's head, in words, accompanied by music: that it might reasonably be hoped that Schuyler VanDyck Ball would want to marry her. Angela's voice, warm and wishing her well, sang solo soprano: *Why don't you marry Van, Ellen Terra?*

Ellen Terra, straightening her plump legs while her lips and her loins lost a little of their lovely, tingling warmth, listened to the music that occurred in her unwitting head.

She heard herself, again, obligingly, lilting: *Tell him to ask me!* And then, antiphonally, herself, with the three of them: *Marry me do. Marry her do. Marry me do. Marry marry marry* $\begin{cases} her \\ me \end{cases}$ *DO.* The organ pealed and lilies grew and the bride in white might have walked up the aisle to the music in her head, but the ladies joined the choir and a faceless chorus swelled: *Marry* MARRY *MARRY, Ellen Terra!* To which a single male voice in the pulpit intoned *No.* And there was nothing and silence.

Van's caresses caught at her attention and her response to them was warm and conscious again in the silence, but she was bemused.

No, sang Mark's remembered voice in her head, *no! Why not?* crooned Ellen Terra, and this was fatal. The choir became a glee club and the glee club sang NO. *Not I,* sang Dugdale. *Not me,* sang Sonny Boy. *NO! Oh,* sang Ellen Terra, *oh, woe. Too cheap,* warbled the ladies pianissimo, *Tooooooooooo cheap. Oh, but we thank you very much,* sang the glee club in gleeful harmony, *we do thank you so very much,* and the ladies shrieked *SEE!* Then the fugue began in poor Ellen Terra's head, the fugue for female voices, led by her mother's resounding voice: *Don't. . . . don't. . . .* DON'T. *. . . DON'T. . . . ELlen TERra. . . .* and resolved in harmony, in an overpowering chord: DON'T!

"Don't," said Ellen Terra, pressing her warm thighs together.

With neither surprise nor disappointment, Van found himself back seducing a hick-town southern girl who was trying to put an exorbitant price on what lay between her plump legs. This was only what he had expected and wanted, and now that all values were established he went about it stubbornly and without illusions.

In a kind of goaded desperation, Ellen Terra held out against him. She did not know what else to do now. She denied even the expertly aroused tingling of her loins, the simpler longing to let him comfort her. Finally, disheveled and defeated, both, they went back out into the enormous night, shattering the night into splinters with the disgruntled speed of his car as they fled from the tattered situation.

In front of her house, he left her with an irritated and confident kiss. It was a promise of more of the same, and they both knew that in the end she would in all probability give him what he was after, and that by then it would not be much.

17.   Man Hunt

The town of Andalusia, which in the spring had become aware of murder done in its midst, now became aware of the man hunt. As the murder had been, and remained, a private family affair, so the man hunt was restricted—this time to the Episcopal fold. The by-standers took no part in it, except to the degree that they felt the shame of standers-by when a man is persecuted, or the shameful rejoicing at the humiliation of a human being other than them-selves.

The affair was prolonged and awkward because there is no convenient way for an Episcopal parish, troubled by its priest, to settle the matter. In Anglican tradition, authority does not rest wholly in the will of the people, or congregation, nor does it pur-port to proceed directly from God, through His official hierarchy. Like all compromise systems of authority, intended for grown people in an atmosphere of rational and spiritual harmony, it falls down badly under the pressure of minority hysteria.

This enabled the white Presbyterians, Methodists, Baptists, Catholics and others in Andalusia to feel briefly superior to the Episcopalians, toward whom they usually felt otherwise. On the whole, they were pro-hunted.

So were the black Andalusians, of whatever creed, who were not supposed to know what was going on but, of course, did. They eyed the hunted with a sympathy that might have been Christian and brotherly if they had felt privileged to feel a sympathy for a white man that was Christian and brotherly.

Most of the Episcopalians, being, as they were supposed to be, fairly temperate and rational people, would have preferred to see the whole thing drift. There were two sides to this question, they felt, as there were to most questions. If Bob White had been by chance born, or even long established, in Andalusia, the church could have contained Mrs. Rook's feud with him, as the town and the church had contained many another.

But no one knew better than Clementine Rook the nature of habit. Clementine was determined to hunt the man, Bob White, out of town before he became a habit, with herself as much as with the town.

Arabella White, on the verge of self-discovery, turned instead to rend the impregnable woman who was her husband's enemy and the impregnable man who was her husband, and, finding no surface sensitive to her fingers, turned again and tore her own brush-fire hair. She squandered such pity as she was able to feel on Alton Rook.

Alton Rook sat enfolded in the huge, overstuffed chair to the left of the mahogany coffee table and scratched savagely and surreptitiously under his right knee. He itched. It was hot. Mrs. Stone, the perfect housekeeper, was unable to cope with heat. She opened the blinds in what she called her "drawring" room in the daytime, closed them at night.

"Don't you agree with me, Alton?" His host, John Stone, inclined toward him from the other overstuffed chair, matching his, symmetrically and exactly placed at the right of the coffee table.

John Stone's forehead, thought Alton, had the most curious contours. John wrinkled one side up and the other side down, adjusting the skin around the equation of his eyebrows. The left eyebrow was lowered to express doubt, the right raised to indicate inquiry. He had used this expression so much and so long that it was grooved into his face, like the lines in a phonograph record.

"You *do* agree, Alton?" asked John Stone, the contours wavering and then deepening anxiously.

Agree about what? wondered Alton. He had been listening to the other end of the room. The three women sat there, hillock to hillock, along the wide, soft sofa. He had been listening to his wife, cunningly using her inescapable voice. She had employed lament, gossip, moral indignation and self-pity in enlisting her friends to aid her against the innocent person of Bob White. She had partially succeeded in rousing the languid, destructive powers of Hannah Madison and in intimidating the timid Anne Stone into fearing inaction more than she feared action. It was an interesting and terrifying performance. His wife would have made an obdurate and vicious general in any war.

"Possibly," replied Alton to John Stone, covering up his inattention to his host with deliberate ambiguity.

"Of course, you fellows have a traditional allegiance to the Democratic Party," went on John Stone.

If John had been talking politics, thought Alton Rook, relieved, the ambiguity was undoubtedly relevant.

"A fine old party, in spite of its trying to make Americans vote for a man like Al Smith," said John Stone considerately. "Naturally, I myself was raised as a Republican . . ." He said this, defensively, at least twice a week. ". . . but I have taken pleasure in voting for some fine Democratic candidates down here. That's beside the point."

Beside what point, wondered Alton, trying to listen to him and not to listen to the women. Clementine was saying with her terrible audibility, "I have been planning this memorial service for my mother so long, but naturally I planned to hold it in the beautiful chapel I wanted to build in her memory. . . ." Pathos and outrage. Very effective, thought Alton. She had also been effective in raising money when a river flood had wiped out a Negro settlement on the banks north of Andalusia.

"I have the greatest faith still in Hoover, as well as in Whitney and in Morgan," said John Stone. "Public-minded men! They'll see us through. No doubt in my mind about it."

"Possibly," said Alton Rook, thinking that it took a great deal to shake John Stone's faith. Well, John had to have faith in something. He had very little in himself.

"Don't you agree, Cecil?" John Stone turned to Cecil Madison, who sat in a stiff chair he had pulled out from the wall and was absently chewing the end of his fine-haired mustache.

"Can't say I do," said Cecil, stiffly, fingering his mustache. "Got to help the nigras quick. Can't let 'em starve. Never have let 'em starve. Can't begin now. Need 'em. Georgianna said 'tother day . . ." He wandered off on a literal quotation from the garrulous, temperamental old Negro woman he loved so well. His imitation of her accent was affectionately exact.

John Stone laughed, assuming that he was intended to laugh at any quotation in the humorous dialect employed by the colored people, and Cecil looked mildly startled. "Serious," Cecil said, reprovingly. "Can't close The Place or they'll starve. Losing money. Explained to Clementine. But need help. Big help. Bank help. Government help. Drastic."

"They're doing the best they can," said John Stone ruffled.

"Insufficient," said Cecil. He added, looking up and inserting all the nouns and definite articles he omitted when he was thinking out loud, "I hope you bankers will use your influence. We have to tide this over. The nigras are in trouble. They have no cushion. You must help."

"Just like that!" said John Stone. "We're having our own troubles."

Hope came into the room and began passing a tray of Nanine's delectable hors d'oeuvre. Conversation stopped at both ends of the room while the three women chose greedily among them and Alton barely concealed his own greed as he reached for several. He wished Clementine had been able to keep Nanine. Mattie wasn't a patch on Nanine as a cook. Food was one of the consoling pleasures of middle age. Still, Clementine could not have kept Nanine. To have two such tempers under one roof was scarcely feasible, even if Nanine was black. Nanine had stayed only one month with the Rooks.

Hope came back to Alton again, after the others were served, pandering instinctively to his male greed before leaving the tray, as

she was expected to do, beside the ladies. He winked at her gratefully. She stared back at him with wide, blind, enormous eyes and he
realized that she was quite drunk. Tut, tut, he thought to himself,
covering a sense of shock, tut, tut, tut, young woman.

She sat down with heavy, wavering decorum beside her
father, who turned to her with the air of one who discarded serious
matters when little girls were around. "Nanine's going to bring
Cecelia in to see us, isn't she?" he asked hopefully. John Stone was
drippy about his grandchild.

There was a general shifting of thighs on the fat sofa, as
Alton heard Clementine cuing in a resumption of the former conversation. "It isn't as if Mr. White didn't know better! He claims
to be a gentleman by birth."

Alton began to scratch again. He wished something would
happen to stop it, to stop it, to stop it.

As if in answer to his wish, Angela and Ellen Terra burst
into the room from the hall.

Alton looked up, grateful for the interruption, and then felt
an inquiring thrill of excitement. They were up to something, the
two of them, swirling and whirling into the room with the defiant
vitality of the young and prettily mischievous.

Angela was as taut as a violin string, down the length of her
thin, tall body. Her long face was vibrant with intense awareness
of her own intelligence. Ellen Terra bounced like a hard rubber
ball on her little round heels, her round, solid, black eyes gleaming
brightly in her round, still, sweet face. The girls were up to something, thought Alton, looking and listening to the overriding rush
of words that matched their movement.

It was Angela who was doing the talking, in a voice high and
ecstatic, a tea-party voice. She had started talking as she came in the
door, her words pelting into the fractional pause that greeted their
entrance. "Mrs. Stone . . . Mrs. Rook . . . Mama, dear . . .
'scuse me for interrupting, I came to get Hope, it's such fun
really. . . ." Behind her Ellen Terra made her pretty manners in a
blurred purr. Angela rushed on, allowing a nominal, inadequate
pause for Ellen Terra, as if too—charmingly—full of herself to wait
politely before telling them whatever it was she was going to tell
them. "Bob White is an angel, don't you think? Such a dear. It's

wonderful to have a real man for a clergyman again. He's all for us, Bob White is, the young people, as it were. He's agreed to help us all he can, and we're going to help him with the nursery. He thinks it's fine. . . ." She was acutely, aggressively innocent in the face of a joint rising of the hillocks, unison indrawn breath, Clementine's mouth opened to interrupt her. Her voice rose a semitone as she answered, as if asked, "The dance, of course, the darling dance . . ." Her words rushed on as swiftly as a gushing waterfall. Clementine would have had to lift her voice and shout to stop her. ". . . not since Mark, you know, has the church meant so much to us, and honestly, the kids need it now, more than we do. Tiny hasn't been to her first dance yet, won't she be darling, thirteen imagine, and it'll be such a lovely one. We're getting a committee of kids, too, enlarging it, with all of us old-timers, of course, Ellen Terra and Hope and I, and Dugdale and Sonny Boy, you know, the whole gang—it's so exciting, it'll be a huge success. But you-all don't want to bother with the details. That's not the chaperones' business, is it? Three weeks from Friday, don't you think? if Mr. White agrees —he will, too, he's *such* a duck, and the nursery needs money *so* badly, no milk—we can't wait to help, it's wonderful—come *on*, Ellen Terra, Hope, we'll go over to the rectory . . ." As she talked, she maneuvered Ellen Terra with her and together they caught Hope's hands and pulled her to her feet, linking arms with her on either side of her, propelling her lumpy, wavering, unresisting body between them. There was no pause in Angela's high, mock-urgent chatter as she maneuvered her trio swiftly toward the door, in a formation politely oblique so that their collective backs were never to the older people. ". . . so wonderful, like the good old days," she gabbled rapidly. "*Just* like the old days . . ." Ellen Terra and Angela had their heads held preposterously high, and the blonde, heavy head between them looked high-held, too, as Hope raised her great blind eyes in ununderstanding. It did not look as if Hope were supported between them. It looked as if the three of them were moving together, gaily, purposeful, linked in frivolous purpose and friendship, propelled by innocent enthusiasm which old people per-force must appreciate and envy. "So . . . See you later, Mama darling, papa, and *thank* you, thank you, all you-all . . ." cooed Angela, her voice again a decibel higher as they reached the door.

Alton, red-faced with amazement and delight, nearly ruined everything by guffawing. The thank-you was such a masterly non-sequitur, a perfect stumbling block in the way of the ominously gathering reply.

At the door, the girls wheeled for an exit, and Angela, wheel horse, continued over her shoulder without even a fractional pause, ". . . you-all, so swell, getting Bob White here, swell, sorry we—can't—stay—and—talk—some—more . . ."

And they were gone.

Clementine's strangled "ELlen TERra" was too late. The noise of the motor outside was like a fleeting giggle.

"Young girls are so insensitive sometimes," said Mrs. Stone artlessly into the explosive silence.

There was no explosion. There was nothing to attack in Angela's behavior or in her pretended assumptions. Explosion would have been undignified and would have put the ladies in a false position.

Hooray for the kids, thought Alton. Good kids, fighting in a good cause. Fighting for Bob White. Any good human was a good cause. The best. For the first time he felt that it was not a lost cause. If the kids had the guts to fight, so did he. Hooray for our side, he said to himself, and chuckled invisibly.

He made his own exit, crabwise and stoop-shouldered, dismissed by, rather than parting from, his wife. At the outside door he clapped on his hat at the usual precarious angle on the back of his head and went down to his office at the Andalusia *Banner*.

In the car, Angela was still gabbling breathlessly, although the flow of her words was gradually lessening. "Did you hear what your mother was saying to Hope's mother while we were in the hall? Gosh, she really is hipped, and I'll have to give her credit, she's impressive. We'll have to make the dance . . ." She felt her fingertips raw, now that they had stopped tingling, as if the skin had peeled from them. The skin inside her elbows was quivering and her hands were slippery.

"You know perfectly well," said Ellen Terra admiringly, "that none of us Rooks can go gallivanting to any dances till after Thanks-

giving, not Mama or Papa or me. The year isn't up since Grandma."
She gestured at the lap of her dress, which was white, with no touch
of color anywhere, correct for youthful mourning in its diminishing
stages, more becoming than the unrelieved black that Clementine
still wore.

"Christ!" said Angela feelingly, gulping a deep breath of the
heavy, hot air. "I outsmarted myself. I forgot that. We'll have to
postpone the damn dance. We'll postpone it in your honor," she
added, slowly now, and thoughtfully. "We'll do it as a magnificent
concession to your mother. We'll say Bob White didn't think it
would be agreeable . . ."

"You're a five-star genius," said Ellen Terra. "Oh, boy! But,
oh boy, will I catch it when I get home."

"Where are we going?" asked Hope. "I didn't mean to
come."

"You haven't done anything bad," said Angela to Ellen
Terra. "Not a damn thing. Blame it on me. You weren't even going
to the dance. . . . Of course you had to come," she remonstrated
with Hope. "You're on the team. You're a grown woman. We have
to stick together." She turned back to Ellen Terra. "It won't take
long!" she said with vigorous optimism. "We must just damn well
hang on and hold out for Bob White until the edge wears off your
mama's mad."

"She sure is all-wool, till-death mad," said Ellen Terra softly.

"Well, so is my mother at Bill! And since God knows when.
Before she was born! I'm holding out for Bill, just the same. I've
held out! *Listen*, we'll make it a dance in honor of my wedding."
Angela, having acted with such superlative assurance, was very close
to achieving it. "For Hallowe'en," she went on gleefully. "By then
everybody will know for sure that The Oaks is going to be a success.
And my Bill is the manager of The Oaks!" She flung out the title
like a banner.

Hope cried, "Oh . . ." and caught herself just as she was
about to cry, "*My* husband will be the manager—mine . . ." wanting to grab the banner, unfurled in the sunshine, to hold it high in
her own clenched hands, to wave it back in Angela's face.

"Whether they like it or not!" said Angela. "He can support
his wife. By then, whether they like it or not! Bob White is my

preacher and Bill is my man, and you can all come and dance at my wedding!"

Hope, sobered at the brink of disaster and betrayal, swayed back from the brink. She had so nearly told Angela what Logan had told her not to tell, so nearly betrayed her husband to this girl who was not as bright as she thought she was. Frightened and sober, she asked petulantly, "Where *are* we going?"

"Oh, anywhere," said Angela carelessly. She rubbed the tips of her fingers on the hard rubber wheel, feeling them healed. "There's no point in seeing Bob White about a dance in November. It's too hot in Andalusia. Let's ride on out to The Oaks and have a drink."

"Can't you do anything with Clementine Rook, Tracy?" asked Andrew Gregory. He and his wife were drinking their cocktails in his den before dinner. Carrie was not there.

"Not I," said Tracy Gregory, shrugging her abundant shoulders. Two perpendicular furrows, which were rarely noticeable except when she thought about her daughter, Carrie, creased deeply into her wide, placid brow. "Isn't it a mess?"

"I'm on a spot," said Andrew, lighting and drawing on his curved pipe. "I wouldn't be surprised if Alton even resigns as junior warden. You women!"

"Don't 'you women' me," said Tracy firmly. "I haven't had a thing to do with this. I haven't even given Clementine the satisfaction of admitting that I agree with her to the extent that I think Bob White has been tactless, to say the least. It's plain foolishness for him to go call on Lucy Cranborne so—so blatantly. And he could have stalled Clementine along on her chapel nonsense."

"Well, it's too bad. We've certainly supported some duds in our day and I've enjoyed giving my money, just when it hurts most, for value received. He's a good preacher. Best we ever had in some ways."

Tracy nodded her head and she and her husband exchanged distressed and sympathetic glances, which emphasized their physical resemblance by being of identical content and duration.

"We do have to go to this memorial service Clementine's cooking up for her mother, I suppose?" said Andrew.

"I'm afraid so," said Tracy. "It'll look like support for Clementine against Bob White, of course, but I don't quite see how we can get out of it. She's been so clever, darn her. Mrs. Terra *did* live in Oakland, and the old chapel there *is* a sort of pre-Civil War monument, and even that dreary dean from Oglethorpe she's going to get to hold the service instead of Bob White *was*, actually, a friend of Mrs. Terra's. You can't prove Clementine's holding it there instead of St. James's and having the dean just to make an issue with Bob White."

"Well, for heaven's sake, get her to hold it right away while it's still hot and nobody goes to St. James's anyway!" Andrew tamped his pipe. "Or to hold off until after Pledge Sunday."

"Oh, dear," said Tracy.

Andrew explained as if Tracy did not understand. "If the annual pledges fall off too much this fall, it'll call the whole thing to the bishop's attention. He'll have to meddle in. And he'll almost certainly have to ask Bob White to leave. Everybody's pinched these days and the diocese can't afford to help support a well-off parish like Andalusia. Even if Bob White would sit there himself and let the old church get cut down to a missionary parish just because he's having a row with the junior warden's wife."

"Or she's having one with him," said Tracy.

"Right. If Alton and Cecil don't ante up, it'll be bad enough, but if a lot of the others don't come through on the dot as usual that Sunday, I don't know what to do. Ask White to leave and get some seminary graduate or an old man for less? Just because Clementine and her rector are rowing?"

"It's a shame," said Tracy. "A shame."

"It is that," said Andrew. "But, darn it, I can't support the man myself unless the others do. Not this year. Why, I can't even afford a new car for Carrie." He plucked at the bulbous end of his nose. The color was rising in his broad, well-fleshed face.

"You'll have to give her one for a wedding present," said Tracy, soothing him, and immediately soothed herself by the pleasure the thought gave her.

"You and old lady Bradford got that all fixed up, too, did

you?" asked Andrew, twinkling at his wife. "I never saw two prospective mothers-in-law so thick before."

"I couldn't help being pleased," said Tracy, beaming gently to herself. "She just really appreciated Carrie. She meant every word of it when she said she thought Carrie was the most wonderful thing that had ever happened to David."

"She kind of overdid it," said Andrew, blowing the words out with a cloud of smoke.

"Oh, don't be so—so Scotch," said Tracy. "David's a charming and lovely boy and his mother is a lady and a gracious one at that, and thank God, that's what I say."

"Oh, I'm happy about it," said Andrew hastily. "I wouldn't think anybody was good enough for our Carrie, I suppose but . . ."

"But still . . ." said Tracy softly and they both thought shyly of their former heart-destroying certainty that their crippled daughter would never, never wed.

A moment later she said, "Did you know that Clementine's so pleased with the way David is handling that little stinker Agrippa at his summer school that she's canceled 'Grippa's reservation at boarding school next year? She's going to keep him with David. That speaks well for our David."

"David's a nice boy," said Andrew firmly. "Nearly studied for the ministry, he tells me."

"What's diabolical about Clementine," said Tracy, reverting to their discussion, "is that she's managed to make it look as if everybody has to choose between her sainted—or anyway, dead—mother and Lucy Lee Cranborne. It isn't fair."

"You women," said Andrew.

"Don't 'you women' me," said Tracy. "But really. That Clementine. Do you know what she told Hannah Madison?" Andrew did, but Tracy repeated it. "That Bob White was urging Angela and Bill to elope, and that he'll perform the ceremony if they do! Hannah's fit to be tied. I think she's going to throw a heart attack, just to keep Angela in the house."

"Hannah gives me a pain," said Andrew, "although I can understand the way she feels about Bill. He's a pretty irresponsible character."

"He's doing very well indeed at The Oaks," urged Tracy with charity.

"He does know how to handle the customers," Andrew conceded. "Takes it seriously, too. Van Ball has done a fine thing for the community there, I must say."

"If Bill keeps on doing well," said Tracy, "Hannah will give in. And when she does she'll act like it was all her idea in the first place. Mark my words."

Andrew laughed. "Marked," he said. "But meantime old Cecil Madison is right on the spot, just as much as Alton is."

"Of course he is," said Tracy philosophically. "After all, the poor man works for Clementine and Hannah, as well as being married to Hannah."

"You women!" said Andrew.

"Don't 'you women' me," said Tracy. "Clementine even tried to tell me that Bob White was having a sinister influence on Carrie, for heaven's sake. 'Talk sense,' I told her. What about the Stones?"

"They're the ones that never did like Bob White," said Andrew.

"But why on earth not?" asked Tracy.

"John thinks they're too loose, offering drinks to the children at the rectory and all that. Some nonsense like that," said Andrew.

"As if Hope couldn't get her drinks at home. Just like born and raised Methodists to think preachers shouldn't drink. Really!"

"It's awkward," said Andrew. "But we'll see what we can do."

"I wish Mr. White had never come to start with," said Tracy, "for all I like him!" And they sighed in understanding unison.

The next morning the Andalusia *Banner* carried on its front page a box announcing that this was the hottest September on record in the paper's files. Equinoctial squalls were predicted for the immediate future, with a seasonal cool spell to follow.

On the second page, a letter to the editor ran for a full column and a half. It was signed "Ardent Episcopalian" and the anonymous writer had an accomplished and amusing prose style. The letter set forth the view that the addition of a chapel to St. James's would spoil the compact and excellent lines of the old church, would interfere with the practice of Christian charity at home, as exemplified by the day nursery, and would serve no more purpose than the gift of a small, white elephant. The author concluded that whoever had proposed such a building—who it was he seemed not to know—must have been carried away, as was natural, by a high-minded wish to contribute beauty to the town and the church. Having recognized his (or her) error, the philanthropist would certainly make better use of his (or her) money and high-minded impulses. It would be difficult to think up anything more useless, said the writer, or sillier.

On the third page, the society column led off with a lengthy announcement of the first of a series of Saturday dinner dances at The Oaks. Local society would be present *en masse*, reservations having already been made by the town's own Mr. and Mrs. Cecil Madison and their popular daughter, Angela, by Mr. and Mrs. John Stone and the young couple, Mr. and Mrs. Logan Knight, and so on. The charming and popular manager of The Oaks, William Shy Bloodgood, formerly of Oglethorpe, predicted a great success for the series. The rector of St. James's, the Reverend Mr. Robert White, and Mrs. White, would be guests of their gracious host, the distinguished Mr. Schuyler VanDyck Ball, to whom the community of Andalusia owed so much. This was in accordance with ancient tradition at The Oaks, and the community was doubly appreciative because Mr. Ball had respected tradition while bringing the new to the county. The article was a sober hairline this side of fulsome.

On the fourth page, it was regretfully indicated in the news from New York that the stock market was again betraying those prophets who said there would be an upswing.

By midnight that same night, the paper's prediction of an equinoctial disturbance was duly fulfilled and the editor of the paper was out in the gale, on the sidewalk in front of his home on Egmont Street.

Alton Rook stood on the sidewalk in front of the wide-porched house on Egmont Street, which had been his grandfather's and his father's and then his and which was now property in his wife's name, and shook with fury. He was unprotected for the first time in years by either humor or detachment. He could feel, like BB shot fired into the back of his neck, the peeks that his two younger children, Tiny and 'Grippa, were quite likely taking at him from behind the curtains of the front bedrooms on the third floor.

They had been sent to bed and peremptorily ordered to sleep, and perhaps they even were asleep, but that did not alter his feeling that their eyes peeked at him, standing, as he was, ignominiously and indecisively on the sidewalk. He knew also that their glances would be frightened, entertained, and complacent, accepting, as children did, that this was how it was. If he moved from where he was, under his children's eyes, the eyes of the whole town would start to riddle him like machine-gun bullets. If he went back into the house, stripped as he was of his armor of humor and detachment, he felt that his wife would shoot flaming arrows from the narrow slits of her eyes straight into his heart and that he would forthwith die, once and forever.

In his ears tingled Clementine's final screaming oath in the night that who was Bob White's friend was henceforth her mortal enemy. Beside him on the sidewalk was the suitcase that Clementine had symbolically stuffed with God knew what from his clothes closet and his bureau drawers. Behind him, where she had flung it, was the old portable typewriter he used at home. It was battered symbol of the fact that he had bartered the financial power, protection and security of his half-interest in the Miller and Rook Pecan Company to his wife in return for the heady privilege of losing money and writing words on paper. Drunk with privilege, he had written a few too many, lost a little too much.

The wind, damp with the promise of rain, blew in sporadic gusts of violence, changing direction with each gust. It buffeted Alton's thin, stooped body. A gust from the direction of the shadowed driveway and portico beside his wife's lighted house brought a sound like that of a kitten mewing in tragic anguish.

"Papa . . . Papa . . ." It was Ellen Terra, a-tiptoe at the edge of the black shadow of the portico. Alton stepped back two steps, as if blown backward by the wind, away from the sidewalk which was lit by two street lamps.

"What?" he rasped, his back still to the house and to his oldest daughter.

"Papa, I'll come with you," she said in pain. "Let me come with you!"

"Where?" he demanded harshly.

Where indeed? Where could a busted middle-aged newspaper owner with a rich wife flee in the night? Out into the depressed world, with a suitcase full of unmatched clothes and a portable not worth the pawning? Could he flee from tyranny, domestic or otherwise, in a penniless panic for the sake of a man who did not know that he was being persecuted? For a man who smiled his provocative, Cheshire cat, innocent pleasure in being alive into the face of man-eating matriarchs, rousing in them the blood lust? Flee in the name of a religion in which he did not even believe, with his plump, pretty, black-eyed daughter with the warm, too eager thighs and the total absence of brains, who believed only in love? Much good it did her to believe in it. Much good it did her to love, his round-bottomed child who was good for nothing else. To love her father, standing before her in ignominy as profound as that in a nightmare or a Mack Sennett comedy. To love Bob White. To have loved Mark Barbee. Poor baby, poor bitch. Poor bitch, poor baby.

Ellen Terra reached from the shadow and caught one of his hands and clung to it. Trying to release his fingers, he realized, humiliated and furious, that she was wonderfully strong. This was no source of pride or appeal to a man who ten minutes before had been shoved bodily out of his front door by his wife, a man who had refrained from physical combat with her not from chivalry but because she was twice as strong as he was. Ah, if he had been pimp for his powerful, deep-loined women, instead of slave to one and helpless idol to the other, he could have lived well.

"Get back in the house and behave yourself, Ellen Terra," he said with bitter fury. Her hand fluttered away and he knew himself a broken idol, deserter of a female. If he had the courage, he would tell her to go without him. He turned to her helplessly. "Honey . . ." he said, and stopped. "Great jumping Jehovah!" he cried, putting his hands to his head and shaking his head from side to side with his hands. An irrational gust of laughter touched him from the south, with the wind, for the crazy, infuriating, insoluble absurdity of everything. A few big, fat, promissory raindrops plopped around him like overripe fruit and one landed right on the top of his head. He would sit down with his daughter on the grass beside the driveway, amid the squashy raindrops, and explain to her about irony and pity, the gods of his youth. Then he would explain about humor and meditation. And then perhaps he could explain to her about humor and honor. Perhaps she could explain to him about good and evil. Only the young could hope to know anything about that. And then they could wonder together about the nature of truth. Surely it was important.

He felt the raindrop soak through his hair and tickle his scalp. "Your mother and I are just having a disagreement," he said with formal asperity. "She's most upset by a little joke I played." It was a serious joke, humor used for the sake of honor. It was a very important joke. "She's annoyed. Well, I expect she's right to be. . . . After all, her mother's loss was a . . . She set her heart on . . ." Oh, the stinking hell with it, he thought. What *was* truth, cried Pontius Pilate, and did not wait for . . . Bob White was a stubborn fool, for all he was a good man. Miss Lucy was a murderess, for all she was a lady. "I'll trot along down to the Andalusia House until your mother . . ." He would spend the night at the Andalusia House, wakefully, among the medium-sized rats and giant cockroaches in the fantastic old building, and come to terms, because there was nothing in the world else to do. The humor, the joke, this time, would be on him. It would be all over town that Alton Rook had been ejected bodily, bag and baggage, onto the sidewalk by his wife, who was richer and stronger than he was. It would be only a joke, too, for he would be back home and un-humiliated. After all, his wife's temper was a local phenomenon, a possession, a landmark, a part of the town, like the courthouse square. To be its victim was no more dishonorable than being caught in a thunderstorm. Nobody thought the worse of you for being caught out in a thunderstorm. He must explain this to Bob White. "Good night, Ellen Terra," he said wryly. "See you tomorrow. Be a good girl."

"Good night, Papa," purred Ellen Terra, sorrowful and helpless. She rocked back on her little round heels into the shadow and protection of the portico. If her mother found that she had been out, offering to go with, in support of, in respect for, her father, for love of Bob White, she would be a sitting target for the full

273

force of her mother's wrath. There would be nothing left of her in the morning except a puddle on the floor. She must slip in quietly and go quickly to sleep. The night had lost its importance.

Alton Rook paused. He owed his daughter at least the minor courtesy of comradeship, in such circumstances. "Quite a temper she's got, your maw," he said, as if rueful, amused, and not unadmiring. Then, feeling like an utter fool, he turned away.

"Good night, Papa," said Ellen Terra blankly, sorrowfully, and went away.

He pulled one of his ears in spent pain. Women, he thought, lumping everything that troubled him into a bundle and labeling it female. Women! It had been a long time since he had *had* a woman. By God, he would go down to the Andalusia House and send out for a five-dollar whore. Why not? The idea invigorated him and he picked up the suitcase and the typewriter and began to walk briskly down the street. He had gone nearly a block before he remembered that the smallest of the three cars was his own and went back for it. Tomorrow he would swear to Clementine that he had not written that Letter to the Editor, which he had.

In the soaking, tranquil, newly chill dawn that followed the gusty storm, Angela awakened hungry. After an enormous breakfast, during which Pinckney hovered over her, enjoying her rare appetite as much as she did, she was replete but still unsatisfied. She thought of scuppernongs and immediately craved them. There might well be no more this year, after the storm. She must go out quickly and stuff as many of the great, bulging globes into her mouth as she could manage, letting the sweet, delicate, inimitable juice trickle down her throat from her mouth.

She called Carrie and spoke to her urgently.

"Wonderful," said Carrie. "Wonderful. Wonderful. I was wondering what it was special I wanted this morning. I'll pick up David and meet you at Miss Sis's . . ."

With an infinitesimal shrug that accepted David, Angela agreed. They exchanged a "See you later," and Angela went out onto the back porch, banging the screen door. She paused on the back steps, her nostrils flaring sensitively to the light chill of the air. She had a second's impulse to go back into the protected house, to go back to bed until the sun should be high and noon upon the no longer chilly day. The door banged again behind her and Pinckney said in his gentle tenor, "Yuh wants uh jacket, Miss Anglah? Jus fuh now."

"No!" said Angela decisively, and ran down the steps and across the wet grass under the branches of the two oak trees. A spray of dampness rose from the grass and settled on her naked ankles and a few drops of the night's rain shivered down from the restless leaves of the water oak onto her hair and shoulders. At Miss Sis's the scuppernongs would be the more delectable for being wet, since they were already sunripe and greengold, speckled with brown.

Hunched over the wheel, she drove straight and fast out the Oakland road and then cut sharply into the narrow dirt road that led to Miss Sis Whittle's cabin in the bamboo thicket. It was as if she were racing to get the last of the scuppernongs before they were gone and the season was over. The road was greasy with the rain and she nearly slid into the ditch at a point where the ditch was deep.

She reached the edge of the field where Miss Sis planted her own year's supply of food and where the corn and potatoes grew that fed the black family who shared the land. Nobody knew whether the ragged bit of farmland now actually belonged to the white old maid or the black family. Angela started to wave at the familiar figure, standing contemplatively among the corn, and then laughed aloud. Miss Sis had dressed the stuffed-gunny-sacks-and-sticks with the clothes she herself wore. The scarecrow Miss Sis, black bombazine skirt touching the tops of high-buttoned shoes, starched white shirt and black bow tie, complete on top with sailor straw, was no less commanding, dignified, and unmistakable than Miss Sis herself. Angela could almost hear the two-fingered whistle, the voice that could be heard across a county, coming from the figure in the cornfield. Surely no crow would dare to steal corn thus valiantly guarded.

In the still narrower lane that fronted Miss Sis's thicket-hidden house, Angela saw a car. She recognized the high-crowned Dodge Bob White drove, and gladdened that she should share the morning's, the last, scuppernongs with him. But it was Arabella who sat inside, pulled up to the scrubbed soft wood kitchen table beside the mammoth coal range, eating scuppernongs out of a brown paper bag. She greeted Angela with a prolonged "M-m-m-m-m-m-m," expressing welcome, polite inquiry as to her health, and Arabella's preoccupation with the huge grapes. Miss Sis took two strides across the room, grasped Angela's hand in her forthright grip, and said, "Hi, there, young one," as if she were indeed calling to Angela from the cornfield.

"Hello, Miss Sis," said Angela warmly. "You're looking pretty perky."

Arabella said, "mmm-MMM-m-mmm," meaning, yes, isn't she?

"I'm feeling perky," said Miss Sis, "and the scuppernongs are pretty near gone, so you'd better get right out there. Fifty cents a bag, do your own picking, and the bag's free." She always said this, to all comers, every September, in just those words. This time she added, "Eat 'em here or take 'em home. They taste better right here, right where they're picked."

Angela, immensely complimented by receiving one of Miss Sis's invitations, took a brown paper bag from the diminished heap on the corner of the table. All year long Miss Sis saved the bags in which she was given her purchases on her Thursday trips to Andalusia, pressing them out with her hands and scrupulously folding them flat to add to the pile. They were of different sizes and you took the one on top. No one ever questioned the authority of pure luck that determined the number of scuppernongs that were yours for fifty cents. Angela's was a big bag, and it made her feel lucky. Happily she went out the back door and along the curling path. The furry, caterpillar-like brushes on the ends of the tall grass in Miss Sis's back yard tickled her, brushing her calves and her knees. The voracious bamboo had perceptibly cut down the space behind the house since her last visit, and the bamboo stood thick and sullen, as if ready to rush across the last empty place. In the middle of the yard was the great old vine, supported on its vast, high frame, the color of driftwood on a beach. At the end of the path, beyond the vine, she could see the little wooden structure, the same color as the frame for the vine, with the door in which a sickle of a moon served for ventilation. She remembered the polished plank on which you sat, and the catalogue hanging from a string within reach, and the powdery, clean smell of lime, the dirt daubers who lived within and how one had once frightened her because she thought it was a wasp. As a child, she had regretted that she had no such attractive place at home in which to sit and think while her body did its pleasant job of relieving her of momentary discomfort.

Inside the house she could hear Miss Sis's unsecret voice and Arabella's mumble.

"I'd shoot her," said Miss Sis. "I'd gladly shoot her dead as a doornail, in broad daylight on Main Street, if I was dead sure I'd only hang for it." Arabella's reply was inaudible.

Angela stopped, her hand arrested high in the air, listening to the vigorous, uncompromising voice.

"Shoot her, sure. But they wouldn't hang me, Arabella White. They'd lock me up in a crazy house. I couldn't stand the crazy house, not for the sake of Bob White or the pleasure I'd take in shooting Clementine Rook. I've known her since she was a black-eyed beauty from Louisiana and I was a plain-jane home-town girl. We're the same age, to a week, Alton and me, and I've known Alton since we were blind kittens. Alton's mother and my mother were best, best friends in the days when that meant more than being kissin' kin."

It still does, thought Angela excitedly, her hands completing their task of reaching for the grapes. She was tremendously moved by the vision of a contemporaneous past that had existed as the present did, when old ladies were young girls and best, best friends. Only academically did you realize that old people were once as young as yourself. You could never really realize that things did happen, over and over. She felt hazy and alarmed. Could it happen that she, Angela, for instance, could one day be Miss Sis's age, an old maid, wearing defiantly her current dresses in the face of changing styles? Of course it could not happen! It was agreed that styles would never really change again. They were too comfortable and too suitable. Life had progressed to a fixed point where it need not change, where there was no reason to defy it because it did not need changing.

"Never could shoot or hang myself," said Miss Sis philosophically. "I can shoot squirrels and coons and all kinds of beasties, but I never could shoot a rabbit."

Miss Sis was the best hunting shot in the county; everybody knew that. She shot her food and the varmints that would eat her corn and sometimes she went hunting with the best of the men.

She answered something that Arabella had said. "You tell your husband to spit right straight in her eye!"

There was a silence that Angela could not interpret. Perhaps Miss Sis had gone out the front door, to feed the chickens or to pluck their eggs. She finished gathering her grapes and went back inside.

Arabella was still sitting at the table. In front of her was a mound of goldgreen speckled skins, squeezed and lifeless. She was scrabbling in the bottom of the bag. Her face wore an expression of inner content.

"First time in my whole life I ever had enough scuppernongs," she said to Angela, inviting her with a gesture to sit down in the other straight-backed kitchen chair beside the table. "And Miss Sis grows the best in the world. They're even better than the ones I remember in the old rectory yard. If they can beat your memories, they must be good. Now why do people go and make nasty, sticky wine out of them? You can make better wine with any little old lousy grapes."

Angela, who had automatically reverenced scuppernong wine as she was told to do, realized that it was too sweet and too sticky and that she had never really enjoyed it. She had a feeling of release.

"Eat away," said Arabella. "I chatter enough for two, anyway. Isn't Miss Sis a dream? I had almost forgotten how delightful southern eccentrics can be. The elderly eccentric. The absolute doer and sayer as she pleases. No other part of this country has produced 'em. They make up for the balloons and the paper dolls."

"I don't know what you mean by that," said Angela, tossing aside the convention that you pretend to understand everything that is said to you by older people, mostly because you are not interested in explanation from such sources. "Miss Sis is a pet, but what's all that about balloons and dolls?"

"I might try to explain," said Arabella. "You're quite a girl, Angela, if you only knew it. Well, balloons. They're the ladies. The kind who run the church. Up North, they're all inflated with notions of equality and covered over with silver paint and they barge all over the place looking for men to tuck into their cabins as pure ballast. Down here they're more or less moored, but they do the same thing from the end of their cables. The thin-skinned ones, up North, have to get reinflated every so often by a lot of men called psychiatrists who blow egos back into them. Down here the thin-skinned ones just flatten out into paper dolls. They paint their flat faces and put ruffles all over themselves and sit up on paper pedestals squeaking through their noses for attention from men. The frailest ones fall off and go floating down the gutter, just like paper dolls in the gutter, eyes open, and on out to sea. Don't think I feel sorry for them because I don't. I am talking a lot of nonsense, the sort of things I think all the time, but to tell you the honest truth I'm just mean. I don't admire anything about anybody but guts. Balloons have lots of vitality, certainly, but no guts. Paper dolls don't have vitality or guts. I object to the word, but I won't soften it."

"Not for me," said Angela, who refused to be shocked by words, "I'm not squeamish."

"It's not a bad thing to be squeamish," said Arabella contrarily. "Never mind what I say, though. I never say what I mean. Miss Sis, you tell me," she said to the straight-backed black and white figure re-entering the room with an empty basket, "you tell me why this whole thing has gotten so out of hand. It's not the first time ladies have been mad at Bob White. He can be very exasperating, but this is pure persecution."

"Sex," said Miss Sis, her voice positive and outdoors-loud. "Clementine ought to've had seventeen children and done the wash. Also she's having change of life, I reckon, and is worse than ever. All she wanted from Bob White was a little attention. He could have had her eating out of his hand with a few ordinary everyday flatteries. She pays a doctor and a lawyer, a couple of them, and a whatdyacall 'em, financial advisor, plenty of cash for a little harmless sex. She's used up Alton. It's plain and simple."

Angela was enchanted. She leaned forward, at one with the previous generation for the first time in her life, partaking on equal terms of wisdom she had never guessed they possessed.

"Of course," said Arabella. "Bob White's such a lazy fool."

"He's a saint," said Miss Sis.

Angela had a mental picture of the tubby, untidy little man with the ineffably sweet and unpretty face and the round, bald head.

"Same thing," said Arabella angrily.

"It's hard for a woman to live with a saint," said Miss Sis sympathetically. "But, listen, lady, you put up with him, hear? Do you know that man is the only man who's ever given me communion on Thursday morning as if he had a packed church and a bishop there instead of a crazy loon of an old woman who goes because she can't stand her fellow humans? He's got respect for God, that man, and for me. So you take care of him. I can't."

The two women glared at each other for an instant of antagonistic understanding. Then Arabella yielded, not to Miss Sis's devotion to Bob White, but to her own respect for Miss Sis. She shrugged obligingly.

"Can't I help?" asked Angela eagerly. "Bill and I would do anything for Bob White."

Arabella opened her mouth and closed it again. The affair of Bill and Angela had already harmed Bob White. Then, on second thought, she said, "Of course you can help, if you have the guts."

Miss Sis ordered, "Eat your scuppernongs, Angela. They've never been better since the day you were born."

Carrie came before Angela was half-through and just as Arabella was rising to leave. She thumped into the room and, over their handshake, kissed Miss Sis on both dry cheeks, though Miss Sis ducked slightly away from her affectionate attention.

David had followed her into the room and stood shyly by the door on his storklike legs, his round, childish head drawn back on his thin neck.

"May I present my fiancé, David Bradford, Miss Sis?" inquired Carrie formally, proudly.

"Sure," said Miss Sis loudly. "Hello," she said to him, pushing her hand at him. She was truly unable to bear strangers, thought Angela.

"I'm awfully glad . . ." began David in his youthful professor's voice.

"Fifty cents a bag, do your own picking, and the bag's

tree," interrupted Miss Sis, adding nothing about eating them there.

"Come on, David," said Carrie, and they bent together over the bags, Carrie's strong, dark profile contrasting with David's soft, intelligent face.

"We're having an argument," said Carrie in her dark, pretty, positive voice. "You and Mrs. White might have an opinion. David says he agrees in principle with the addition of a huge chapel to St. James's. I say it's the bunk."

David reddened very slightly under his fair skin. "That's not quite a just presentation of my side," he protested. "I mean I think we lack what you might call Cathedral faith these days. We admit Andalusia will grow, but we seem to maintain that our church won't."

"Something in that," said Miss Sis grumpily, interested but hating to talk to a stranger. She addressed Carrie. "It's called being realistic, instead of having faith."

"Oh, faith!" said Carrie. "I object to a big old Grecian *thing* where children ought to play. I should think David would be the first to agree. Now, really! St. James's hasn't been jammed except Easter time since Grandma was a pup. There's no use pretending it has."

David protested, reddening still more. "It needn't be Grecian. That's an error. I know the architect very well. He was only trying to do first what Mrs. Rook already had in mind. That could be modified, would be, with a little persuasion used on Mrs. Rook. And adding a piece of permanent beauty these days is so rare. I have a—cousin—who could explain better than I can what I mean. It's the principle of the aesthetic future, the contribution to the artistic heritage . . ."

"Every time I hear the word aesthetic," said Arabella meditatively, "I react like an American Legion meeting. Suspicious. Isn't that odd of me? Reprehensible."

"Come on, darling," said Carrie to David, blithely enough. "Let's finish arguing while we pick. Don't they look luscious?"

"They are," said Angela fervently. "They're divine. Have you ever had any scuppernongs before, David?"

"Never," said David. "They look really wonderful. Thank you, Miss Whittle . . ."

"Pays your money," said Miss Sis, "and picks your own."

"Andalusia's been a wonderful town to me," said David nervously, obviously unwilling to leave on unfriendly terms with Miss Sis and Mrs. White.

"Glad you like it," said Miss Sis heartily. "I'm told you're doing a fine job with the young ones. Keep it up."

She bustled Carrie and David out of the room through the back door, patting Carrie on the arm to assure her that there were no hard feelings because Carrie had brought a stranger, and a talkative one at that, into her house. She turned back and eyed Angela and Arabella with dismissal in her look. Enough for one day, she seemed to think.

At the door, she took Angela's hand and frowned at her. "Good luck, young Angela," she said. "You and that Bloodgood brat of yours."

Before Angela could reply from the tight fullness of her happy heart, Miss Sis turned abruptly to Arabella.

"I wish I could shoot that woman!" she said. "See you Thursday, maybe, after church. Give Bob White my warmest regards."

Outside, under the slow climbing sun, Angela wondered how in the world she could get around back to meet Carrie and David without going through Miss Sis's house again, from which she had been dismissed. There was no way through the bamboo. It was at least a quarter of a mile to get around it and into the field where a path led back to the outhouse. After hesitating, she decided, resigned, to sit in her car until they came out. There was still some chill in the fresh breeze that blew outside, but if she sat very still, with her face up, within the protection of her windshield and side windows, the sun would warm her through and through.

18.   **Party**

Clementine Terra Rook's memorial service for her deceased mother, Marguerite Thibodeaux Terra, was announced for Sunday, October 4th, at the Chapel of All Angels in Oakland. The service would be held under the ancient, pre-Civil War oak trees outdoors in order to accommodate the numerous guests who wished to pay their respects to the so honored departed. The Very Reverend Mr. Withers, Dean of the Cathedral of St. Matthew in Oglethorpe, would preside. This Sunday was, as the whole town knew, the all-important Sunday for St. James's, when its members pledged, with the day's offering, like contributions for every Sunday the following year, whether they attended service later or did not. It was, of course, possible to make one's pledge *in absentia*, but, like the use of absentee ballots, it was not often done.

Dressing for the dinner dance, which was in effect the grand opening of the finally completed Oaks, on the Saturday afternoon of the week before, Andrew and Tracy Gregory were still discussing the affair in terms of their personal quandary.

There were ways of dodging the issue. They could go away for the week-end, and were strongly tempted to do so. They could attend the early service, leave their two pledges, and go to Clementine's eleven o'clock memorial service. But the only way they could affect the outcome of the showdown, which this was intended to be, was to announce in advance that they would attend St. James's on Sunday, October 4th, and considered it the Christian duty of other parishioners to do likewise. Mrs. Gregory, for all she gave few parties, was a matron socially even more respected than Mrs. Rook, and Andrew Gregory was not only the church's senior warden but the town's leading citizen. It would make quite a difference. It would also mean an open and ugly social break with Clementine Rook, which would make for personal unpleasantness in their pleasant lives for some time to come. It would mean public flouting of the respect traditionally and publicly due the dead in Andalusia, in the name of private morals in defense of a living man, which was the sort of thing you were expected to defend privately. It was all very difficult.

"She'll try to pin us down tonight," said Tracy, with a sigh.

Clementine Rook had announced that she and her family would attend the dinner dance at The Oaks. A full year of mourning, she explained widely, was an anachronism of which her dear, dead, modern-minded mother would not have approved. If the fact that Mrs. Terra was modern-minded came as something of a surprise to most people, enough time had elapsed so that appropriate virtues could be assigned to the no longer living by those who had known them best.

"Clementine could make a scene," said Andrew.

"Oh, dear," said Tracy. "Oh, dear, oh, dear."

"If she only hadn't chosen Sunday week, Pledge Sunday," said Andrew once more.

"It may even be my fault," said Tracy unhappily. "I asked her not to."

"That wasn't very bright," said Andrew.

The two looked at each other with rare antagonism. Then Andrew patted his wife's heavy shoulder and went out of her room, untying the cord of his dressing gown as he went. He had no objection to being viewed by his wife in the nude, but he drew the line at appearing before her in shirttails and shorts. This costume reduced, as he knew, any living man to the ridiculous.

She heard various noises in their joint bathroom, and then the door into his room close behind him. Sighing deeply, she went over to her dressing table and sat down before the mirror. She contemplated unhappily the unhappy expression on her broad face before becoming absorbed in removing the few blackheads that occasionally marred her healthy, ruddy skin.

Without knocking, Carrie stumped into her mother's bedroom. She said, in a flat, harsh voice, without preliminaries, "You might as well be the first to know, Mother, that David and I are all washed up."

Mrs. Gregory's heart gave a great, lurching thump. She got up from the dressing table, started toward Carrie, and then sat down abruptly on the edge of the bed, which was still mussed from the nap she had taken thereon before starting to dress. Carrie stumped over and stood spraddle-legged in a way that emphasized her lameness leaning one elbow on the white, carved mantelpiece that surmounted the small fireplace. She looked at her mother with an expression of cool, amused detachment. So Carrie had often looked at her mother when she was in the greatest pain, warning away and warding off her mother's intimacy, her sympathy. A cigarette burned in the corner of Carrie's mouth and the smoke curled up so that she squinted one eye.

"I'm sorry, Mother," said Carrie, as if it were her mother who was to be pitied under the circumstances.

"But, Carrie, darling . . ." said Mrs. Gregory in a tight, bewildered voice. She put her hands, arms crossed, to her bare shoulders, as if she were cold.

Carrie turned and looked down at the fireplace. Removing the cigarette from the corner of her mouth, she threw it into the still empty grate. "God damn it," she said.

"Carrie!" said her mother, in automatic reproval.

"Sorry. I get mad when I even think of that whited sepulcher, that rotten spoiled, bad-tempered, stinking bitch . . ."

"Carrie!" said Mrs. Gregory.

"I told David that no decent human being could put up with her, the way she's acting, and that if she has her way the whole town should be ashamed. There's no such thing as decency if she gets away with it. I told him nobody but softies would let her pull this my-sainted-mother crap . . ."

"Carrie!" said Mrs. Gregory.

Carrie went on, unheedingly, her skin drawing finer and finer over the high cheekbones of her narrow face. "People like you and Dad and the Winthrops have the guts to stand up to her, thank the Lord. Mrs. Winthrop is going next Sunday, even if she has to go in a wheelchair—never liked the old hypochondriac before, with all that old aristocrat invalid humbug, but when it comes to a showdown . . . David says there are two sides to every question, but there aren't. There *are not.*"

"There are to this one, Carrie, for heaven's sake, I never saw you so excited," said Mrs. Gregory, crying out in protest. "Your father and I think there are very much two sides. I do admit Clementine has been high-handed, but Mr. White was also pretty high-handed about refusing the chapel. . . ."

"Don't quibble!" said Carrie loudly and scornfully.

"Keep your voice down, Carrie," commanded her mother sharply.

"I will *not,*" said Carrie, dropping her voice. "If St. James's nursery school isn't worth a million chapels, I'll . . ."

"Be reasonable, Carrie," said Mrs. Gregory. "The nursery school would go on."

"Sure, in those stuffy little rooms with four feet of front lawn! Have you ever watched those kids playing out there where that God damn chapel would be, in sun like today's?"

"Is *this* what you and David quarreled about?" asked Mrs. Gregory unbelievingly.

"He agrees about the chapel," said Carrie, suddenly calm. "We argued about it a lot. But he does agree. So it's over Bob White."

Mrs. Gregory felt a sense of such relief that a deep sigh escaped her. "Well," she said, exhaling. Carrie could not stay angry for long with David for the sake of the tubby clergyman. It was not possible. "That's absurd," she said.

"Is it?" asked Carrie quizzically. "No, it's not. Right's right and wrong's wrong. And that's that. And if that doesn't matter, what does? Love? Go around loving everybody and let a good man get hounded out of town for making an honest decision? Even if he's wrong!"

"You really go too far," said Mrs. Gregory gently. "After all, darling, it's not David's church or his business, is it?"

"Certainly it's his church," said Carrie. "He was going to that memorial service just because Mrs. Rook bullied him into it and because Agrippa Rook goes to his school. He's just as much a member of St. James's as I am, even if he's new. He'll admit that. It's your Clementine who made it pretty clear that she'd take Agrippa out of school if David went to St. James's with me next Sunday."

"That seems a good enough reason for David not to," said Mrs. Gregory. "Really!"

"Oh, hell," said Carrie. She flung the stub of another cigarette into the fireplace and lit a fresh one. Then she turned quietly, blinking in the smoke, and spoke to her mother as if her mother were her daughter. "I won't argue, dear," she said. "David can do what he likes, for all of me now. He's no man for me, and that's all there is to it."

"I must say I find this very, very tiresome," said Mrs. Gregory, exasperated and worried. "I, for one, don't propose to fight with one of my oldest friends—and Clementine may be the limit, some times, but she is an old and dear friend—over a man I scarcely know, really, even if he is my clergyman. I'll not turn against Mr. White, of course, but I do think he's been tactless. After all, he should compromise. Besides, though I hate to talk about this, Mr. White really seems to be championing Lucy Cranborne. It really is a little hard to take. It confuses everything so. After all, she . . ."

"*Do you mean to say you'll go on Sunday?*" asked Carrie ominously.

"To Clementine's service? Yes, I shall," said Mrs. Gregory, making up her mind finally, with a sense of relief, as she spoke. "It's all too dreadfully messy, really. And I hope David can still come to dinner afterwards."

Carrie flushed a dark red and Mrs. Gregory, frightened, stopped short, both in her words and her thoughts. She looked anxiously at her daughter, who was staring at the floor. Carrie looked up and spoke, her voice as toneless and harsh as a marsh hen's. "Funny," she said. "This seems to have become a match between you and David's mother. Very funny. I'm not mad, Mother, at you or anybody. But I won't marry to please you, or his mother either. And I won't marry because the chances are nobody else will want to marry me, either. David is a nice boy, but that's not enough for me. Bob White's a man and I'll stick by him against all you women and his wife and all the cowards in this town."

"Good heavens, are you in love with him, Carrie?" asked Mrs. Gregory, thinking of Mark.

Carrie laughed tonelessly. "Of course not. Not the way you sound like. But I'm not in love with David—any more—either. If I ever was. He just isn't—anybody, Mother. He's sweet. He was sweet to love me. Poor guy."

"You really mean to say, Carrie Gregory," said her mother, harsh herself, because she was so unhappy that she could scarcely breathe, "that you won't marry David because you insist on going and he won't go to church with you next Sunday?"

"Something like that," said Carrie, smiling. "Except that he says he will, of course, since I want him to so much."

"Well, then . . ." said Mrs. Gregory pleadingly.

"God damn the day of my birth," said Carrie, lifting her head, "but that's how it is."

The Hunt Club at The Oaks was, actually, a speakeasy. To "play cards" there, you had to be a "member," or be introduced by one. It was also designed with its conversion into a legal barroom in mind, the moment the Volstead Act should be repealed. The iron grille in the close-fitting, solid door was of light and exquisite design. It was temporarily backed with inch-thick wood. The peephole was of ornamental stained glass. The solid mahogany bar with its polished brass rail was backed by shelves containing nothing more illegal than old-fashioned sarsaparilla. Liquor, both moonshine and smuggled, was brought by way of an underground tunnel, which would later serve as a wine cellar, and in through a trap door hidden beneath a white bear rug with a long-fanged, glass-eyed head. When the glass eye of the stuffed fish on one wall turned red, it was the signal to hide current bottles behind the antlered deer head on the other wall. The furniture was rich and decorous and the wallpaper, above the dark, waist-high paneling, was old-fashioned. There was a real, wood-burning fireplace, but the windows were fake. The final effect was disturbing: staid and lawless, dignified and furtive, solid and brittle, respectable and disreputable.

The Hunt Club closed at three A.M., by arrangement with the local police, who knew all about the Club, as did everyone else in Oakland and Andalusia. That Saturday night, after the dance, the remaining "members" were bowed out personally by all three of their hosts, Van Ball, Bill Bloodgood, and Logan Knight. Bill, Logan and Van, accompanied by Angela, Hope and Ellen Terra, decided to have one penultimate drink in the privacy of the closed "club," in accordance with the superstition that no drink should ever be called the ultimate.

They were all in a highly stimulated frame of mind, so that the alcohol already consumed had had little effect on any of them except Hope. The dinner dance, their first at the new Oaks, had been an unqualified success. The townspeople of Andalusia had turned out in numbers, and there had been gratifying contingents from Marianna and Oglethorpe. Furthermore, the hotel had garnered a small but respectable group of week-enders and weekers from varying distances. After most of their names, in his meticulous private notes, Van had been able to mark MA, WH, WB, his designation for perfect guests, which meant Middle-Aged, Well-Heeled, and Well-Behaved.

Nearly all of the out-of-towners and most of the "locals" had worn evening clothes for the dance, which made for decorative and decorous success rather than a raucous party. The two guests of the owner, the Reverend Robert White and his wife, had likewise dressed for the occasion.

"I told you so," Bill had said to Van triumphantly, looking over the crowd.

Van had started to argue that Bill's reasoning was faulty, that he had not "told him so," but he contented himself with a petulant grunt. He was too pleased with the evening's success, which enabled him at least to whisper "I told you so" in the direction of his trustees in New York, to pick any of several small bones with his subordinate. He was also, on the whole, pleased with Bill. Bill had been not only reasonable but gracious over the matter of Logan Knight's job. He had even insisted that Logan be given, as was proper, the title of manager and that he be called assistant manager, or anything else handy. He admitted that he was casual to a degree about finance and said he was glad to have somebody else handle that part. Logan was his friend. It was his own job he liked, and to hell with titles. Van was too relieved to recognize the fact that he also considered Bill unduly cavalier about the matter. He had insisted that both have the title. Logan was the manager of the Oakland Corporation and Bill was manager of The Oaks. It gave Logan the edge, but Bill made no comment on this. Bill ought to know that titles were important in a competitive society. Van was only mildly irritated that Bill took credit not only for the presence of most of the guests but for the fact that almost all of them had dressed. It was, in fact, Bill who had insisted that Van refrain from making evening dress obligatory.

"It's not the depression or anything political," Bill had argued, "but class down here sometimes looks like it came straight off the dump heap. Nobody likes rules about it. Take old man Winthrop. He's got some money still, but I bet he hasn't bought anything since he got married in that old cutaway he wears to church on Sunday. You can't snub him and you can always discourage the ringers some other way."

Van had given in, although he was privately of the opinion that if the third generation could not hang onto what it took, and look as if they had, it was better for them to go back to overalls without dallying over it. It was in the same way that he had yielded to Bill's insistence that he invite the Episcopal preacher and his wife as his personal guests. It was an old custom, arising from the same impulse that got for Bob White free passes to the moving pictures, however lurid, and a permanent invitation to the dog races in Marianna. Nonetheless, an honored custom. Van commented that it might be more to the point to invite the mayor and the chief of police, as a guarantee of moral purity. But Logan had begun by backing Bill up, although he, like Van, disapproved of giving things away. Bill had said, a little too patiently, "There are back-door handouts and front-door handouts, my friend Van. Cash and kind. What's-his-name, the mayor, gets a Christmas present. Lucas takes care of the police. He knows that score, all the way down to the six-bit colored boys that stick the labels on the bottles of booze."

"Lucas is cheating me," Van had complained, momentarily sidetracked.

"Some," Bill had admitted indifferently.

Van had decided then to put Lucas and the bootlegging under Logan's jurisdiction, but had not yet gotten around to it. Before he could reopen the argument against inviting Bob White, the announcement in the *Banner* had settled the question.

Settled it for one Saturday night, thought Van now. He would have to settle with Bill for the future.

"*El penúltimo*," said Bill joyfully to them all.

Angela did not want any more to drink, but she could think of no way to refuse. Van was ceremoniously opening a private bottle, which meant that the whiskey therein was slightly older and slightly less lousy than what they had been drinking. To refuse such a drink was a personal insult. Angela thought there was something to be said for the days when ladies were not supposed to drink. It was a reflection on his bathtub or his mother, these days, for a lady to turn down a gentleman's lousy liquor.

"Here you are," said Bill and, sensing her demur, added, "Don't be a snitface. Let's have fun."

"All right," said Angela, and smiled at him sunnily. She could refuse her true love nothing. She touched for luck the ring, bought the week before, and felt its small diamond cold against the bony cavity between her breasts. She could always induce with her thin, brown forefinger her thin, nervous stomach to give up its load if the load became too ungraceful to carry. She would drink with her true love, and with his boss, and with his co-equal, Logan Knight, the other manager.

"How," she said.

"You're sweet," said Bill, and winked at her before he turned to Logan. "Can I get you yours, partner?"

"But why not, partner?" asked Logan, his boyish, handsome face radiating vague good will.

291

Hope lifted the lids over her eyes with the aid of her eyebrows for leverage and lifted herself a little in her chair before falling back as if partially attached to it. "Want me to fix some baconneggs?" she asked agreeably. "I love to fix baconneggs. I fix wonderful baconneggs."

"She certainly does, too," said Logan to them all.

Hope beamed and groped for the drink beside her. "For all you wonderful people," she said, letting the eyebrows drop down, the lids following, falling of their own astonishing weight.

Logan sat down beside her and surreptitiously pinched her thigh, not too hard but hard enough for her to know that her fair skin, easily bruised, would be black and blue when she next looked at it. She suppressed a yelp and the impulse to pull up her skirt and examine the spot now, and nodded, opening her eyes again, to show that she understood that she must not, naturally, go to sleep. This occupied her thoroughly for the next ten minutes, and she felt that she was leading a busy life as a good wife to Logan. To Logan, who was now the manager of the Oakland Corporation, a successful man, a wonderful young man, partner and friend of her friend's Bill Bloodgood.

"Did we break even tonight?" asked Van of Logan, with mock humility, for the sake of hearing the answer.

"We did indeed, boss," said Logan. "Plenty and lots more besides. Subtracting free rides and all."

"Oh, don't talk business," said Ellen Terra plaintively. "It makes me feel like it wasn't a party. It was a lovely party."

"I'm just a hotel keeper," said Van, sure that he was also a gentleman. "Parties are business to me."

"Poor Van," said Angela, faintly mocking. "Don't you ever have a good time?"

"Wonderful," said Van. "I enjoy myself both ways. Ellen Terra, I fell in love with one of my customers tonight!"

"You did?" said Ellen Terra equably. "Now I think that's right much of a good thing."

"With your mother," said Van.

"You *did*?" said Ellen Terra, staring at him with her raisin-black eyes.

"I certainly did," said Van admiringly. "I haven't met anybody like her since my Aunt Rosalyn Stuyvesant used to terrify Newport. She's *quelqu'une*, that one, your mother!"

"You talk so fun-ny," drawled Ellen Terra. "I just lo-o-ve to hear you talk."

Logan said, "Van, there's one thing about these dances, especially, that worries me."

"Oh, business," said Ellen Terra. "I wish you-all wouldn't go on and on and on about business."

"What?" asked Van.

"Lucas's cut for producing the liquor," said Logan. "He's getting away with murder."

"That's what he's paid for," said Bill, "getting away with murder."

"It's been worrying me, too," said Van. "Seriously. What do you say, Bill?"

"Look," said Bill, as if Van were a child. "None of us can afford to be mixed up in the liquor end. You can't. Logan can't. I could, maybe, but I won't. It's illegal, for the Lord's sake. You can go to jail. So. You've got to have your dirty work done for you and the risks run by somebody else. It comes high. Lucas is as good a man as any. Better."

"Never trust a black man," said Van. "I'm sure you trust him too far, Bill."

"Better black than po' white," said Bill, turning patient again, "for God's sake. And there ain't any other sort in the business of trafficking in liquor. We're lucky to have Lucas. His grandfather worked for mine."

"Ah, nepotism," said Van, irritated at Bill's use of ain't as if it were an exact, correct word, and irritated because he sensed that Bill was exactly right about Lucas. "Oh, well. Happy days."

"Happy days," said Hope, responding unexpectedly. "I know," she said. "Let's play a game . . ."

"Let's don't and say we did," said Van.

"*Why do I love you?*" sang Ellen Terra, purring slightly off key.

In a minute they were all singing. Bill went out and came back with Angela's ukulele from the car and she took it from him and began to tune the strings. The brief instant in the fresh air had brought back his usual high color. Angela looked at him with that start of appreciation which, even after so long a time, she felt for the rough beauty of his face. She began to strum and, finding a key, began softly, "*Who stole my heart away?* . . . *Who made me dream all day?* . . . *Dreams I know can never come true* . . ."

One song spawned another, or several others at a time, and the music made a linked chain of live and wriggling memories of moods. Oddly enough, it was Van, with his tenor which had been good enough for him to make the Princeton Glee Club's quartet, who began the hymns. Not with the generic Christmas carols, either, but with the substantial, triumphant, and dignified "Rejoice Ye Pure in Heart." The white-surpliced, black-cassocked choirs of his New York Fifth Avenue boyhood, as well as the Episcopal choirs of Andalusia and Oglethorpe, had swung to it into the church behind the golden, uplifted cross of Christ. He thus laid aside the mass of his pretensions and asked wistfully to be one with them, to share with them not only the decade of their titillated adolescence and urgent tries at love-making, but their childhood and, such as it was, whatever they had learned about God and good and evil. Angela turned to him, happy again. Hope's sure, trained soprano cleared and steadied and the words she sang were blurred no longer. Bill, who had been an angel-faced choir boy before his voice changed and his early pimples sprouted, strained his low baritone to produce a deep bass to do credit to the rumbling, harmonius "Re-e-e-e-ejoice" of the final bars. Logan was the one who remembered also the words of the second verse.

Ellen Terra slipped her hand into the crook of Van's arm, and he squeezed her hand to his side with his elbow. She had long since given in to him and she had long since given him up, so that she was again unself-conscious with him and undemanding and full of love. She delighted him thus, for he understood, from out of his own complicated inability ever to be natural, the strength and charm of her naturalness. It made her public behavior as impeccable as her private behavior was wanton. This was a personally satisfactory combination, as well as one that, having lived several years in England, he considered eminently ladylike. He was beginning to feel that this place would bring him success and that this girl was one with this place. He loved Andalusia. And this girl satisfied him more than he was willing to admit. He had commanded and received her fidelity, offering her nothing whatever in return. It bothered him a little that he could not settle it by giving her money in payment for fidelity.

Drunk, as they were now all finally very drunk, their singing of the stately, full-worded hymns that followed each other, each one sealed with an harmonious *Amen,* was stately and respectful. They sang them as they had been written, in solemnly joyful tribute to the traditional, dignified and Godlike Anglican God. Before the hymns gave out, Van began, "Praise God from Whom all blessings flow . . ."

The sextet swelled into exaggerated harmony with the firm chords of the ancient doxology.

> *Praise Him all creatures here below.*
> *Praise Him above ye heavenly host*
> *Praise Fa . . .*

"No, no," said Van, his speaking voice cutting across the music. "Bill! *Fa* ther, like that." He was waving his finger imperiously up under Bill's nose in the intensity of his sudden perfectionism. "Not *Fa*-ther."

"All right," said Bill, drawing his cleft chin a little higher so that he looked directly down at Van's head, "*Fa* ther . . ."

"Not—quite—" said Van judiciously.

They tried it again, but it was ragged now. Van said cantankerously, "No, *not* like that."

"Hooray, hooray, my *fa-ther's* gonna be hung," sang Bill. "How's that?"

"Wonderful," agreed Van, and they were off, fully launched into a new group of songs, a fresh attitude, new and slyer harmonies, singing the barroom bawdy songs they also shared.

"She was pore but she was honest . . ."

"I wish I were a fascinating bitch . . ."

The drinking went faster and the singing grew louder and their high approval of it even less justified. There were trips to the bathroom by baritone-bass, tenor, and baritone-tenor, by the two sopranos and the one alto. Someone discovered then that dawn was arriving somewhere outside, over by the edge of the vigorous-smelling pine forest. They all went out to see and approve vociferously, and then, shivering and partially sobered, came back into the thick fumes of whiskey and tobacco smoke in the cardroom.

"Absolutely the penultimate," said Bill.

"Let's drink to the black," said Logan drunkenly, "the little old wonderful old black . . ."

"The what?" said Ellen Terra, toying with her glass, able, as always, to drink less than she appeared to be drinking.

"The black," said Logan with a radiant poet's look, "is the ink you use when you make money. The opposite is red. Tonight . . ."

"Oh, *business*," said Ellen Terra.

"Oh, be*fore* I forget it, Bill," said Van, tapping his forehead with his forefinger, "I want you to take Mr. Robert White off the invitation list tomorrow. No more free rides. No more free rides AT all. Up your kilts with tradition. This is business."

"Now, look, Van," said Bill ponderously, as he was only ponderous when he had drunk too much. "We went over all this. It's for our own good. We like tradition. Besides, Bob White is such a hell of a good guy . . ."

"You explained," said Van. "You certainly did. You explained and explained. But I never did get convinced. Remember? I gave in. Didn't matter. Gracefully. Well, I've ungiven in. Personal reasons. Ellen Terra's mother, to whom I am ardently attached . . ."

"How you do talk," said Ellen Terra.

". . . has told me," Van went on, ignoring Ellen Terra, "that she considers an invitation to Mr. White a slap in the face to her. I wouldn't dream of slapping a lady's face, and besides she's one of our best customers. She had twelve tonight. Count 'em. Twelve."

"Listen," said Bill, straightening his massive shoulders and wishing that he were slightly soberer, "it all depends on whether you act like people are customers or *all* honored guests. If one honored guest doesn't like another honored guest, the honored guest that doesn't like the other honored guest can go home if he wants to go home, but the host doesn't throw out the honored guest that the other one doesn't like, just because the other one doesn't like him. In other words . . ."

"Never mind the 'other words'," said Van almost good-naturedly. "I follow you. I'm not a host. I'm a hotel keeper. I don't want to get mixed up in any little old town arguments."

"That's what I'm saying," said Bill. "We shouldn't. In our book, Bob White's as welcome as the biggest spender in town. He's a gentleman and we invited him and nobody can make us back down on our principles."

"You got me wrong, buddy," said Van, pretending to talk tough in order to mitigate the snarl in his voice, which had been trained into it and which sounded provocative at such a moment. "I *ain't* arguing, about principles or anything else. I'm telling. After all, pal, somebody's gotta be boss. I guess it'll have to be little old me." He paused and looked directly and almost shyly at Bill.

Bill lifted his glass to his mouth and took a long swallow. Angela, paralyzed with indecision, opened and closed her mouth twice, soundlessly. Bill was so right, so beautifully, heavenly right. She had never loved him more. Bill was defending a code of manners, but he was also defending a man. Bill loved courage and he was defending the man who had had the courage to say that he would marry them without her parents' consent, which took a great deal of courage in Andalusia. It was curious how much it had meant to her, to know that, if she chose, she could be married in St. James's, by her own rector. If she must defy her parents to marry, this made everything all right. Her act would be no longer a deliberate defiance, a running away from everything she was in order to do what she wanted to, but merely a difference of opinion between her and her mother, in which her God and her mores were on her own side. Thank the Lord for the way Bob White made her feel.

He had made her feel good enough to stand against her mother for a great many long, nightmarish days now. Since her game, the one she had played so gaily in the Stones' living room, her mother had been working on her. She had not yet gone into one of *those*, the stubborn withdrawals that made her agony to live with until she was appeased, but she had argued, sideways and around corners, day and night, trying to catch Angela out. And she had had such headaches. The headaches were real enough, and they hurt Angela. But she had to hold out. It was her luck she was fighting for, and her love.

But how could she be strong if Bill lost his job? If it grew cold again and they could not marry again. How could they marry if Bill fought with Van? On nothing, with nothing, dowryless and cursed, out in a jobless world with all familiar doors closed behind them? She did not think she was afraid of being poor. What had Bill ever been else? But proud! You must be proud to live. Could Bill be proud, taking his wife to the gutter for her bridal bed, living on charity, or what else, until he could "find something" again? Her proud Bill! What good would it do for Bill to fight with Van over Bob White's right to come to a party. Maybe that's all this was. Parties were different from principles. Bill was prepared to accompany her to church the next Sunday, on principle. Perhaps it did not matter whether or not Bob White came to a party.

Ellen Terra said reprovingly, "You mustn't let Mama make you rude to Bob White, Van Ball. That's not right. That's wrong. There's almighty right and there's dreadfully wrong!"

Van glared and then stared at her. She was solemn and earnest and there was a radiant inner light shining in her raisin eyes. She was also convincing and adorable. He did not reason it out, but he knew somewhere in his devious and overlaid being that if this girl knew almighty right from dreadfully wrong, he should grab her and keep her for his own. If this girl knew in her heart almighty right from dreadfully wrong, you could come very near to trusting her. "Dear heart," he said, and then, suspicious as ever and shrewd in suspicion, "darling, are you going to be in Oakland next Sunday? Are you coming with your mother to your mother's little showdown with the Reverend Robert White, our rector? Your very smart mother. You are coming, aren't you? You won't be at St. James's on the almighty right side, will you?"

Ellen Terra dropped her eyes and then peeped up at him pleadingly from under the fringe of her hair. The light in her eyes was gone and the light he saw did not dazzle him. She wriggled self-consciously, her body lush and desirable. "Well, honey, that's sort of different. After all, I don't see how I can . . . Papa and Grandma and—you see . . ." She pouted and looked as if she would weep and that they would be dry tears, like those of winsome babies.

"I see, honey chile," said Van, possessive and contemptuous. "I agree with you. That's exactly what I mean. Now you hush your pretty mouth while we men talk business. I'm talking business and I want to get this settled. It's no moral question."

Logan said gently, "Of course it's not. It's absurd to make it one." He looked vaguely inspired and made a sketch in the air. "Interesting face, Bob White has, hasn't he?"

"It's an old custom to invite the rector," said Angela painfully and slowly. "A very old custom . . ."

"Nuts," said Van, with an arrogant wave of his hand, contemptuous of them all. "It's no old custom of mine. If the cloth wanted to stay at The Schuyler, you can bet old Schuyler VanDyck got the bill paid, for all he toted the plate on Sunday. Now, let's drop it, huh? It's settled."

"I don't *care*," said Hope suddenly, loudly. Then she said cloudily, "Open a window. Please, somebody open a window in here. I just don't *want* Bob White to go away, you hear?" Her voice rose.

Logan put his hand gently over her mouth. For a terrible instant, she thought she would suffocate. Then she found that she could breathe quite nicely through her nose if she did not struggle. Nobody paid any attention to them.

"Somebody will invite him as their guest," said Bill, sullen and indecisive. "They like him."

"That's not *my* business," said Van, poised and tense as if ready to fight.

"I suppose," said Bill, drawing a deep, reluctant breath, "that inviting the preacher is no real honor to him. Since it's really done so we can say look who was here and said grace in case we are accused of breaking the commandments. Not that Bob White took it that way. So . . ." His eyes met Angela's and their eyes pleaded with each other, a confused pleading. He shrugged and took another swallow of his drink. ". . . to hell with it. It's your show, Van. You're the boss."

"Good boy," said Van jovially, his body relaxing. He would

have touched Bill as a token of friendly good will, but Bill moved, as if by accident, away from him.

"Absolutely the penultimate," said Bill, picking up the bottle.

"Let's go, Van," said Ellen Terra softly.

"Oh, not yet," said Van. "What's your hurry? Party's getting good now. I'll fix you a drink and how about drinking it this time? No more of that stalling, Missy Ellen Terra Rookie. Every drop. There's a good girl. I like a girl that can hold her liquor and not waste it." Perversely, having admired her technique of shamming the amount she drank, admired her ability to seem to get drunk and retain a graceful sobriety, he was determined to get her drunk. He watched her like a hawk, and she submissively did what he wanted.

They spent a desultory fifteen minutes trying to bring the party to some other conclusion. Van was overly friendly and, together with Logan, tried to make Bill join them in a final rejoicing over the success of The Oaks this night, over the prospects for a long and gala future. Ellen Terra and Angela joined forces in a corner, feeling the need to be close together. They imitated gaiety, as only the oldest friends can be gay together, drinking in swift sips and acting as if they were at one with their beaus in a splendid, nearly ended party. They wished that all of them would go home and they were only glad that they were together.

Ellen Terra felt the down-spiraling chill that preceded the possibility of being very sick. She wondered if she could manage to spiral back up again without having to dash for the bathroom to throw up. She hated being sick worse than anything in the world. She closed her eyes for a second and then quickly opened them again, got up suddenly, clutched the bar, and fixed a hunting print with a desperate focus that might save her.

"Bob White's my friend," she said, speaking to no one. She was rocking on her little round heels and no one was listening to her.

"Absolutely the penultimate," said Bill.

Angela said, "No . . ." and then hushed. She knew better than that. Bill would drink as much as he wanted to drink.

"This last was my penultimate," said Van, the sses washing.

"It's time for baby to go bye-bye." He leered at Ellen Terra. "Pick up my hat, Bill, and let's get the hell out of here."

There was a second of silence in the room, during which the room stopped spiraling around Ellen Terra and the cold sweat dried under the bangs on her forehead. Van's commanding, querulous tone was absent-minded and the content of his imperious order accidental. The hat lay, where it had long since fallen, near the bear rug beside the bar and near Bill's feet. If Bill had tossed it to Van carelessly, in the first instant, as carelessly as the order had been given, it would not have mattered. But the pause was too pregnant and Bill's mood too clear. For one staggering second Angela thought Bill was going to pick it up anyway.

"Pick up your own hat, chum," said Bill, "and let's go."

"I think I made a very simple request," said Van, and his lips folded inward, making a thin, tight line of his small, well-cut, drooping mouth. He added, almost immediately, self-pitying and committed, "I don't *feel* well," considering this an impressive and generous apology.

"That's one great big request to anybody but a nigger boy," said Bill, "and you can say please." He hauled his body backward, as if it might accidentally topple in the direction of the hat, and added his own generous concession, "Terribly sorry you feel bad." He felt himself sober, in the center of himself, where it mattered.

"God damn it," said Van, anger coming to the support of the inadvertent folding in of his mouth that had committed him. "Will—you—pick—up . . ."

Ellen Terra leaned slightly forward from the bar and vomited deliberately in a long arc down the rug, from fat fur tail to glassy-eyed head.

In the confusion that followed, the hat was kicked behind the bar, where it was found the next day by Lucas's wife, who cleaned the Club Room. Bill found time to say to Van, in the formal manner of a man slapping an erstwhile friend and social equal across the cheek with a white kid glove, "If you want me back on the job, you may say please."

That ties it, thought Angela foggily, wishing that she had drunk less. Thanks all the same, Ellen Terra.

She clung to Bill's arm as they made their unsteady way

to the car. She wondered what it would be like if her darling, her lovely, her handsome love had kept his job by picking up a hat, or had let himself be saved by a lady who lost her lunch.

"I love you," she crooned. "I love you I love you I love you."

"That's fine," said Bill, as if he were entirely sober. "You keep right on, honey."

"Le's go ri' down and ge' Bob White to marry us ri' now," said Angela.

"By the time we can get married this time, baby," said Bill, grinning down at her, "Bob White'll be right where I am. Out of a job. Your mamma and Mrs. Rook'll get him, sure as God made little apples and Schuyler VanDyck Balls."

"No," said Angela uncertainly. "No, no . . ."

When they got to the car, he ceremoniously helped her in and kissed her once. Climbing in on his own side, under the wheel, he put his hands high on the wheel and leaned his head down on the wheel for the briefest of seconds. Then he threw back his shoulders, started, and roared the engine of the car he so carefully tended.

"*Then I wish I was in Dixie,*" he sang loudly in his near bass-baritone.

"Hoo*ray,* hoo*ray,*" Angela chimed in, swallowing the honeycomb of tears in her throat.

"I'm goin to church," said Mercy Church. "I'm gonna take yo mammy's white gloves for my hands and I'm goin." She was sobbing continuously, as she had been sobbing ever since she had started. Periodically she wiped her nose with the skirt of her dress, but she made no other gesture in the direction of her swollen, weeping face.

"Naw yuh ain't," said Georgianna. "Yuh's gonna stay home. Dat ain no church tuh mek no fuss in and yuh ain duh right tuh mek no fuss nohow. Jus let him go, daughtuh Mercy mine. D'ain nothin else tuh do."

"I'm goin," said Mercy.

"Naw yuh ain," said Georgianna. "Yuh's gonna stay wid yo maw. Ain nobody goin but Miss Lucy an Miss Carrie."

"An me," said Mercy.

"Miz Rook she mark yuh down in duh black book. Miz Rook she duh she devil who is wussen duh devil hisself. Miz Rook she fix yuh, and Gawd he fix yuh too, yuh try tuh be so uppity when He done mek yuh black," said Georgianna. "Heah me, Mercy Church?"

"Don't heed you," said Mercy. "Don't never heard you talk so."

Georgianna was silent for a long time and there was no sound except Mercy's steady sobbing and no movement except the steady coursing of Mercy's tears.

"I'm gonna work for Miss Carrie when she done marry. That's what," said Mercy defiantly.

"Miss Carrie ain gonna marry," said Georgianna with scornful wisdom. "Mistuh White done save huh fum dat. Dat boy he jus fightin himself wid Miss Carrie. He uh sick boy. Doan tell me. Now yuh listen tuh me. Mistuh White he goin. Yuh gonna stay. Yuh ain gonna wuk fuh Miss Carrie an yuh ain gonna wuk fo Miss Lucy and yuh ain gonna go to church."

"You ain't never talk so, Mama," said Mercy. "You always been brave."

"Ah knows duh beginnin," said Georgianna. "And ah knows duh end. An ah knows duh middle. Yuh cain't do whut yuh cain't do. Dey is dose could do ain do and dey is dose shouldn't do is did, but yo—yuh cain't. So go right ahead an cry real good."

Mercy sobbed quietly and steadily.

"Ah dunno," said Georgianna at last. "Ah is so ol mebbe ah los somepn. Mebbe. Deys somepn yuh cain't risk tuh lose. Eensy lil thing tis too, an yuh hardly knows when yuh lost it. Its uh stone no biggern uh pebble in duh middle uh yo heart. Yuh go ahead an cry, Mercy Church, and mebbe ah go wid yuh."

19. Eighteenth Sunday After Trinity

In St. James's congregation, on the Eighteenth Sunday after Trinity, which was also Pledge Sunday, were Mrs. Robert White, Miss Carrie Gregory, Miss Lucy Lee Cranborne—for the first time since her mother's funeral—Miss Sis Whittle—for the first time on Sunday in fifteen years—old Dr. Dandridge and his wife, Mr. and Mrs. Matthew Dugdale Winthrop and their tall son, the mothers and fathers of two of the children who went to St. James's nursery school, who were not Episcopalians, the local plumber, who was also the local Socialist and his wife, two members of the eight-voice voluntary choir, a substitute acolyte named Jockey who picked his nose solemnly through the service, the organist, who was paid, and three visitors from The Oaks. The drunken and disreputable sexton, "Uncle Jimmy," whom no rector, let alone Bob White, had ever quite managed to fire, tolled the bell as if for a funeral until Carrie Gregory stumped down the aisle into the entry where the bell rope hung and told him sharply to stop. Mercy Church and her mother, Georgianna, slipped in after the service began, sat primly in the last pew with their white gloves folded, and tiptoed out before it ended.

No one listened to the sermon, which was a sedate and interesting discussion of the day's lesson and which had no bearing, moral or otherwise, on the dramatic issue of the day. Everybody listened to the Anglican service, which Bob White read with reverence, sincerity and attention, as he always did, in his high, sweet voice. The light, filtered through the huge, red east window behind the altar, fell on Bob White's bald head like coals of fire.

At the end of the service, Arabella left quickly and started across the street to the rectory, where Mercy Church had preceded her to prepare their lunch. She saw Carrie emerge and went back, drawing Carrie aside on the strip of lawn between the church steps and the choir room door.

"You're somebody," said Arabella, "For all the good it'll do you. I want to say good-bye."

"Are you leaving, then?" asked Carrie grimly. She looked exhausted and hollow-eyed and she lit a cigarette as she spoke.

"I am," said Arabella. "Bob White can do as he pleases. He won't fight. So I am no help to him. When Bob White's dead, I'll come back and spit in everybody's eye. Or maybe I won't. I'll outlive him, you know. I'm too mean to die."

Carrie shifted uncomfortably on her bad leg. "I hoped you and Mr. White would stay," she said formally, twisting her mouth, the cigarette bobbing at the corner, and squinting her tired eyes against the smoke. "This unholy mess will clear up. Everything calms down in time."

"No doubt," said Arabella. "No doubt the meek will one day inherit the earth. But not in my day. If Bob White turns his cheek again it'll be me that slaps it. I'm going. He can stay if he likes."

Bob White came hurrying out of the choir room door minus his surplice and stole. The fringe of one end of the sash of his cassock trailed the ground while the other end was tucked into the careless knot across his billiken belly. Arabella's fingers twitched and relaxed.

"Ladies," said Bob White, bowing genially and then pausing to shake hands with Carrie. "You're looking mighty handsome this morning, Miss Carrie."

Carrie pulled nervously at the light coat she had over her

shoulders. "I enjoyed your sermon, Mr. White," she said. "Thank you."

"Thank *you*. I'm glad you did. I'm afraid there weren't so many here to hear it," said Bob White and hurried on to catch Miss Lucy and Miss Sis, who were calmly descending the steps of the church and discussing the weather, which was clear and crisp.

"We'll go back to Texas," said Arabella, grinding her teeth lightly as a child might in its sleep. "Texas understands largeness, even of spirit, and has no time for subtleties. They love Bob White out there. In a simple-minded way. It suits them to have a chunk of goodness around, so they don't have to bother. You don't know what I'm talking about."

Carrie said nothing. She yearned after Bob White, who did not seem to be disturbed. There was nothing, really, that she could offer him and he offered her nothing, except now the knowledge that she was courageous in her heart as well as in her body, which was important but not comforting.

"I hate Texas," confided Arabella. "They don't hate me, though. They don't bother. It's easy for me to be any of the things I am supposed to be in Texas. Nobody examines your pretenses there. As long as they are proper pretenses, of course. I don't really hate Texas. We'll go back there and leave Andalusia to *rot*."

Carrie repeated this to Angela at Angela's house, where she went directly after she left the church.

"I feel like I'm rotting already," said Angela, touching her temples gingerly. She huddled deeper into the big chair by the fire and wrapped her dressing gown tight around her legs. "I feel awful —just awful—and so cold."

"That bad?" said Carrie unsympathetically. Mrs. Madison had told her brusquely that Angela was sick when Carrie had called.

"Really it is," pleaded Angela. "Carrie, I just couldn't go. I had to not go. I have to stay in this house for God knows how long." She looked around her, at the bright, well kept, orderly room and down at the glowing fire. "Oh, God," she said.

The big house was silent. The older Madisons were in Oakland, to attend the memorial service and to stay afterwards for Mrs. Rook's luncheon party at The Oaks. Pinckney had the day off.

"All right," said Carrie at last. "It doesn't matter."

"Yes, it does," said Angela, her face pinched and pale. "But it's too late. Mama would never have forgiven me."

"No," said Carrie. "She wouldn't have. Public humiliation. I don't blame you."

"I do," said Angela. Mama would never have forgiven her through the long, long days to come. There was so much time in a winter and the coldest of cold things was a placid and loving woman's unforgiveness. There was too much time when it was cold. "I blame myself."

"Oh, can it," said Carrie. "It doesn't matter."

"Did David go with you?" asked Angela gently.

"Hell, no," said Carrie. "I wouldn't let him. He didn't go to the other, either. He went up to Oglethorpe to meet some cousin or other of his. He says he may not come back."

"Who was there?" asked Angela, averting her face so as not to see Carrie's.

"Nobody," said Carrie grimly. "A cripple, an old maid, a crackpot medico and Mrs. Crackpot, two antisocial aristocrats, a couple of po' whites, some strangers, and two niggers. I think quite a lot of people stayed home, for all the good that'll do."

"I feel so rotten," said Angela violently.

"I'll fix you a Martini," said Carrie. "That'll help."

"Make it a double," said Angela. "Did Hope and Ellen Terra go to Oakland?"

"Sure," said Carrie. "What difference does it make? Don't think I feel holy. Where's the vermouth?"

"Over there. Stay for lunch, Carrie. Pinckney left me enough for a party. Bill's in Oglethorpe, having Sunday with the cousins. Penalty of living at home again. Poor angel. *Please* stay for lunch."

"Sure," said Carrie. "Well—here's to Bob White."

Angela drank. "I wish I'd gone with you," said Angela.

"I wish you had, too," said Carrie. "But you didn't. So it's no use moaning. It doesn't matter. Bob White won't cry. Drink up."

"I wish I had gone," said Angela. She fetched a sigh that trembled up from her toes and sustained itself in the room like a long-drawn note on the cello.

"Oh, stop sounding like the mock turtle," said Carrie, turning on her. "In a hundred years, we'll all be dead."

"Damn," said Angela. "Damn, damn, damn, I wish to hell I'd gone."

"Hang on to that, then," said Carrie. "That's a God damn sight better than nothing."

Nor for Good

nor Evil

1947 3

20. # June Wedding

Angela put her brush down and got up from her dressing table. She tacked aimlessly across the wide, bareboarded floor as if propelled by an inadequate breeze. When she reached the window, she stood still in front of it, wishing there were a balcony outside her window so that she could step out into the sunshine. She shoved the screen up with her palms and propped it there with her back and leaned out into the warm June afternoon. It was a beautiful day. It was an entirely suitable day for a wedding.

In the back yard the water oak trembled with its indomitable summer youthfulness. A thousand gray beards nodded as if from sun-warmed rocking chairs on the great ancient branches of the live-oak. The delicate red camellias and the white ones on their dark green bushes were dying, turning brown at the edges from the rough fingering of the sun. In their narrow beds, the zinnias thrust the bright thickets of their heads upward, staring at the sun. It was a real summer day, her kind of day.

Pinckney said it was a good-luck sign when your wedding day was a fine fair day. Angela wondered. She tried to total the score on her friends, but the memories of other marriages blurred in her mind. At any rate, it had certainly rained the day Carrie and the doctor were married.

Pinckney bustled out of the kitchen door onto the back porch, followed by the slam of the kitchen screen. From the porch steps he threw the water from the dishpan in a long arc so that it fell along a stretch of earth, bare of grass and smelling faintly of the dirty water already absorbed. He looked up and saw her.

"Miss *A*nglah," he said in a scandalized voice. "Anybody might see yuh, anybody comin up duh alley. Jus *any*body."

The alley was almost buried from her vision beneath its many-layered archway of thick oak limbs dripping with moss. It was even doubtful whether any of the Negroes who lived along the alley were passing now, under the archway, in the early hot afternoon. Still, she was dressed only in her slip and she drew in from the window. She let the screen crash down behind her and steadied the bamboo prop that held the window open.

"Mama told you to stop throwing the water so near the house," she called down affectionately. Nobody, but nobody, could ever fix that kitchen drain so it stayed fixed, she thought.

"Ange*lah!*" Her mother's voice took the stairs in a practiced curve.

Angela frowned. Mama had promised to leave her entirely alone while she dressed. "If you need help, you just have to call," Mama had said, and lingered. "Just think. After today, I won't have any daughter to help." Angela had not replied. It was an exhausted topic. If she encouraged it, Mama might say again, "I'm not losing a daughter, I'm gaining a son," and she would scream.

Angela stared at the screen that blurred the perfect day. It would be a perfect night, too, clear and with a full moon. A perfect night for a wedding night. A wonderful night for a chivaree. She clasped her hands and twisted them.

It was one of the town's traditions, and she had always loved the town's traditions. She loved its formal yearly cotillion, contrasting with the yearly riotous celebration of Shrove Tuesday. She loved its wanton treasure hunts, already traditions, and its rigidly chaperoned, old-fashioned Sunday-night suppers. She loved all form and ceremony. She loved the funerals at St. James's, in the somber light of the black-draped church, and the winding processions afterward when the flesh that was grass was taken to the grass-bright, cypress-dark burial ground. She loved the high Episcopal weddings. Hers would be such. The town would wait for her, in hushed, stained-glass shadows, while the tiptoeing acolytes lit the huge wedding candles standing in stately procession on either side of the long aisle, lighting them two by two in front of the coming bride. Thus kindly lighted by tradition, all brides were blessed with the beauty brides were supposed to have. And afterward and equally, by bawdy and ruthless tradition, the bride must be made to blush and to weep, and the man whose sacred right to her had been sanctified must be made ridiculous.

Bill had sworn that they would escape. She would not be exposed, stripped of her inviolate raiment, publicly blushing to public leers. She knotted her fingers. There must be no chivaree after their wedding. There must be no clamor heralding their accepted mating. They had no defenses against the town, if the privacy of their loins was violated.

"With my body I thee worship . . ." thought Angela reverently. This wedding vow, long since censored from the Anglican service by the prudish or the prurient, was the one she had already taken in her heart. And kept. She had kept this vow and the secret of this vow. And the town had never known.

They had known so much. So much of their love, hers and Bill's, had been conducted in the distorting goldfish bowl of the town's curiosity. So many people had watched while they fell in love and had regarded throughout what was known, with the town's avid detachment, as the Madison-Bloodgood affair. Had deplored, or enjoyed, the chill reluctance of the welcome given Angela Madison, daughter of Andalusia's Hannah Miller, by Alicia Shy Bloodgood of Oglethorpe. Had enjoyed, or deplored, the retaliatory heat of Hannah Miller Madison's judgment on "that good-looking, good-for-nothing, no-account, stuck-up Bill Bloodgood." Had known well enough when Bill, miserable and frustrated, had taken his momentary revengeful pleasure elsewhere, and had poked and pried at Angela's momentary jealous misery. Had known that Bill begrudged the brief plighting of her prior troth to Logan Knight. . . . They had known so much! Had known the perennial decision she and Bill took to defy town tradition and marry without parental consent.

Had known the wherefore of each failure. Had, as if they had the right, taken "sides," admiring or deploring the enduringness of the romance. Had even claimed to know, and had repeated, the bitter dialogue, diversely reported, when the struggle had ended, when Hannah Madison and Alicia Bloodgood had yielded up to each other the use of their first names and had settled the date for the wedding.

But they did not know the secret of their fulfilled and loving loins. They had always, accounting it to Bill's honor and to her purity, granted and conceded to Angela, together with her constancy, her virginity. Now they would make rude and public clamor over it.

Oh, Lord! It was Bill who had perpetrated the most legendary outrages in his adopted town's tradition of wedding-night outrage. He had forged a cowbell onto one Andalusia bride's dressing case and had led the posse to the next town to prevent its removal there by blowtorch at the forge. He had cut off Mary and Morton Hadley with a hired truck and made them drive back through Andalusia while he fired his pistol in the air over their heads. As the slow southern train meandered its way to the seashore, carrying decorous Hope and dreamy Logan Knight to the honeymoon cottage by the sea that Mrs. Stone had given them, Bill had met it at each station with a six-piece brass band and a fresh supply of rice. He had kidnapped Sonny Boy and kept him from his hysterical out-of-town bride until after midnight. Sonny Boy had been a "good sport"—you had to be a "good sport" in a summertime town —but he would pursue Bill tonight with cheerful revenge in his cheerful little heart. None of them would understand that Bill had done these things in support of his wild, necessary pride and that it was necessary to his dear pride that he escape them now.

He had to hold his head high in this town, "stuck-up" Bill Bloodgood from Oglethorpe. In the commercial judgment of this also modern and commercial town, he must be accounted a failure —that unreliable Bloodgood boy who had lost his big chance with Van Ball at The Oaks, who would never amount to much. Sonny Boy was a success, Logan Knight was a noble success, Dugdale Winthrop was—had been—sufficiently a success. Even Morton Hadley "did well." They could all buy their cars from Bill because he had forced them to respect his failure and they need not turn away their eyes. After all, he had quixotically snubbed Van Ball in order to fail, and he had succeeded, gloriously, at play. He could secrete his chagrin, make light of his old hopes, treat work as his avocation, and accept with reasonable nonchalance the meagerness of his income, so long as he outjested, outsmarted, outdrank, outshot, and outplayed the town's own. While the long-faced girl of his quixotic choice smiled on him from the pedestal of her purity . . . He must outjest, outsmart, them now, on his wedding day.

Angela wiped the sweat of fear from her palms, sliding them along the silk slip that covered her long, bony thighs. She stood still, her hands straight at her sides, her head lifted as if she were listening, but she did not hear, or did not heed, her mother's importunate "ANGelah!" hurled this time, like a dart, in a sharp half-whisper at the thick wood of her bedroom door. Bill's pride, thought Angela, his beautiful, sinful, shaky, erratic, necessary pride.

There was a restrained knock on her door like a voice toned down to a whisper.

"Oh, come *in,*" said Angela testily. She sat down quickly at her dressing table and bent her head so that her shoulder-length, light brown hair fell forward over her face. She fumbled for her brush and began brushing her hair in long, vicious strokes.

Mrs. Madison came on loud tiptoe into the room. She was panting from the stairs.

"It's *Carrie,*" said Mrs. Madison in a hissing whisper that reminded Angela of Mrs. Rook. "She says she came over to help the bride. I told her you didn't even want your mother in this last precious hour, but she said ask you anyway."

"You send her on up," said Angela from under her hair. "I don't want to hurt her feelings."

She wanted Carrie to be with her now. She would have liked Ellen Terra to be there, too. And Hope. It was so much harder to imagine leaving the three of them than it was to know that she was leaving her own home. She did not want her mother with her.

"You're so sweet and thoughtful, Angela," said Mrs. Madison. "I declare you certainly will make Bill a happy man."

You had to say for Mama, once she gave in she gave in. You

would think Bill was the King of Sheba now, to hear her talk. She was pouring honey over all the old wounds. Buckets of honey.

Mrs. Madison went out into the hall and called over the bannisters, throwing her voice downward like a thin, weighted fishing line. "Come on up, Carrie!" She came back to the door of her daughter's room. "You'll be—good, darling?"

Angela nodded. She was still brushing her hair upside down and her eyes were closed. She felt pleasantly dizzy. She had the very best kind of hangover, she thought approvingly. The floating kind, the milky kind, the thoughtful kind, the soft kind.

She heard Carrie coming up the stairs with her signature of a walk. Her good leg hit with a thump that counterbalanced the scrape of the leg she was saving. Only at moments like this, unduly sensitized, when everything familiar seemed a little strange, did Angela realize that Carrie was a cripple.

"Hi, toots," said Carrie in her harsh, pretty voice.

"Hello, honey," said Angela through her hair.

Mrs. Madison hesitated near the door. Angela and Carrie said nothing more. Their silence was respectful and tranquil.

"I'm really glad you are here, Carrie," said Mrs. Madison. "Really. Angela is nervous as a—as a *bride*." She laughed, her constant and not unattractive laugh. "You make sure she looks pretty as a picture, won't you, Carrie?" she said as she went out.

Angela threw back her hair and straightened up. She and Carrie exchanged amused and cynical glances. Carrie closed the door.

"How do you feel, sweetie?" Carrie asked.

"I dunno. Funny. How did you feel?"

"It was different," said Carrie.

It certainly had been different, thought Angela, wondering to what extent she was envious. It had been brief, violent, unexpected, unorthodox. Jack Maitland had lumbered into town to take over the new hospital. Mr. and Mrs. Gregory, twin pictures of ruddy health, had been struck, as similarly as they had lived, with heart attacks. The Gregorys had no regular doctor, after Dr. Dandridge folded his long, tortured, uncertain hands, since it was clear that no doctor could help their Carrie, who was as tough as a twisted tree. Carrie called in Dr. Jack Maitland for her parents, and not even the town's inordinately sensitive antennae detected romance. He was an older man, self-styled a misogynist, a towering, homely, rough-voiced man, immediately popular enough, but not with those he called, in a way that made it opprobrious, "the ladies." He respected, he declared, the female ability to bear pain, but he also respected, he added, booming, the female ability to cause pain, and he wasn't having any. Carrie was destined in the collective town mind to be an old maid. She had lost her "only chance" in her "silly row" with the schoolmaster, David Bradford, over the uncomfortable Bob White affair. Bob White and David had gone away and afterwards Carrie drank heavily, in a controlled fashion, her misshapen body emaciated and her face sullen and gaunt. Jack Maitland was scornful of the flesh, whose traps and flaws he knew well. He told Carrie her parents would die and he eased their way to death and he watched Carrie nurse them, with tenderness and patience, in the agony of her love for them. He saw the luminous resistance of her spirit and he loved her. The week after the Gregorys' very nearly simultaneous deaths, he had married her. "To hell with that," he had roared, in Angela's presence, when Carrie had protested that she must wait and wait. They had been married at the dusty registry in Andalusia's city hall, with only Angela and Ellen Terra and Bill, with whom Jack had immediately made friends, and Jack's brother from Atlanta, for witnesses. The town had been wild with astonishment. They had forgiven Carrie, because they forgave Carrie everything, and because Jack was not one of their own.

"I almost wish we could do it like you-all did," said Angela. "I'm terrified."

Carrie nodded. She said, "Well, Bill's a smart one. I'll help you get away any way I can."

"Thanks," said Angela. "Thanks, Carrie."

"I must say I'll miss you," said Carrie harshly. "Both of you. I wish you weren't going to New York."

"Thanks," said Angela, breathing lightly. Carrie was feeling very tender to say such a thing.

"Do you really want to go?" asked Carrie.

"It's such a chance for Bill," pleaded Angela, feeling fear again at the pit of her heart, at the pit of her belly. She rubbed the moisture from her hands surreptitiously. She had definitely been drinking too much.

Carrie shrugged. "Sure," she said. "By the way, if you—that is, if you don't want to . . . Oh, hell! Jack's a doctor and you don't need to have a baby unless you want one. I suppose you know the stork doesn't bring 'em." She laughed at her own embarrassment. The things people never said to each other, and the things they did.

"It's all right," said Angela, her eyes lighting up with triumphant amusement at this proof of how well she and Bill had kept from the whole town their secret.

Carrie looked at her shrewdly. "Why, Angela Madison!" she said. "Damn. I do believe . . . Well, you certainly fooled the world and your old Aunt Carrie."

You might have known, thought Angela. You might have guessed how Bill would need and how I would give to his need and how good it is with us and how much it's meant to us. You know how close we came sometimes. You can't get that close any other way. "You'll never know," said Angela lightly, "because I'm going to go right ahead and have a baby just as fast as I can. Why not? Bloodgoods must have sons—from virgin brides," she added deliberately. She said this to tantalize, because their secret must be forever kept, even from Carrie.

"All right!" said Carrie. "I must say this is a hell of a conversation to have just before your wedding." She smiled affectionately. "Can't I help you dress?"

"Make me look pretty as a picture?" Angela refrained from looking in the mirror. The circles under her eyes would show through any makeup. She had been drinking too much. "Let's have a cigarette first." She offered the package to Carrie.

"This is eight," said Carrie, refusing Angela's and taking a cigarette from her pocket. "I have to keep track. I only smoke a pack a day now."

"Good Lord," said Angela. "Jack's a miracle worker. You must be in love." She lit her own cigarette and drew deep on it.

"Have you heard from Bill since last night?" asked Carrie. "Jack said the dinner was super."

"Bill said even your precious Jack got tight," said Angela,

not unmaliciously. "And Sonny Boy decided he was Salome and did the dance of the seven veils. He even took off his underpants. And Logan, of all people, hung them on the chandelier and nobody could get them down. They're still there."

They both laughed, easily and gaily.

"Too bad we weren't allowed," said Carrie. "What did you do with yourself?"

"Played bridge, with Mama and Hope and Miss What's-her-name, Hope's 'friend.' It was a bore, but Bill called me up every half hour and proposed a toast. I got drunk with him over the telephone."

"Does she play, What's-her-name?" asked Carrie.

"Badly," said Angela. "She's so stupid I thought I'd go nuts. Hope stakes her. She did promise to have Hope at the church in good shape."

Carrie nodded. "Hope certainly tied one on the other night," she said. "I swear, it was a relief. She's been so pathetic since she got sobered up. And she enjoyed herself so much, outwitting What's-her-name. Hope has pretty good fun when she's drunk. She's right good fun, too, even if it gets to be a bore."

"Well, I hope she never goes off for another cure," said Angela. "I nearly bawl every time I look at the underwear she made for my trousseau while she was 'away.' It must have taken a hundred hours. I did want to ask her to be my matron of honor, but I couldn't be sure . . ."

"Oh, she knows that," said Carrie. "It wouldn't hurt her feelings."

"Yankees always carry things too far," said Angela, complainingly.

Carrie nodded. She pinched out the end of her cigarette, laying it carefully aside to finish later. "Give me the tongs," she said. "I'll work on your hair."

Farther down Norwich Street, in her big bedroom in her parents' house, surrounded by the neat accumulation of her lifetime there, Hope was also working on her hair, preparing herself for Angela's wedding.

"I still can't quite believe it," she said to What's-her-name, who did have a name, which was Betty Jones. "After all this time. I've known Angela, you know, since we were tiny tots. She's one of my very best friends. She never was terribly good-looking, really, but she always had charm. She was vivid, that's it, and she was brainy. Fairly brainy. Don't you think she has charm?"

Betty Jones said soothingly and noncommittally, "She is very charming, Miss Madison is, Mrs. Knight." She had been invited to call Hope by her first name, but she felt that this would only make her job more difficult. It was difficult enough. Mrs. Knight looked stupid, with those huge, blind-looking honest blue eyes, but, like all alcoholics, thought Betty Jones, she was sly.

"And Bill Bloodgood was the best-looking thing you can imagine. He really was. We all fell in love with him." Hope realized then that she was confusing Bill Bloodgood, the handsome beau from Oglethorpe, with Mark Barbee, the minister, who had come from Mobile or somewhere, and with whom they had all fallen in love. She was thinking simultaneously of the night Bill had kissed her many times, oh, before he had ever even looked at Angela who had been so much less pretty than Hope, and the night of the treasure hunt when Mark Barbee had kissed her just once. It did seem long ago. There was really no confusion in her mind, but her memories were all shaken down and packed too tight. She had to shake each memory loose from its wrinkled clinging to the others. It was like the boxes you packed so beautifully in the fall. When you got them out next spring, your summer clothes never looked as fresh as they did when you put them away. She started to shake out and sort her memories in order to display them to—Betty, that was it, Betty Jones—but decided it was not the time. "Anyway," she went on, gossiping now, as with any semi-stranger, "we never really thought it would come off, you know. Not actually. Bill is so wild and Angela's gotten so bad-tempered. And Angela's mother really hated the Bloodgoods. She hated Bill. I honestly thought Bill would give up. He went off to New York, too, once, but he came right back. Anyway, in—in thirty-five minutes!" she exclaimed fussily, staring dimly at the ivory traveling clock that stood on her dresser. She consulted the list that lay on her dresser, weighted with a ruffled

pin cushion Cecelia had made for her with fat baby stitches. The
list read, in her precise, pointed script:

> bathe (pine scent)
> shave under arms
> shave legs
> Chanel #5 (before dressing)
> nails
> hair
> dress
> corsage (orchids)
> Cecelia's corsage (spring flowers) (check
>   Cecelia's back hooks)
> Betty's corsage (gardenias)
> Logan's carnation
> church at four

It was her afternoon list, to follow her nap, and the first five items
had been crossed off. She could give five more minutes to her hair.
She undid and started to roll again a curl that might be further
perfected.

"I've left everything open after the reception," she told Betty
Jones with decision, waving a hand at the list. "You never know
what will happen, after the reception. They are really planning to
'get' Bill. Isn't it awful?" She giggled. "They do the worst things
in this town. Bill's been the ringleader ever since he first came
down. Did I tell you about the chivaree when Logan and I were
married? The brass band that followed us across the whole *state*?
Bill did that. I thought I'd die."

"You told me, Mrs. Knight," said Betty. "It sounded kind
of embarrassing."

"It was awful," said Hope, and then, staring at the mirror
with the big, blind eyes, said honestly, "but I thought it was fun,
too. I really did. Truly. Logan did, too, I think, although he pretended to be furious. It *was* fun. The boys all laughing and screaming and all the noise and Bill introducing us at each station and
firing off that little pistol of his and then the terrible music and
everybody laughing at us and knowing we were just married. I really
didn't mind, although I blushed. Did I blush! But Angela's funny.

321

She'll mind. And Bill will *die*. He can't stand to be outsmarted. He just can't stand it. *Now* my dress. But first, I have to go to the bathroom . . ."

"Now . . ." said Betty Jones. "Now . . ."

"I won't," promised Hope sincerely. "Really. I'll leave the door open, too."

She went in, turned on the water in the basin, and did what she must in the privacy of the noise. She did not so much as look at the medicine cabinet where she kept a little bit of whiskey, just in case she felt faint in her bath. But a wee nippie, she thought, keeping her eyes cast downward, the wee-est of nippies would make her feel as if she were really going to a wedding. To Angela's wedding. A wee nip never hurt anybody when anybody had such a lot to do. Nobody really minded, she thought, nobody except Betty Jones, who was paid to mind. Logan didn't mind. He was so kind and forbearing, and he knew she could be counted on whenever he needed her. She felt so heavy in the afternoons, the long and increasingly hot afternoons. She felt so *fat*. Whiskey lightened you, in the afternoons. In the mornings, you never drank. No matter how much of a hangover you had, you never drank before noon. If you didn't drink before noon, you were not incurably bad, she thought precisely. That was the rule. Her mother would not even notice if she had a nip. Her mother never did notice. She started to lift her eyes to the medicine cabinet, but she thought of her rector, St. John Rand, and cast them down again. He would be at the church, of course, and he would notice and *he* would mind. I mind, she reminded herself. She had crossed that precise and particular and all-important line between the lady, the southern lady, who had taken a wee nippie too many to be mildly reprimanded and easily indulged, and the unmentionable un-lady who could scarcely be forgiven. She had crossed that line the night she had passed out, so briefly and comfortably, on the rectory lawn. She had seen it in the Reverend St. John Rand's gray elephant eyes, that she had crossed the line. She had seen that she had crossed the line, and she had punished herself. She had gone 'away' and been cured of being an un-lady. It was good and sufficient punishment, she thought, shying away from the memory of the cure. She had brought Betty Jones home with her, her 'friend,' who would help her so that she would never see that look in anybody's eyes again. She would take no wee nip today, she promised herself. No, no, indeed.

She returned to her room without once looking, even, at the medicine cabinet. Betty Jones smiled at her approvingly, as the Reverend St. John Rand must now smile at her. "That's a good girl," Betty said.

Logan knocked, in deference to Miss Jones, and came into the room. Looking through her open door and the open door of his room, across the hall, she could see the debris of his dressing. She frowned. She must speak to Nanine about getting that lazy Clara to clean up after Logan. He was so messy, and he said he didn't care, but he did.

"Hello, sweetheart," he said gently. "Hello, Miss Jones. Now do I suit you?" Facetiously he half turned for her approval.

Hope studied him carefully, her head on one side, her blue eyes going in and out of focus. The morning coat was very, very successful. She had slaved with the tailor in Oglethorpe over it, getting Logan there for three separate fittings. The trousers made him look flat, hiding the little paunch that he blamed on Nanine, and the coat broadened his shoulders without looking in the least padded. Above it, the feathers of gray were beautiful to her in his dark brown hair, and his brown eyes looked amused on the surface, over the look she could never read. He switched impatiently.

"You're perfect," she said positively. "You look so distinguished."

He made a face at her, mildly mocking, as if looks were absurdly unimportant.

"I suppose you have a flower for me," he said carelessly.

"Oh, it's the prettiest one you ever saw," said Hope eagerly. "I picked it out myself. It's the—very—best . . ."

"You're a silly fusspot," said Logan, kindly enough. "See you downstairs . . ."

"Oh, Logan, is Cecelia well enough to go, do you think?" She had completely forgotten to check on her daughter's health.

"The little flower is fussing a bit, but she's all right," said Logan with fatherly lack of concern. "Don't fret. Maw is with her."

He went out and Hope stood uncertainly between the bed

and the door. She had better put her dress on. It was time. She wished she had invited Ellen Terra over to dress with her. Ellen Terra was so sloppy and she loved to just relax and let Hope dress her, replacing the safety pins with which Ellen Terra habitually repaired her clothes with Hope's strong sewing, buttoning her up and bullying her into the girdle she always took off and hid somewhere. Hope used to take nips with her, when they did this, while Ellen Terra pretended to. It was fun, getting Ellen Terra ready, but lately she found herself disapproving of Ellen Terra, not just occasionally, but all the time. She moved heavily over toward the bed where her dress lay, keeping her eyes away from the clothes closet. There was a pint of whiskey hidden behind the hats, where she had left it before she went 'away.' She should, on the other hand, have gone over to Angela's and helped the bride to dress. That would have been the thing to do. Nobody would remember any more that Angela had been briefly engaged to Logan Knight.

When Mrs. Madison came into the room again, it was a quarter to four. Appreciating her mother's forbearance, Angela smiled at her warmly. Her mother returned the smile.

Angela was very nearly ready. Her long, sheathlike dress was hooked up to its lace turnover collar. Cunningly designed, it made the most of her bony, long-legged figure, emphasizing the slimness of her waist, cupping her small but firm breasts, concealing her rounded and sharp-boned shoulders. Carrie had fluffed her soft hair until it curled softly away from her thin, long-jawed face and fell neatly and softly to her shoulders. Her face was carefully powdered all over, with a tan powder that matched her early sunburn. The color contrasted pleasingly with the old ivory of the fragile, lace veil. Carrie was pinning the veil into place, her mouth full of pins so that she could only bob her head in acknowledgment of Mrs. Madison's return.

"Why, baby, you look just perfectly lovely," said Mrs. Madison. She groaned minutely, shifting the rolls of her stomach within the tight confines of a new corset. "Just lovely."

"She does," said Carrie rolling the pins to one side of her mouth, where she habitually clamped her cigarette.

"Like a bride!" Mrs. Madison clasped her plump hands in front of her stomach and gazed at her daughter. Angela took a deep puff of her cigarette. "Now don't you go burn a hole in your great-great-grandmother Madison's veil!" Mrs. Madison warned sharply.

"No, Mama," said Angela.

The telephone rang.

"That's Bill," said Angela, standing very still, her face lifted. "He always calls me when I want him to. Always."

"Just a sec' till I get this fixed for sure," said Carrie.

Her father called up the stairs in his thin, remote voice. "Bill, Angela."

"I'm coming," called Angela.

Her father pattered up the stairs. "No, no," he said as he came. At the door, he stopped politely, regarding his daughter standing there in her wedding dress. "Hung up," her father explained. "Told him you were dressing. Said he forgot you couldn't speak to brides. Said to tell you he'd see you in church." Mr. Madison chewed the end of his fine-haired mustache and said, "Why, hello, Carrie . . ."

"Come on, girls," said Mrs. Madison, shooing Mr. Madison ahead of her and starting out the door. She pitched her voice for the kitchen as she reached the stair railing. "PINCKNEY!" She started down the stairs, her voice diminishing with the distance between her and Pinckney. "BRING Miss *Angela's* bouquet out of the ice box!"

Angela and Carrie embraced gingerly, avoiding each other's ceremonial clothes. Angela followed her mother out without waiting for Carrie. You never waited for Carrie when she had to negotiate her leg on stairs.

Angela walked sedately down the stairs with her veil gathered over her arm. Her father was waiting in the hall, fingering his vest pocket watch.

Pinckney said softly, coming in the front door, "Ah puts duh flowuhs on duh back seat in duh box, Miss Anglah. Good luck, Miss Anglah."

"Thanks, Fate," said Angela, the rare use of his given name making her thanks warmer and more intimate.

"Gawd bless," muttered Pinckney to himself.

"Ready to give me away, Papa?" Angela asked.

"Certainly, baby," said Mr. Madison. "Reluctantly, of course . . ."

He had been ready from the first, thought Angela, ready to accept anything she did, a natural-born fatalist. He may have disapproved of Bill in his own mild fashion. He also seemed to like Bill, in his inexpressive way. He was a sweet, remote man to have for a father.

Usually Angela drove when they went out together, but today her father helped her carefully into the back seat and waited while her mother dabbed at the veil Angela had spread carefully on the seat. Then he helped his wife into the front seat and went around to get in himself behind the wheel. As they started off, they were all solemn and self-conscious. Even Mrs. Madison was quiet. Pinckney watched them quietly from the front porch. Angela had invited him to the wedding, but he had refused, as Mrs. Madison had refused for him, because he had too much to do with the last-minute preparations for the reception. Even with the Rooks' Mattie and Carrie's Annie and Mattie's sister, dependable Mercy Church, to help him, there was too much to do. Angela twisted herself carefully and waved to him through the window. She was also leaving Pinckney behind her.

Angela wondered what she should think about, on the sedate trip down Norwich Street that was actually taking her to her wedding. The undirected thoughts awash in her mind like Hallowe'en apples were insufficiently grave, even though they were relevant. She had been wondering idly whether the champagne would go around and whether Bill would decide on clocked or plain socks and what in the world Miss Sis Whittle would wear to the wedding. Poor Miss Sis. St. John Rand had announced the Sunday before that he was discontinuing the Thursday-morning communion services and substituting a Bible class on Friday nights. This was hardly even relevant, thought Angela wryly. It was only coincidence that her wedding was this particular Thursday afternoon. Her wedding!

It would sound, in the society columns of the Oglethorpe *Sun*, like any other June wedding of any other socially prominent local couple. Even the blurred pictures would look the same. They always did. In the Andalusia *Banner* it would sound even better than that. Editor Alton Rook was fond of her, in his curious way, and he would pay her the compliment of writing about it himself. But there wasn't much even a man with his gift for words could do about a wedding. "The radiant bride," composed Angela with mild cynicism, ". . . lovely daughter of. . . . The many friends of the popular groom. . . . With the Reverend Robert White officiating . . ."

She paused, startled at the error of her thoughts. What in the world made her think that? "The Reverend St. John Rand, D.D. . . ." she corrected herself. With an unexpected leap of longing, she wished that Bob White were marrying her to Bill today. She wished, with a swift downward drag of her spirits, that she had gone to St. James's that Sunday. . . . It was too late. It was the wrong thing to think about, a foolish, long-over thing to think about, as she drove along the familiar street to the familiar church on this particular errand. This was a beginning for her, and an end. The past was over and done, and the future would begin.

In a way, she thought, feeling herself thinking clearly this time, it was quite fitting that the Reverend Doctor Rand should marry her to Bill. In a way, he had finally brought the wedding about.

He had come to Andalusia a stranger in their midst, and he had looked at Andalusia, looked at them all, with his little, ordinary gray eyes. His eyes were mirrors, conventional and polished of surface, reflecting flatly the images that crossed their surfaces. You could see in his stranger's eyes just how you looked to him. He was thrust there, in their most intimate midst, and they had seen themselves as he saw them.

His attitude toward the "Madison-Bloodgood affair" was as plain in his eyes as the thick nose on his face, as plainly visible as in twin, flat mirrors on a wall. He seemed all but to say that if that noisy auto salesman really wanted to marry that old skinny, battered female, what in the world was all the fuss about?

Angela made a face. The tic began to beat in her cheek, at the end of the long scar from the automobile accident. It was a keepsake of the rainy November night when she and Bill had skidded off the road into the tree, the other side of the bridge across the river, on their way to Marianna to defy, once and finally, their families and be married there by an unsanctified justice of the peace. They had been drunk and were not too much hurt. She put her finger on the tic, gently, to stop its beating. Mama had tended her as though Angela were on her deathbed, and the hue and cry she had raised after Bill was worthy of criminal kidnapping, with, thought Angela, snorting lightly, intent to statutory rape.

It was not until St. John Rand had looked at Angela that Mama had ceased to behave as though Angela were a beautiful, moneyed, under-age heiress recalcitrantly in love with the decadent scion of a ruined enemy nobility. As if Bill were a calculating rake and his mother a vampire, seeking money in order to spurn its source . . . Mama had decided, after looking in St. John Rand's eyes, that perhaps after all Bill was better than nobody whatever for her Angela, and then—rather gallantly, Angela considered—that Bill was perfectly wonderful. But she had refused, Mama had, to see Bill as the stranger, St. John Rand, saw him, as a small-town failure. . . .

Such a new kind of man, and so efficient, thought Angela of her new rector. He had fired Uncle Jimmy, after all these years, and sent Lucas to jail for making moonshine by the river, which he had done before, during and after prohibition. He had got Hope cured and Angela and Bill married. He was so efficient!

Angela found herself staring, surprised and resentful, at the stucco cottage sitting across from Miss Lucy Cranborne's, between the old Lovell house that was now a boarding house and the rectory. It had been there as long as the Rands had been in the rectory, nearly eight months, but she never remembered that it was there. She was too set in her bony ways. Bill was quite right that they should go away, leaving Andalusia and St. James's and the stranger-rector, St. John Rand, and go where everything would be strange and everybody stranger. If only they could get away without humiliation, outwitting, at the last, the town.

Afraid to wipe her hands on the exquisite dress or on the wisp of lace that was her handkerchief, she held first one and then the other outstretched to dry.

They were upon the church.

As they drove past the church's choir-room door, Angela saw Bill and Dugdale Winthrop, who was Bill's best man, through the open door. Bill looked out and gave her a warm, impudent little flip of his hand. Her heart gave a queer little thump.

"Ready, baby?" asked her father. His voice was tender and his look was tender and remote.

Ready?

Surely she must be ready.

In the vestibule, Angela disentangled herself from the twittering group of her assorted bridesmaids and from the matronly fussing of her matron-of-honor, who was Mary Hadley. They looked silly, she thought coolly, surveying the group, dressed in the pastel-colored, floor-length organdy dresses designed for the wedding. A bunch of wilted flowers, she thought unkindly. She had not given a tinker's damn who attended her, since none of the three could attend her. Carrie would have hated to hobble up the aisle, and Angela had not asked her. Hope could no longer be trusted not to fall on her fat prat. Ellen Terra had refused. Her response had been spontaneous, unconsidered, and undecorated with regrets. "Not me," Ellen Terra had said, her voice full of warmth.

"Ready?" said her father remotely in Angela's ear, and offered her, with elderly grace, the thin crook of his arm.

"Not as a bridesmaid, honey," Ellen Terra had said cheerfully.

Ellen Terra turned her body with the rest, craning her neck as the rest craned theirs. The organ was pealing to herald the bride. The lights from the first two candles, lit by the solemn little acolytes on tiptoe in their long red cassocks, were supplemented by the next two. The bride appeared between them on her father's arm, her face a lighted blur, haloed by her veil, distant as a dream at the end of the long aisle.

Ellen Terra was not crying now, only sniffing a little. Her round moon of a face was stained with the tears that had rolled, fat and round, from her screwed-up eyes as she sat waiting in the dusky church, while the organ murmured as restively as the murmuring crowd, waiting for the bride. Her handkerchief was a wet

329

ball in her hands, and her purse, with its fresh supply, slid to the floor from her plump lap as she turned to look for Angela. Alton Rook, sitting beside her, leaned from his narrow haunches and picked up her bag. Taking one of her fists in his, her father patted it and then slipped the strap of her bag over her hand and along her arm, pinching the plump arm near the elbow as he did so. The tears welled up again, but she stared through them resolutely at Angela's blurred, approaching face. If she cried again, her mother would lean over again, across the narrow separation of her father's body, and say in her carrying whisper, "*Stop* that, Ellen Terra!" She did not want to cry, but to smile with all her heart's benevolence on the bride, who was Angela.

If she could not summon her heart's smile now, the smile that would include the whole past and beam on the future, she saw herself never smiling again. She saw herself spending the rest of her life with her face swollen and her eyes squeezed and her hands clutching only a damp handkerchief. Blinking wildly, she looked up toward the altar where the Reverend St. John Rand stood, bulky and strange and male in the robes of a priest. He seemed to be looking straight at her with his clear little mirrors of eyes. Guiltily she suppressed her tears, knowing that they were not for Angela, but for herself. Guiltily she longed to weep so as to wash away her sins.

Sinful, that's what she was. Verily, a scarlet woman. She saw herself painted a brilliant, sunset red, only her wildly blinking eyes and her short mop of hair the color of black. She saw them looking at her, every one, as she had seen St. John Rand look at her, not with hatred, but with distaste. She wanted to cry out for shame and to hide her round face behind her hands, to sink to her plump knees, pressing them in the hassock on which she would kneel until the buttons made round black marks on her knees. She had been no better than the little dogs that roamed the streets in the summertime, and she had been as merry and remorseless and as patient as they were.

Since she had first offered Mark Barbee her tingling virginity, since Dugdale Winthrop had refused her, and since Sonny Boy Lovejoy had taken her—in brief pain—since she had tried to lie herself virgin to Van Ball and then had given him her fidelity and love until he went away . . . She could no more help flirting than she could help breathing. Her body seemed to flirt for her, in a way. She had even flirted with Bob White, she thought, astonished, even though it was ever so respectfully. She had never flirted with David Bradford or with Logan Knight, but, oh my, with practically everybody else. Then it always seemed so rude and unnecessary to refuse what they wanted and needed and she had to give. To try to refuse them made her feel so shy. It still did. Or downright mean. So, oh woe, she could no longer count on her fingers the sum total of her willing generosities, her *sins*. Until St. John Rand had hove into town and she had flirted with him, oh very respectfully, because he was big and sort of homely and flat-footed, and then she had seen herself in his eyes. Blowsy, thought Ellen Terra, shopworn, and put together with safety pins. And so very much worse than that! Oh woe, thought Ellen Terra, oh woe, woe, woe.

She saw Angela's face coming closer now, still and set and lifted to the altar. She managed, somehow, to smile a watery, weak, guilty little smile, wrenched from her misery, that Angela did not even see.

Angela did not see Carrie smile at her, either, from the pew two rows ahead of Ellen Terra. Lounging beside the rough, impatient man who was her husband, Carrie smiled in the motherly fashion of one who is older and who got there first, withal a very little cynically, but warmly welcoming.

Nor did she see Hope smile, with her eyes wide and blind, smiling sentimentally because all weddings were beautiful, and all brides.

Angela was looking only for Bill, who waited for her in the shadowy chancel. She could not see him. The soft flattering light from the candles on her face blurred her vision, the looming bulk of the preacher was in her way, the pace at which she moved was prescribed and sedate. Then she found him. When she saw him she smiled and he smiled back, tenderly, topping the tenderness by dropping one eyelid in the barest suggestion of a wink.

Her wedding dress and veil lay limp and done with on her narrow bed. Beside them, fresh and ready, lay her new traveling dress in lettuce green linen, her small green linen hat with the off-the-face brim, her spanking white gloves. Angela moved over to her dressing table as though she were swimming under water. The high-ceilinged, wide-floored room had not changed and did not seem to know that she would no longer be its maidenly occupant. Outside the trees were unchangeable and the birds chittered agreeably far up in the high, late sunshine of the June afternoon.

The sound of the birds blended with the sounds from the wedding reception below. Distantly, together, Mary and Morton Hadley were singing "Gonna lay down my sword and shield." They were trying to start group singing, but it was too soon for that. They sang well together, but they always tried to start the singing too soon, doggedly singing the same songs over and over, until somebody joined them and then somebody else, until you could not talk and might as well sing too. The same songs, thought Angela, over and over and over.

It was still quite decorous, the party, while the men who would make up the posse for the chivaree, and the girls who were watching to see what would happen, waited, bridled, for the time to come. Some of the older people who took no part in the traditional indecencies had left. St. John Rand had left, taking his pale stick of a wife who lagged always one step behind him. He had said good-bye as he might have said "That's that," shaking hands with Bill with his thick, pudding handshake, and kissing Angela with the air of performing a ritual that was not quite suitable on this occasion. The elder Stones were gone, Angela thought, but she could not be sure. She was never entirely aware of them, present or absent. The Winthrops had gone, and Dugdale had gone with them, supporting his fragile mother with his long, drooping frame, but he would come galloping slowly back. . . . Miss Sis Whittle had not come to the reception. It was a real tribute, thought Angela smiling, that Miss Sis had come to the wedding, the shirtwaist above her rusty old skirt starched until it crackled. Maybe she came to make up for missing, after God knew how many years, her lone communion through her priest with God on Thursday morning. No, thought Angela, the smile lingering, Miss Sis had come because that old hermit liked Angela. Angela and Carrie, the preacher at St. James's, the preacher's wife, and the nigras were the only people Miss Sis permitted any more to find their way through her thickening bamboo.

Angela and Bill had stayed downstairs until Mrs. Alicia Shy Bloodgood had taken her leave, escorted by a male cousin. The twins, thank heaven, had been too ill to come. Mrs. Bloodgood—her mother-in-law—had behaved with such unruffled dignity, only the number of times she lifted her thin hand to cover her ruined mouth with its lumpy china teeth indicating her nervousness, with such level graciousness, that Angela had very nearly loved her. She had been proud of her. If she never saw her again, she could, quite possibly, remember her with love.

Mrs. Rook was not gone. She could hear the old she-bat, with her dyed hair piled above her dead-white china face and the voice that turned corners and went through doors and up stairs. Alton Rook had jumped up to kiss her good-bye seeing her intention to leave the reception. It had been a surprisingly tender kiss, almost embarrassing, thought Angela. She always forgot how sweet Ellen Terra's father was. Almost as sweet as Ellen Terra, who was sweet. Her moon of a face was still stained and she clutched two handkerchiefs, in a wet ball, while she flirted, rolling her hips and her eyes, if a bit dolefully. Flirting at, of all people, thought Angela, smiling, Carrie's Doctor Jack. Carrie, sitting by Mr. Rook, had watched her with peaceful, assured amusement. How she would miss them, Carrie and Ellen Terra, Angela thought.

How she would miss the minute conversational post-mortem they would hold over this day. They would talk so, after such an occasion. They would talk about how Hope had taken "wee nippies" while Miss What's-her-name made impotent efforts to stop her. Because Hope must, just simply must, drink wee nippies to the bride because the bride was Angela. Angela was—was she not?— Hope's best, best friend, although it was Hope who had married Logan. Drunk, Hope always tried to act as if she had taken Logan away from Angela. As if Angela had wanted Logan for one single second after Bill had kissed her for the very first time, thought Angela, mildly indignant. Hope could have Logan, the dreamy, frustrated artist, the handsome, unmistakable success. Angela could not even remember what he looked like. Though he had been, yes, he had been, her first and only other lover, she could never recall him unless he stood before her in his dreamy, careless impeccability. He had ceased to exist for her when Bill kissed her. She had tried to reassure Hope, but Hope was so persistent.

They would talk and giggle over Sonny Boy, who went round and round the reception declaring to those who would listen and those who would not that he had been madly, desperately in love with Angela Lord Madison Bloodgood until Bill had broken his heart by stealing her away. It was only after Angela had broken his heart, he said, that he had looked into another pair of eyes. It was what he said to, and of, all the town's brides. It was his bouquet of flowers for the bride. His out-of-town wife must be bored with it by now.

They would talk.

Her mother's voice rose above the distant babble and the stubborn singing of the Hadleys below. "I cried *buckets*! My only little girl!" Angela grimaced ruefully. Someone called "PINCKney" and he answered in his rich, brown mumble. She heard Hope giggle shrilly.

Well, she and Bill would hold their own post-mortem, lying together in peace in a double bed. After they had escaped . . .

There was a scratching at the door and Bill peered in at her and then came in. He was dressed in flannel trousers and a tweed jacket and was ready to go.

"Oh, my God," he said. "You aren't ready. Hurry up, honey. We've got to get out damn fast."

Bill's expression was intent and remote. In his hand was a big pair of steel wire-cutters. She stared at them stupidly. "Listen," said Bill, "I'll explain while you finish dressing." He grinned at her standing there stupidly in her slip. "Get a move on, honey. I'm your husband now." He slapped her lightly on the thin silk that covered her buttocks.

"Oh, Bill," she said, wanting some kind of comfort, some kind of reassurance. But he was intent and remote.

"They're watching the front and back doors," he said. "And a ladder's no good. Too corny. But listen—this is it. I didn't dare tell you before. You blab so. We're going out by the screen porch!"

Angela thought quickly. The only exit from the screen porch

downstairs was at the front, onto the front porch, but you could enter it from the pantry at the end of the back stairs.

Bill waved the shears. "We'll *cut* our way out the side and go through the Fox's yard to the alley. See?"

It was a feasible, clever plan. "Mama will be furious about the screen," said Angela, feeling suddenly hopeful and light-hearted.

"Sure," said Bill absently. That kind of furious did not matter. "I've got the agency sedan hidden at Pinckney's house in the alley and Pinckney sneaked your bags in while you were at church."

"Does Bucky know you took the car?" she asked anxiously.

"Hell, no. He'll have a fit. So what? They won't find out till tomorrow."

"Bucky'll be mad." Bucky Lassiter had given Bill the job with the agency. She hated to make him mad.

"Come *on*," he said. "I hid my car where those bastards could find it, and Pinckney says it's got bells and shoes and signs and God knows what-all *chained* all over it."

Angela shuddered and then laughed. "You are a smarty, Bill Bloodgood, darling," she said. "I'll say that for you."

She slid the fresh linen dress over her head and buckled the belt.

"Hurry up," said Bill. "Want a nip?"

She nodded. He got a glass from her bathroom and poured into it half an inch of bourbon from a pocket flask. He took a drink himself direct from the flask, patting it as he put it back on his hip.

Angela swallowed the whiskey in quick gulps while she adjusted her round hat that matched her dress. She checked the contents of her bag quickly and pulled on her spotless gloves. Her heart ran like a sewing machine. "All set," she said.

At the door she hesitated, overwhelmed by the panic she had kept herself from considering. "Then where?" she asked in a terrified whisper.

There were only three ways to go: down the long, straight, shadowless road to Marianna, up the long curving, tree-shaded road to Oglethorpe, or to Oakland, five miles away. Down highway and byway, they would be pursued. Sonny Boy, cheerful and relentless, the town's second gayest clown, would shriek in their wake. Logan, absent-minded and carelessly impeccable, would be intolerably, gently persistent. Dugdale Winthrop would seek them, needing, for his own sad need, to share in Bill's humiliation. Doleful and determined, apologetically, he would come after them. Morton Hadley, who had long ago sworn his revenge, Bucky Lassiter, in whose car they were fleeing, would chase them. In the name of the tradition Bill had so spectacularly re-enforced, how could they hope to escape the town?

"Trust your old man, honey," said Bill, pinching her gently. "We aren't going anywhere."

Downstairs Carrie felt her nerves tighten as the minutes passed. She watched Jack, rarely tolerant, as he always was with Ellen Terra, benignly letting her flirt with him. Sober, because he had patients to see later, politely sociable, because he had agreed beforehand to take part in this particular social occasion, dutifully watchful because he had agreed to keep watch at the west window, he bulked there, filling that corner of the living room. She was prickly with annoyance at him and she bared her teeth at him and defiantly lit a cigarette. He would not—he had completely refused to—understand why Bill should be let off. "He dished it out," Jack had said flatly, in his loud, positive, no-nonsense voice. "Why shouldn't he take it?" And, even knowing how she felt about it, he had agreed, benignly, to keep watch at the west window for the posse. Oh, he would not go with them. He was too old and too busy to take part in such games. He had patients to see. But he had agreed readily to watch for them. Damn the thickhead. There was no arguing with Jack over subtleties. There was no explaining to him why Bill and Angela alone among couples must manage to get away. Black was black and white was white and that was that.

There was no arguing with Jack, anyway, unless you had something you could shout about, at the top of your lungs, which made you mad enough to throw ash trays at him. Which, she smiled to herself reluctantly, he threw right back at you. . . . And you settled it, loudly, one way or another, flat out and no residue, and went off to bed together. That's how it was. That was what made it a marriage.

Nobody ever told you anything about marriage that made

any sense. You started from scratch. Two people—like cats in a paper bag—trying to make room for each other, trying to get comfortable. It was hell, and it was heaven.

If she owed it to an old loyalty, an old and subtle understanding, to disagree with him, not flatly, but subtly, over Bill's and Angela's special right, or special need, to escape what was only justice in view of Bill's own behavior, she would plead Jack no special pleading. She would do what she could herself, which was damn little, and let the consequences go. She would not chew over it, to herself, or with Jack. He hated the chewed-over. You did what you did and thought what you thought. If you did wrong, or changed your mind, you admitted it. You were only unremittingly and squarely honest. No woman was really honest, he said. He had never trusted them. No woman in the world was honest, he said, except his Carrie. Carrie was the only woman in the world he could have for wife. It was exaggerated, even absurd, but it was what he thought.

His high, uncompromising opinion of her frightened her as nothing had ever frightened her except that one moment when she had found out all there was to know about David Bradford. It frightened her because it made her distrust herself again. Because it was so terribly precious to her. There was nothing that could shake it, really, his opinion of her, as long as she, Carrie Gregory, was the very best she knew she was. That was all Jack wanted of her. That part was up to her. Only one thing could shake it—the delayed and painful knowledge of the one thing she had kept from him. If she had told him at once, it would have been bad enough. It would have made him blasphemous and furious. It would, even then, have shaken his faith in her final integrity, or her judgment. Now, it would be pure hell. God damn the man, thought Carrie explosively, God damn the God damn preacher. Why had St. John Rand come to Andalusia, from Louisville, mirroring his special knowledge of David Bradford in his flat, gray eyes when he looked at her? She had sweated it out long enough, that somebody might find out what she knew, and nobody had. Then this man had come, knowing, too late for her to tell Jack, as she might have told him at the very first. If St. John Rand were not there, she could even tell him now, trusting to the violent security of their growing marriage. But she could not tell him cravenly, with the man Rand there, in the obvious fear that he would find out. God damn Rand. He had said nothing so far, hinted no hints. She had given him no chance. She had not even been to church since Bob White left Andalusia except for the funerals, and this, Angela's wedding. But the fact of his existence made her crawlingly watchful.

As she had been crawlingly watchful of herself for so long after she found out that David Bradford, the young schoolmaster, the boy she had loved, if not with passion at least with tenderness, was a—oh, all the hideous names, a queer, a pansy, a homo, a wretched, unhappy pervert! At first she had felt the simplest and blackest despair. She was one of the damned, an outcast and a cripple, who was loved by the outcasts and the crippled. She had hated David and hated his mother, savagely, because they had tried to compound her damnation with their own. When David's mother had pleaded, "I had to send for you, Carrie. You are my son's only hope. Don't you see? If he could love a woman and have a son, he could let them alone, the little ones he loves so much. He tried to save himself with that man, the one he calls his 'cousin.' It doesn't run in the family, Carrie, that man is no kin to David. . . ." As if this helped, as if this meant anything to Carrie, as it seemed to mean something to the desperate, thin-skinned, treacherous woman who had tried to entrap her into marrying her son . . . "But that dreadful man was unfaithful to David . . ." It was unbearable, every bit of it, every word of it. ". . . and then David thought if he only had his own school, so he would be as much father to them as teacher, or brother, it would keep him from ever touching one of the little ones, the father relationship, you know, and then you were there, and Carrie, believe me, he loves you. He was so thankful. . . ." He had been thankful because he could make love to her, because he could, somehow, endure her female body because it was misshapen. Hell beneath hell beneath hell. "When you sent him away, he tried to die. Carrie, he cut his wrists in the tub! You can't let him die. Marry him, oh do, and have a son by him." Carrie had burst out, black words and honest, "I'd as soon have a son by a cannibal!" And Mrs. Bradford had looked at her with such hatred as Carrie had never seen in a human being's eyes and let her go.

There had been a hushed-up scandal later at the school in

Louisville, where David had gone back to teach. Carrie knew because Mrs. Bradford had written her for the last time, ten pages of furious venom, blaming Carrie. She had burned the letter and thrown the ashes in the wide river. Symbolic gesture of hope, no doubt, and justified, since the river had flowed and flowed and gradually carried the ashes so far away that David's mother and David were truly gone from Andalusia and almost gone from her. No one in Andalusia had found out any more than that Carrie had been a mulish sort of fool who, having small enough choice with only one good leg to stand on, had so quixotically rejected a perfectly eligible suitor schoolmaster over a silly row between Bob White, the preacher, and the town's own Mrs. Rook.

Turning to Alton Rook, who sat beside her, chewing the cud of his hidden humor, Carrie said viciously, "How in hell will Bill and Angela get out of the house?"

"Beats me," said Alton Rook, who shared Carrie's wish with all his heart that Angela and Bill would be spared on their wedding night. "But Bill's clever about such stunts."

They spoke under, rather than over, the noise of the party, leaning their heads together. In the backwash of listening to Mr. Rook, Carrie heard the noises of the party, heard its increasing tension. The Hadleys were no longer singing, but were quarreling over a song to sing. Mrs. Madison was aimlessly repeating "I cried buckets . . ." but no longer assuring herself of an audience. Sonny Boy was paying such absent-minded and unsuitable compliments to Rachel Mirimar Mandelstan that Rachel was laughing at him. Dugdale stood in the middle of the floor, talking dolefully at Hope, who talked back at him in the repetitious little gushes of her drunken enthusiasms. There was no connection whatever between the things they said to each other. Bucky Lassiter, who was stationed to watch the front door, passed Carrie in hasty search of a drink and a second later she heard the faint sound of a crash. Her hunter's ear located the sound and she acted with the swift reflex of a hunter's shooting.

Thumping to her feet to cover any echo of the crash, she cried out, as if at one with them, "Glory, I heard a car. . . . Out front . . . Over the roof, down the drainpipe, out to the STREET . . ." That did it. There was a stampede to the front door and a grand confusion of delay.

"We aren't going anywhere," Bill had said. "We're going to stay right here, at the Andalusia House, smack in the middle of town."

Not even the crash of the cut screen wire, thunderous in her ears, had put the pursuers on the track. It had taken them less than a minute to run, hand in hand, across her yard, to scramble through the hedge into the yard next door. The yard was empty. The Foxes were at the reception. They had run, breathing rapidly and scuffling up clouds of dust under the overhanging trees, down the alley to Pinckney's little gray cabin.

Now Bill was driving the agency car that belonged to Bucky Lassiter with rapid caution from the alley into Somerset Street, where nobody lived except some people, and down toward Main Street. Angela felt the muscles at the back of her neck relax, although the moment of their greatest danger would be when they must cross Main Street to reach the nameless little street that ran behind the Andalusia House. Bill was handling this. Bill was wonderful. Whatever his unsteady relations with the rest of the world, he would take care of her, now and for the rest of her life.

When the light went against them at the corner of Main, Bill cursed tensely, while the car, under his nervous foot, bucked gently, like a horse reined up to a racing tape. Angela huddled down into the seat, the skin inside her elbows and under her knees crawling and dampening while they waited, her arms and legs fluid and impractical at the joints. This was the danger point. Sliding her eyes along the street without turning her head, she thought she saw the Reverend St. John Rand looking at her from a car halfway down the block on Main. She seemed to see his gray eyes guessing their destination, his expression of disgusted disapproval that they should make such a fuss over the traditional pleasantries of the chivaree. She was imagining things.

They were over Main and on down Somerset and around onto the nameless cross street and drawing up in back of the hotel. A strange colored boy slept alone in the cluttered dusty space that was still called the hotel garden, leaning upright against the closed doors of the carriage house that now served as a garage. Bill shouted at him imperiously and he came slowly to life, astonished at this invasion of his dead world, bowing to them with quaint, quizzical welcome. Bill did not attempt bribery or explanation, but ordered him to put the car away, to lock it away, quickly, leaving the rest of the luggage and bringing in the two small cases and the radio. That is, if he could drive . . . The boy was still explaining, with pained indignation, that he was, indeed, a chauf*feur*, when they turned from him, forcing themselves to move slowly toward the hotel.

Nobody except strangers who were unwarned had stayed there for years. The wide, back steps dipped toward the center with the empty weight of an echo of feet. Behind the splintery bannister rail, a row of green chairs tilted variously on their rockers as if just vacated the moment before, still animate in their long lack of motion. Above the extravagant length and width of the enormous porch rose the skinny, yellow columns fringed by a serried row of diamond-shaped shingles that supported the roof, full five stories up.

Angela and Bill climbed the dipping center of the steps, crossed the wide, creaking porch beneath the distant roof, went through the long, open double door in the thick brick wall and into the wide, dim hall.

The fat clerk was nodding in his shirtsleeves at the reception desk and he jerked wide awake with surprise when they came up to the desk. "You have a room for Mr. and Mrs. Walter Bly?" inquired Bill with faint belligerence.

"Yeah, suah, suh," drawled the clerk with his pimply, half familiar face. Then he looked closely at Angela. "Why, Miss Madison . . ."

"Listen," said Bill violently. "We just got married and we don't want *anybody* to know we're here. You understand? Not God almighty or Mrs. Madison. If anybody finds out where we are, by God, I'll burn down this lousy mausoleum."

"Take it easy, suh," said the clerk, unperturbed and companionable. "Good riddance if you did. Ah won't tell nobody. I get you. But I cain't register you under fake names. Tain't legal."

Angela rallied all her resources, even somehow managing to remember the semi-stranger's name. "My husband," she said primly, slipping not at all over the term she was using for the first time, "is William Bloodgood from Oglethorpe, Mr. Weir. I'd be awfully grateful if we could be left in peace." She smiled wanly. "You can imagine . . ."

"Of course," said Weir, conspiratorial and friendly. "Why, certainly, bless your heart. Miss—Mrs. Bloodgood, you and your husband go right on up and don't worry a bit. I'll send your bags along and you just order dinner any old time you feel like it."

"Right now we feel like some ice, soda, lemon peel, glasses and sugar," said Bill, partially jovial.

The elderly Negro in the wire-cage elevator untilted his chair and his uniform cap and slid to his feet. "Nice day, it sure is, ain't it?" he chattered, as he pulled the wire cable that started them on their leisurely course to the second floor. "Right putty day. Suits me right down to the ground—and then back up to the fifth floor." He laughed in a musical trill at his pridefully repeated joke.

Their bedroom was enormous and dim. A gigantic double bed covered with a red damask spread stood under a looped-up mosquito net suspended from the high ceiling. From the center of the ceiling hung a chandelier with many of its crystal droplets broken and with only a few bulbs screwed into its numerous outlets. A ceiling fan hung stagnant below the chandelier. Under the light and the fan, on the floor, was a round table and beside the table were two big soiled arm chairs. The door was open into a bathroom the size of an ordinary room. The green outside shutters were closed against the sun. It looked restful and impregnable.

"Want them open?" The elevator man was moving toward the windows.

"No!" said Bill violently. "Thanks. You go hurry up that ice and stuff I asked for at the desk. I'm a man who needs a drink."

The old man departed, closing the door, and they were alone. Bill took his hat off and sailed it across the room onto the bed. He stripped off his jacket and threw that, too, missing the foot of the bed. In his shirtsleeves, he stretched, showing the clean sweat under his arms. Angela sat down in one of the big overstuffed chairs and pushed her round hat farther back on her head. Bill came over and took her limp hands.

"Well, here we are, honey," he said. His voice was triumphant. "You and I. Married. By damn." He patted her hands together. "I love you, Missus Bloodgood," he said, quickly and gently, diffident and almost embarrassed.

She disengaged her hands and caught his face. They kissed tenderly and lingeringly and for a moment everything was all right.

There was a discreet knock at the door. Angela got up and moved toward the bathroom.

"Wash my face," she said over her shoulder. "While you mix. Make it stiff."

"One of my best," said Bill, "in honor of the occasion. I sure as hell do need it."

There was a giant cockroach in the bathtub. Angela eyed it with distaste, but without alarm. There wasn't a thing you could do about cockroaches in this place. Only Mrs. Stone would not acknowledge their incontestable right to share your house and still carried on her ceaseless, useless tirade of a civil war with them. Angela hoped there were no mice, but there undoubtedly were. She remembered the annual cotillion held once again at the Andalusia House, in the gigantic ballroom, when Van Ball was in the middle of rebuilding The Oaks. A mouse had got loose among the dancers and there had been pandemonium. Somebody had turned out the lights—Bill, maybe—and every woman had shrieked in chorus and clutched the nearest male. It was terribly funny. But she still hated mice.

She washed and repowdered her face and put on fresh lipstick. The bathroom mirror was speckled, green, and distorted. She rather liked the mirror. It was false, like those in funny houses. At least, you did not look like *that*.

Bill's voice called happily, "Come drink with me and be my love!"

"Coming, honey . . ."

The cocktails were strong and tasted wonderful.

"The best bourbon," said Bill with satisfaction, "and damn the expense. You only get married once. Drink it up. There's lots more where it came from."

Angela took a long swallow. "You certainly mix the best old-fashioneds in the world, Bill," she said.

"Good ice, too," said Bill. "Proper ice. Hunks out of an ice box. None of those damn stinky modern ice cubes."

This was a nice, old-fashioned room, too, big and cool and so quiet. "You don't think they'll find us?" Her fingers tightened convulsively on her glass.

"No," said Bill judiciously, "I do not. I honestly don't. Sonny Boy will split a gut!" He threw back his head and laughed victoriously.

She wanted to be altogether with him, there, feeling victorious, laughing victoriously. She said slowly, seeking to join him, "Honey, you don't mind—you don't mind because this isn't. . . . You wouldn't a little bit rather this were—the first time? Truly don't mind, I mean?"

"No, I don't," said Bill. "Why bring that up now? Since you did, I wish there'd never been anybody else. And God damn I wish to hell it had not been—who it was. You know that. But what the hell? We've been all over that."

She wished, too, that it had not been Logan. She did not know why, but she would rather it had been anybody else. Still, it was perverse of her to remind Bill now. She wished she had not.

"Unless," said Bill angrily, burning up his resentment against what was irrevocable in anger at what he should know was not so, "there was ever anybody afterwards. There wasn't, was there? If there was, tell me now. If you ever went back to Logan, even once, or if anybody else—I have to know. That's the only thing on earth that could make me not want you for my wife. Not to know. If you lie to me now. We've had it pretty rugged, you and I, and I don't mind if you've lied to me up to now. Honestly I don't. But don't now."

It does so matter if I had lied to you up to now, thought Angela, mildly indignant. That part was a trap. But her heart went out to him, as her hands did, wide, and without reservations.

He held back from her, waiting, not really wary, but insistent. "Be sure. . . ."

Oh, Bill, thought Angela, thanking her stars fervently that she never had, not once, not since the night Bill had only kissed her, not ever, not even when *he* did, to revenge herself on him. "No," she said, almost wanting to laugh joyfully, but matching his solemnity. "Never, never, never, after. Honest, cross my heart, and hope to die. I'm not lying. I may sometimes about little things. It's a bad sort of habit you get into when you aren't happy." She knew he was touchy about honesty and she wanted to be entirely honest. "But not about that. Never."

He hesitated, wondering whether to press her about little lies. He wanted to have it straight about lying. You could destroy a man by lying to him. He was too close to her, when he was sober and went out to her, not to suspect it when she lied even a little. He was pretty sure she was telling the truth now. But he did not want to be picked at by any lying. You could hurt a man by lying. But she understood about hurting a man, his girl. "Okay," he said. "Don't any more. About anything. Long puss. I'm *glad* it isn't the first time with us, if you want to know."

She sighed luxuriously, resigning without pain her own right to jealousy in their shared past.

The colored boy who had put their car in the garage brought in their suitcases and Bill's portable radio. He eyed the dollar Bill gave him with disfavor. "Oh, nuts," said Bill, and added another fifty cents.

"My God," he said when the boy was gone. "I remember when they'd kiss your feet for a half-buck tip."

Bill opened his suitcase and took out a full bottle of bourbon and put it on the center table. In the top of the open suitcase, Angela recognized Bill's favorite apple green shirt and the polished leather case that held Bill's favorite toy. He had had the little 25-caliber pistol that just fitted into his big hand since college, where he had once shot out a street light in front of a professor's house with it, from a motorcycle, on a bet. No one else could hit anything at all with it, but Bill said it was glove to his hand, and understood him. He shot rats with it, in Oakland, for practice. It lay now, familiarly nestled into the familiar shirt, next to the stiff blue cotton pajama top she had never seen. She felt very pleased because Bill wore pajamas with collared tops.

At home and humming to himself, Bill put the radio on the bureau against the wall and fastened the ground wire to the cold radiator and turned the radio's switches. He fiddled with the dials and nodded when he found the station he wanted, as the volume swelled.

Angela watched him idly, calm and at home with him. She

was draining the last of her cocktail. Bill came back to the table and started to mix another.

The announcer on the radio said loudly, ". . . continuing our program of old favorites . . ." There was a trumpet note and a drum beat and then a clarinet went straight into the refrain. "*Who stole my heart away? . . .*" Bill tapped his foot and sang the words in his near-bass baritone. "*Who made me dream all day? . . .* remember, honey? *Dreams I know can never come true . . .* the first night. *Seems as though I'll never be blue . . .*"

Angela put her hand up, palm out. The tears were gathering within her like swift rain clouds on a midsummer day. It was playing on the victrola in Carrie's living room. She had wandered out on Carrie's front porch with wild young William Bloodgood from Oglethorpe, for whom she felt only the mild titillation of her mother's command that, alone among men, she should have nothing whatever to do with him. The porch was a nest of shadow between the brightly lighted room and the brightly moonlit yard. They began to dance to the music that filled the shadows from the open, lighted window. "*Who stole my heart away . . .*" It was understood that they would kiss, and kiss they did, easily and practically, with due regard for stance and balance, for the anatomy of the nose. In the middle of the kiss, the kiss had changed, and their two lives with it. He had said afterward, in disturbed amazement, "But you aren't even pretty!" It was a tremendous statement from Bill, to whom pleasant compliments were the bread and butter of his bred and born speech. It was a measure of his shocked sincerity. Then he said, ardent, and almost humble, "Angela! You're so strange and it's so different. You're so gentle. Angela, Angela, Angela. You're, good Lord, you're *you,* and you're mine. You hear? You're mine!"

Angela got up quickly and went over to the mantelpiece that topped the empty iron grate. She turned her back to Bill. She fought her tears. Bill hated her crying jags, she reminded herself. If she started to weep now, she would never stop. But there was reason enough to weep, verily, verily, reason enough to weep.

There was a mirror over the mantelpiece and she saw her face.

The longest scar from the accident lay like a welt across her cheek and the nerve end at the top of it was pulsing. They had had her green car then, the old Buick, and her last allowance, and birth certificates to prove that they were old enough, even disinherited and jobless, if they were foolish enough. They had Bob White's blessing, though he was long gone, and they had their love to keep them warm. But they had been too drunk to see the sign marking the washout on the familiar road, the other side of the bridge. The scars of her patched-up face had healed, and his fractured leg had healed in his big, healthy body, though he had never quite thinned down again. . . . The pulse at the end of the scar had gradually stopped beating, except to warn her that she was about to cry. She had acquired other scars, since, on her long face. Scars called wrinkles. Some of them were war wounds, she thought, from the long days and long nights when Bill had been an overage corporal, foolhardy, they said, more than brave, in a front-line company, when the tic had pulsed without ceasing and she had cried for days and nights. Some of them were the marks of later fretfulness prolonged, and some were from laughter. It was a wounded face, all right, a ruined face, hateful and ugly. And behind her, more clearly in the mirror, she saw Bill's face, fat, red, ruined and ugly, too.

"*Who . . . who . . . no one but you!*"

How long ago? Nineteen years ago! This was 1947. She was forty years old and it was too late. The tears broke like a midsummer storm. "It's too late—too late—too late," she wept. "Bill, it's too late."

"Oh, Christ," said Bill. "Don't cry."

St. John Rand had looked at her face, and she should have known. Her voice rose. "It's too *late!*"

He came close to her and caught her wrists.

"Stop that," he ordered sharply. "Right now."

"Too *late*," she said into his face, wrenching at her wrists to free them.

He held her a little away from him with one arm and slapped her. It was businesslike and essentially friendly. She gulped, drew in a long breath, and almost smiled at him.

"That's the girl," he said. "Take it easy. Listen! We're married. Get that through your head. We're married!"

The incontrovertible fact of their marriage amazed her.

"We got away. We're off," he said. "Maybe it's not too late."

347

21.   A Little Fortitude

"The radiant bride," wrote Alton Rook, and paused. His forefingers hovered over the rickety keys of his typewriter. He exed out "radiant" with his left forefinger. Turning the roller back a notch, he wrote "charming" in the space above, and paused. That made three "charmings"—one substituted for "beautiful" and one for "lovely" and this one for "radiant." He exed out the "charming" and paused. You could not call her "intelligent." That was an insult in a social note. Besides, he doubted whether she was, any more. Intelligences could go as dim as beauty, after twenty years of misuse. Angela had never really been beautiful. But she had been, to him, radiant and lovely. "Gracious"? The mothers were "gracious"—at least, Mrs. Madison already was. Oh, hell, "lovely" . . . He should have let Gloria May go ahead and write it. It would sound ridiculous, but it would have been unself-conscious. To Gloria May, who did the social notes, a bride was a bride. He had stuck himself with a tizzy problem. If he toned it down too much, it would only point up the disparity between Angela and the radiant, beautiful and lovely brides for whom such prose was invented. He admired Angela's spunk. She had seen it through, with orange blossoms on her great-

great-grandmother's white veil and rosettes on the wedding cake she had cut with dead General Bloodgood's pappy's Civil War sword. The "spunky" bride? Her long jaw stuck out and she had exactly what she had held out for—for twenty years.

Alton lifted his eyes to the plate-glass window he had installed in his office the week he moved in. It was protected by a wrought-iron railing of exceptional grace that he had bought in New Orleans when he was courting Clementine Terra. There was a view of the wide, sluggish river from his window. He had loved that view. He peered out the window now, the slow-moving water barely visible through the accumulated dust on the window, the muddy water the color of the dirty window. The late light of the June afternoon lay above the muddy water, among the particolored dust. In a moment it would be gone and he would see nothing but the black square of the window and the blacker tracing of the wrought-iron shield. He worked best in the isolated well of light from the single green-shaded bulb over his head. He would wait now for the black southern twilight.

Lately he had used this time of day to reminisce. He had written a number of nostalgic pieces about the old Andalusia. Perhaps today, at twilight, he could write a little poem of a social note for Angela Madison that would not make her even faintly ridiculous. God knew he did not find her ridiculous.

Alton Rook took down his forefingers and folded his hands and waited patiently for the dark. Twenty years ago it would have been so easy to write it for her. Twenty years ago, thought Alton Rook, when Angela was twenty years old.

That was the year they had all fallen so ridiculously in love. He had scarcely found them ridiculous, even then, they had been so touchingly, appealingly young. All four of them, falling, bump, elbows over teakettles, in love with the minister, Mark Barbee, who had to run away . . . He had not laughed then, but had yearned over them, when Mark left them. Publicly wounded and publicly proud, they had held their feathery heads so high. Like wounded pines, visibly tapped and bleeding, they had held themselves straight and proud. He had been so damn fond of them, and so solemnly hopeful.

Life was so ridiculously repetitious that it was not surprising

349

that a second priest, in the staid, unexciting Episcopal pulpit at St. James's, had brought Angela and the other three, including his own daughter, once more close to him. Bob White had created a joint crisis for them, just as Mark Barbee had done, wounding them, tapping their hearts' juices at another vulnerable time in their lives. Alton had loved them all then. They had been gallant about Bob White. Bless Angela, bless them all, they had understood for the moment the rare, clear choice you could only occasionally make between right and wrong.

The third priest, who came, finding them vulnerable, was no young God to love. He offered them no gallant choice of good or evil. St. John Rand was not so different from the preacher before Mark Barbee and the one after Bob White—just a biggish, moderately sanctimonious, sensible sort of stupid fellow, like any other poky man of the pulpit. Except that he was not a proper Anglican priest at all because he had mirrors for eyes. Mirrors were a form of judgment. Anglicans should not make judgments. That was the pride and the beauty of it. Your sins were up to you. Your priest did not make judgments.

St. John Rand had judged them. He had looked with the flat mirrors of his stranger's eyes and he had seen: a ridiculous, middle-aged, virgin bride, a whore, a drunk, and a cripple. Alton Rook put his hands over his eyes to cover his pain and his anger and the things he saw with his own eyes. He put his thoughts into parentheses.

(Let them alone! The town had taken care of them. It took care of its own, in its own blind, instinctive way. Once you were taken care of, you could get away with murder. If you were Lucy Lee Cranborne, you could get away with murder. If you were Alton Rook, husband to Clementine and labeled a wit, you could be as subversive as you pleased. If you were Miss Sis Whittle, you could whistle through your teeth at the world.

(You could still play Juliet, if you were Angela Madison, with waspish touches of Kate the Virgin Shrew, at forty—at fifty, if you liked—to your fat, overage Romeo from Oglethorpe. Scarred and battered, Angela Juliet could watch demurely while her Lord of the Universe brawled away in the streets. And fail to observe or remark that Billeo looked less and less like a Lord of the Universe and more and more like a Life of the Party . . .

(The town took care of its own in its own way.

(His darling daughter could sleep with the world and his brother and still be no whore. Whom the town could not countenance, and still must take care of, it institutionalized. Damn useful institution, Ellen Terra, never, ah, never a whore, but the town's own *Lady* Whore. In the name of southern hospitality, in the name of the town's self-created ante-bellum dreams, now that gentlemen guests no longer had the time or the manners to lay siege before southern purity, Ellen Terra was a necessary institution. She never wasted anybody's valuable time. Ah, poor baby, poor bitch, who had been his pinchable pretty, whom everybody pinched and petted. And if she lived long enough to outlive her usefulness, she would be most honorably demoted—from everybody's sweetheart to everybody's aunt—and would be buried in the end with the full Episcopal honors accorded the town's old maids.

(As Hope would, if she lived long enough to drink herself to death, be buried to mournful music under the Stars and Bars. Hope had become the town's own. The Confederate convert was a full-fledged southern lady at last. Oh, not because she married the town's own Logan Knight, its private frustrated artist, its handsomest success, but because she was a lady drunk. Every southern town must have its lady drunk. Meticulous and letter-perfect, as only converts can be, square-cut and unbeautiful, Hope wept her ladylike tears and sighed her harplike sighs and giggled her little giggles and suffered her wretched hangovers. And did the right thing at parties, the talkable aboutable, not too disgraceful thing.

(Let them alone! It was too late. It was too late to make Ellen Terra see herself guilty, to sober up Hope, to send Angela and Bill fleeing the town to seek new destinies. The town had taken care of them. It was too late to make a cripple of Carrie.)

The daylight was quite suddenly gone, and Alton took his hands from his eyes and the parentheses from his thoughts. He had sat beside Carrie the day St. John Rand, newly down from Louisville, had looked at Carrie. He had felt in the hidden, nervous interior of his heart that Carrie became crippled when he looked at her. For this, he truly hated the Reverend St. John Rand. He had so often taken heart from Carrie.

Take heart now, Alton Rook, he told himself in the dark twilight, staring at the newly black window with its blacker tracing from the graceful iron casement. You once helped a fine young man to flee who might have loved and married your child or one of your child's friends if he had stayed. You once left your child and your child's friends in the lurch when they were fighting on your own side for a good man against an evil woman, who is your wife. You have done those things you ought not to have done and left undone etcetera etcetera. And it's too late. But you have a little fortitude. There's that. If you have never burst the confines of your foolish life, you have never quite given in and you have never, not once, asked for help. There's that. That's something. It's better than nothing. So take heart.

He turned on the green-shaded light and tore out and replaced the piece of rough copy paper in the old machine. "Lit by the long candles of tradition," he hammered out carefully with his forefingers, "came the proud bride . . ." It would not do, but before he was through he would compose his tribute to Angela. A little fortitude. To hell with St. John Rand! Angela was a bride. Hope was a southern lady. Carrie was no cripple. And his Ellen Terra was sweet.

22. The Kiss, the Tree and the Bullet

"It's too late," wailed Angela softly. She was crying quietly now, with tears like summer rain.

"Maybe it's not," said Bill.

Angela drank cautiously, coddling her glass, savoring the taste of good whiskey and quiet tears. There was a state of being drunk that lay just beyond this one, a rosy state, subdued, controlled, and hopeful. You could hold an old conversation when you felt that way, and it sounded like new, only better. You could perform the comforting act, with the well-known lover, desire and ability in balance, and the act was sufficient unto itself. You were intimate with the moment, discounting the past, disregarding the future.

Bill turned off the radio and came over to sit beside her.

"Honey," he said, "just get it through your thick head that we're married, you and I. Married, honey. You and I."

The amazing, final, accomplished fact of their marriage was difficult to encompass. She stared at her ring in wonder through the last of her tears.

"Listen," said Bill, his voice youthful, "we've licked this town. You hear? We could stay here if we felt like it. We would, too, and spit in the Reverend Dr. Rand's eye. By the same token, we can go. We can lick any other, see, since we've a mind to. We decided to go, didn't we? Six months ago. All right. It may not mean much to be a Bloodgood up there . . ." He hesitated, unable to believe that it would mean nothing at all. "Not much, but they won't remember every time I ever got tight, either, or talked myself out of a job. Forty's not even old up there."

It's old enough in Andalusia, thought Angela. You can add till you're twenty and hold the count till you're forty, but then you have to start subtracting.

"It's the prime, that's what they tell me. Hell, I'm almost forty-four and I never felt better in my life. Sure, it didn't work for me before, in New York, but I had to come back for you, honey. You're my girl. I couldn't do without my girl. Hell, honey, I've loved you for twenty years. That's a damn sight more than most people can say for themselves."

It was true. It was wonderful. It was rare. It had taken all Bill's stubborn pride and all her stubborn devotion to his pride for their love to survive. But it had survived. Everything it had to survive: Bloodgood snobbishness and Hannah Miller Madison's tenacious hate; separation, a whole war, and even two weeks entirely alone together—exhausted and debilitated by the network of deceit necessary to the two weeks, when they were afraid to look even strangers in the face; Bill's desperate infidelities and the unalterable fact that she had once slept with Logan Knight; sober quarrels and drunken ones, and physical combat—the time she put her heel through Bill's windshield during a fight, the time Bill had quite simply blacked her eye; the advice of friends and the sneers of enemies, the eyes of St. John Rand and the interference of everybody.

"If people would only let people alone," said Angela.

"Well, they don't, but to hell with 'em. We got away from them this time."

Until, on a perfect June day, they were married. Until they escaped them all and they were alone together, one in the sight of only God, who was incurious and respectful.

Hope had been married all those twenty years. Hope would become a grandmother while Angela was on her honeymoon. But what had really happened to Hope in twenty years? Nothing—she was still waiting for it to happen, drinking away the time that nothing happened in. She was still waiting to love and serve the man she had married in place of the man she had loved. She had never found Logan's heart in order to give him her own. She was still a girl with her heart in her hand.

No one would marry Ellen Terra, who had refused to be her bridesmaid. She was everybody's sweetheart, and no one's. She would be no man's woman until she died.

Carrie had married her opinionated, elderly doctor, but he had not been her young heart's dream. Carrie loved him, no doubt, with a good, gruff, middle-aged love, but Carrie's youth was dead. Carrie had never had her youth.

Only Angela was whole and complete. Only she had been young and was no longer young, but grown and fulfilled. Only she had what she had always wanted. She had it, just as she had always wanted it, and she must take heart. Take heart, Angela.

"Oh, Bill . . ." said Angela.

"Here's to our future, Mrs. B., honey," said Bill.

They clinked glasses, and drank. Angela smiled and the welt in her cheek, reddened by tears, creased across the faint dimple in her smile.

Cautiously they began to erect a tower of hope, among strangers. The tower grew solid as they dwelt upon its details. No one would find them among the strangers to point out what they had been, and they could be what they would.

Bill paced the faded roses on the carpet, earnest and voluble. His face grew leaner as the muscles of his padded jaw hardened with fresh determination. Angela sat in the faded arm chair and followed him with her eyes. Her eyes were soft and she saw him still as the man of her dreams. She was prepared to give him whatever he wanted of her, even faith that the future would be wholly different from the past. No other stranger would look at them as St. John Rand had looked at them. No other stranger would know whether they had been married an hour or a month or all of the twenty years.

She was surprised when Bill stiffened mid-step and hushed mid-sentence. She listened, trying to hear what he had heard, straining and puzzled. There was a rustling somewhere. Mice, thought Angela, distressed. She did so hate mice.

Bill's face bewildered her. His eyes were hooded and his lips had fallen open into a slack puffiness. On tiptoe he crossed over to the baggage rack where his suitcase lay open. He thrust his hand between the green shirt and the blue pajama top and took out the leather pistol case. He often shot rats, thought Angela again in mute incomprehension. He could shoot with it. It was his favorite toy. He shot rats in Oakland, but you did not shoot mice in Andalusia. He slid the revolver out of its holster as he moved, dropping the case on the table beside her.

She followed him with her eyes as he ran across the room, still on tiptoe. The revolver was almost hidden in his hand. He turned the handle of the door with a wrench and opened it suddenly inward. Sonny Boy, on his knees in front of the keyhole, saved himself from falling into the room by falling backwards against Dugdale's high-set knees. A poised spoon fell on a held dishpan and the noise was thunderous.

"*Got* you," cried Bucky triumphantly, poising the spoon again to take his part in what would become general cacophony. Sonny Boy, on his knees, lifted his tin horn. Logan reached one hand toward Bill. There was a split second of silence, as when a falling baton precedes the opening chord of a symphony. There was a steely whisper in the silence, as Bill released the safety catch on his little pistol. The whisper engraved itself on the silence.

Angela sat sprawled timelessly against the faded red plush background of the chair, her spread hand over her mouth, her middle finger touching her nose, her eyes bright with a wild, dead light. Bill was in front of her, his powerful muscles caught tensely bunched under the layer of his fat, his body springing forward like a statue's, half a-tiptoe, his arm in front of him, his finger tense and light on the toy trigger of his little gun. Sonny Boy seemed to fall farther back without moving, his head pushing against Dugdale's bony knees. Logan, dreamy and relaxed, stretched his hand toward Bill, and behind him stood the posse. The various members of the wedding party, now in pursuit of the groom, were impeccably dressed and ridiculously still, holding their soundless, childish instruments for the chivaree.

In the middle distance, down the path of faded roses that carpeted the wide, high hall, Carrie contemplated them, saturnine and composed, the coal at the end of her cigarette hissing and glowing alone with life. Beside her, Ellen Terra rocked back on her round heels, her arms folded under her full bosom, her black eyes solid with indignation. Behind them, Hope clung to the arm of her nurse, and behind them the worried face of Mr. Weir of the Andalusia House was as comical and inconsequential as the black face of the elevator man peering under his elbow.

The scene was bereft of any purpose whatever.

Then Hope cried, in a high, piercing, delighted shriek, "Shoot 'em, Bill. Shoot 'em all!"

And Carrie called gruffly, "Do put that silly thing down, Bill, for God's sake."

And Bucky spoke at the same moment, tentatively hilarious, uneasily gay, "Man, man, you sure were smart." He held the dishpan and spoon apart, with a faint juggling motion.

And Sonny Boy said, aggressive and aggrieved, "I've waited fifteen years for this."

And Morton started immediately to sing. He was extremely and foolishly drunk. "Hooray, hooray, my father's gonna be hung . . ."

Bill grimaced in a travesty of the expression required of a "good sport." "Okay, my friends," he said in a travesty of the voice required of a "good sport." "You win, and the drinks are on me. Downstairs. SHUT UP!" He spoke to Morton, his voice deadly and without concessions to sportsmanship. Morton stopped singing with his mouth open. "But that's all, my friends. Downstairs and then outside. Sorry to spoil the fun, but I'm not having any!" He fanned the pistol at the group, which instinctively recoiled, all but Logan. "This is a *private* honeymoon."

"Oh, hell," said Sonny Boy, "I wish old St. John Rand hadn't told us where you were! After all these years, and I ain't enjoying it . . ."

"It's the same one," said Morton crossly, recognizing the pistol that Bill had flourished in the chivaree on the night he married Mary.

Dugdale reared to his inordinate height and looked down his

long nose, which sniffed up all pain and all frustration. "Let's go, friends," he said. "The elderly gentleman here says he's got other things to do. . . ."

Logan said dreamily, "He's bluffing us, fellow countrymen. Are we mice or men? The lady can wait. . . ." He looked with the cool, dreamy surface of his eyes at Angela, who stirred for the first time. "In*deed*, she can."

Bill said, "Get out, Logan! Get out."

"He *dished* it out," said Logan, dreamily, with rhythmic accent, "and he's *bluff*ing it out now."

There was a rallying movement in the posse. Bill's head snapped back and then went forward again; the dark, ugly color flooded up from the V neck of his shirt and over his face and into the scalp where his hair was thin. Angela felt as if she were endlessly sinking into the dusty cushions of the chair. Bill would shoot Logan and she could stop it, if she would. But she would not. Bill's pride.

"And *stay* out." Bill's voice was deadly and steady and Logan moved dreamily and steadily and inexorably toward him with his hand stretched out. It was as if Logan, the forgotten first lover, had come to reclaim his own. Bill stared into the eyes of the man who had had his girl. Sonny Boy was suddenly in action beside Logan.

There was an explosion and then silence.

Angela felt the chair, with her body in it, stop stone still while the earth plowed on its stately way on its axis around the sun.

In the middle of Bill's first kiss, on the night when their car hit the tree on the other side of the bridge across the river, she had stopped thus, utterly still, while time and the earth moved on without her.

She caught up with the earth, with a gasping lurch, and lifted her finger to touch the top of the long scar to still the tic that was beating like a heart. She opened her eyes and saw Logan try to fall, upheld in the arms of the posse. She saw Bill's arm drop and she heard Hope's voice, high and delighted, "You shot'em, Bill, good BOY!"

There was a brief time of unsortable confusion. She met Bill's eyes and his eyes were humbly pleading and she smiled at him and his eyes went proud. Someone said urgently, "Stay here!" and everybody left her.

Except Ellen Terra who came back and sat beside her, gabbling. The gabble had been going on for some time while Ellen Terra held Angela's hand tightly in her plump, sweet hands. Angela heard her, finally, saying, "I bet it's just nothin' 'tall. Why I bet Bill hardly scratched him with that silly little thing. Just scared him silly. He's hollering for a duel at dawn, to shoot it out with Bill at sunrise, isn't that just like Logan Knight? But don't you fret, Angela. Bill's fine. And here he is. . . ."

"Of course he's here," said Angela, lifting her face to Bill.

"I'm going," said Ellen Terra then, bouncing to her heels. "'Bye. I'm going with Hope and get her drunk. Carrie is going to call Papa and tell him to keep it off the wires and all that, and out of the paper. Don't you fret. Don't you even worry. 'Bye now . . ."

Angela watched Bill close the door behind Ellen Terra and put a spindle-legged chair under the knob. Then she heard Carrie's voice, gruff and affectionate, through the door.

"You'll stay where you are?" she asked.

"Yes," said Bill coldly.

"Hope's gone for bail in case you need it and I guaranteed to that cop you wouldn't budge. Chief Black's out, but he'll be back. He'll fix everything. You can trust him. Don't let anybody else in. Don't talk to anybody. Jack's meeting Logan at the hospital. It'll be all right. Hear?"

"I hear," said Bill coldly.

"Angela okay?" called Ellen Terra.

Bill turned his head slowly as if he had a stiff neck and looked at Angela. "I reckon so," he said. "Sure."

"See you later . . ." And there was silence again.

Bill said, "I think it went right through his shoulder without hitting a bone."

He came over and sat down quietly in the other chair beside the table. He slowly tilted his head so that his profile lay in one palm and bent his other hand down to cover hers. His smile was wry and enigmatic.

They said nothing. For the moment, there was nothing to say. There was nothing to do but wait.

Well, thought Angela, we ought to be good at that by now. Why did the hours just ahead of them stretch longer in her mind than the twenty years gone by?

They began to talk in little, restless dribbles, not to say anything, not even to communicate, but for the sound it made in the big, quiet room.

Bill got to his feet without warning and lifted up his big arms. "Nuts!" he said. "Hell's bells. So I'm supposed to sit here while it gets fixed up for me. Not me! I'm not going to sit around and let a lot of women fix things up for me. Men ought to settle things between themselves. If you've never lied to me . . ."

Not about that, thought Angela, I haven't. Thank the Lord.

". . . I know where I stand with Logan. And he knows where he stands with me. We're even now. We can start fresh. Unless he thinks he's got to shoot back. I'm not afraid of him or anybody. Listen, can I leave you here alone, honey? Can I? Can I? I want to go over and see Logan, damn it. Not leave it to a lot of women. Listen, will you stay right here and cover up for me? Will you? Say I'm in the can if Chief Black or the cops call? Or anybody else except Carrie. You can trust Carrie. Will you do that, Angela?"

She could keep him here. She could keep him here with her and out of trouble. Maybe she could keep him out of trouble for the rest of his life. He was shaken to the bottom boots of his courage. He might have killed Logan. She could keep him now. But she would not. Not now or ever. "Sure," said Angela. "Go ahead. Go ahead, Bill."

"Good baby. You're my baby. See you later, honey."

Before she could know what it would be like to be alone in this strange room, he was gone.

There was nothing to do but wait. She should be good at that.

Twenty years was a long time. She must think of it as a long time. She thought of movie sequences in which the passage of time was indicated by calendar leaves fluttering down into space. The image was imperfect. Time was more like an overturned pot of glue. It poured down stickily and slowly, flowing like the slow, muddy river beside the town. The years, months, weeks, days, hours, minutes were all sticky and inseparable. Tomorrow became yesterday and it was never today. It was almost never now.

Once in a while it was now. The first time Bill had kissed her; the instant they hit the tree; the moment the revolver fired the bullet. Those were nows, belonging to her and Bill. Beginnings and ends encompassed so quickly that they belonged, separately, to themselves, distinct, complete. But what happened between the kiss, the tree, and the bullet?

The same things, over and over.

The river of glue had incorporated the kiss which had become a thousand kisses. The river of glue had flowed around the tree and left it standing, distantly, bending to the stream.

There was summer which was long, and fall, and winter, which was short, and spring. There was Advent and Epiphany and Lent and the innumerable Sundays after Trinity.

What had happened between Mark Barbee and Bob White and St. John Rand? Baptisms and funerals and weddings. Service at eleven on Sundays and communion at dawn on Thursdays. There was the Thursday morning when you actually went to communion because of Mark Barbee. There was the Sunday when you intended to go, but you did not go to church for Bob White. There was the Thursday when there was no communion, but you went to your wedding in the afternoon.

Then there you were back waiting again. You ought to be good at it. Even in a strange, new place. You'd done a lot of it. You knew how to wait. . . .

There was the telephone ringing like church bells, over and over, to wake you up. Bill always called you when you wanted him to.

She was awake and she had been asleep. She got up and went over and lifted up the telephone. Her mouth tasted sandy. She must have slept with it open. She said, "Hello," prosaically.

"Listen, chicken," said the voice. It was Carrie's voice and not Bill's. Angela was disappointed and she yawned. Then she noticed with surprise that it was dark. It was dark and she was hungry. It must be around dinner time. It was quite, quite dark. "Are you listening?" said Carrie sharply.

"Yes," said Angela. "What, Carrie?"

"First of all," said Carrie, and her voice was matter-of-fact as it always was over the telephone, "Logan's not hurt worth a hoot. Bill's under arrest, sort of, but Hope's got bail money and I've been down swearing that Bill won't leave the hotel until Black says he can. If I can fix it with Black, why don't you sneak out to dinner with me? Annie's cooking up a big shrimp *paella*. Anyway, honey, everything's all right. It won't do worse than cut out Logan's tennis for a while! Listen, is Bill right there?"

"Bill's not here," said Angela flatly, sounding more like Carrie than Carrie had.

There was a second of silence. "Oh," said Carrie. "Where is he?"

"He went out," said Angela.

"How long ago?" asked Carrie.

"Half an hour—an hour," said Angela. "I really don't know."

"Stay where you are and don't speak to anybody," said Carrie, and she added, "for God's sake."

Angela nodded and hung up the telephone. She went over to the wall and pressed down the switch. The few irregularly placed bulbs in the chandelier over the center table went yellow with light. The light pushed the shadows into the corners of the big room and shoved them under the looped-up mosquito net over the huge bed. She went back and sat down in the chair by the table under the light. There was nothing to do but wait. She ought to be good at that.

The town took care of its own, the same way as the river flowed. You only had to wait. The shooting of Logan would be buried in diminishing whispers in the capacious closet behind the door that was never opened to strangers. There the bones of it would rattle with the other town skeletons. It was not even a very impressive skeleton. Rather a gay little dog of a skeleton. It was certainly not too big for the town's capacious closet.

"Everything's changed," Carrie had said one day as they drove out through the forests of new little houses that had supplanted the pines on the way to Oakland. "Everything's changed but us!" It was not true. The town had not changed so much in its heart. Only a little. If St. John Rand would go away . . . The town, in its heart, was the same.

Angela turned at a sound and the door opened and Bill came in the door toward her. He looked tired and blotched and almost pathetic, but he walked with his pesky pride. She lifted her face in the chair and he bent down over her and gently they kissed.

Bill said, "Give me a drink, honey. Me and Logan are pals."

He laughed. Then he bent down again and kissed her with closed lips, hard.

Why, it's all over, thought Angela. He has it all settled about Logan. He knows, now, it was nothing to me, and that it never happened again, afterwards. It won't ever matter again. He knows all about it now. Everybody finds out everything in time, she thought. Maybe everybody knows now. All about everything. About Logan and me, and about me and Bill. It's so hard to keep a secret. It's so wearisome and hard. Because why else would Logan have been so—contemptuous—and Bill angry enough to really shoot him, to maybe kill him. Unless, of course, Logan had had me once and knew all about me and Bill . . . She felt a sharp pang at the loss of their beautiful secret, and a sense of relief that she no longer had to keep so fragile a thing safe in her clumsy fingers as a secret. Besides, she thought, carelessly and coolly, probably no one really did know. It was only that it no longer mattered. She and Bill were married and they were the town's own forever now. They would never go away.

Bill pulled at the sleeves of his shirt to loosen them from his underarms. "No hard feelings," he said. "We *both* apologized. After all, we called each other's bluff. He had to keep coming and I had to shoot him. There wasn't anything else to do. It went right through his shoulder and he ain't more than uncomfortable. Hope's had a wonderful time, acting like he was on his deathbed. She's drunk as four goats and thinks we're both heroes. It'll be something for everybody to talk about."

"Does Mama know?" asked Angela.

"Sure. Everybody knows. Jack says he sent over a sedative that would knock her out for a week. Don't fret."

"That's fine," said Angela.

"Listen, honey, the one thing I can't stand is this lousy

363

mausoleum. I've squared it with Weir, more or less. Let's get the hell out of here."

"Fine," said Angela.

"Let's go out to Carrie's and get good and drunk. Ellen Terra's gone out already, buckety-buckety, with Dugdale. You don't suppose those two will get around to it at last? Okay with you?"

"Fine," said Angela. "Just fine." She would get in on her own wedding's post-mortem after all. And she did love Annie's shrimp *paella*.

Bill picked up the pistol from the floor near the door, where he must have dropped it, and set the safety catch and put it on the table. He poured a slug of whiskey into his glass and chunked in the rest of the ice. Angela got up and picked up the little gun gingerly and buttoned it into its holster. She corked the whiskey bottle. Then she carried them both over to the suitcase and put them in between the familiar shirt and the unfamiliar pajamas. She saw Bill's hat this side of the line of light near the foot of the bed and started over to get it.

"Oh, let it lie," said Bill in an odd, truculent voice. "You don't need hats in this town."

Angela nodded and buckled the suitcase. She picked up her too-young hat and tugged it onto the back of her head. It seemed to her that her fingers were sticky with glue. In the mirror, she saw Bill's face, sagging a little, but not gone slack, his expression touchily gay. In the mirror, she saw the giant bed in the shadows, covered with its unwrinkled red damask spread.

"What'll we do when . . ." She tilted her head in a backwards jerk toward the bed, a little shyly.

"Walk straight upstairs in front of everybody and his goddamn uncle," said Bill. "It's no secret. We're married."

Angela smiled and turned to him. She had on her gloves. "Ready," she said.

At the threshold of the room, Bill set down their two suitcases to open the door for her. Pausing, he tipped up her chin, running his finger down the long, sharp jaw. Lightly he kissed her once.

They left the bridal chamber and descended into the town.

23.   White and Black

Georgianna Church, having achieved her ambition to be the oldest woman alive in the county, white or black, was enjoying her deathbed. Jack Maitland said she would probably stay alive just as long as she enjoyed it and no longer. There was very little left of her except the enjoyment of dying.

Miss Sis Whittle whistled once, piercingly, through her teeth, outside the gray board cabin, and then came in the door. Her shirtwaist crackled faintly above the shushering of her black bombazine skirt.

"What are you making all the fuss about, Georgianna?" she demanded in her voice that could be heard across the county. "You look fit as a fiddler's frog."

"She am putty poly, Miss Sis, ma'am," said Mercy, whose dialect had thickened as she nursed her mother, daughter of a slave. She moved backward, with ponderous grace, making way for their visitor.

Georgiana made no attempt to speak, but the gray-black lips in her gray-black face worked themselves into a smile.

"I brought you some junk and I want to ask you something," said Miss Sis.

"Thank yuh, Miss Sis, ma'am. Yuh know Mama doan heah so good now. . . ." said Mercy.

"She can hear me!" said Miss Sis.

"Yes'm," said Mercy.

Georgianna's voice issued from her body. "Yuh is mos welcome, honey, Miss Sis."

"Mr. Rook sent you this—and Miss Ellen Terra this—and Miss Carrie and Doctor Jack this—and Miss Angela and Mister Bill this. . . ." The fruit in its basket, the dark, webbed bed jacket, the bottle of old sherry, and the soft, down pillow with the soft pink cover glowed newly in the austere room with the gray board walls and the uncertain floor.

"Thank em suahly," said Georgianna, the whisper of her voice gentle and emotionless, "an tell me how dey does."

"Everybody's perky," said Miss Sis. "And Miss Angela and Mister Bill are the cooingest newlyweds the county ever did see. The very cooingest."

There was a ghost of a lively chuckle from the bed.

"I brought you some scuppernongs," said Miss Sis, and she held up the big, brown paper bag full for Georgianna to see.

The dark eyes gleamed and laughter passed without sound like a current among the three women.

"He asked for some of my scuppernongs," said Miss Sis in her mighty voice, "and I swept him out of my house, with my broom to his backside, Georgianna."

The dark eyes in the gray face rolled in their yellow liquid, wild with glee. Standing beside her mother, Mercy opened the broad mouth in her broad, placid face and the laughter poured out in a blissful peal, the more glorious because she had laughed for a week now over the same monumental jest. Amanda's big bastard son had been witness and tale-bearer when St. John Rand had come to the house in the bamboo to make his preacher's peace with Miss Sis and to take his tithe of her grapes. The laughter had spread like fire in the dry pine needles that littered the county in the fall and had swept the county, leaping even the moat that lay between black laughter and white.

Miss Sis stood astride in the middle of the little room. Her voice filled the room. "I honored him with curses, as if he were the devil's own, Georgianna. As if even the devil would pester his purely ordinary soul. I flattered that man with curses and I swept my house clean of him with the straw end of my broom!"

Georgianna's cup of joy in life ran over and the last of her tears spilled out of her ancient eyes with delight. She was willing to die.

Miss Sis said flatly, "Now I want to ask you something, Georgianna."

"Honey, Miss Sis," whispered Georgianna.

"Can I ask the black preacher to bury me when I'm dead, Georgianna, if that man outstays me? Can I do that, for the peace of my bones?"

The dark eyes swam over and held her daughter's for a brief, communicative second.

"No'm," said Mercy. "Mama say no'm."

"It's too late and too soon," said Miss Sis. "Too late and too soon. Well. That's what I thought myself and that's all I wanted to know. What you can't help you've got to abide. I hold no more communion with my Lord, but my grape vine is still blessed by the Lord. The Lord said a long time ago that from him that had not should be taken away . . ."

Georgianna's voice was thin and whispery and indignant. "Everybody got Gawd wrong," she said. "He doan take nothin. He know somepns betterirn nothin an sometimes it's mohn plenty. Doan yuh fret, honey, Miss Sis."

Miss Sis nodded, once. Then she turned to Mercy. "You tell that biggety son of Amanda's that if he steals my scuppernongs, I'll shoot him dead," she said ferociously. "He can have some if he asks for them."

"Ma'am, Miss Sis," said Mercy.

Miss Sis took two strides to the door. She stopped and looked back. "It's a mighty puny time, Georgianna, when you can't laugh a stranger out of town!"

Georgianna's eyes were closed and Mercy had adopted the mantle of her mother. "We got us somethin," she said, "an dat's betterirn nothin."

367

"Tell that Georgianna not to die 'til I get back!" said Miss Sis.

Outside, in the alley, there was a piercing whistle as Miss **Sis** summoned, through her teeth, Amanda's biggety son.